Leaf and Flame
Coin of Rulve Book Four

Acclaim for *Leaf and Flame*

In a story about suffering, healing, and the search for reconciliation, *Leaf and Flame* offers a suspenseful feast of possibilities with characters and plot. While the evils of betrayal and brutality are palpable, tenderness lies beneath. I could sense it throughout, and it brings hope. In all, this layered novel is a timeless allegory depicting the great agony of fulfilling one's destiny in the face of deception and physical pain.
—**Iris Lee Underwood.** Poet and author of *The Mantle*, American fiction Awards Finalist and Silver Medalist in the Illumination Book Awards.

Dale weaves a captivating conclusion to her excellent series with this final volume, in which the central heroes are put to their ultimate test. Thanks to Dale's emotional resonance in her character development, and her inventive and compelling dialogue, I felt insight into the twin brothers' mindset as tension builds. The plot contains more than one surprise that brings about a truly thrilling conclusion to this poignant and action-packed narrative. Five stars.
—**K.C. Finn.** Readers' Favorite Book Review

This is a good book. The novel's climax is spectacular, consisting of slam-bang action that captures the sheer physicality of the whole experience. Filled with impressive visuals, that entire section is worth every page given to it. In all, *Leaf and Flame* is a worthy wrap-up to the *Coin* series. It plays out at a satisfying length so that the reader won't feel cheated. It's

annoying when a plot builds up to the Big Climax and then fizzles. This book doesn't fizzle!
—**Debra Doyle, PhD.** Award-winning author of many novels and short stories in science fiction, fantasy, and mystery genres. Co-winner of the Mythopoetic Fantasy Award.

Dale's concluding story offers many surprises that will delight her fans, making it an essential addition that cleverly sums up the power of all three previous books in a crescendo of action and revised fates. The novel definitively answers the question posed from the beginning: How can a dark spiritual journey lead to the providential grace of dawn?
—**Diane Donovan.** Midwest Book Review

Dale has created a world like no other in her *Coin of Rulve* series. In this powerful payoff, *Leaf and Flame* fulfills every promise of the earlier works in that the story takes readers further into the darkness of a cursed world and into the brave hearts of its most significant characters. The author engages with that basic question with which all humans grapple: the meaning hidden under the mystery of our existence. Dramatic, cinematic, and at times terrifying, this novel offers a roller-coaster ride between some wicked cliffhangers.
—**Cynthia Harrison.** Author of the multicultural crime novel *Lily White in Detroit* and the popular Blue Lake novels.

In *Leaf and Flame*, Veronica Dale again does elegant, poetic work, using everyday items to create powerful, emotional scenes set in an intriguing alternative world. After a careful, emotionally charged buildup, the latter chapters are full of thrilling conflict, action scenes and the heroes' creative responses. Kudos for

the spectacular ending. Bravo for a work that is taut, exciting and full of creative imagery.
—**Robert Neil Baker.** Classic car enthusiast and author of *Gasoline, Coffin Gold*, and other humorous, auto-related mysteries.

Dale's work contains such vivid imagery it definitely needs to be portrayed on the screen. I have been struck through all the *Coin* books by the humanity of the protagonists Sheft and Teller. They are not comic book superheroes, but real life flesh and blood human beings who struggle under the burden of their calling. The novel is lyrically written and full of profound spiritual significance regarding the themes of good, evil, and redemption. This book is truly the author's Magnum Opus.
—**Roberta Brown.** Musician, writer, and poet; president of Detroit Working Writers (2017-2021)

Exciting storytelling that kept me on the edge of my seat. I liked the back-and-forth between the brothers and the bigger-than-life battle between good and evil.
—**Christian Belz.** Architect, award-winning short story writer, and author of the Ken Knoll Architectural Mysteries series.

Dale presents profound insights into despair and acute anxiety, as well as into empathy and healing. The author creates word pictures that enable readers to see the characters as if on a professionally staged set. Her sensitive observations reveal how a devastated land can ache, how people can experience the deep intimacy that arises from bearing each other's pain, and how tenderness and kindness are redemptive.
—**A.M. Andino Rochon MA, MSW.** Educator, psychiatric therapist, and author of *Fatherless* and *The Piece to Peace Cancer Quilt*.

Leaf and Flame is the stunning conclusion of a brilliant series. The twin brothers are well-rounded characters who are now working together to achieve their redemptive goal. The plot is rich, complex, and well woven. The descriptions are vivid and the atmosphere just perfect. I will miss these characters! Five stars.
—**Rabia Tanveer.** Readers' Favorite Book Review

Leaf and Flame brings the *Coin of Rulve* series to a triumphant and satisfying conclusion. The author conjures up the land of Shunder in vivid detail without ever losing track of her characters' internal struggles. This book is an enthralling adventure tale for young and old alike.
—**Richard Rothrock.** Freelance editor, teacher at the Motion Picture Institute in Troy, Michigan, and author of *Sunday Nights with Walt*

Dale is an incredible writer with an astounding imagination.
—**Sarah Katreen Hoggatt.** Book Designer, Lucky Bat Books

Leaf and Flame

Coin of Rulve Book Four

by Veronica Dale

Published by Nika Press
Macomb, MI

Leaf and Flame

Copyright ©2020 by Veronica Dale

All rights reserved. No portion of this work may be reproduced or used in any manner whatsoever without the permission of the author. For permissions contact the author.

ISBN-13: 978-0-9969-521-6-3

Cover Design: Christa Holland, Paper and Sage
Map: Jaimie Trampus

Published by Nika Press
10 9 8 7 6 5 4 3 2 1

With thanks to the many people who helped me bring this book into being, including my patient husband Tom; Bob, Cindy, and Tom in my novel critique group; my editors Debra and Adele; book designer Sarah; artists Christa and Jaimie; and all my supporters at Detroit Working Writers

A Note From the Author

At book fairs or interviews, people sometimes ask me why I write. Now that the *Coin of Rulve* series is over, I've gained enough insight to answer that question. Here's the story.

I started out surrounded by great writers. Our mom and dad saw to that. They were both born of immigrant parents into large families and were the only ones on either side to finish high school—my dad in his twenties and my mom in her sixties. When my sister and I were kids, Mom took us to the library a lot, where I devoured everything from fairy tales to books about raising horses. (I saw no reason why our tiny backyard couldn't house a pony). I went on to read all kinds of things: mysteries, fantasy, nature, Uncle Scrooge comics, and science books for kids.

After high school, I told my parents I'd like to go to college, not realizing that many people at the time believed daughters weren't worth the cost of tuition, because "all college girls want is their 'Mrs' degree." Luckily my parents didn't buy that: women had brains too. So thanks to a tiny scholarship (a one-time $450 valedictorian award) and a work-study program, I paid the university tuition. It took three busses to get to Wayne State University, but my classes were a real game-changer for me. I discovered a bevy of outstanding writers who made me think and feel, but the most impactful of these was J.R.R. Tolkien and his *Lord of the Rings*. I must have read it half a dozen times over the years.

After graduation I became a librarian. Surrounded again by great authors, I felt like a happy duck in a great pond. But something was missing. All this time I had a big thing swelling in my heart, but I didn't know what it was.

I'd been writing since grade school and had written a few short stories in college. After getting married, I began working on a short story called *Rue*, but put it aside in a turn away from fiction and toward journalism. I edited and wrote feature articles for newspapers and magazines while Liguori Press published my booklets and pamphlets. *Rue* sat in a drawer.

Now a stay-at-home mom with four children, I volunteered to serve in our church's Christian Service Commission while hubby watched the kids. Soon one of the staff at the church, located in a large parish in the Detroit metro area, encouraged me to think about a ministerial position there. So, while completing an MA in pastoral ministry, I found myself surrounded by more great writers. They helped deepen a faith that hadn't really grown for years. After I was hired at our church, I was surrounded again, this time not only by an amazing staff but also by people who came to our church because they were hurting. Part of my ministry was to help the needy, and I witnessed the hope and courage of many people, mostly single moms, struggling with two strikes against them.

All this input was filling the well. The thing in my heart began rising again, becoming insistent, and threatening to overflow. Only lately did I discover it was the drive to articulate, to put words to so much of what I had inside. *Rue* seemed to cry out from its drawer, and in 2003 I pulled it out and began to work on it. I never dreamed the story would grow into a four-book series, the *Coin of Rulve*!

While I was writing the *Coin* series, my first fiction book was published in 2014. It was *Night*

Cruiser, a collection of my short stories that had won commendations over the years. Starting in 2016, the *Coin* books were published.

Then, in April of 2018, my alma mater, Wayne State, put out their list of the "ten top words that deserve to be used more often." I was amazed to see "eucatastrophe" there. The word was coined by Tolkien, who was a linguist as well as a writer. Eucatastrophe refers to a devastating event, a catastrophe, that is redemptive. The Greek prefix "eu" means good or true. Because of my background in pastoral ministry, putting these two seemingly opposite concepts together into one word had a deep meaning for me.

I got pretty excited about this because I hoped "eucatastrophe" might describe my own writing. At first I wondered if the term was, well, a little pompous, but then I found to my surprise that people were interested in it. This may be because many of us are looking for a deeper meaning in our chaotic world, and because the word references spirituality, rather than any specific religion.

With this last book of the *Coin* series now published, I want to thank all my readers for sticking with me. I hope that you will add my books to your list labeled "eucatastrophe," even if only at the bottom! I wrote the books because my desire as an author is to involve you on more than a superficial level. Of course I want to keep you up at night immersed in intriguing plots, fascinating worlds, and characters you want to spend time with. But I also want to satisfy our need for hope by showing how failures and losses can lead to providential victories, how Sheft and Teller in the *Coin* series can be an inspiration in our ordinary lives. In short, I write so we can look up in the midst of our hardships and see the overarching wonder of a divine light.

    Godspeed.

Veronica "Vernie" Dale (www.veronicadale.com)

P.S. A heads-up: Questions for Discussion are listed at the back of this book. These might come in handy if you belong to a book club, would like to start one with your friends, or just want to explore *Leaf and Flame* at a deeper level. If you're like me and want to be on the lookout for these questions as you read, take a glance at them before you begin.

Characters

Rulve—(*ruhl*-vay) the Creator. Neither male nor female, but spirit. Referred to with either male or female pronouns
Teller and Sheft—twin brothers, grandsons of Se Mena
Mariat—Sheft's wife

Childhood friends of Teller, now adults
Avia—Se Celume's assistant, Deoner's wife, ward-mother
Deoner—Rift-rider
Eiver—candle-lighter
Hirai—(*here*-eye) brewer, ward-mother
Ianak—(*ee*-uh-nahk) Se Utray's assistant
Lir—Se Druv's assistant
Taisa—(*tie*-suh) healer's apprentice
Yuin—musician, Hirai's husband, ward-father

The Se *(say)*—leaders of the Seani, a walled hillside community
Se Abiyat—chief healer
Se Celume—(*sell*-oo-may) musician, seeress
Se Druv—eldest of the Se
Se Komond—in charge of Seani defense
Se Mena—teacher, Teller and Sheft's grandmother
Se Nemes—counselor
Se Penan—scholar and linguist
Se Ukaipa—(yu-*kai*-pah—woman in charge of the nursery
Se Utray—(*uht*-ray) botanist

Other Seani residents
Afer—Rift-rider captain
Larrin—captain of the guards, married to Se Celume
Tema—Abiyat's assistant, widow, ward-mother of Taisa

In Oknu Shuld *(ahk-new)*
Eyascnu Varo – (eye-*ahsk*-nu), Lord of Shunder, the Spider-king
Rigiati—head of the lord's army
Rivere –imprisoned healer, former assistant to Se Abiyat
Vol Kuat—the Delver, a shape-shifter

Table of Contents

1. Taisa — 1
2. Shadowed Faces — 10
3. Night Watch — 22
4. The Weshnik' Aseah — 26
5. Passageways — 40
6. Laying Bare the Bones — 44
7. At a Complete Loss — 51
8. A Hidden Drama — 61
9. At the Foot of Two Trees — 67
10. Works of Art — 77
11. Teller's Choice — 84
12. Currents — 90
13. Spending the Night — 106
14. A Figure Blocks the Path — 119
15. The Mirror Pool — 125
16. Summons — 139
17. Fire Ghosts — 150
18. Journey — 159
19. Into the Shadow of Insheer Cliff — 166
20. Deoner's Mission — 176
21. The Jeweled Spider — 182
22. Without Sound or Hope — 194
23. Uprooting — 199
24. Inside the Vora's Domain — 207
25. Time Sliced into Now — 213
26. Black Tears — 219
27. A Glancing Shaft of Sun — 226
28. Heart-Sight — 231
29. Hand and Claw — 237
30. A Small Brave Fire — 241

31.	The Simulacrum	247
32.	Varo	249
33.	Inside	256
34.	Apotheosis	263
35.	Nihilarist	271
36.	Orders	275
37.	Sh'kier in Deed	281
38.	The Node	291
39.	Too Late to Love	299
40.	Vol Zero	307
41.	Acorn	313
42.	Eyasc-perjabik	321
43.	Down the Drain	332
44.	The Ghosts of Oknu Shuld	340
45.	Exaltation	346
46.	Twice Given and Yet Again	357
47.	The Rolling Crown	367
48.	Falls	372
49.	Going Home	379
50.	Log Jam	389
51.	Unfettered	394
52.	Elementals	397
53.	Far-off Graves	401
54.	At Enlen's Roots	408
55.	The Third Day	412
56.	A Strange Liturgy	417
57.	Greenmist	422
58.	Flowers in Footprints	425
	Questions for Discussion	431
	About the Author	435
	About the Coin of Rulve Series	437

The Quela

during the Weshnik' Aseah

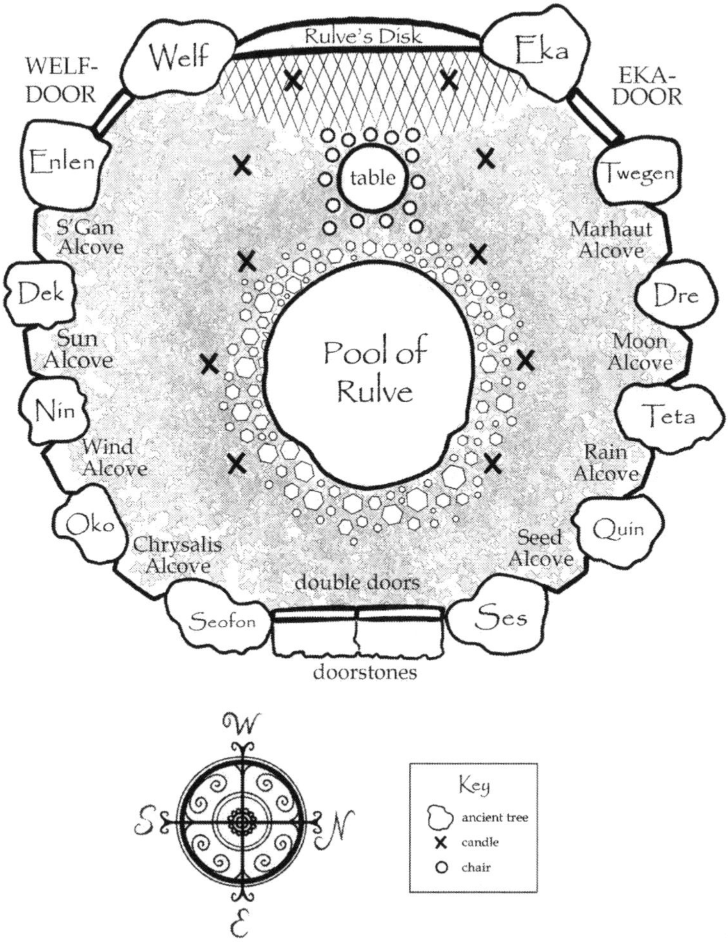

People who pray for miracles—like good grades, bicycles, or boyfriends—usually don't get them as a result. But people who pray for courage, for strength to bear the unbearable, for the grace to remember what they have left instead of what they have lost, very often find their prayers are answered. They discover that they have more strength and more courage than they ever thought.
Rabbi Harold Kushner

God's dreams do not suffer defeats; they just become more circuitous in their fulfillment.
Michael Simone, SJ.

No single act of love will be lost, no generous effort is meaningless, no painful endurance is wasted. All of these encircle our world like a vital force.
Pope Francis

Chapter 1

Taisa

Teller had been hearing the constant warm hissing and crackling for some time. He found the noise soothing. Until it struck him what it was.

His eyes flew open. He was lying on his back, and orange light flickered on the ceiling. He raised his head. Flames were leaping at the foot of his bed, flames about to engulf the young woman standing there.

"Get back!" He threw off the blanket, jumped to his feet, and pushed her aside.

Fire burned, but not around her. His power of skora had not started it. The flames were safely contained in—he searched for the once-familiar word—in a hearth. He felt its heat on his body and looked down. He wore nothing but a bandage around his thigh.

The young woman was staring at him with large brown eyes.

"F-forgive me," he stammered. "I thought"—her face began to blur, to break up into dark motes—"thought you were on fire." He had gotten up too fast and the blood was draining from his head.

"I'm not on fire," she said, spreading out her arms. "See?"

He nodded. She guided him back to bed and tucked a woolen blanket around him, and the black motes faded away. She was the most beautiful young woman he had ever seen. Her skin was a soft fawn-brown, her lips were full and pink, and tight coils of shining black hair fell over her cheeks. Those eyes looked down at him, liquid with concern.

"Are you thirsty?" she asked.

Immersed in her eyes, he had to blink, and then found his throat was dry. "Yes," he croaked.

She turned away, and he realized that he recognized, not so much her voice, but her—there was no other word for it—her presence. But from where, he couldn't remember.

Now all was quiet. The skora simmered low inside him as usual, but a while ago it had been a raging force eager to flare out—at her and at everyone or anything that it deemed was attacking him. He had fought to control it, to keep it leashed as if it were a vicious beast, and thankfully someone—his twin brother—had helped him. Teller glanced to the right. Covered with a brown wool blanket, Sheft was sleeping in the bed next to his.

Turning his head to the left, he looked around the dimly lit room. He was in the infirmary. It had changed hardly at all since he'd been here as a boy. The beds used to be bigger, but of course he'd been smaller then. The rocking chair, the counter along the wall with its basin, the south-facing window, now tinted a pre-dawn grey, the door that led into the Garden of the Sick—all were familiar. His gaze, however, hesitated at the blazing hearth, and then at the burning time candle in the corner. So much fire in the room made him uneasy.

But fire hadn't bothered him when he was six years old. He remembered peering through the embers in the two-sided hearth and seeing the healer's sleeping-room next door. Yet now he perceived everything as if recalled from a dream. A dream from thirteen years ago, when he'd been a different person.

A person who'd now come—home? Or merely back to the place where he'd been born?

A sudden memory jolted him, and he sat up. "Where's Mariat?" he asked sharply. "Where is Sheft's wife?"

The young woman stood over him with a cup of water, and lines of concern appeared in her lovely face. "Drink this first."

She waited until he gulped it down and, after placing the cup on a small table between the beds, she answered him. "We don't know where Sheft's wife is. Se Komond and Deoner rode out in search of her. They followed the tracks of a pony, found footprints of umbraks and"—she swallowed—"traces of blood. But the rain had washed everything else away. I'm so sorry, Teller."

Remembering the chaotic skirmish in the Riftwood, he sank back onto the pillow. His band of 'braks had run into three Rift-riders who'd been searching for Sheft. Both he and his brother had been wounded by arrows poisoned with ineerva. The Rift-riders had galloped off with Sheft in one direction, and his 'braks had gone off with Mariat in the other. As Vol Cinc, he'd been in agony, and his subaltern had galloped away to report to their Lord Eyascnu Varo, so there'd been no one to take command of the 'braks.

He knew 'braks, had lived with them for thirteen years. The boar-men were brutal when they felt they had lost face, and at least two of them had seized Mariat's pony during their failed attack. The other three 'braks, all of them excellent trackers, would've surely made an effort to join their companions. Which meant that a gang of enraged boar-men, determined to restore their *jukh*, or manhood, would have had the entire night to take their revenge on a helpless prisoner—Sheft's newly wed wife. Teller's heart plummeted. Mariat, who had called him brother, who had trusted him to lead her and Sheft home, could not have survived.

"Does Sheft know?" he asked.

"Not yet."

He put a hand over his eyes, but could not stop the flood of anguish and anger.

The woman leaned over him. "Has the ineerva pain returned, emjadi?"

Emjadi. The word pierced him like a dart. Voices from the past rushed into his mind. His own as a child: *"Grandma, what does 'emjadi' mean?"* The falconform Yarahe calling after him as the wyvern bore him away: *"Have courage, emjadi!"* A silver-eyed woman with a basket of seeds: *"Set fire to this thicket, emjadi, and burn it all away."*

"No," he said. "That pain is gone."

"But your loss remains," she said gently.

Loss? He rode out of Oknu Shuld with nothing more to lose. He felt crushing remorse for what happened to Mariat, but his brother would feel a much greater grief.

She sat on the bed next to him and, as she did so, Teller remembered who she was. "You—you were with me, when I was dying." She had laid her hand gently over his throat, over his spirikai. She had helped him bear the pain. During the worst of it, she had been with him. Such undeserved kindness swelled in his throat, and in view of what she had done for him, he couldn't even find the words to thank her.

He started to reach out to her with his right hand, but the glitter of the vol-ring stopped him. At one point she must have cleaned the blood and dirt off it, must have actually touched it, and now it leered out at him. It had grown roots into his hand, and he couldn't claw it off. A low groan escaped him, and he slid his hand under the blanket. As if he could hide what he was from her.

"A massage will make you feel better, Teller. Your muscles are all tense, and you're still sore from the seizures."

He realized two things at once: she was addressing him in the mind-speech, and every muscle in his body ached for a massage.

But not at her hands. She must never touch him.

"I've already touched you, Teller." Her cheeks turned a little pinker as she looked down at him. "In quite a few places, actually. You've been in the infirmary for two nights, after all."

So she had heard his thoughts somehow. When he was with her, did his thoughts verge into mind-speech? He'd have to watch out for that.

"I'm Taisa, by the way," she said. "Do you remember me?"

He recalled the face of an eager little girl in the nursery, toddling up to him with a red ball. *"Pay baw, Tewer, pay baw."* But the six-year-old boy that used to play with her no longer existed. "I remember," he said. Even in the tunnels of Oknu Shuld he had remembered.

"Ah," another voice said. "You are awake." Se Abiyat, holding a steaming cup, entered the room from the hall door. Teller had glimpsed his face between bouts of pain and, even after all the time that had passed, had recognized it.

"I was just going to get you," Taisa said.

The healer put down his cup and bent to look fixedly into Teller's eyes, then felt the sides of his throat. "Good, good," he muttered. He folded the blanket back from

Teller's thigh, removed the bandage, and examined the skin around the injury. "We don't need that anymore," he said, tossing the bandage into a basket beside the bed. He covered Teller with the blanket again and smiled at him. "We have you back at last."

His kindness was like salt rubbed into a wound. Teller had found safety here, while Mariat had found nothing but a degrading death.

"He's already tried to get up," Taisa said with a healer's pride.

"None of that, lad, at least for now. The ineerva appears to have gone, but I am not certain if the apsura has left any lingering effects."

"Apsura?" Teller asked.

"A potion we had to give you, to save your life. Unfortunately, apsura may have damaged the nerves and left them more sensitive to pain."

That would be ironic, a modicum of justice, since he had made the poison that almost killed him and Sheft to begin with.

"He asked about Mariat," Taisa said to the healer, "and I had to tell him."

Abiyat pursed his lips and shook his head slightly. "I'd hoped to inform you later, emjadi, when you were feeling stronger. Please accept my deep condolences. I understand Mariat was your sister-in-law." He expelled a deep sigh. "Unfortunately, we must deal with our loss and move on."

Another man, who had come in after Abiyat, stepped closer to Teller's bed. It was Se Druv, the eldest. "Hold on a minute, Abiyat." He placed a hand on Teller's shoulder. "Our healer spoke frankly, son, but perhaps without sensitivity. We must indeed move on. Yet we're not asking you and your brother to do anything we here in the Seani have not done. "

Teller understood what Druv meant. When Teller was just an infant, the Se leaders were forced to make a difficult decision. In order to protect him and his twin brother from the Spider-king, their mother Riah had to flee their homeland with Sheft.

"After you were abducted, Teller," Druv went on, "we were faced with the fact that we had lost both niyalahn-ristas, both the emjadis whom Rulve had entrusted into our care. For years, we were overwhelmed by grief and guilt."

And for much of that time, Teller remembered, he had believed no one in the Seani had cared.

"Yet," Druv continued, "we learned we had to come to terms with the past. That took time for us, and it will take time for you and Sheft. But it must be done. Actually, as many of us are well aware, it must be done over and over through the years. So Abiyat may have spoken harshly, but he told you the truth."

"Thank you, Druv," Abiyat said, and then looked down at Teller. "They tell me I over-extended myself these past few days, and that my bedside manner flew off somewhere. In any case, there is a meeting of the Seah tomorrow, and you must gather your strength for it. Taisa, the massage please."

He tapped Teller on the knee. "The technique is one I introduced here several years ago. I taught it to the medicants, and they use it down in the villages. I maintain that massaging with healoil alleviates stress, and it should be an integral part of every treatment regime. You have certainly been through the mill, my boy, and a massage will do you good."

Taisa came to his side with a small pitcher she was warming between her hands. "Se Nemes says grieving people in particular benefit, because they feel so isolated."

She was innocent. She should not touch one who had done what he had done; should not touch the marks Shacad had left on him. "Sheft's the one who's grieving," he said. *And I'm responsible for that.* "Give him this massage."

"We already have. Now roll over, Teller."

Abiyat fixed him with a stern eye, as did Druv, and in spite of the emotions that beset him, Teller was too exhausted and wanted the massage too much to resist. Cursing his weakness, he turned onto his stomach, every muscle tight, and kept his scathi ringed hand hidden under the pillow.

At the first touch of her hands, he flinched.

"Oh! Are my hands cold?"

"N-no. I just—wasn't ready."

"Are you now?"

"Yes," he said helplessly.

Healoil dripped onto his back and her strong, warm hands rubbed it into his skin. "These scars don't look so bad now," she assured him. "They must've faded a little in the Pool of Rulve."

He did not want her to see them, felt hot with the shame of his ultimate capitulation at the hands of Vol Tierce.

She started at the back of his neck, and her fingers dug into the soreness on either side of it. "So tight. Just relax a bit, emjadi."

He tried, but had to keep at bay the intense awareness of her touch, and then a rising desire that made it difficult to lie face down. She found knots around his shoulder blades that he hadn't known were there and kneaded them away. She poured out oil like forgiveness and rubbed it into his back; her hands like salvation smoothed away the tension.

But then a chilling thought swept over him. For him there could be no redemption.

Awkwardly he reached back to push her hands away, but she must have misunderstood. She took his extended arm between her hands, laid it down on the sheet, and rubbed oil into it. Her thumbs made small circles in the muscles of his forearm, around his wrist, over the back of his hand. Then she went further. She gently began to work healoil into the scratches around the vol-ring.

Even that she tried to heal, even that she tried to rub away. He made a fist against her efforts, but her thumb slid in and opened his hand. Their fingers briefly intertwined as she moved her oily thumb into his palm and around the base of the ring. Leaving his hand open at his side, her fingers flowed away to massage his other arm, the muscles of his shoulders, and down his spine to the small of his back. She dripped more oil over his thighs and kneaded it in, smoothed it over the tender spot where the arrow-wound had been.

He remembered how Mariat had tended to Sheft's scarred back in the henge. A wife comforting her husband, love spilling from her hands.

There could be no forgiveness for what he had done to her.

He forced himself to turn, to push Taisa gently away. He wanted to thank her, to explain, but the words caught in his throat.

She drew back, surprise and then hurt filling those liquid brown eyes. "As you wish, emjadi." She wiped her hands and left his side.

Teller sat up and watched her go.

"A mild draught," Abiyat said, handing him a cup. "To aid in sleeping."

Desperately, cowardly, he drank it down.

Chapter 2

Shadowed Faces

GREY LIGHT SEEPED THROUGH THE WINDOW when Teller next awoke. He discovered he was wearing a clean small-cloth. He was now free, he thought wryly, to leap out of bed like a fool, as he had done a few hours ago. His brother, sitting on the edge of his bed with a blanket over his shoulders, was attired likewise. He was bent over, holding his head in his hands, the toltyr dangling from his neck.

Sometime during the night, Teller had half-heard a whispered conversation between Sheft and Se Nemes. From his brother's posture of despair, Teller knew that Sheft must have asked about his wife, and the counselor must have told him.

Abiyat's voice rang out from behind him. "Time for breakfast, emjadis. Time to get up and walk a bit. Sheft, lean on me. Teller, go with Tema."

Teller sat up and pulled the blanket over his back, noticing as he wrapped it around himself that the wool no longer caught on the rough scars. Tema, someone had told him, was Taisa's ward-mother, who ran the hospit building further down the hillside. He looked around for Taisa, but she wasn't in the room. Thinking he didn't need the older woman's support, he swung his legs out of bed and almost immediately was glad when she took his arm.

They walked around the beds a few times, and then sat on the chairs, which had been moved next to the hearth. Across from him, Sheft looked up at Abiyat. Purple bruises under his eyes attested that his twin had spent a sleepless night. "My wife came to me," Sheft said to the healer. "When I was under the apsura. She came to say—goodbye." A troubled look crept into his unsettling silver eyes. "But wouldn't I have known, Abiyat, wouldn't I have felt it, when—when she…" Jaw clenched, his throat working, he leaned his head back and stared blindly at the ceiling, trying to hold back tears.

"I am truly sorry," the healer said gently. "We all like to think we would know when an absent loved one dies, but that is very rarely the case. It is a sign of Rulve's compassion that you and Mariat were afforded the opportunity to say farewell, even if only in a vision. Mariat is with Creator Rulve now, and he loves her even more than you do, Sheft."

"But what happened to her? How did she—." He couldn't finish, but Teller saw how his eyes pleaded for answers.

"I'm sure Nemes told you, niyal'arist, that we may never know. There are too many ways to die in the Riftwood, and the tracks were obliterated by the rain."

"What if she's still alive?" Sheft choked out. "What if she suffers, lost and alone?"

Abiyat grasped Sheft's blanket-covered shoulders and gently shook him. "Do not torment yourself, emjadi. Your wife would say the same, would she not? You have taken leave of each other, and now she is beyond pain. Be comforted that Rulve enfolds her. Trust that our loving Creator will give you the strength to bear this."

By now, Teller knew, the 'braks would be riding as fast as they could out of Shunder, and the violated body of the young woman who had tried to befriend him would be left for scavengers.

Tema gave them both some sort of cool liquid that Abiyat urged them to drink. It was, he said, a mix of goat's milk and herbs that would build up their strength and help them rest. "We'll be giving you some of this every few notches," the healer explained.

Notches? Teller suddenly remembered the word. In contrast to the gongs he'd grown up with in Oknu Shuld, notches on the time-candle were used to measure the hours here. He glanced at the time-candle in the corner by the hearth. Its flame rested just above the sixth notch after midnight, which meant dawn at this time of year. He and Sheft were escorted back to bed, and some time later he awoke to two strange sensations: full sun flooding the room and a bird chirping on the sill. He hadn't experienced either of these events for most of the thirteen years he'd lived in the lord's underground domain. Someone was speaking to Sheft, and Teller turned his head on the pillow to see who it was.

Se Gremez was sitting in a chair between the beds.

Teller drew a sharp breath. The man seemed to have two faces, one superimposed on the other. The first belonged to a shadow, but the other was that of Greaz, the mind-prober who had tried to pull his soul apart in Oknu Shuld. The man he had engulfed in flames and burned to death when he was only six years old.

He squeezed his eyes shut. But as the man spoke, Teller realized the low-timbered and patient voice belonged to Se Nemes, the person who'd had been whispering to Sheft in the night. Teller opened his eyes, and Greaz faded away, leaving the kindly, crinkle-eyed counselor he had trusted as a boy and could trust now.

Sheft listened intently while Nemes explained to him how things were in the Land of Shunder. He told how the Spider-king had dammed the waterfall that once had renewed the Eeron River and had thereby wiped out Shunder's entire fishing industry. He told how year by year the soil grew poorer and the harvest grew less, and how taxes were raised to compensate. And then he told Sheft about the ahn, children ripped away from their niyal twins and taken as slaves into Oknu Shuld.

Sheft said nothing throughout all this. His hand went up to grip the toltyr around his neck, and fevered spots of emotion formed on his planed cheeks.

Teller had known these facts even as a boy, and for thirteen years had lived with the ahn-pain in Oknu Shuld. But now he heard the story as if for the first time, a tale of poverty, addiction to morue, and child slavery—suffering caused by the lord to whom he had pledged his body and soul, whose orders he had obeyed, whose ring he wore even now.

As the counselor went on, Teller learned what had changed in the Seani the last thirteen years. Medicants secretly going out to help the sick. His childhood friends married and caring for both natural children and wards. Two new Se, to replace those who had died. Dangerous trips down to the villages where Seani and Sperians conspired against the Lord of Shunder.

There was silence, and then Se Nemes turned his gaze toward Teller. "Emjadi, while we were treating you, I discovered that you suffered mind-damage in Oknu Shuld; that your memories had been twisted. May I now tell you the truth? I promise you may stop me at any point."

Pulling his blanket around him as if it were armor, Teller nodded. The telling took a long time, and the hearing was like peeling the scab off a wound. He had already begun to recall some of what Nemes said, but now the past became crystal clear. The Seah had never told him who he was, not because they feared his power of fire, but to protect him—and thank God they had. The Se had never pushed him out of the gates. In reality, Se Ísavin and Suver had given their lives in an attempt to rescue him, and the Seah had sent the falconform Yarahe after him, that time on Insheer Cliff.

He had spent years hating them. As Vol Cinc, he would have used skora to annihilate them. He wore the ring of their deadliest enemy, yet every day the Se had been praying for him. Because of him, the Seani died to what it had been, and in the hope of carrying out the niyal'arist mission, rose to what it could become.

"Enough for now," Nemes said. "We will speak more deeply at the Weshnik' Aseah tomorrow." On his way out, he passed Taisa quietly coming in.

With her mind closed to Teller, she mixed Abiyat's prescribed drink and gave one cup to Sheft and the other, her eyes askance, to Teller. He wanted to put the cup on the table, to take her hands and draw her toward him, to tell her how much her massage had meant to him, to say what he felt in his heart. But he had no words for any of this, and she turned her back on him to work silently at the counter. Once or twice he opened his mouth to speak, but could not. In the end, he gave in to the medicine and allowed it to take him once more into sleep.

A CLATTER WOKE HIM, FOLLOWED BY the distant sound of people talking and forks clinking against dishes. He had heard that sound many times as a child, sitting next to his grandmother in the dining room. It was located, he recalled, out the half-door, whose top half was open just now, past the kitchen, and down the hall to the left.

Tema, carrying a tray, pushed the bottom half of the door open with her hip. She smiled at him and nodded toward the chairs flanking the hearth. "Over there, Teller. Do you need help?"

He shook his head, pulled himself out of bed, and with the blanket over his shoulders, made the short trek. After spending the whole day resting, the effort was still harder than he thought it should be. Sheft sat nearby, his eyes downcast. Tema put the tray onto his bed and gave each of them a plate.

Teller looked at his, which was full of unfamiliar objects.

"Eat up," Tema ordered. "Keppit prepared a special meal just for the two of you."

A face flashed into his mind: the cook brandishing a wooden spoon at Eiver years ago, for filching cookies, as he remembered. "It's fine," he said hastily. "We just had different food in Ok—" He choked back the word. They didn't say "Oknu Shuld" in the Seani.

Used to cold food, he found everything too hot to eat, so he waited until the roasted chicken and buttered white chunks of something had cooled down. There were also long green things on his plate, like little spears, and tiny green balls whose skins popped when he chewed them. He made himself eat it, for Keppit's sake.

Abiyat came in with two heavy-looking cloaks, which he tossed onto Teller's bed. He glanced with approval at Teller's mostly empty plate and frowned at Sheft's mostly full one. "You should finish this," he said.

Sheft reluctantly took a forkful of chicken, chewed it, and clearly forced it down.

"It's that ache in your spirikai, is it not?" Abiyat asked. Sheft looked to the side and nodded.

"Our land suffers, lad, and it is that which you feel in your own body."

"Rulve also suffers," Sheft said in a low voice. "He feels the sickness in the soil, but can't heal it. He feels how his children are crushed and trampled, but can't in his tenderness lift them up." His eyes liquid with unshed tears, he glanced up at the healer. "Rulve has no hands, Abiyat. He needs ours."

The healer laid his hand on Sheft's arm. "Most of us do not realize Rulve suffers. It is a very tender revelation, emjadi."

Desolation filtered over Teller. He too had felt the ache in his spirikai, felt the ahn in torment in Oknu Shuld; but while his brother had come through the Riftwood to reach them, he had raised a skora barrier against them. Rulve had spoken to his brother's heart, but not to his. A bitter, silent laugh rose up at the thought. Why should he expect anything different?

Abiyat was still speaking to his brother. "Nemes explained many things to you, emjadi, but he left it to me to inform you about what else causes us pain. An herb called sweet-rue was once common here. Its roots used to be plowed under as fertilizer, and its leaves were one of our most powerful pain-relievers." His voice turned bitter. "The Spider-king wiped it out. He hybridized it to form the addictive morue, and an outright poison would have been better. At least we could have used it to kill rats. Morue is that damned Purple by which the Eyascnu Vora controls the people and enriches himself."

Teller had known all this but felt a chill at the forbidden mispronunciation of the lord's name. In Oknu Shuld, only "Eyascnu *Varo*" was correct. Voras were blood-sucking monsters, and varos were sources of light. If spies from across the valley could hear how the Seani spoke of their lord, the entire complex would pay a price.

"On a brighter note, niyal'arists," Abiyat went on, "everyone is asking about you both. Many people wanted to visit you, the children bringing flowers and such, and they were disappointed when I advised against it for now. The Weshnik' Aseah will be meeting at dawn tomorrow, and you will need all your strength for that."

He motioned to Tema, who began collecting their plates. "Tomorrow we will discern what Rulve has called us all to do. For now, however, there are two chairs out in the garden. The gate is shut, and you will not be disturbed. Go out and sit in the last of the sun's rays, for there is great healing benefit in that."

The prospect of being alone with his brother struck Teller with a sudden cold dread. Yes, they'd been together, but too much separated them. "I'm not used to sitting in the sun," he said.

"I'm afraid I must insist." Abiyat took their blankets, replaced them with the cloaks he'd brought, and escorted them to the wooden chairs in the Garden of the Sick. He disappeared into the infirmary, leaving the two of them sitting in awkward silence.

Even though it was an early evening in Seed, the sheltered garden faced south and still held the warmth of the day. On their right, tall yews separated the Garden of the Sick from the kitchen garden; on their left, a high stone wall marked the edge of the Quarantine Garden next door. In front of them, in the corner formed by the wall and a loosely woven fence made of willow branches, grew a grey-barked tree covered with violet blossoms. A few had already fallen into the small spring that bubbled out of the mossy rocks beneath. A bush outside the window behind them filled the area with a clean, soapy scent, and purple, yellow, and white flowers grew everywhere in the new grass. Teller ran his gaze over them and couldn't recall seeing such flowers before.

"Teller, I—I have to"— Very haltingly, Sheft was trying to mind-speak to him.

"I can barely understand you. If you must talk, do it out loud."

"Se Nemes said that in this—language, there are no lies. This way of talking is part of—who we are, together. Our heritage. In it, I want to thank you."

Teller shifted in his chair. "You owe me no thanks. Believe me."

"You helped my wife and me. You witnessed our marriage. You fought with the boar-men so that we and the other Rift-riders might escape."

"Don't look at me like that. You have everything wrong."

"I was there, Teller."

"I was never a Rift-rider. The truth is I was in command of the group that attacked."

Faint confusion crossed Sheft's face, as if he hadn't heard him correctly.

"You asked how Mariat died?" Teller continued. "My umbraks killed her. It's what they do. They used your wife, and then they killed her."

The silver eyes widened. Sheft stared at him for one frozen moment, then abruptly turned away.

While under apsura, a link had been forged between them and now his brother's emotions poured through it. Teller did not block any of it. He forced himself to stay open to everything: the shocked incredulity, the sting of betrayal, the wrenching failure to protect the wife he would have died for—all wound through with torment over the brutal way his beloved must have been killed. *Oh God, Sheft, what have I done to you?*

His brother, white-faced and rigid, clutched the wooden armrests. Sensing a coming burst of rage, the skora rose up. Teller forced it back. "It would be justice"—and he would not defend himself from whatever Sheft did to him.

Sheft turned to face him. "Justice?" The word seemed to unearth some deep memory in Sheft, a memory that allowed his brother's angry, chaotic emotions to drain away, into a void of loss.

Teller forced himself to be clear, to confess everything to his twin. "I was bringing you and your wife into Oknu Shuld."

The silver eyes clouded. Sheft had no idea about the lord's windowless domain.

So Teller showed him: the dark passages, the crawling globes, the luniku pits, the isav, the rista students who swarmed inside the corridors like vicious ants.

"Why? Why would you bring us to that place?"

The mind-words came with an anguish that cut through Teller's heart. "I was ordered to do it. And Vol Cinc," he spat out, "always obeys orders." There could be no forgiveness. Even to ask for it would be the greater sin.

Sheft took a deep breath, more like a shudder. "Oh God. I know what it's like not to be forgiven."

A stream of images rushed through the link, and in moments Teller saw years of his brother's life. He saw rejection in his father's face, suspicion in his mother's. Children laughed at him; villagers spat at the ground in front of him. Roots writhed in his veins. His blood called to darkness, and numbing ice set him apart. He denied the truth of who he was even as the pain of a suffering land throbbed deep in his spirikai. He was responsible for the deaths of two villagers. He let his dying mother bear the toltyr, and took it from her only when a falconform shamed him into it. He was accused, blindfolded, expelled. Out of pure grace he found someone who loved him, and after one night saw her ripped away. He looked down at a white flower that had fallen into his hand. A flower with a blood-red center.

A stream of empathy rushed out of Teller, raw and useless and rightly to be rejected.

But it wasn't rejected. Incredibly, it washed back upon him, coming from the brother who was himself, was his own twin, who looked upon him with a compassion that made forgiveness unnecessary.

"Don't do this!" Teller cried. "Don't leave me to forgive myself!"

Looking away, Sheft slumped back against his chair. "That's the only forgiveness there is."

The sun had slipped behind the yews and left an empty, twilit sky. Across it two birds streaked toward the shelter of the trees.

Sheft's gaze followed them. "In the Riftwood, and now, just a minute ago, you told me your name. Vol Cinc, you said. Repeat that name in the mind-speech."

Teller tried. He could number all four Vols, but not the fifth. In the mind-speech there was no Vol Cinc. So he just sat there, the ring heavy on his hand, while the small spring in the corner of the garden bubbled in the silence.

"What happened to you, Teller? What happened to you in Oknu Shuld?"

The vol-ring constricted around his finger, and the reality of it tightened around his throat like an ahn-collar. He owed his brother an answer. It was the smallest part of what he owed him.

It was like digging a hole into his own chest, but he deserved to feel the pain. The past welled up, muddy at first and dark; then spurted out, as red as a severed artery.

Chapter 3

Night Watch

SHEFT LAY SLEEPLESS IN HIS BED. All around him the land was aching. He had felt it, far-off when he lived in At-Wysher, and then more strongly when he was sent across the Meera into the Riftwood. But when he entered Shunder, when the Rift-riders were rushing him away from the umbraks and he was constricted with ice and lashed by ineerva, it had fallen upon him even more. Now, because of what Nemes and Abiyat had told him earlier, he knew exactly why this land was suffering so badly.

He rolled over to stare at the window's black rectangle. When he had been with his brother in the Garden of the Sick, he could sense the underlying desiccation all around him. It was as if the newly budded crocuses and anemones were withered at the heart, as if the deep green yew-hedge were already turning brown.

The hall door opened, admitting a slant of light. Sheft lay still as a woman with grey hair quietly placed a pile of clothing on the foot of his bed and departed. The light winked out.

Sheft rolled off his mattress and fingered the clean clothes the woman had just brought. By the light of the time-candle he saw that his shirt was neatly patched where the arrow had torn it. He brushed his hand over the garment. Mariat had thought to pack it for him when she left her home to follow him into the Riftwood. He put it on, along with his pants and his now clean boots, but his sheepskin jacket had been tucked in front of Mariat on her pony. Had she draped it over her head when it started to rain? Was she wearing it when—

Quickly he shook out a cloak, made of the same brown wool as the blanket on his bed. It smelled like it too, like the camphor crystals that repelled moths. Sheft quietly opened the door to the garden. He thought he could find his way back to the great hands, to the circular hall of Rulve. The Quela, Abiyat called it.

The willow-wood fence ahead of him shimmered with frost. In the southern sky above it hung the bright Sickle, followed by the Seed-sower with her bag of stars. He wondered what these constellations were called here, in this far country. Everything was still as he pushed open the gate, turned to the right, and followed a path lit by red lanterns that took him to the double doors of the Quela. He pulled one of the doors open and slipped through.

All the effervescence had gone from the pool in the center of the hall, and it lay as still as a shadow. Also dark was the great jade disk, Rulve's Disk, which took up most of the front wall. Barely two days ago, when he'd seen the disk for the first time in his life, sunlight had transformed it into a magnificent jewel that bathed the hall in a forest light. That's how his mother's dreamy voice had described Rulve's house to him when he'd been a child beset with nightmares. But now, only two of the twelve tall candles were lit, one on each side of the disk, and they cast glowing, slightly shifting circles onto the floor.

He turned to the left and sank onto a massive root. It extended from one of the twelve ancient trees that supported the circular walls and roof. Like silent, shrouded giants, the trees loomed all around him. Small walk-in alcoves, built in between the trees, formed a row of dark doorways around the hall.

A shadow emerged from the closest one. It was Druv, who stopped, peered at him, and then came to sit quietly at his side. For a long moment both looked straight ahead, and then, without turning his head, the eldest of the Se spoke. "I am so sorry about your wife, emjadi."

Sheft bowed his head. "I thought she was with me," he said. "I thought she was there in the infirmary, helping me when the pain came rushing back. But Se Nemes told me it was Avia, one of the pain-bearers."

A small regretful sigh came from the man beside him. It shivered into the stillness and prompted Sheft to go on. "It felt like her, Druv. Her compassion. Her strength." He lifted his head and looked away from Druv. "I should've known though. Somehow I could tell that the woman touching me was, you know, a mother. I thought, for a minute there, that we had children." He swallowed. "That I was—a father. But later Nemes told me it was Avia."

Druv was silent, as if waiting for him to continue, but Sheft could not. The old man climbed to his feet, reached down to squeeze Sheft's shoulder, and then left the Quela.

Sheft stared at one of the candle flames, now an utterly motionless teardrop of light. He made his way forward to stand before Rulve's open hands. They were carved into the base of the jade disk, bigger than they had seemed from the pool yesterday, yet somehow far more vulnerable. Anything so open could be deeply hurt.

The weight inside him dragged him to his knees. He reached up, grasped the thumbs with both hands, and rested his forehead against the smooth jade. *Oh God, keep Mariat's spirit safe. Let me quickly join her.* He tightened his hold. *Whatever you want, Rulve, make it happen soon. Please make it happen soon.*

High above him, unseen among the shadows, he knew words were carved. Long ago his mother had told him what they were, and they had flashed into his mind the moment he came up from the Pool of Rulve.

My life is in your hands.

At length he left the shadowed hall and returned to the infirmary, to sink back onto his rumpled bed.

Chapter 4

The Weshnik' Aseah

Teller sat on the edge of his bed, waiting for their escort to the gathering of the Seah. If its purpose was judgment, he would have no defense. If it was to discern what must be done next, he would have no answer. Through the garden door he could see Sheft and Abiyat also waiting, their breath steaming in the cold air. The sun had not yet risen over Insheer Cliff, but the sky promised a sunny day. Yet a grey haze seemed to hang over everything—the legacy, he knew, of the vol-ring.

He was wearing clean clothes, his own boots, and his camouflaged dead-leaf cloak, but apparently his black shirt and pants could not be salvaged. They had been replaced with simple homespun. With clothing like an ahn's.

Taisa came into the infirmary, and he rose. For much of the night he'd been alternately assailed by—and then trying to push away—the sensations of how she had been with him as a pain-bearer. He had never been with a woman so intimately and probably never would again. Her tenderness, the feel of her hands resting upon his spirikai, his throat—she didn't know what she was doing to him then, what she was doing to him now. She didn't know she offered an impossible salvation.

Without looking at him, she hung up her cloak, opened a drawer under the counter, and took something out of it. Turning, she said, "I believe this belongs to you."

It was his dagger. He'd been thirteen when he found it in the treasure chamber of Oknu Shuld, just before the full power of skora flared through his spirikai for the first time. Its hilt was made of green jade, and the blade held the wavy shape of a flame. The other side, however, was faintly scored like a leaf. He took the dagger and pushed it into place at his belt. Only then did it dawn on him that no one he had yet seen in the Seani was armed.

"This is yours too." Taisa opened her hand, which held the blue and red knotted cord. "Susera found it when she was going through your pockets at the laundry shed."

Taisa, he sensed, was deliberately avoiding the mind-speech, and he could detect no wisp of emotion behind her words. She was able to guard herself, apparently, far better than he.

He took the cord from her. On the night before his Acclamation as Vol Cinc, he'd savagely twisted the two strands together and tied tight knots along its length. It was the end of the life he had known, the end of Teller and the beginning of Vol Cinc. He made it knowing he must completely destroy the faith the ahn had placed in him.

"This blue hair ribbon," he said, "belonged to an ahn named Keya. When I was first brought into Oknu Shuld, she disobeyed orders and befriended me. She died for that. But for years I thought I'd saved her."

But he hadn't. Instead, the ahn Gorv had saved him. In the desolate tunnels of the final exam, Gorv had given his life for him. Rife with renunciation and failure, Teller had stuffed the ribbon into his pocket. He lived with it there, a symbol of all he had done and all he did not do.

Still not looking at him, Taisa raised her eyebrows. "And the red cord?"

"I cut it off the wrists of an ahn." Off the beautiful slave Liasit who was the first to mind-speak to him in the depths of Oknu Shuld. She too had suffered because of her faith in him.

Now Taisa's great eyes fully met his, and he realized once again that she must have heard him. She must have felt the emotion he thought he had quelled.

"I am sorry, niyalahn-rista."

He crushed the cord in his hand. "Don't call me that! There are no saviors in Oknu Shuld."

She didn't flinch at his harsh tone, and her gaze remained steady. "Are you saying that because you believe it, emjadi, or because someone convinced you it was so?"

Dismay twisted through his stomach. She hadn't been there, couldn't comprehend what it had been like. Yet he owed her the truth and tried to explain, to her and perhaps also to himself. "I kept this cord to remind me—" his throat tightened and his words came out in a voice he barely recognized as his own—"that I didn't wear an ahn-collar."

She leaned toward him but did not touch him. "A collar you felt you deserved, Teller?"

He couldn't answer her; the question was too hard. His throat still tight, he could only stare wordlessly into her eyes.

"Rulve wants us to dwell on her love for us, not on our failings."

"You don't understand!" he cried. "You don't know what I have done. I don't want you to know." Appalled, he realized what had just happened. The mind-speech could not lie. At some level, he very badly wanted—needed—her to know.

Now she did touch him, gently on the arm, and Teller caught a glimpse of a purple ribbon around her wrist. The mark of mourning, worn in memory of a loved one. She dropped her hand, and he struggled to continue.

"I'm sorry, Taisa, for… what you could not do for me." To his surprise, he'd spoken the last words aloud. They weren't true, he realized, and the mind-speech couldn't say them. With an impatient gesture, he flicked the spoken words aside and tried again. "I'm sorry for what I wouldn't allow you to do for me." He had wanted her touch, oh God he wanted it, but he couldn't—." He stopped, hoping she hadn't heard him yet again.

For an instant she looked as if she would answer him, but just then someone came into the room. Taisa turned away to greet a guard she called Larrin, and Teller was bustled away.

Outside, the sun slanted through the trees, and a light frost lay in their shadows. In spite of the early hour, a crowd of people lined the Red Lantern Way. Larrin and Abiyat propelled him and Sheft along, making apologies for their haste. Teller held his right hand at his side, where his cloak covered the vol-ring. With their faces alight, everyone greeted him and his brother. Their eyes were filled with expectancy and hope. Like Liasit's eyes had been, and Gorv's.

"Welcome home, emjadis!"

"Bless you, niyalahn-ristas!"

The undeserved titles were like blows. These people deserved to know the truth, and he had chosen the vol-ring as his truth. He flipped his cloak aside so everyone could see it. Looking straight ahead, he walked in the much-washed garments of an ahn, under a cloak designed to hide him, one hand clutching the red and blue cord hidden in his pocket, but the other hand wearing a ring now clearly visible. Yet beyond his humiliation, like a lovely moon blurred by clouds, lingered Taisa's beautiful face.

As they walked through the crowd of well-wishers, Sheft realized he was searching faces for the one he loved. Grief welled out of his spirikai yet again, always fresh, seeming without end. Mariat had held him inside her in the henge, pressed full-length against him under their blanket—all in a dream of only one night.

Many eyes were looking at him, and out of long habit Sheft lowered his gaze. But these people had been with him in the Pool of Rulve. They had entered his pain and brought down the light. They had held him upright when the call of the great bell welled up with such strength that he felt it throughout his entire body.

He glanced up, ready for rejection, braced for revulsion, but everyone met his silver eyes with gladness. Hands reached out to touch him, not knowing of the roots that lay only skin-deep, not seeing the ice that could prevent a wound from bleeding but would also trap him in frozen isolation. If Mariat had lived, they would surely have welcomed her as they now welcomed him. They would have supported their marriage, been their friends, rejoiced in their children. For her sake, Sheft reached out, and eyes lit up in response, and smiles bloomed, and hand after hand brushed against his fingertips as he passed.

But oh Rulve, the ground all around him was hurting; parents and children were hurting, and their wounds throbbed continually in his spirikai.

Waiting with the others for the niyal'arists to arrive, Druv sat facing the double doors of the Quela.

For the first time in years, he had dreamed of his wife last night, dreamed of his green-eyed Laena. She had possessed a gentle spirit, one which would have been utterly crushed had she stayed with the ambitious young scholar Nosce once had been. At least that is what he always told himself. It was only when he had become an old man that he wondered if he had taken away Nosce's only salvation. Their paths had diverged. He took the one that led to the fair Seani, and Nosce chose the one that ended with disfigurement of both body and soul in the tunnels of Oknu Shuld.

The door opened and the niyalahn-ristas entered. I could have been their true grandfather, Druv thought. Leana had died after giving life to Neal, and that boy could have been his son. Druv, however, had had his doubts. He told the Seani that the infant Neal was his ward-son. But did any of that matter now? Whether Neal had been his son or Nosce's, he'd spent a lifetime loving the boy, and wasn't that all Rulve cared about?

Yet he lingered for a while with Leana in the dream. To this day no one knew how Neal's name reflected his mother's, how similar had been the color of their eyes.

The brothers, Druv saw, looked drained. Having barely recovered from ineerva poisoning, they must now face virtual strangers who would question them not only about their traumatic pasts but also about how that would affect their ability to discern and fulfill their future mission. Sheft was also enduring a staggering grief, and Teller a burden they did not yet know. These boys were too young, he thought sadly, to have lived so long.

The big round table had been brought in sections from storage and set up between the Pool of Rulve and the Great Disk, the place where liturgy was usually held. On the table stood a jug of water with several cups, a time-candle, and Mena's carved, open box. Inside glinted a toltyr. Teller's eyes fell upon it and quickly darted away. Ah, Druv thought with dismay, he both recognizes it and repudiates it. We have a long way to go.

Eleven chairs had been set up around the table, with four more arranged slightly behind the others to form a square outside the circle. The eleven chairs were for the Seah and the emjadis, while the young assistants to Se—Avia, Lir, Ianak, and Hirai—occupied the four corners. According to the seeress Celume, the result was a powerful circle-square arrangement that symbolized earth and heaven interwoven, a mandala that entwined them all. Six of the big candles were lit, two flanking Rulve's jade green disk and the other four around the table. The emjadis were ushered into the last of the empty seats, save one. Utray's chair, directly across from Druv, was still vacant.

The two brothers had barely been seated, facing each other over the table's expanse, when the main doors opened to a bright rectangle of morning sun. A backlit figure entered and cast a long shadow, which abruptly disappeared as the doors banged shut. His lips tight, Utray walked stiffly around the pool, past the unlit candles, and stood behind the last empty chair.

Celume leaned sideways to whisper to Druv. "Poor man. His back is still bothering him. I told him it might have helped if he had deigned to enter the Pool of Rulve with the rest of us."

"I'm sure he appreciated that remark," Druv muttered. He stood and addressed the group. "The Weshnik' Aseah will begin. Let us stand and place ourselves in Rulve's presence." Chairs scraped back, garments rustled, and hands were raised. Teller, standing next to Celume on Druv's right, quietly took a step back, his hands at his sides.

Utray's voice rang out. "Is the Seah now to pray with a Vol?"

Heads turned and hands fell. Teller stood motionless.

"That's an interesting question," Penan said, "since I see no Vols here." The scholar stood at Druv's left, beside Sheft, and his mild eyes glanced around the table. "I see only the Weshnik' Aseah and the niyal'arists of Rulve."

"Don't play games," Utray retorted. "He wears an evil ring."

"Evil does not reside in any artifact, but in the heart. You know that, Utray."

"Evil resides in the will and is revealed by one's decisions. He chose the vol-ring."

"Look," Teller said. "I stepped out of the circle and do not pray."

"Is there anything else, Utray?" Penan asked, his eyebrows raised politely.

Utray adjusted his cloak. "Not at the moment."

So we begin, Druv thought with a sigh.

After they prayed in their own hearts and then reseated themselves, Druv turned to the young emjadi sitting next to Penan. "On behalf of us all, Sheft, I express our deep condolences. Others here know the pain of losing a spouse." The flash of last night's dream brought a tremor into his voice, and to cover his emotion, he nodded briefly at Komond and Penan, as if referring to them. "We pray that Rulve will grant you the peace that we trust Mariat has already found." He spoke too formally, he knew that, but at least Sheft's eyes turned from staring at the table-top to look for a moment into Druv's own.

"Emjadi," Komond interjected, "I must publicly acknowledge that, in regard to your wife, I failed you not once, but twice."

"Please don't," Sheft said. "You did everything you could to find her."

Druv addressed Mena, who had received the news of her daughter's death from Sheft only yesterday. "We grieve with you also, Mena, for Riah. She was a courageous woman, close to our hearts, and chosen by Rulve to be the mother of our niyalahn-ristas." It would have been easier if he and Mena could have comforted each other, for this loss and others, but that could not happen. A part of Mena still blamed him for exiling Sheft and Riah and had never really understood how necessary it had been.

Everyone was looking at him attentively; it was time to begin. "This meeting is to help us discern what Rulve has called the emjadis to do and what we of the Seani must do. All of us have a part. The emjadis were born to us and through us, and we have come to realize that the entire Seani shares their mission. Both Sheft and Teller have been informed about what happened in the Seani during their absence. Now we must know what happened to them. Teller, please describe to us your life in Oknu Shuld."

Teller's shoulders tightened. He turned to Sheft, and they exchanged an anguished look across the table.

"I think," Celume said to Druv, "each twin already knows what happened to the other."

"I agree," Druv answered. "Abiyat reported that he insisted the twins spend time together in the Garden of the Sick. They came away from that, he said, looking subdued. Maybe they found compassion for one another."

"Always a good thing," she said with a sigh, "always a step forward."

Teller, meanwhile, had turned slightly away from Sheft. Looking straight ahead, his eyes hooded, the dark emjadi did as he was asked. In a voice devoid of expression, he told them about his education under the Vols, about the suffering he had felt in the ahn but did nothing to alleviate, and about the time he escorted ahn-children into Oknu Shuld. He told them that he chose the name Teller-of-Lies, chose the vol-ring, chose to serve the Lord of Oknu Shuld as Vol Cinc. He told them about the deaths for which he felt responsible: that of the mind-prober Greaz, the young girl Keya, Yuin's ahn-twin Gorv—and worst of all, Sheft's wife Mariat. The entire time Mena stared at her grandson, her eyes bereft, her knuckles white bumps on her thin fists.

At one point, Abiyat asked Teller about the scars on his back and cheek. If Druv had not been watching closely, he would have missed how Teller's eyes jerked down and to the side, the fleeting tension in his jaw, the faint flush of shame. Yet he answered Abiyat's question in the same expressionless voice. Brows creased around the table and, to Druv's gratitude, Ukaipa, the Se in charge of the nursery, reached out to take Mena's hand.

At last the dark emjadi's tale came to a close. He continued to stare straight ahead, but now Druv noticed he had withdrawn a twisted piece of cord from his pocket and was clutching it tightly.

"Thank you, Teller," Druv said. "That could not have been easy for you."

With this, the grip of the painful narrative was loosened in the room, and several people wiped their eyes. The morning sun had risen high enough now to illuminate the stained-glass windows in the eastern alcoves, and it cast shining images of blue-white Chrysalis and golden Seed onto the earthen floor. Hirai passed around the water flask and the cups.

Druv called the meeting back to order, and then nodded at Komond, who wanted to speak. The Se turned to his left to address Teller. "You have answered many of our questions, but being responsible for Seani defense, I must ask another. What are the Spider-king's future plans?"

Teller lowered his eyes and a look of anguish passed over his face. It was quickly repressed, so that when he replied, it was in the same dead tone he'd been using most of the morning. "The Eyascnu intends to spread his domain throughout Shunder and beyond. I was ordered to find and fortify the ancient towers on the edge of the Riftwood. He wants to use them as a base to cut off the rebels of Bellstone Forest and then raze the Seani to the ground." He swallowed, and then went on. "He will condemn the Se to the Skewrong Grabe. He has promised Se Druv to Vol Nosce."

A short cry escaped Hirai, but Komond merely compressed his lips and nodded. Druv knew that Teller was only confirming the Seah's long-held suspicions, but to hear that those suspicions had become the lord's immediate intentions, and to learn of the viciousness of those intentions, chilled even himself.

Utray's eyebrows came down as he leaned forward to glare at Teller. "So tell us," he asked, "would *Vol Cinc* have been part of these plans?"

Teller cut his dark eyes to Utray. "What do you think?"

His tone was half-defiant and half-tormented, as if the emjadi had put the question to both Utray and himself.

"You would see your home destroyed?" Utray pressed on. "Your grandmother horribly tortured?"

"Leave off from that!" Sheft demanded. At this sudden exclamation, several people started in surprise, but Sheft never took his eyes off Utray. "Endure what he endured and then ask such questions."

"Before this goes any further," Nemes interrupted, "I wish to remind everyone what my examination of Teller revealed. He was made to believe that the Se feared him, that his grandmother tried to drown him, that he had no real home."

The counselor, Druv knew, was firmly reminding not only Utray, but also Teller, of pertinent facts that neither of them were taking into account.

"When only six years old," Nemes went on, "Teller endured a brutal mind-probing. He also was subjected to multiple interrogations conducted by a skilled Vol over a period of two days. In all likelihood, substances were used to implant false memories and confuse others. Following this experience were thirteen years of indoctrination and coercion."

Nemes looked down at his clasped hands for a moment. "I believe it shows Rulve's providence," he said, "and perhaps the emjadi's resilience and early upbringing, that he was not completely corrupted. He was able to come home to us."

Utray looked as if he might argue with that, but Abiyat took one glance at Teller and put up his hand. "The emjadi has had enough questions for now."

"Let us then proceed with Sheft," Druv said.

Now it was Sheft's turn to seek and meet his brother's eyes. Druv could not overhear mind-speech directed toward someone else—no one could—but he sensed that Sheft needed to know if his brother was there for him.

Whatever passed between them, Sheft seemed to take courage from it. With his silver eyes fixed on the table in front of him, he described his life in At-Wysher. Twice Utray told him to speak louder, but both times meeting a black look from Teller, did not ask again. In a voice as rigidly toneless as his brother's had been, Sheft told them about Wask, an entity that haunted their village, an entity so lethal it took three names to describe it. He said he saw it for the first time when he was six, when it had crept out of the Riftwood under the form of a black ground-mist called the Groper. He said that his appearance repelled the villagers and they suspected him as a foreigner, that he used an inner constriction he called ice to prevent a wound from bleeding, and that he believed—like his brother, Druv noted—that he was responsible for two deaths. Again like his brother, he was brutally honest and made no excuses for anything he'd done.

During the narration Penan had quietly gotten up to pace in front of the nearby Marhaut Alcove, and dim spots of light from her stained-glass window—silver, slate, and pearl—passed across his form. Some of the others asked Sheft several questions, and from his answers, everyone learned that his injuries were the result of a field-burn accident, discovered what the so-called council of elders had planned to do to him at the K'meen Arûk, and found out what had transpired after Sheft was expelled into the Riftwood. Relating all these events was clearly difficult for the young man, yet Druv felt that Sheft had glossed over certain details. He knew from Nemes that the emjadi had not told them about his greatest fear.

Sheft finished to a prolonged, heavy silence. Having observed his reticent nature, Druv guessed that the emjadi had been talking longer than he ever had in his life and motioned for Hirai to bring him a cup of water. This the lad gratefully gulped down.

Celume had been listening with her head bowed, her long brown hair a curtain around her face. Now she straightened, pushed her hair back, and addressed Druv.

"They have been gravely wounded, not only in body, but also in spirit."

Druv answered with a heavy heart. "Only time can heal the double burdens of grief and guilt. It seems we have a long road ahead of us, Celume."

Neither was looking at the other, but when Celume answered him, he knew by the quality of her mind-speech that she was no longer herself. She was now the seeress who saw deeper and farther. "The Creator has taken them and blessed them, broken them and forged them anew. Rulve has given them to us so that our land might live. Now the Coin of Rulve is being made ready for the spending yet to come."

Druv closed his eyes, aware of the great disk behind him, of the open hands. *You brought us here, Rulve, into this mixture of failure and pain. Now what are we supposed to do with it?*

Chapter 5

Passageways

Mariat raised her head from the pillow she had made of Sheft's jacket. In the murky light, two slanted ovals glowed down at her. They were eyes, blank white eyes without pupils, embedded in a tree-bark face. She gasped and sat up.

The lipless mouth opened and emitted a voice that echoed strangely. "I am called Vol Kuat, the Delver." He wore a cloak that looked like it was made of dead, vein-threaded leaves, and he held as a lantern one of the larvae-filled globes.

The last person Mariat had seen in this opulent rocky chamber was the silver-eyed woman who had saved her in the Riftwood. But the woman had made a demand that had broken her heart: she must free her beloved Sheft and allow him to be who he was, the Coin of Rulve. Mariat did not know what that phrase meant, but knew deep down the truth of what the woman had told her. And so, whether it happened in a vision or in some greater reality, she had embraced her dearest heart for what might be the last time and torn herself away from his side.

Now she found herself alone, sitting at a wooden desk in this oppressive, rock-bound chamber with no windows and no comforting hearth. She met the figure's gaze as levelly as she could. "If you are Vol Kuat, then you must know Vol Cinc." Even to her own ears, her voice sounded too high, and she lowered it. "I was traveling with Vol Cinc and"—she swallowed—"another man. We were attacked by umbraks, and now I'm here. What is this place?"

"It is called Oknu Shuld."

Teller had mentioned the name, and even in the forest, it sounded ominous. Here it sounded deadly. Yet Sheft's brother had told her that if she was captured, she must play the haughty lady and show no fear. "I demand," she said, standing up to face the Delver, "that you escort me to Vol Cinc."

The figure turned toward the blank wall to his left, muttered a word, and the outline of a door appeared. It rumbled open, and he gestured for her to enter.

She could see nothing but blackness beyond the opening. "I'm not walking in there."

"It is the only way. I always point out the only way."

A part of her mind clanged a warning; another part knew she had no choice. After making the decision to release Sheft, she had no choices left.

Her heart in her throat, she threw on her green cloak and ducked through the opening. They made their way down a maze of narrow tunnels. Perhaps because of the lack of ventilation, or the smell of mold, or her own fear, she couldn't seem to get enough air. An open window would have allowed the cold wind of Seed to swirl through the passage and clear her head, but there seemed to be no such thing in this vast crypt. They went down a long curve of rocky steps built into the wall while the Vol's lantern-globe cast his monstrous shadow against it.

They passed the dark mouth of a tunnel, which exuded the odor of old blood. Vol Kuat unlocked a rusty gate, ushered her through, and shut it behind them. As they walked, the walls and ceiling receded into the shadows, and the tunnel became a cave with an uneven floor. The Delver led her past an array of side-passages and through open areas where water dripped from above. At one point they skirted a deep pit, its bottom lost in obscurity. Mariat tried to remember the turns but soon lost track.

At last Vol Kuat stopped and raised the lantern. They were standing at the bottom of two shallow, terrace-like steps. Not far off gaped a pair of black passageways.

The fear that had been skittering in Mariat's stomach now spread into chills along her arms. The Delver lowered the lantern, and the ghostly light under his face turned his eyes into inky pools. "You're not leading me to Vol Cinc, are you," she said. It was a statement, not a question.

"Wait here," the Delver ordered. "Wait for the Vora." He placed the lantern on the ground and made as if to turn away.

Mariat grabbed his arm. "What is the Vora?" The Vol said nothing, only looked straight ahead, but beneath his cloak the limb she clutched was crawling like a sack stuffed with cockroaches. In horror she let go, and Vol Kuat glided away.

She started to follow, but he had already been swallowed by the dark. "I've done nothing to you," she cried after him. "Don't leave me alone here." She heard no footsteps, and the echo of her quavering voice was the only answer. She shuddered; those pupil-less eyes must be able to see in even in this blackness.

Mariat pulled her cloak closer around her. Oh god, she'd left Sheft's jacket behind. She'd been wearing it ever since she'd been taken from his side, had clutched its sleeves when terror stalked her, and now it was gone. Tears stung in the back of her eyes.

From the direction they had come, she heard the faint, far-off clang of a gate. The Delver had locked her in. Blackness pressed against the lantern's dim circle of light at her feet, and all she could hear was her own breathing, as if she were confined in a closed, stone sarcophagus. Wiping her eyes, she sank down to the floor and huddled close to the repulsive globe. How long would the trapped worms continue to glow? She could try to find her way out, but in the wavering lantern-light she would risk stumbling into a shaft or trapping her foot in an unseen crevice. She pictured herself groping through endless passageways as the light grew fainter, until it died and left her smothering in airless black.

She listened for any sound, for the rustle of the approaching Vora, whatever that might be. Fearful images jumped before her mind's eye, but she firmly shoved them aside. She still had some light, some hope. Yet the hairs rose at the back of her neck, as if hostile eyes were staring at her. Like a foolish child, she pulled her hood over her head to hide from them.

But she could not hide from the darkness, for it arched over her like a waiting spider.

Chapter 6

Laying Bare the Bones

Druv sat back, took a deep breath, and addressed the Weshnika. "We now all know some of what the emjadis experienced while they lived apart from us. They are dealing with failure and grief, and are unsure of what they are called to do." He paused, then went on. "They are, in fact, much like this gathering here. All of us in this room have failed. We have struggled for years to do what we could to help our land, yet the Spider-king continues to grow stronger. This morning we learned much to sadden and dishearten us. But we cannot lose hope. Sheft has taken up the toltyr and sits here with us. Teller has found his way back to us. It's a beginning."

"It may be a beginning," Abiyat said, "but for now it must end. The niyalahn-ristas almost died. They are only one day out of their sickbeds, and these past hours have been hard on them. They must return to the infirmary and rest. We will continue tomorrow."

Utray pushed back his chair and stood. "Much as some of us might want that," he said, "I cannot agree just yet. I have another question for Teller."

"Utray," Druv said, "for heaven's sake. Listen to—"

"Let him ask," Teller said wearily.

Utray turned his head to the emjadi. "You have not explained to my satisfaction why you accepted the vol-ring."

"I would think," Penan said with a sigh, "that it was obvious. He was coerced under torture."

"Many men would not be so easily persuaded."

"Easily?" Sheft asked. "Have you seen his scars?"

"He wanted to save the little ahn boy, Utray," Mena said, speaking as if to a child.

Teller, who had been sitting with his elbow on the table and his hand shielding his eyes, put his hand down and turned to Utray. "I saved myself. I took the ring and became Cinc. I was no ahn, Utray. I had choices, just as you said, and I made them."

Utray crossed his arms. "So you took the Vol-ring to obtain power. To escape pain."

The emjadi regarded him steadily. "Correct," he said.

"And how did that work out, Teller?" Celume asked. "Did you in truth escape pain and acquire power?"

The dark eyes turned to her. "It brought more pain. For the ahn. For me. It brought power, yes, but not enough to free anyone."

Including yourself, Druv thought.

"Your motives are skewed," Utray said. "They go deep into the dark."

A tight, ironic twist touched Teller's lips. "It's where I lived, Utray."

Behind Druv, Lir stirred. As his assistant, he sat in one of the seats that formed a square outside the circle of chairs around the table. Having recently returned from a night journey across umbrak-infested territory in order to help the emjadis, Lir seemed in no mood to tolerate anything he disagreed with. "Your remarks, Se Utray, accomplish nothing. Blame and guilt are like vultures that tear at the dead."

Utray raised his eyebrows at Lir's tone. "Didn't I teach you, lad, that vultures have an important purpose? That they lay bare the bones and dispose of rot? And surely you understand this is what the Weshnika is designed to do." He transferred his look to Teller. "So, Teller, what about the ahn? What, ultimately, *did* you do for them?"

A flush rose to the dark emjadi's cheeks, but he met Utray's gaze. "I took their hope away."

"And by doing that," Sheft interjected, "saved their lives."

Hirai, who sat in the corner across from Lir and who had been sighing and frowning and clearly expressing her disapproval, finally spoke up. "You're making this into some kind of trial, Se Utray. We're not here to deal with bones and rot, but to discern the Heart of the Seah."

Utray spread out his hands and appealed to Penan. "Surely you support me in this. The heart must be informed by the mind, or the truth will never be revealed."

The scholar smiled. "Do you really want me to expound on the subject of truth?"

"It is time we move on," Druv said hastily. "The past is beyond our ability to change, and the truth—as both of you will certainly agree—consists of many facets, some of which may be visible to Rulve alone. The Vols did their worst to twist Teller's nature, and no one instructed him about who he was. Now please sit—" Before he could finish, Teller interrupted.

"They told me who I was," he said. "In Oknu Shuld they told me. Gorv and Liasit, even Mochlos. They all told me."

"But you denied it," Utray said.

Teller met Utray's stare. "I denied Rulve first," he said. "With my body and soul I denied him. How could I be anything of his?"

"You thought you could save Keya," Sheft said. "They told you that your rejection of Rulve would save her, but they lied."

Teller's eyes turned to his brother. "I couldn't be who Gorv wanted me to be, or who Liasit wanted. I burned with hate and fire, Sheft. I made collars for ahn. I brought children into Oknu Shuld. For God's sake, I made the very poison that almost killed us."

Nemes leaned across the table. "Teller, they mind-damaged you. They drugged you and lied to you and hurt you. Your intellect knows this, but your heart does not."

"I betrayed my own brother! I was on my way to take him—and his wife, Nemes—to Oknu Shuld."

"But just before the attack," Sheft protested, "you tried to help us."

"His efforts coming," Utray pointed out, "just a little too late."

Teller said nothing, and Druv saw only the side of his rigid, dark head.

With a sigh, Nemes rubbed the bridge of his nose between thumb and forefinger. "It is to the emjadi's credit that he has confessed all these things, even though he could easily have hidden them from us. In the final analysis, Teller turned away from evil and tried to do good."

Utray arranged his cloak around him and sat down "Yet," he murmured, "Mariat is dead."

Teller took a shuddering breath. "I would give my life to bring her back."

Druv could feel the emjadi's agony of soul, but he must speak honestly. "It is true, Teller, that you have done grave harm to innocent people. That burden is indeed heavy, my son, and you will carry it all your days. But the deaths you blame yourself for, especially in the cases of Keya and Gorv, were not entirely your responsibility. Others make choices too, and there's nothing we can do about that."

Something hard passed over Teller's face. "What choices did Mariat have?"

No one spoke, and neither twin looked at the other. Druv decided it was time to end this niyal'arist flood of guilt and remorse. "I suspect that young people judge themselves so severely partly because of immaturity and pride. They find it hard to admit how weak human nature can be, how some events are out of their control. It is the elderly, with a lifetime of experience with such things, who value mercy."

He turned his head to address first Teller and then Sheft. "We are not here to judge you, and neither must you judge yourselves. As Rulve's niyal'arists, you have a mission, and this mission is not about you. It is about redeeming our land. It is about taking back our people and our soil from the evil that has stolen it. You must acknowledge—both of you—that you are as prone to failure as the rest of us. Your brother, Teller, was one of those most hurt by your actions, and he has forgiven you. Now you must accept his forgiveness and move on."

Abruptly, Teller slapped his right hand onto the table, deliberately exposing the vol-ring. "All morning every one of you has been trying not to look at this ring, but here it is. I can't get it off. It's grown into my hand. Is this also what I must accept?"

Every eye darted to the ring, and then away.

From her chair at Teller's left, Celume reached out to touch the young man's arm. "Soon after you were taken, the Seah learned you are t'lir and s'eft, the opposite sides of one coin. Whether you are worthy or unworthy in your own eyes or in ours, and for reasons we may not understand, Sheft needs you to complete his mission, and you need him. This fact may be denied or rejected, but it remains a fact."

She stood, reached across the table to take the toltyr from Mena's box, and held it out in front of Teller. "This toltyr belongs to you and to no one else. Will you take it up?"

Teller's face was so white that the scar on the side of his face, lightened by the healing waters, now seemed to burn. "I can't wear this ring and Rulve's holy toltyr. I can't."

"You are right," Utray said, "for you cannot hold both in your heart."

The dark eyes burned. "This ring was *never* in my heart!"

Celume took Teller's hand and gently rubbed the scratches around the vol-ring with her thumb. "You accepted this ring to save ahn, to flee from a greatness you thought you did not possess. In spite of what happened to you, in spite of what you have done, Rulve calls you, Teller. She has laid her hands upon you, upon you and your brother. Accept the toltyr, and even this vol-ring will be redeemed."

The emjadi withdrew his hand from hers. "I can't wear both."

Celume gazed at him a moment. Then she quietly placed the toltyr back into its box and sat down.

Teller raised his eyes to his brother, sitting across the table from him, and said, "I can never make up for the hurt I have caused you. But when you discover your power, Sheft, when you depart on Rulve's mission, I'll go with you as your servant—if you'll have me."

Penan, who had again left his seat and was leaning against the great tree Twegen, now stepped forward. "Without the toltyr," he said to Teller, "you will go with only half your soul. And Sheft will have only half his power." He narrowed his eyes at him. "Who are you, Teller? Vol Cinc? Teller-of-Lies? Or the T'lir of Rulve's Coin? You are free now to decide, free of the influence of the Vols. You must set guilt aside, set the past aside, and decide."

Teller flinched as if he had been hit, but said nothing.

"How free," Nemes murmured, "can he be, after spending most of his life as a captive in Oknu Shuld?"

"I could have left whenever I wanted," Teller insisted. "I was no ahn."

No one answered, and both twins kept their eyes averted from each other.

"He would rather believe," Celume said to Druv, "that he freely chose evil than that he fell victim to it."

Druv opened his hands and then let them close. "Wouldn't most people prefer to think of themselves as powerful instead of weak?"

Without looking at him, the seeress produced a sad, one-sided smile. "It must be a man thing, Druv."

CHAPTER 7

AT A COMPLETE LOSS

AT DRUV'S RIGHT, REFLECTIONS FROM THE alcoves facing southwest now lay on the floor: oranges and yellows from the Sun window and red light from the window of S'gan pooling like blood on the ground. According to the time-candle in the middle of the table, it was already after noon, and the Seani's heart had discerned little but tragedy.

Keppit the cook brought in a lunch of herb tea, hot soup, and warm brown bread, which they all ate at their places. Afterward, Abiyat insisted that mats be rolled out for the emjadis in the now dim silver and grey recesses of the Marhaut Alcove. Both twins, looking exhausted, took advantage of them.

The rules of the Weshnika did not permit anyone to leave until the meeting was declared closed, so everyone tried to relax. Ukaipa opened the Welf door, which faced the southwest, and placed rugs in the bright sunlight that poured in. Avia and Hirai joined her, where they sat cross-legged and talked about their children. Others walked briskly around the Pool of Rulve or poked their heads through the Eka door for a breath of cool air. One of the guards delivered a letter to Abiyat, who read it and, with a significant look, passed it over to Druv. At last the bowls and cups were taken away, the side doors were closed, and everyone returned to their places.

Turning to Sheft, Druv said, "Before we go on, I've been asked to explain that when we speak about Rulve, we use both masculine and feminine references. This is to remind ourselves that the Creator is not male or female, but spirit."

Sheft had barely nodded before Utray started in. "This skora of yours," the botanist asked Teller, "how powerful is it?"

Several people around the table leaned forward.

"I don't know," Teller said in a dull voice. The short rest had not erased the bruise-like shadows under his eyes.

"Can it kill?"

"I never tried."

Penan chewed his lips as he considered this. "How does this fire differ from the power of sh'kier?"

"Sh'kier?" Teller's forehead creased, as if he were trying to remember something. "I saw the word once, in an ancient manuscript. I didn't know what it meant then, and I don't know now."

Penan produced the small rolled-up scroll he always carried and tapped it absently on the table, where it made a hollow, popping sound. "Even when you were a boy, Teller, we suspected you held the seeds of skora. Over the years, however, we have learned much more." The scholar glanced at Celume, but she gestured for him to continue.

"Skora is a great power, but with its roots in anger or fear, it is not a specific niyal'arist power. But sh'kier is. According to the ancient writings, sh'kier in its first stages may be confused with skora, but it is a very different fire. Empathy releases it; compassion kindles it. Skora is defensive, often self-serving, something sh'kier can never be. It is"—he thoughtfully held the scroll against his lips for a moment—"the fire of justice."

Druv glanced at Teller. A movement too bitter to be a smile jerked briefly at the corner of the lad's mouth, then was gone. Justice was undoubtedly a foreign concept in Oknu Shuld.

From the chair behind Celume, Avia spoke up. "As is true with much that has been written about the emjadis," she said, "the word has other connotations. Sh'kier is not justice in the sense of punishment, but it is the power that restores balance. The *Tajemjadi* says, '*When opposites build up like storm-clouds, sh'kier lights up the darkness like a bolt from the sky. It rips through lies and cruelty, and justice pours down, and peace is born in the thunder of its passing.*'"

"Compared to this fire," Celume added, "skora is but a candle's flame."

No one said anything, but an unasked question floated over the big table. Ianak speared it like an egret spears a fish. "Teller, has Rulve given you this power?"

Every eye leaped to Teller's face. But he answered like a dead man. "No."

"Are you sure?" Hirai asked. "Maybe this sh'kier is bottled inside you, and skora is, well, like the cork."

"If Rulve laid this great thing inside me," Teller answered, "the Vols would have known. The Lord of Oknu Shuld would have known."

"But would *you* know?" Penan asked.

"How could he?" Mena cried. "The Vols made sure he didn't know his own name!"

"Perhaps," Utray said, "Rulve did place sh'kier inside Vol Cinc here but, because of the choices he made, it withered away into skora."

The dark emjadi, sitting under his heart's shadow, made no answer.

Druv heaved a great sigh and glanced at Abiyat. Now they must, however reluctantly, reveal what he and the healer had just discovered during their break, "At best," Druv said, "the emjadis are only half ours. We know Riah was their mother and that Mena is their grandmother, but we do not know who their father was."

"What!" Mena exclaimed. "For God's sake, do we have to go over this *again*? It's been years, and still we—"

"What do you mean?" Teller asked Druv. "We were both born in the Seani, sons of Riah and Neal."

"Riah told me," Sheft added, "that she had been raped while a prisoner in the lord's dungeon. But she was sure Neal was our father."

"*Is* your father," Mena corrected in a high, strained voice. "He could still be alive, a prisoner in Oknu Shuld."

Druv stifled a groan. On this topic Mena stubbornly refused to give up hope, no matter how unwarranted. But even if she were right, and Neal still lived, no one really knew who Neal had been: the son of Nosce, Vol Prome of Oknu Shuld, or the son of Druv, the Seah's eldest. The lineage of the emjadis was shrouded in uncertainties, lost in shadows. Why would Rulve choose to place two damaged young men who were supposed to save her people into such a chaotic situation?

Everyone was looking expectantly at him, and this was not the place to dwell on his own lack of faith. "While we were having lunch," Druv said, "Abiyat received a report from Ullar-Sent. He will now share it with all of you. Mena, please calm yourself and listen to what he has to say."

The healer folded his hands on the table and, running one thumb over the other, addressed the group. "As is my custom from time to time, I traveled last year to Ullar-Sent to meet with a small but renowned group of healers there. They were engaged in a study of the swelling sickness, which has now been concluded. Their report"—he tapped it with his finger—"has confirmed something I had long suspected about this disease."

Ukaipa blew her nose. "Sorry," she said. "I feel the sniffles coming on. Anyway, emjadis, this swelling sickness is fairly common in children. Its main symptom is a swollen throat. Most often the little ones get better without any problems."

"That's true," Abiyat went on, "but this report has corroborated my suspicions that this disease is far more serious when the patient is past puberty. Only eight weeks before Neal's wedding, a particularly virulent form of the swelling sickness struck the portion of the Spider-king's army that was garrisoned in Rydle. Neal, who was working as our spy in the bakery at that time, came down with it. Although he was a healthy young man, it took him some time to recover, and even then I wondered if damage had been done. I said nothing about my suspicions at the time because I wasn't certain. Now, however, we know"—he placed both open hands on the letter in front of him—"that a severe case of the swelling sickness in adult males inevitably causes testicular inflammation and sterility. I am sorry, emjadis, but the evidence tells us that your father could not have been Neal."

"But," Sheft objected, "even before they were married, our mother and Neal might have—"

Abiyat shook his head. "The timing of your births shows that you could not have been conceived before Neal's illness."

Everyone sat in stunned silence. Mena leaned back in her chair, her face deeply lined.

"Then who?" Teller rasped.

"We don't know," Abiyat answered.

Mena moaned. "We discussed all this long ago. It has nothing to do with what we're talking about here."

"I disagree," Utray retorted. "Who their father is, or was, might have a bearing on how the power that Rulve gave your grandsons has been affected."

Mena looked away from him, her throat working.

Utray shook his head. "Many times I've asked the Seah to consider this matter. No one listened to me, and now my suspicions are proved true. We may now know the reason why Teller is sitting there wearing a vol-ring. It comes as an evil heritage from whatever spawned him in Oknu Shuld."

"Sometimes," Lir said in a tight voice, "I wonder who in hell spawned you, Se."

"You're being illogical, Se Utray," Sheft said. "My brother's father must be my father too, and I'm wearing the toltyr."

"But only because," Utray said, "by your own admittance, you were shamed into it. A decision, it seems to me, of a weakling."

Sheft said nothing; but his cheeks flamed, and he lowered his head.

"My God, Utray," Mena exclaimed. "Are you attacking Sheft now? Now *neither* emjadi is to your liking?"

"Liking has nothing to do with it," Utray retorted. "*Someone* must point out the obvious here. Do you think I enjoy sitting among you as the only open-minded inquirer? It takes courage, Mena. I'm sure you teach your students that it is not easy to go against the crowd. But"—truly angry now, he raised his voice and thumped the table with his fist—"facts are facts!"

"Indeed," Penan said. "So let us deal with facts. We know what we know, and now we must continue with our investigation of what powers Rulve has bestowed upon his niyalahn-ristas." He turned to Sheft, sitting at his left. "We have heard that you used an inner constriction you call ice to stop yourself from bleeding. This is indeed unusual, but it is never mentioned in the writings we have studied regarding niyal'arist abilities. It seems to be a negative ability, a preventative not on par with the positive nature of sh'kier or even skora. So I ask you, emjadi, what power do you possess?"

Sheft did not lift his head, but Druv could see that all the color drained from the young man's face. "None," he said in a low voice.

Utray threw up his hands. "Of course not. Why would we expect anything different from a weakling?"

"Why are you so confrontational, Utray?" Ukaipa burst out. "So angry? Don't you trust Rulve anymore? You used to have a kind heart. You used to take the children sledding, take them on hikes through the woods. Teller was there, one of the youngest at the time. And you loved him. Like you loved all of them. You taught them the names of the stars, Utray. What *happened* to you?"

"What happened to *me*?" Utray retorted. "Ask rather what happened to *Teller*." He fell back against his chair and blew air out of his cheeks. "We are wasting our time here. Druv, you said the emjadis were much like ourselves. I don't see it. I see two young men who never helped anyone and exhibited a life of almost complete self-absorption. Now we hear that one has only a debased gift to offer, and the other none at all. Of course I trust Rulve. But how can I trust a Vol and his weakling brother?"

Teller jerked his head around to face Utray. Druv couldn't see the look on the emjadi's face, but whatever Utray saw was enough to cause his eyes to widen. "Weakling!" Teller grated. "That's three times you've thrown that word at Sheft. The wounds on his back almost killed him, but you know nothing about the courage that put them there."

"If I do not," Utray snapped, "then in Rulve's name, inform me!"

Teller turned to look at Sheft, who raised his head. They regarded each other, probably mind-speaking. Then, in that dead voice that both emjadis used when talking about emotional events, Sheft filled in what he had earlier omitted. During a field-burn accident, he had thrown himself over a young boy and took the damage that would have torn the child apart.

The silence that followed was so deep that Druv heard Celume, at his right, take a long breath and quietly exhale it. "So now we see it," she said. "The mysterious parallels that emerge in the lives of twins, even though they have long been separated. Both emjadis have saved a child's life at considerable cost to themselves. To this day, they bear the scars. A foreshadowing, perhaps, of what Rulve has called them to do."

Utray's eyebrows turned down. "I understand that, Celume. Yet both Sheft and Teller have told us that people also died because of them." He shook his head once, as if to clear it. "There is too much a mix of good and evil here. I am"—his whole body sagged—"at a complete loss."

The man was truly discouraged, Druv saw. His last words had come from the heart. Druv studied both emjadis for some reaction. They sat as rigidly as they had for hours now, but a flush had returned to Sheft's cheeks, and Teller's jaw clenched.

Ukaipa, looking contrite, reached over to pat Utray's arm. "Have patience," she murmured. "With yourself and with the Weshnika. These things take time. Rulve created all things good, so let her deal with what we call evil."

Utray maintained his dismal look, but did not shrug off her hand.

Druv sighed, reluctant to subject either of the emjadis to yet more pressure, but he had to go on. "Sheft," he said, "when Penan just asked you about your power, you said you had none. This morning, when you told us of your life in At-Wysher, I sensed that you left out something important. That isn't helpful, to us or to you. When you were half-conscious in the hospit, Nemes ascertained that your fear of bleeding arose from a frightening experience when you were a child. Was this when you saw the black mist, the Groper, for the first time?"

"Yes," Sheft answered.

The doors remained closed, but the tall candle behind Sheft guttered. It stood in front of the ancient tree called Twegen, its trunk inscribed with a leaf, and it seemed as if the candle flame had been disturbed by an invisible passage. Air movements in the Quela, Druv had noticed, were often strange and wayward, as were its shadows, caused by nothing he could discern.

"Emjadi, what was it that drew the creature to your blood?"

Sheft turned his silver eyes on him, looked quickly away, and then deliberately back. It was as if he realized that, in this time and place, he could allow others see him the way he was. Progress, Druv thought, of a sort.

"It was," Sheft said, "the plants." He took a deep breath, glanced at his twin, and then, clearly hesitant, told them about the afternoon when, as a young child, he saw how drops of his blood that had fallen onto the ground made the earth stir with roots. His father had been appalled and hacked away what was sprouting. That night, as a black mist, Wask the Groper had approached the spot. It seemed in some horrible way to savor the blood in the soil, to taste it and want more. Twice more in his life, Sheft admitted, ice hadn't been enough to stop himself from bleeding, and both times the obscene plants had sprung up, and both times he had done his best to annihilate them. Yet Wask had still sensed the blood that was their source, evil within calling to evil without, even to the beetle-man coming to his door.

Soon after Sheft began talking, Utray's face sharpened with a peculiar intensity. Now he leaned forward, placed both hands on the table, and interrupted him. "You said your blood made the earth stir with roots. What do you mean by that?"

A look of distaste passed over the young man's face. "The ground," Sheft answered, "erupted with a mass of tiny plants. It was as if my veins"—he swallowed—"were packed with roots, infested with disease. And everyone in the village could somehow sense that."

Utray jumped up with a cry. His chair scraped on the floor. "S'rere, Druv! Oh my God, I think he's talking about s'rere!"

CHAPTER 8

A Hidden Drama

"What's the matter, Se Utray?" Hirai asked. "Are you accusing Sheft of something else now?"

Utray turned to her, his whole expression touched with wonder. "S'rere, Hirai. The restorative power of growth!"

"They know of this power in Oknu Shuld!" Teller exclaimed. He stared, ashen-faced, at his brother. "They call it the 'blood that makes the earth dance.' The lord searches for it, tests every rista for it. I was tested. If the Eyascnu Varo knew this power was within his grasp, he would attack the Seani for it."

Alarm rippled around the table, and Komond sat back grimly, his thumbs in his belt.

"Surely our wards—" Mena protested, but Druv put out a hand.

"One thing at a time, please," he said. "Penan, what do you know about s'rere?"

Penan rolled his scroll thoughtfully between his palms. "Only what the ancient escrimages have written. S'rere is the earth's powerful ability to grow and regenerate."

"There's also," Celume said, "an old rhyme in the *Tajemjadi* that says:

'Twin-self maimed, evil claimed; s'rere stained and waned.

Twin-self faced, death embraced; s'rere deeply graced.'"

As if it had suddenly sprung out at him, Druv saw the leaf carved on the great tree Twegen to his left. His eyes jumped to his right, to the flame etched on Enlen. Leaf and flame, facing each other in the Quela. It was as if they crossed invisible beams in front of Rulve's Disk, as if their lines of force met and sparked over the emjadis' heads, the dark and the light. He had never thought much about the symbols, assuming them to represent earth and fire, two of the four great elementals, and that the other two, air and water, had been lost or never carved. The symbols had been there long before he'd arrived at the Seani, and no one seemed to know anything about their origin.

Some shifted in their chairs after Celume's recitation, but Hirai voiced what they all must be thinking. "I don't understand that poem," she said, "and I don't like that 'death embraced' part."

Celume smiled faintly at her. "What about the 'deeply graced' part? Doesn't that ameliorate all the rest?"

Looking unconvinced, Hirai didn't answer.

"I'm not sure," Celume went on, "if this verse describes what happened to niyalahn-ristas of the past or what they will face in the future."

"Or," her assistant Avia put in, "it could refer to choices that lie before ordinary people in every time."

"Perhaps both," Nemes suggested.

The rhyme troubled Druv, yet, as their seeress had pointed out, a hint of hope gleamed inside it. He turned to Sheft. "Emjadi, you fear the power in your blood that produces these roots. What about ice, this ability that prevents a wound from bleeding? It may not be a niyal'arist power, but do you feel it comes from Rulve?"

Sheft looked down at his hands. "I only know," he said, "that both come from here." He touched his spirikai.

The solar plexus, the fifth node and the seat of niyalahn-rista power.

"Sheft," Utray urged, "you must demonstrate what your blood does."

The young man stiffened.

"It would be difficult for Sheft to do this, Utray," Nemes reminded him.

"Yes, yes," Utray answered, "but he must! S'rere is what all of Shunder aches for. For years I have been searching for any trace of this graced herb, in the fields, in every kind of weather. But I never found it. Niyal'arist blood may draw it out of the earth again!"

Ianak broke in, his eyes alight. "It may be that your skora, Teller, will burn away the evil morue; and your s'rere, Sheft, will restore the healing rue." He spread out his hands to the assembled group. "This must be Sheft and Teller's mission: to burn away and then replant. This would uproot the Spider-king's hold over all Shunder!"

"His hold certainly involves morue," Komond warned, "but it also lies in strength of arms, in fear, and in collusion with corrupted power and wealth."

"We can go no further with that discussion," Utray insisted, "until Sheft bleeds."

His features gaunt, Sheft tapped a spread hand over his closed fist—in desperation, Druv thought. "You don't understand," Sheft pleaded. "My blood always summoned a black mist out of the Riftwood. A mist that killed."

"Perhaps," Nemes said, an edge of excitement in his voice, "that is the origin of your ice. It is the opposite of green and growing things. You must have developed it, Sheft, as a barrier against s'rere, which you learned from an early age to misunderstand and fear."

"The lord believes he once possessed s'rere," Teller said. "I know that because in Oknu Shuld all the ristas had to read his autobiography. His *L'garza Wadek* tells how twin voras came out of the Riftwood at the command of Rûk and infiltrated Oknu Shuld. The lord maintains they were niyalahn-ristas, and that they sucked away the kingly power he was born with. He seeks always to get it back."

"But why?" Mena asked. "Why bother to restore a land he had poisoned?"

While the discussion had been going on, Penan rapidly seesawed his scroll between two fingers, as if it were some kind of engine that powered his thoughts. Now he put the scroll down and said, "I, too, have read the *L'garza*. I believe the Spider-king has no interest in restoring sweet-rue. I believe he wants s'rere for purposes of his own. *L'Garza Wadek*, by the way, means something like *Irrefutable Witness*." He smiled grimly as Hirai snorted.

"It is rumored," Teller said, "that the lord's hands are afflicted with a skin disease. No one ever speaks of it, but the lord sometimes wears black leather gloves. And a mask."

Unease stirred around the table. Then Nemes the counselor said, "If the lord indeed once possessed s'rere, but lost it through some evil choice, his affliction might make a kind of sense. The result when good is twisted and begins to fester."

Penan spoke over the tent of his hands. "The *L'garza* also maintains that these supposed niyal'arist voras so corrupted the lord's brother, Varo, that the Spider-king was forced to kill him in self-defense. The author wrote that he calls himself Eyascnu Varo in memory of this brother." The scholar glanced at Sheft. "You should understand, emjadi, that to this day, the Spider-king hunts for anyone who purports to be niyal'arist. He has vowed to recover both s'rere and skora and avenge what was done to him and to his brother."

"Why then," Komond asked, "does Teller still possess skora? He was under the Spider-king's control for years."

They all turned their heads toward Teller, who produced a sardonic half-smile. "Whatever a Vol has," he said, "the lord will surely use."

The room went silent.

"The Spider-king tells a shadowed story," Celume murmured, "with puzzling motivations. The characters seem to have faces that slide away as soon as one looks closely at them."

Utray, apparently losing patience with the direction the group had gone, made a gesture with one hand that erased it from the air. "No matter what happened in the past, Sheft, you must not fear what s'rere will bring here and now. We are protected."

"But the Riftwood surrounds you," Sheft protested. "Wask must be even stronger here."

"Wask is a creature of the borderlands and has no business with us. In ancient times Marhaut made a bargain with Rûk, the Shadow-King of the Riftwood, to protect the Seani. As long as Marhaut remains his queen, Rûk will not break his bargain. Nothing from the ancient forest has ever come out of it to harm us."

"Yet," Teller put in, "Vol Kuat told me that the king of the Riftwood also looks for s'rere."

Penan raised his eyebrows at this. "So Rûk must have sent Wask to find it. And Wask did find it, according to what Sheft told us. Yet he didn't seize Sheft when he was at his mercy in the Riftwood."

"The ice, Penan," Druv reminded him. "Perhaps he could not."

"Perhaps Wask could not, but I would think the King of the Riftwood could do whatever he wanted in his own domain, ice or no ice."

Druv frowned and leaned back in his chair. Penan, as usual, had an excellent point, but an unsettling one. It seemed as if some hidden drama were being enacted, but all they could see of it were the characters' shadows, silent and inscrutable, flitting across a blank wall.

"Free will," Celume murmured from beside him. "The emjadis must act of their own free will, and both the Spider-king and Rûk would know that."

At this, Sheft looked up, met his brother's eyes, and then looked away.

"We have gone too far afield," Utray said firmly. He pointed across the room. "We will use the ground there." He pushed his chair back and made his way to the great tree behind Sheft, Twegen, into which the leaf was carved.

Sheft cast a pleading look at Druv. "The biggest temptation," he said, "the worst lie, might be to presume I have any power to make a difference."

Druv placed his hands on his thighs and rose with a grunt out of his chair. "We must get to the heart of your doubt, emjadi. That is what this Weshnika is for." He walked stiffly to the ancient tree. The others rose and gathered around him.

It was now mid-afternoon, and the entire Quela was bathed with the leaf-light that streamed through Rulve's Disk. It reflected off the pool and shimmered in the rafters, and for a moment it seemed to Druv that the entire Quela existed within the heart of an emerald. Reluctantly, Sheft joined the group.

Utray called for Larrin. The double doors opened a crack, and the captain of the guards poked his head in. "Please bring a scalpel from the infirmary," Utray ordered.

Sheft turned pale, and Druv sympathized with him, but this test had to be undergone.

CHAPTER 9

AT THE FOOT OF TWO TREES

SUFFUSED IN GREEN LIGHT, IN THE midst of a group of people he barely knew, Sheft stood in front of the tree they called Twegen. A long veined leaf had been carved into the ancient trunk at about head-height. It looked like the leaf on his toltyr. Except for the veins, the shape could be mistaken for a wavy blade or a tongue of fire.

He now faced the blade.

"Don't be afraid, Sheft," his grandmother whispered to him. "Nothing can harm us in Rulve's house."

Someone had opened the Eka-door, and a shaft of sunlight fell over the hard-packed earth at his feet. Even here, in this holy place, he felt its pain, and the longing to heal it swelled in his spirikai. Was this s'rere? Was it s'rere that throughout his life had ached to respond to the cries from far away? The thing in his blood had a name now, and what he had imagined as a curse—as alien roots tightly packed into every vein and welling out with every cut—the people all around him saw as a blessing. Was this what Rulve had called him to do: shed his blood on this holy ground? He remembered his vision, remembered sitting under a white tree with the old man who was Rulve. *"Will you do what you most fear,"* the Creator had asked, *"if love demands it?"*

Rulve's question could be the answer, come soon, an answer that he had begged for only hours ago. Perhaps his grandmother was right. The Quela was the dwelling-place of the Creator, and surely everyone was safe here. Surely he could bleed without fear at the foot of Twegen and in front of Rulve's open hands.

Larrin returned and passed the scalpel to Abiyat.

It glittered, like the knife used at the Rites had glittered; and too many people encircled him, too many eyes were watching him. The earth opened beneath him like a dark mouth, and what it had always disgorged sent a chill up his spine.

Instead of blessing the Quela, what if his blood defiled it? He had no idea what his blood on the soil of this land would produce. A sudden grotesque picture flashed before him, of vines bursting out of the seeds his blood engendered, twining rapaciously around the Quela trees to pull them down; of hordes of beetles, chittering with an avid hunger, streaming out from under the great roots. He felt a sudden urge to dash out the door, into the sun, but his own footsteps would follow him, crawling with roots. It had been his worst nightmare when he was a child: he and a boy whose name began with T running happily through the fields, not knowing the horror that stalked so closely behind.

Someone put a hand on his arm, and he flinched. It was Mena, who claimed to be his grandmother, who was smiling at him, but what if it were Wask's insidious temptation that looked out of her eyes?

Abiyat stepped beside Sheft, his face backlit by the green light. Another face jumped into Sheft's mind, a face alive with beetles under the skin, opening its lipless mouth. *"Pour out your life, niyal'arist. Bleed freely and water the earth."*

"How can I make this easier for you, emjadi?" Abiyat murmured.

His throat was too dry to answer.

"Perhaps on the back of your hand?"

Sheft extended his left hand into the shaft of sunlight; made a fist to keep it from trembling. With his other hand he clutched the toltyr around his neck. Was this what Rulve wanted? His eyes sought the green hands carved into Rulve's disk, but all he could see past those who surrounded him was the top part of the massive disk—a bloated green sun looming over him.

The cold point of Abiyat's knife pressed down. It broke the skin, incised a red line. It shrieked in his head like a nail on metal. Instinctively he constricted his spirikai, and ice closed the cut.

Sheft swallowed. "You'll have to go deeper."

Abiyat did, but ice still gripped Sheft. He tried to loosen it, tried to relax the spirals of his spirikai, but his ears rang with the chittering of night-beetles, and he was frozen by a lifetime of fear. "Deeper," his cold lips said.

Abiyat took a breath and complied.

Sheft willed the vein to melt and flow. *Oh God Rulve, redeem this cursed blood!*

The wound on his hand glistened scarlet in its depths, but receded and did not bleed.

He tried to concentrate on what the Seah had just told him, tried to focus on the toltyr and summon the power of s'rere. But there was nothing in his spirikai but ice. All around him brows creased; faces that had been full of hope now fell.

Hot shame washed over him. He was guilty of a monumental pride, had convinced himself that Rulve wanted him, had snatched a toltyr that belonged to someone else. Sheft tugged at the medallion in angry despair, trying to pull it off.

But then he remembered. They said the toltyr was a coin, that the other side of s'eft was t'lir. He remembered the vision he'd seen under apsura, when his ice had enabled Teller to control his raging skora. Now Sheft looked through the crowd around him, searching for his brother—for fire that could melt ice.

W<small>HILE EVERYONE WAS FOCUSED ON</small> S<small>HEFT</small>, Teller slipped out of the Quela through the Welf-door. After the green light in the hall, the late afternoon sun blazed into his eyes, but he found the trail just as he remembered it. The path led through the woods to the Pool of Compassion, to the quiet pond at the gentle mother's feet. Marhaut would understand what he had to do.

It was a longer walk than Teller remembered. His battle with ineerva poisoning must have drained him more than he thought, and he stopped to rest under a tree.

"Teller, help me!"

The call startled him. It echoed from the past, from a green-eyed man who had begged for help from a six year-old boy. The words had been the plea of a devisement, the beginning of a nightmare; for somehow an evil entity had lied to him while using the language of truth, and he could never understand that betrayal.

"Teller, I need your fire!"

This time he recognized the voice. It was his brother who called him, not a shape-shifter from Oknu Shuld. In his mind's eye he saw him, encased in ice and needing to bleed.

When skora had struggled to break from his control and engulf the infirmary in flames, it was Sheft who had helped him. His brother had somehow passed over to him the ice that kept the fire in check. Now he must return the favor.

"Hold out your hand," Teller said.

SHEFT FELT A SENSATION IN THE palm of his cut hand, as if someone had placed a warm stone there. He closed his fist around it, and slowly the ice retreated. Warmth returned and traveled up his arm. Blood melted and flowed. He unclenched his hand, and the stone, never there, was gone.

Blood trickled through his fingers to the ground. Drops of it trembled on the hard-packed earth, and then slowly sank in. The soil between Twegen's great tree-roots began to bubble, .to stir with life.

Sheft backed away from the sight. His stomach twisted at a memory that had stalked him for thirteen years: his father's horrified face as he looked down at a rash of green plants, the vicious way he hacked at them with his spade; then himself as a boy in the moonlight, frozen with fear as the black mist crept out of the Riftwood. It came as if following a scent, its leading edge stopping inches from his foot, where its wispy fingers sifted through the recently disturbed soil.

With a cry, Utray sank to his knees to examine the roiling earth. People crowded around, exclaiming. Tiny seed-heads bobbed, split, swelled into thick green dicots. These folded down, and true leaves sprang out, a bright lacey green. Seeking the sun, they turned toward the open door.

"It's rue!" Utray cried. "Oh God Rulve, it's sweet-rue!" He held his hands over the rising mat, as if it were a green fire that would warm all of Shunder.

Sheft recognized the tiny plants. From the field-burn, when he watched them sprout as his blood dripped between the slats of the ruined cart. From the wheat field, after Gwin hurled the sickle at him. From that day when he was six, when he had been so proud of what he'd done. *"Father, come see! I bled on the ground and grew these plants."*

They were Rulve's healing, the salvation of his homeland, and they had come out of him. All along, they had been his blood's redemption. Sheft's heart leaped up. *Oh Mariat, you were right. You had faith in me and you were right. If only you could see this, my dearest heart.*

"Emjadi!" Hirai whispered in awe. She went down on one knee, partly to him, partly to the new life at his feet. "Oh Emjadi Sheft, it's the healing rue!" Her face beaming, she burst into tears.

Everyone pressed closer, exclaiming and craning their necks. Some raised their arms in thanks to Rulve.

But then everything changed.

"No!" Utray cried.

With a sharp breath, Hirai stood, her hand at her mouth.

Sheft shifted his eyes to the ground. The seedlings were withering, were turning brown, and swiftly became nothing but ash.

He let the ice flood back and turned aside, shivering from the inevitable ice-reaction. Someone closed the side door, and the sunlight disappeared. His fingers were sticky with dried blood.

All day Teller had been fighting skora, reining it in against its perception of attack; but then, in order to help Sheft, he had to release it in a controlled and careful way. Now, knowing what he intended to do, the fire was rising even further than it had before. He had to move on while he still had the will.

His stomach knotted as he passed under trees tinged with the green buds of Seed, and he barely noticed the still-brown grasses that brushed against his pants. At last he entered the clearing beside the Pool of Compassion and fell to his knees before the white stone bench.

From behind it, the sad mother looked down on him. Marhaut's eyes were of blank, unseeing stone, not the demanding silver eyes that had challenged him in the Riftwood. Not his brother's eyes, which would never again look with love upon his wife.

He didn't have much time before they realized he was missing and would come searching for him.

Teller pulled his dagger out of his belt, laid it on the bench, and placed his right hand flat next to it. The sight of the vol-ring made his stomach lurch; the thin twisted wires clutched his finger like spider legs. He pushed the ring up toward the knuckle as far as it would go and, pressing all his fingers down against the rough-hewn edge of the bench, left only the ring finger extended on top of it. Reining in the frantic skora, jamming his hand tightly against the edge of the bench to keep his other fingers out of the way, he picked up his dagger and positioned the sharp blade just below the ring on his extended finger. He tightened his muscles in determination, then pressed down hard.

Pain shot through his hand and blood swelled, but he bore down harder, seesawing the blade through the skin and into the bone. He hadn't realized how clumsy he would be with his left hand, how awkward the angle would be at the base of his finger. Nausea rose in his throat but now he had a groove he could cut into.

With the point of the dagger he sawed at the bone from one side and then the other, working mostly by feel because of all the blood. The pain ground into his stomach, and he had to blink away a swarm of black dots that crowded into his vision. At one point he had to turn his hand over and cut through the other side. Finally the bone was severed.

But now the blade encountered something it couldn't cut through. What looked like two grey roots ran close to either side of the bone, extending their tendrils into his hand. He had expected this, had felt the progress of its growth only days after the ring had first bitten into his finger.

Holding his dripping hand away from him, he climbed to his feet. His finger dangled, attached now only by the tough grey roots. Again his stomach turned. He bent over, which helped, then placed his maimed hand flat on the ground and planted the heel of his left boot firmly on the bloody finger. He took a deep breath, then pulled back on his hand.

Fresh pain exploded as he twisted his hand back and forth, as if he were uprooting an entrenched malignant weed. A vein in his hand jumped and something cracked. With a sickening squelch, the roots slid out of his hand. Red splattered over his boot, and he fell sideways. He caught himself on his left arm, and only a flare of skora kept him conscious.

His finger lay not far from his foot, bloody roots trailing out of it and writhing on the ground. He shot skora at it, and the skin blistered, then fried, and the roots convulsed like lethal snakes. The smell of burnt flesh hung over the ground.

He engulfed the whole obscenity in flames, until the living thing that had once been attached to his hand fell into ashes.

Except for the ring itself. It was barely charred. Teller sent flare after flare into it until the wires curled inward and fused into a metallic lump. A wisp of smoke rose from the spot.

He was shaking, and his right hand dripped blood. With skora he seared the place where his finger had been and stopped the bleeding. The black spots surged once again into his vision, so he lowered his head and took deep breaths until they subsided. Fighting nausea, he wiped his hand on a patch of newly sprung grass, crawled to the Pool of Compassion, and plunged his hand into the cool water. He lay there until he could stand up again.

The front edge of Marhaut's white stone bench was stained with red. Teller tried to carry water in his hands to wash it off, but most of it leaked out of the gap in his right hand, so he used his boot. At first he succeeded only in spreading the stain, and it took several trips until everything was clean. He wiped his dagger on the grass, awkwardly pulled his boot back on, and stuffed the now-cool metallic lump into his pocket—the left pocket, where it would not touch the blue and red cord. Stumbling, he made his way back to the Quela.

Inside, he could hardly see, and sounds echoed all around him: people talking, then crying out. "Over here! He's returned."

Teller dropped to his knees in front of Enlen, the great tree upon which the flame was carved. With the dagger in his left hand, he hacked a small hole into the hard-packed earth. Pant-legs and the hems of robes surrounded him, people bent over him.

"What's he doing?"

"Oh God, look at his hand!"

He fumbled for the remains of the vol-ring, pushed it deep into the hole, and then covered it with dirt. Fighting off the black motes, he climbed to his feet and somehow made his way to his place at the table. Mena's box, sitting in the circle of the time-candle's light, swam into his vision. The box was still open. Trembling badly, Teller leaned over the table, reached out with his left hand, and took the toltyr. One-handed, he struggled to get it over his head.

Then his brother was bending over him, his pale hair shining. Their eyes met, and Teller saw in Sheft a light he could not understand, and Sheft seemed to see in him a darkness he knew only too well.

Suddenly he had two hands again: his own the left, his brother's the right. Together they got the cord around his neck and settled the toltyr over his heart.

Help had been given and received. An exchange had been made—compassion from Sheft and a gasp of gratitude from Teller—and for an instant these emotions mingled in each other's spirikai.

Teller heard a voice, and he turned his head to see a shadowy figure standing tall and confident against the low green light streaming through Rulve's Disk.

"Now at last they both accept the toltyr," Celume's voice proclaimed. But as she went on, as Teller's consciousness drained away, her voice wavered and echoed. "But s'eft and t'lir are not yet one. Before you, Teller, still lies a choice. Do you understand?"

He did not, and her form, her voice, the meaning of the words—all seemed to pass down a rapidly dimming corridor, and he slumped gratefully into its darkness.

Chapter 10

Works of Art

Across the valley and deep inside Insheer Cliff, the Eyascnu Varo, Lord of Oknu Shuld, bent over his bloodwood worktable, his tightly gloved hands shaping a mound of wet black clay. His palms smoothed an oval thorax, his long, tapered fingers shaped an abdomen and two eye-mounds, and the tips of his thumbs incised grooves under the bulbous head. Completely absorbed, he worked under the single globe suspended above him. The light from the slowly writhing luniku larvae within cast shadows that crawled in the folds of the lord's robe. A cowl hid the top of his face, and only the lips were visible, a red gash above the chin.

"Ah, the wings, Kuat," the lord murmured. "They will consist of black glass, exquisitely thin, veined with purple and garnet and a deep, dark green." He indicated a sheaf of black wires bent at different angles. "Note how these legs are feathered at the ends, just as they are in life. The front two will be raised, as if this creature had paused for a moment to rub them. Flies constantly rub their front legs together, and I intend to catch the deep sensuality of that motion."

Vol Kuat, the Delver, stood wrapped in his dead-leaf cloak, his pupil-less eyes blank. "You are wearing gloves. It must be time for another treatment."

The hands worked silently for a moment. "I suffer, Kuat. That is true. Yet for the sake of my subjects I keep on. Only my vision can give them hope."

"'My vision'—a strange turn of phrase for one born as you were."

The red mouth-gash within the hood twisted for an instant, and then the lord continued to select several tiny hexagons of glass from a heap at the side. "What, Kuat, does a fly's compound eye see? Compared to the single opening in a human eye, how many facets of truth are reflected in it?"

The Delver spread out his arms and the sharp cut of his sleeves hung down like bat wings. "A light shines in the Seani. It is an aura in the dark."

The lord bent to carefully position a single hexagon to one of the eye-mounds. "That has been reported before. Thirteen years ago."

"They were infants at the time, then were separated and hidden. Now they have grown, and now they are together."

The gloved hands stopped moving. "The niyalahn-ristas." He spoke in measured tones, his pronunciation precise, but it now contained a clicking quality.

"One carries the blood you seek," Vol Kuat said. "The other carries the fire."

The lord straightened, his cowl directly facing the Vol. "Tell me," he said, "of the blood."

"It makes the earth dance. It is the heritage that was stolen from you. It heals permanently, not like other blood."

A long hiss came out of the cowl. "S'rere." He repeated the word, as if his tongue were licking the edges of it. "S'rere. And the other? The one with fire?"

"He is Vol Cinc, the one you call Teller-of-Lies."

The Eyascnu's entire form stiffened and the red mouth tightened. For a moment he held himself perfectly still. Then, in a sudden vicious movement, he swept everything off the worktable. Metal legs and mouthparts crashed onto the stone floor, along with the squelching mass of clay. Glass hexagons flew through the air, glinted in the dark like tiny mirrors, and tinkled down. The Delver extended his palm, and a hexagon fell into it. In the ensuing silence, breathing heavily, the lord surveyed the mess.

The Delver turned his hand and allowed the hexagon to drift down to the floor. "Cinc has run to the Seani," he said, "with your skora. His brother has returned, from his hidden exile. The Bellstone called them forth."

Abruptly the lord turned away. His low, tightly controlled words came out of the darkness. "Summon Shacad."

"You are thinking," Vol Kuat said, "of abakal. You are thinking how well it worked against the falconforms. You are thinking of using it to crush the Seani and seize the niyalahn-ristas."

The Eyascnu Varo's voice growled out of the shadows. "Abakal will punch through their wards. It will bring down their gates."

"In time."

"I will burn the Seani and take the Se. I will make the niyal'arist voras wish they had never been born."

"Druv will slay them first. He will take their powers for himself."

The figure in the shadows considered this. "You see another course."

"I will bring the niyal'arists before you in chains. Do what you must with them. Then destroy the Seani with abakal and rule the Gap."

The lord emerged to stand once more under the light, the top half of his face still hidden. "How do you propose to capture the twin voras? They are crafty and ruthless."

The Kuat bared his sharp teeth. "They will come of their own free will."

Intense power poured out of the cowl and focused on the Delver.

"Have I ever failed you?" the Vol asked.

"Not yet."

"And still," the Delver placed a hand lightly on his chest, "I remain Kuat and not Prome."

The lord moved a gloved finger over the worktable. "Perhaps that will change. After I regain my s'rere and my skora. After my Apotheosis. Many things will change after that."

The Vol dropped his hand to his side. "Yes, many things."

"When will you bring the niyalahn-ristas to me?"

"Before the next rota ends."

The tight gloves creaked as the lord formed his hands into fists. "Drag them through the streets of Rydle, as if they were pretenders like the others. Make sure all know they were the best the Bellstone could draw forth." He grinned and rapped on the worktable. "Bring them to me, and I will take what I need. Then arrange an assembly in the Hall of the Eye. Call my archons, their officers, and dignitaries from Rydle and Baenfeld. Summon every rista, teacher, and foreign guest in Oknu Shuld. Before my throne gather them, to witness my Apotheosis. There the eternal king shall be revealed, his eyes blazing with fire and his hands full of life."

He tore off one glove and threw it onto the floor. "These I will utterly destroy!" A rotting stench rose from his hand. "With my flesh forever whole, when skora has burned Rûk's vile Riftwood to the ground, s'rere will replant it with morue. An endless vista of purple will cover its ashes like a mist. Production will increase a thousand fold, and my kingdom will expand in like manner. Every rebel will be routed, Kuat, every uprising put down. And under my hand, peace will at last settle upon Shunder."

The cowl turned to the Delver and radiated a warning. "Let not a single scratch come to the one with s'rere."

"Every drop of his blood shall be yours." The Delver retrieved the glove and tossed it onto the worktable. "And Vol Cinc?"

"I laid my trust in him, as tenderly as a mother lays a child to rest. He was to complete my hand." The Eyascnu shoved his hand into the glove and stared at it as one by one he extended a finger. "Prome, Segun, Tierce, Kuat, and Cinc. But again the terrible drama is being replayed. Again, one I trusted, one I brought close to me, proved to be a vora seeking my life. The niyal'arist cycle must be ended." The hand clenched. "The niyal'arist weed must be pulled out of my land and its root annihilated."

"Vol Cinc served you poorly in life."

"In death he will do better," the lord grated. He thought a moment. "If his eyes were removed and the sockets filled with luniku larvae, how long, Kuat, before they ate through to the brain?"

The Delver tilted his head. "How unflinchingly you face your own depths, Eyascnu."

"I require retribution."

"Then give him instead to the Vora."

"I also require a slow death, Kuat."

Two stony pupils sprang into the Delver's eyes. "You are artful. You can devise ways to restrain the Vora, ways which might allow it to rend, but not kill. Let Vol Cinc fully experience what his niyal'arist forebears brought into existence."

"Ah. So the wheel turns toward justice at last."

"And also toward mercy."

The red lips pursed. "You understand me very well, Kuat. You challenge the artist in me, as well as the king." The lord settled himself onto the stool, his cowl bent in thought. "I will be merciful, Kuat, as well as just. I will allow the Vora its diversions, but at precisely the right moment, I will gather up Teller-of-Lies. Out of something riven I will create something new, a new evocation of horror and pity. Is that not the goal of every tragedian? This work will test both my skill and my patience, for what I envision has never been done to a living man before. I shall fashion a Volghast Cinc, completely subservient like my other volghasts, but unlike them, capable of feeling and remembering."

"Such a work," the Delver said, "would surpass even Arachniman." He gestured toward the lord's masterpiece, a statue of a man morphing into a spider but without a mouth with which to scream.

"Yes, Kuat. Volghast Cinc will become my crowning artistic achievement. When not serving me, he shall be prominently displayed in the statuary hall."

"And his brother?"

The lord reached down to a box at the side of the worktable, flipped aside the leather flap, and withdrew a fistful of damp clay. He began to roll it slowly between his gloved hands, his breath coming slow and deep. "He shall become mine, Kuat, in the most intimate way possible."

The Delver stood silently until the lord, without looking up, spoke again. "There was a foreign woman traveling with Teller-of-Lies," he remarked. "The subaltern reported you took her away."

The Vol's pupils faded back into the white. "It was Rûk who seized her."

"For what purpose, do you suppose?"

The Delver shrugged. "He is the shadow-king. Perhaps he has hungers of his own."

The lord carefully placed another lump of clay on the table. "Ah. The rising sun of Oknu Shuld will scatter such shadow-kings. There will be only one king."

"And what will be his name?"

"At my Apotheosis, I will be called the Eyasc-perjabik, for my gaze will pierce all enemies. But my warrior name will be Nihilarist."

"A clever turn of phrase. But what of the other Vols? The Prome sought to deceive you. The Ségun tried to seize the skora. The Tierce could not quell the chaos in your land. Did they not all fail you?"

The lord sneered, revealing a sharp incisor. "My Kuat, ambitious to the last. Now go. Do as you have promised."

The Delver bowed and departed.

"It was my other three Vols," the lord muttered. "They turned my Cinc into a traitor. They twisted my most promising Vol into one who betrayed my trust." He took another fistful of clay from the box and squeezed the mass until it oozed between his fingers. "The Lord of Shunder, Eyasc-perjabik the Nihilarist, does not take lightly the loss. Their time will come. But first," he spoke to an apparently empty room, "Volghasti, obud."

From the dark behind the worktable, two hulks emerged, their eyes opening red.

"Go to my private audience chamber," Varo ordered them, "and prepare the earthen circle beside my throne."

Without a word, the volghasts obeyed.

CHAPTER 11

TELLER'S CHOICE

THE TOLTYR LAY AGAINST HIS CHEST, under the homespun shirt. Above him, in the twilit lavender sky, the pale green disk of the moon hung over the shadowy fields of emerging morue. The lunar surface was inscribed with what seemed at first to be a wavy blade, but as thin clouds passed over, it was now a leaf and now a flame. Teller was dimly aware that his physical body was off in the Quela, where his maimed hand hurt.

He sat with his back against one of the massive oak buttresses that supported the East Dam atop Insheer Cliff. Its log cribs, filled with rocks and earth, formed one side of the larger of the two dams that held back the accumulated waters of the lake. Not long ago he had followed the lord's orders and repaired it. Now the irrigation sluices built into it were all closed, for the spring had been a wet one, and the air smelled of disturbed, damp earth. The wood buttress creaked, as if the great mass of the lake pressed forward, testing the strength of the barrier.

That didn't bother him as much as it should have, nor did being so close to Oknu Shuld. He was in a place far more real than those, even though his body, as well as Sheft's, was actually somewhere else.

"I was always with you," the One next to him said. The speaker's face glowed too brightly to quite come into focus. It seemed to change from that of an elderly sage, to a handsome youth, to a middle-aged woman. The eyes merged from one color into another—as sparkling brown as a deep well, as opalescent as a twilit lake, as wild a blue as the legendary sea. Qualities also flowed among and through them: gentle strength, stern compassion, tender wisdom. The One sat cross-legged between Teller and his brother, the stars on his night-blue robe and the crescent moons on her gown glimmering in the dusk, and he/she was speaking to them both.

"My spirit lived with you always: in those who befriended you, who challenged you, who bore your pain. Sheft, I lived in your mother, in your friend Etane, and in your dear Mariat. Teller, I acted in Rivere, in the Se, and in the ahn Liasit and Gorv and Hanat. All these, and many more, gave so freely, and I delighted in them and in you." The person between them laid one hand over Sheft's shoulder and the other over Teller's. "My beloved sons, you faced and overcame every bitter challenge. You have more than vindicated the trust I put in you."

Sheft leaned out to look up at the One sitting between them. Although his brother's face was grooved by pain both past and yet to come, his silver eyes twinkled ruefully. "I have the feeling, Rulve, that there's more trust you'd like vindicated."

So this is Rulve, Teller thought. It felt as if he'd always known him/her, even as a small boy.

Rulve turned to him. "Do you remember the green room, when you were just six years old? I sat you on my lap and rocked you."

He did. He remembered the gentle old man whose comfort had saved his sanity, not to mention his soul, at a time when the Vols were trying to destroy both. "I didn't know it was you. I thought you had abandoned me, because I first abandoned you."

The old man smiled and shook his head. "Your names are engraved on my hands, deeper than the wounds on your backs. I am closer to you than your small-cloths. There is no abandoning."

The deep reassurance poured over Teller's head like oil. It flowed over his body and touched every scar. It permeated his spirikai and flooded his inmost being with a sweet and aching pain. It was a caress that both hurt and healed.

"This is how I love them all," the woman's strong, clear voice said, "ahn or rista, priestess or shamana, village elder or Se, those who recognize my many names or those who kill for the only one they know. I hear all of them, whether they cry out to me or to the demon in the dark or believe they speak merely to themselves. I even hear the Eyascnu Varo, who still bears my promise, though refused and buried deep."

Even awash as he was in Rulve's love, Teller felt a tendril of protest stir inside him. How could the Creator see any promise in the Lord of Oknu Shuld? How could he even pronounce his name?

Rulve answered his thought. "My dear son, freely you cut off your finger in order to come into my hand. Freely you have taken up my toltyr. Now you must come a little further in your understanding of what that freedom means. As we received freedom from those upon whom we once depended, so must we now bestow it upon those who depend on us. Sheft has accepted the consequences of his choice, and now, Teller, I ask if you will too.

Rulve's eyes beheld and encompassed him. They were the eyes of an ageless being, the Creator of worlds, full of a boundless tenderness that called out of the wastelands to Teller's heart. "You wear my Coin, but will you be my Coin? Will you consent to be spent, to buy back the lost?"

Even now he had doubts about himself. He did not want to fail this being, did not want to promise more than he could give. "What do you mean, Rulve? What must I do?"

The great Lord turned to him and bent over him. The Creator held Teller's cheeks between her hands and spoke with tears in his eyes. "Trust in what I have given you, my son, and act with an open heart."

Would he choose to turn away from this request, in order to live and find love and grow old through autumn days; or would he trust this One who begged for his help?

The Creator's gaze filtered down into Teller's heart. "If you agree, my son, you must go to a place where there is nothing but my grace."

Teller leaned out to look at his brother. Cries from the land had pulled at Sheft the same way cries from the ahn had pulled at Teller himself. They shared a passion that felt like blood to Sheft and to himself like fire—a passion to surrender to the persistent longing in their innermost core; to be a salve spread out and rubbed in for the salvation of all Shunder.

The longing would die if he refused to acknowledge it. It would shrivel and waste away. It had almost happened inside Oknu Shuld.

But somehow he knew there would be a terrible cost. Somehow he knew they must be stripped, down to the kernel inside; must be shelled and husked and buried, must fall empty into the great hands. His brother had already assented, and now they waited for him. There could be no s'eft without t'lir.

A memory rushed in, not his memory, but Sheft's, yet it also pertained to him. "*You will be wounded,*" Miramakamen had predicted, *"by a child, by your brother, and by the dark."* And so it was. First by the boy Aron, and then by Sheft, and now…. All he could envision was the spider-hole, black and expectant.

He didn't want to face that. When he'd been on the lord's mission in the Riftwood, surrounded in a dream by a net of thorns, he'd met a silver-eyed woman who carried a basket of seeds in one hand and a silently burning torch in the other. He'd taken the flame and set the thorns on fire, but he had caught fire too. He stood upright, burning like a lightning-hit tree, until he stood charred and alone in the center of their circle. The woman walked around what he had been, sowing seeds that melted like snow into the fertile black earth.

Abruptly he had awakened, and never knew if they sprouted.

"Teller-of-Lies never knew," the youth said. "Vol Cinc never could know. But you, emjadi T'lir, will truly know. Look at what you hold in your pocket."

He fished around for it, drew out the cord, and a loop of it sagged through the fingerless gap in his hand. Teller-of-Lies had knotted this cord like a tourniquet against the flow of despair. For even though he had fought for years against the name imposed on him, Vol Cinc had won out at the end.

Except he hadn't. The missing digit in his hand proclaimed that loud and clear. Vol Cinc had been cut off, his past uprooted, and his power buried at Rulve's feet.

He leaned into the love beside him, grasped the strong arm. There was no name left but his own, the one by which the Creator had just called him: Emjadi T'lir.

Yes, Rulve. He and his twin were light and dark, fire and ice, hidden magma that supported the green and growing earth. They were obverse and reverse, alike yet diverse. The toltyr marked them, *yes*; bound them, *yes*; leaf and flame, all one thing: the Coin of Rulve. *Yes.* For complete disbursement was why they had been born, and in utter freedom they would be spent.

The rising cry spilled out of him: "Yes!" and the great warm hands moved to rest upon his shoulders.

Chapter 12

Currents

Rulve's jade disk glowed with the setting sun and filled the Quela with a green-gold light. It cast long shadows of the candle stands across the floor, as if they were young trees. Teller sat at his place at the round table across from Sheft, and everything had changed for him. The vol-ring's dimness had fled from his eyes, and he felt washed clean and full of light. His bandaged right hand lay in his lap. It hurt too much to lift it onto the table—it hurt wherever he put it—but that didn't matter. He was Rulve's undeserving T'lir, and with amazed humility, he wore the holy toltyr brand.

The link with his brother was wide open. It was a strange sensation, more than mind-speech, for now emotions surged through from both sides. They both felt what the other felt: Sheft's ongoing grief and Teller's piercing regret; the tension of an unknown future balanced with new-found hope; affection for each other permeated by the intimacy of having experienced the same all-encompassing divine love. Their feelings washed back and forth like different-colored dyes that changed hues as they mingled. His end of their link shone with a lilac dawn—with the assurance that his failures were exonerated and that he had finally accepted not only his true name, but also the stunning fact that Rulve had chosen him.

Sheft had come further than he in the knowledge of what Rulve had done for them, but his brother's end of the link lay pooled in the numinous indigo of a spring night. His brother not only feared a granite demand, an arduous trial he might not have the courage to bear, but also an empty life without his wife. Nonetheless, they both looked for the distant coming of rest and joy.

Their toltyrs pulsed with Rulve's acceptance, unconditional and forever. What they had thought failures were a series of muddy, floundering steps by which Rulve had led them back to this place where they had been born. They would, they both knew, be sent out again; but all along, the deepest of their prayers had been answered, and always would be.

The Weshnik' Aseah briefly adjourned when dinner was brought in. Teller had an appetite now, and everything tasted delicious, especially the crunchy brined cucumbers that were never served in Oknu Shuld. It was difficult to eat with his left hand, but Avia helped by cutting up his meat. When everyone had finished eating, plates were taken away and Larrin, who with Afer had been conferring quietly with Komond and Druv, departed, shutting the doors against the twilight. The green light had faded from the hall, and the time-candle in the middle of the table seemed to shine brighter.

Mena took the now empty box that had held the toltyrs to Quin, the fifth great tree at the back of the hall that separated the Rain and Seed alcoves. Their grandmother then reverently placed the box in the tree's niche and returned to her seat.

All the colored windows in the alcoves had faded to grey, and the far end of the hall lay in shadows. The only illumination came from the tall candles around the meeting table, which surrounded those sitting beneath them within intersecting spheres of orange light. In contrast, the polished round table shone under its time-candle like an island in the darkness. Everyone waited in silence for the council's summation. In union with his brother, Teller felt a summons tremble in the air, like the anticipation before a name was called or a great bell sounded.

Across the table, the brothers regarded each other with new eyes. They were battered yet strong, grief-stricken yet standing, set apart but no longer alone. Teller saw in Sheft a finely wrought nobility of soul, and Sheft saw in him an unrelenting perseverance, and both were astonished at what the other beheld. Like the confluence of two streams, they exchanged these currents and were changed by them, and now the link between them flowed with the deep humility necessary for interdependent strength.

Se Druv stood up to address the gathering. "We began the Weshnika this morning," the eldest said, "with doubt and sadness. Now that Teller has chosen the toltyr, our land can look forward to the coming of our salvation."

Everyone turned to Teller, some even applauding, and Teller felt himself flush with embarrassment. To his great relief, Druv soon brought the meeting to order.

"This morning we began with three main questions," he said. "The first has been answered: we now know what Sheft and Teller have experienced while they were apart from us. The second question was to discover what powers Rulve has placed in their hearts. These seemed to be s'rere and skora, but we saw how Sheft's s'rere failed, and learned that Teller's skora may not be a niyalahn-rista power at all; so that question still remains for Rulve to answer. The third question we will address this evening: what does Rulve want us to do now?

A ripple of dismay ran through Sheft and Teller. The high and timeless place they had shared with Rulve, the closeness they had felt with the Creator and with each other, must of necessity be brought down now to the challenge of finding an uncertain path.

"Let us," Celume said, "return to our second question for a moment." She stood and pointed at the base of Twegen. "I know that the barren earth there is a bitter disappointment to us all. Particularly to you, Sheft. And you, Utray. We so hoped sweet-rue would bloom again in Shunder. It almost happened. For a moment, we saw rue again."

Dismal images from Sheft flowed through the link and unearthed images of Teller's own. Together they had produced only a withered s'rere and a barely controlled skora.

Celume now pointed to the base of Enlen, into which a flame was carved. "At first all we see there is more barren ground. But another seed is planted there, a charred ring buried by Teller, and is that not a cause for hope?" She smiled at them all, but then her smile faded.

A deep stillness seeped into her body, and her eyes seemed to focus on something not quite present. Her voice emerged in a lower timbre, one which reverberated in the quiet room, and both twins suddenly saw her for the first time as a seeress, as one who looked where others could not. "Quietly and without our notice," she said, "the emjadis have gone to another place and have now returned. The Coin of Rulve is made whole. S'eft and t'lir, obverse and reverse, are now joined." With eyes blind with seeing, she turned her head toward first one emjadi and then the other. "Hear me, niyalahn-ristas. You were made to redeem not only what is precious to Rulve, but also that which—in her mercy, because of a love we cannot fathom—she has made necessary to herself."

Although the candles all around them burned serenely, the Pool of Rulve shivered as from a stray gust of air. "When utterly bound, emjadis, you will be utterly free. Then s'rere shall pierce the earth like a green dagger, and up its blade shall run sh'kier."

A different kind of shiver—one of foreboding—ran along the arms of both Sheft and Teller.

"We don't understand." Hirai spoke softly, as to a dreamer who should not be awakened.

Celume gazed through the flame in front of her as if it were a doorway. "One niyal'arist will help the other die, and all who bear s'rere must be buried."

Her words rippled through the link, then coalesced into a cold stone. It sank into the pit of Teller's stomach, heavy not only with his own dread, but also that of his brother's.

"Who will die?" Penan asked. "Celume, who will be buried?"

The time-candle, and the seeress who stood behind it, were like a single calm pillar, unmoved by portent, unperturbed by the surrounding shadows. "It is our part to tend what grows," she said, "and gather up the harvest."

Penan sighed and folded his arms across his chest. "With that," he said, "I believe our seeress has returned us to our third question: what does Rulve want us to do now?"

"I believe," Nemes said, "that is exactly what Celume has been talking about: what must be done now.

Prophecy is not so much a prediction of the future but a deeper perception of the present. We must be careful, then, not to misconstrue what Celume has told us." He turned to include everyone at the table. "We of the Seani must indeed help each other die, but in a figurative yet very necessary sense. We must die to our impatience, to our lack of trust in the slow unfolding of Rulve's plan."

Celume appeared not to have heard him, but only looked deeper into the flame. Now her eyes widened. "There are three coins. One long broken, one to be spent, one yet to be forged."

Heads turned and brows creased, but in the midst of all the puzzlement Utray put his palms flat on the table and leaned toward the young woman. "Celume, the plants *died*. We need to know why."

The seeress blinked, looked away from the candle flame, and came back from her seeing. "I believe I have already explained that." She stood quiet for a moment, and then sat down.

"Perhaps," Hirai ventured, "the plants died because the—the soil wasn't right."

"What do you mean?" Penan demanded.

Hirai sat with her elbow on the table, her hand propping up her chin and hiding her mouth. The hand moved to touch the base of her throat. "Perhaps s'rere must fall on good soil. On the only ground in Shunder where the lord's killing mist never penetrated."

"But it seeped into everything," Mena reminded her.

"There was one place where it didn't." Hirai stared steadily into Mena's eyes for a moment, and then looked aside.

Penan leaned back in his chair. "In Oknu Shuld itself," he murmured.

"It's like balm," Abiyat exclaimed from the other end of the table, "applied to a wound! In order to heal, s'rere must go to the source of the hurt."

"In the *Tajemjadi*," Avia added, "it is written that the power of Rulve's Coin is released when it is spent. When the price is paid."

Teller glanced at his brother. "Rulve told us the same thing."

Without returning the glance, Sheft nodded. And then, to Teller's dismay, he quietly closed the link between them. The hall changed focus, seemed to turn cold, and having just found the essence of who he was with his brother, Teller felt suddenly alone.

"I don't like where this is going," Mena protested. "Surely the Creator of the stars doesn't care about paying some kind of bill." She lifted a contemptuous shoulder. "As if Rulve were a shopkeeper."

Penan pulled out his little scroll and tapped it rapidly on the table. "I agree, Mena. Celume said that the one most bound is the one most free. I think she meant that you go through life making choices, and each choice eliminates a host of others. Each choice sculpts you, defines you—a painful process, I might add—until you emerge as yourself and no one else. You are completely bound by the decisions you've made, and completely free from everything that is not you. Only those so liberated, and so committed, can use the power of Rulve's Coin."

Hirai spoke up. "I always thought that freedom means having many choices."

"Then my nine-month-old ward-sons," Avia answered, "are freer than any of us here, because they have many choices yet ahead of them. But the poor little things are still ruled by their impulses."

Teller stirred in his chair. The time he had spent with Rulve and with his brother seemed to recede even further into a dream from which he was being increasingly forced to awaken. He looked at Sheft, but his brother sat with his eyes lowered, locked within himself.

Utray, who'd been tapping the table with his knuckles, now thumped it with his fist. "Forgive me," he said, "but we don't have time for more talk. We all saw the emjadis' aura in the Quela, and must assume our enemy has seen it as well."

Sheft looked up. "Aura?"

"Forgive us, niyal'arists," Druv said. "We should have told you." He explained how a sphere of light hovered above the heads of the emjadis as they slept, how it had almost winked out when they had been suffering from the effects of ineerva poisoning, and how the aura had been renewed in the Pool of Rulve by the efforts of the entire Seani community.

Sheft stared at him, grooves digging between his eyebrows and around the corners of his mouth. "I have brought danger into your house."

Just as, Druv knew, the young emjadi believed he had brought danger to his own far village across the Meera River. He was about to speak, but Utray cut him off.

"We know that the Spider-king wants both s'rere and skora," the botanist said. "Those powers are now within his reach. Therefore he will be planning a full-scale attack on the Seani."

"Our wards will protect us," Mena insisted.

"Will they?" Ianak asked. "Last summer," he explained to Sheft, "a falconform eyrie was completely wiped out by the Spider-king's army. It was said that the colony was destroyed by a powerful sorcery that this land has never seen before."

"There are always such rumors," Mena said, "no doubt started by the Spider-king himself. In any case, it only makes sense to strengthen our wards. We must also renew our alliances. When the falconforms and the Bellstone warriors hear that the emjadis have returned, they will rush to unite with us in defense of our land."

"So we would hope," Ianak said. His face grim, he chewed for a moment on his lip. "I agree with Mena that we must attend to our wards. But there's one thing that we haven't even considered, and that's a possible siege."

"We believe that—" Komond began, but Utray interrupted.

"*Possible* siege? Of course we'll be besieged. And to what end?" He put out both hands, as if to offer an obvious observation. "Sheft is handicapped by grief, and Teller is weighed down by guilt. It is possible that their powers have been weakened considerably—or even destroyed altogether—by past experiences. The Spider-king will besiege us, and our people will die."

"So what do you suggest, Utray?" Penan asked. "Hand the emjadis over to the Spider-king immediately? Take steps to save ourselves even before he acts? Rulve gave these boys to us in trust, and we cannot betray this trust again."

"We never betrayed it!" Utray thumped his fist on the table. "We did all we could to protect their power. They are the ones who betrayed it. They did not have the strength to overcome the challenges that faced them."

Immediately Mena made a hot reply, but Teller wasn't listening. He saw in Sheft's face a reflection of his own deep distress, but felt nothing else through the closed link. His brother must have blocked him because he knew Utray was right. They were bringing war to the gates of the Seani, to the home that, against all hope, had just been restored to them. Many would die for them, kill for them, and for what? The forest people risked decimation, farmers and villagers would be slaughtered, and the innocent ahn enslaved in Oknu Shuld—Liasit and Aron and Rivere—would continue to suffer. Children all over Shunder would suffer, and the land would continue its dying.

And what about the beautiful young woman who had captured his heart? What would happen to Taisa if the lord invaded the Seani?

Sheft stood, and the room suddenly fell silent. "I've brought danger to your community," he said, sweeping his silver gaze around the table, "danger to you and your children. It would be wrong for me to stay here any longer." Protests sprang up, but they faded away as Sheft continued. "I have no wife anymore, no children. Nothing to keep me here. Innocent people shouldn't suffer because of my useless blood. I came here on a perfectly good horse, and in the morning I'll ride it into Oknu Shuld."

A silent wave of shock rolled across the room. Then several people gasped, and cries of "No!" rang around the table.

So this, Teller thought with a sinking heart, is the plan that his twin wanted to keep from him.

Mena, red-faced with fury, stood and confronted Utray, "Look at what you've done! Open your mouth again, Utray, and I swear I will hit you." She turned to Sheft. "You dare to speak so? You would toss your life on a dung heap after all we've done to save it? After the Creator Rulve brought you home to us? For shame, flouting us in such a way, but also for spurning the will of the Lord God!"

A flush rose in Sheft's cheeks, but he didn't look away from her.

Teller leaned across the table toward Mena. "Grandmother, please. Sheft is right. It would have been better if neither of us had entered your gates." He switched his gaze to his brother and swallowed the dread of what he was about to say. "Sheft, I won't let you go anywhere alone."

Another clamor began to arise, which Druv immediately quelled by standing up and slicing a hand through the noise. "Mena," he ordered, "be seated. You too, Utray. Sheft, please sit down."

He waited for complete silence and then addressed Teller and Sheft. "Your offer, emjadis, is unbelievably courageous, but the Seah will not accept it. Frankly, you have spoken with the rashness of youth and without mature consideration. Giving yourselves up to the Spider-king would be wasting the power Rulve has laid upon you. In the long run, it would accomplish nothing."

"But what about the aura?" Utray insisted.

"Listen, all of you, to what I have to say. During dinner this evening, I withdrew to discuss our situation with Komond and his captains, Afer and Larrin. I told them I called this Weshnik' Aseah so quickly because I believed the Seani was running out of time, that the Spider-king would detect the niyal'arist aura and would immediately come against us. The captains, however, differed with me on that." He gestured for Komond, the Se in charge of Seani defense, to continue.

"Even though it has been two days since the aura shone out," Komond said, "the Sperians in Rydle have reported nothing unusual around Oknu Shuld. Yes, the king's armies are on rotation, and there is the usual coming and going, but this is to be expected at this time of year. Whether the event in the Pool of Rulve has hidden the aura from detection, or it hasn't grown strong enough yet, or whether Rulve is protecting us, or for some other reason, we have no evidence that the Eyascnu is aware of the aura at all. What we do know is that there's been no unusual activity within the Rydle garrison, no loose talk from soldiers in the alehouses, no stir in the umbrak camp. In view of that, any precipitous action on your part, Sheft, or yours, Teller, would be disastrous."

Teller cut his eyes from Komond's face to Sheft's. He saw his twin's downcast gaze, the tension around his mouth, the furrow between his eyes. Sheft felt him staring and looked up. He was not convinced.

"We also discussed Ianak's concern about a siege," Komond went on, "and concluded that such an action on the part of our enemy would be unlikely. A siege would place the Spider-king directly between the anvil of our wards and the hammer of the Bellstone warriors. Given the rising tension in the countryside, it could be the spark that would ignite the entire populace, including the Sperians and the falconforms, against the Spider-king. He and his Vols must be well aware of this.

"There are other factors involved; but, in short, the four of us believe the Spider-king has no reason to come against us now. We are of the unanimous opinion that strengthening both our wards and our alliances are far more effective options than what Sheft and Teller have proposed. Rulve has given us time, precious time, for the emjadis to heal and to rise to the full extent of their powers." He tapped his fingers firmly on the table to punctuate each of his next words. "We must—use—that—gift."

Druv looked from Teller to Sheft. "Even though we do not yet know what precisely Rulve requires of you, we do know that the Creator would never demand that you act beyond your present limitations. You are not yet who you will become. That much has been shown here. But Rulve is not mocked. S'rere and skora can be healed. They will be healed. When all doors close save one, then your way will be made clear."

With a thumb and second finger forming a circle, Penan offered a scholarly thought. "All this time," he said, "we have been focusing on s'rere and skora. But these may not be Rulve's focus at all. An entire generation"—he waved a hand to include the four young people sitting in the corners of the square—"will eventually govern the Seani. The wisdom and the power of the niyalahn-ristas must be a part of that. I don't mean to denigrate your offer, emjadis, but hasty action on your part may be dodging the *true* mission Rulve has laid upon you: a long-term and very difficult mission as future leaders of our land."

"You may be right," Lir put in. From his chair between Penan and Druv, the young man leaned sideways to look first at Sheft and then across the table at Teller. "We must consider Penan's insight, and we may have been given time to do that; but it might be the case, emjadis, that foolish heroism right now will ruin the Creator's plan for the future of our land."

Many nodded at what Lir said. Druv placed both hands on the table and pushed himself to his feet. "No matter what the Spider-king is planning, and no matter what Rulve intends for Sheft and Teller, our immediate course is clear. We must prepare for every eventuality by seeing to our wards, by strengthening our alliances, and by assisting our emjadis to grow into their full power. I propose we close this Weshnika and get some rest. All who agree please raise your hand."

No one moved, but then a few hands went up, until one by one all went up.

"Very well," Druv said. "Tomorrow morning we will reassemble in the Sky Tower and begin our work to connect with our allies and strengthen the wards. The Weshnika is closed."

With a scraping of chairs, everyone stood and faced the great disk. All around Teller people lifted their hands to Rulve. Teller felt the familiar stab of loss and isolation, and for a moment did nothing. Long ago he had renounced Rulve and pledged himself, body and soul, to the Lord of Oknu Shuld. But now the toltyr lay against his chest, warm with Rulve's anointing, and a charred and rejected ring lay buried at Rulve's feet. Slowly, and for the first time in thirteen years, he raised his hands—the one whole and the other truncated and throbbing—to a love so great it subsumed all evil. After a brief time of silent prayer, the Weshnika was over.

Another look at his brother, however, told him Sheft was still uneasy. "What's wrong, Sheft? Please tell me."

Sheft hesitated a moment, but without opening the link, finally answered. "I don't know, Teller. I wish I did."

Druv spoke to various people who crowded around him. "Komond, have Larrin get word to the Bellstone Forest defenders. Ask them to double their watch on Oknu Shuld and to keep silent about Sheft and Teller's presence here. Then you and I will consult with the captains on how best to proceed with the falconforms. We can use their visual reports. Ianak, Utray, get word to the resistance leaders in Rydle. The rest of you, get some sleep. You will need all your energy to power up the wards."

Everyone was flexing cramped muscles, retrieving cloaks from the backs of chairs, and gathering around Teller and Sheft to bid them good night. Mena gave them both a warm hug, and as she left the Quela, Druv approached them.

"This has been a trying day for you both," he said. "You were exhausted even as it began, and the Weshnika is not always known for its tact and gentle handling. Your hand must be hurting you, Teller, and both of you need to return to the infirmary and rest. Tomorrow we will arrange more permanent lodgings for you."

"Thank you," Sheft said, "for everything. For your healing and your patience. For accepting us both. Mariat would have felt at home here. But my presence is causing—"

"A little humility, if you please, Sheft. The Creator has reunited you and your brother for her own good purpose, and you must trust that. Rest easy, emjadis. For now, there is nothing to fear. Go back to the infirmary in peace." He turned to leave.

Sheft stopped him. "If it's allowed, may we sleep in the Quela tonight? Our blankets and mats are already here, and we'll take up only one alcove."

The request deepened Teller's sense of foreboding, which had been getting darker, moving closer, all evening. Sheft still had not opened his side of the link, but enough of his emotions leaked out for Teller to know that his brother was deeply troubled.

A look of suspicion crossed Druv's face. "If you still have thoughts of leaving the Seani, emjadis, kindly banish them. You are needed here. We have few enough guards as it is, to waste any on watching for foolish behavior."

"I will stay as you said, until all doors save one are closed." Sheft spoke with conviction, and Teller knew he meant it.

"I accept your word." Some of the lines of tension in Druv's face softened. "And of course you may sleep here. You are niyal'arists and need to be with Rulve."

But Teller knew it was more than that.

His twin needed to be with Rulve because he needed the Creator's strength. His brother knew that something was coming, and he was afraid.

CHAPTER 13

SPENDING THE NIGHT

JUST AS DRUV LEFT BY THE Welf-door, calling for Larrin to get his guards to dismantle the round table and carry it back to storage, Abiyat bustled over. Before he could say anything, however, Sheft put a hand on his arm. "I heard that some of the people in the hospit never got into the Pool of Rulve in time for the healing. That they're still in pain, and some are children."

"Unfortunately, that is so. It is a grievous thing for them to bear—and for us as well. We didn't understand what was happening quickly enough to move them."

Sheft had opened his end of the link again, so Teller knew what his brother wanted to do. Teller was reluctant to do it, though, and tried to hold back the reason why.

Sheft cast him a curious look, then turned back to Abiyat. "Can we," he asked, "visit the hospit?"

"Now?"

"Is it too late in the evening?"

"No, no, no. It is fairly early yet, but both of you need rest. The visit would be especially hard on you, Teller." Teller winced as the healer proceeded to explain to his twin what Teller had tried to hide from him. "Even as a boy, your brother felt the pain of those in hospit. But" he glanced at Teller, "forgive me, lad for underestimating you. No doubt you learned well in Oknu Shuld how to bear the pain of others."

He had learned it, but not well, and Teller knew any visit to the hospit would entail raising the skora barrier. Despite his best efforts, Sheft felt this through the link, and a non-verbal discussion, of which Abiyat was completely unaware, ensued. Sheft insisted that Teller not come, but Teller refused. He had too much to atone for. Plus, came the sudden thought, Taisa and her mother lived in the hospit. Perhaps a glimpse, a word.... He stopped. He'd forgotten to block this part and Sheft, with a grin, gave up trying to persuade him to stay behind.

Abiyat steered them out the double doors. "Our patients will be greatly encouraged by your visit," he said, clearly pleased, "and we certainly do not have to stay long. But I insist we take the shortcut through the Seani House and stop to rest in the Common Room."

"All right."

"And while we're there, we might speak with some of our residents who haven't gotten a chance to welcome you home yet."

"That would be good," Sheft said. His twin was tired, Teller knew, as tired as he himself was; but Sheft was feeling a desire, even an urgency, to be with as many of the Seani people as he could, however briefly, before—and here Sheft quickly repressed the rest of his thought.

"We'll just pass through," Abiyat assured them. "But the contact might actually aid in your recovery, emjadis—not going to extremes of course—but a moderate amount of socialization has been proved...."

He kept on talking as they left the Quela. The mildness of the day had softened the edge of the mid-Seed night, and spring frogs were weaving their choruses through an intermittent damp breeze. Just before they turned onto the slope of the Red Lantern Way, Teller glanced up at the sky. A golden half-moon hung low above the hillside as a few high clouds hurried toward it, like wraiths on a mysterious mission.

They approached the lights of the Seani House without encountering anyone but Deoner. Carrying a squirming twin under each arm, he greeted them as he hurried toward the trail to his and Avia's domicile.

Abiyat shepherded them past a shadowy area that smelled like the herb garden, through the side door, and down the hall between the dark infirmary and the well-lighted kitchen. Keppit the cook and her helpers were busy washing dishes, but as soon as they saw Abiyat and the emjadis, they excitedly wiped their hands on aprons and followed the three of them down the hall.

The dining room still contained a crowd of people, including a few children, who were just finishing their dinner. With a clatter of forks, they jumped up and surged forward, smiling broadly. People hugged Teller and thumped Sheft on the back; and at the shining look in their eyes, both twins felt the same initial reticence, a slight pulling back, for how could either of them live up to that grateful admiration?

The welcomers all seemed to talk at once. "And to think Teller was once my little bean!" Keppit exclaimed. "Now look at the tall stalks they've both grown into!"

"...won't recognize things around here anymore, Teller. We've got a new barn over there by the front gate and a new wing on the hospit."

"You can have the rest of my cookie, emjadi Sheft. I don't really want it."

"...meet us down by the lower creek, them speckle-backs is that long I swear, an 'a course we'll bring the poles."

Every pair of eyes, Teller noticed, sought out Sheft's toltyr, which lay in plain sight. His own pendant was hidden, and the gazes of many followed the black cord as it disappeared into his shirt. The Seani people loved him for who he once was, and for who he was now, but what about that person in the middle? Could love ever absolve Vol Cinc?

It became very warm in the dining room, for the defensive skora barrier was building up.

Over Abiyat's shoulder, he glimpsed Taisa at the edge of the group. Their eyes met. "It's all grace, Teller," she said. "Nothing can be given unless it's received."

People crowded around him and he lost sight of her. Across the room a little girl raised her arms to Sheft, and he picked her up. His shy smile and the dazed thankfulness that shone from his face showed how his brother's lifelong isolation was melting away. The Seani had done that for Sheft and could do it for him. If he accepted it.

Teller came to stand at Sheft's side and lowered the skora barrier down to thin, blue flames. He leaned into the link with his brother, and his brother leaned into him, and they allowed the distinction between them to blur. The surrounding people disarmed them of fire and took away their ice, looked unflinchingly into one's silver eyes and at the scar on the other's face. An aching gratitude filled them, like water filling a dry leather flask.

A little boy tugged at their sleeves. "Are you really the emjadis?" he asked, looking up at them. His eyes were wide with innocence, yet his question felt like a demand.

"Yes," Sheft said.

Teller hesitated. Even now, it was a hard thing to admit. The boy waited, his gaze piercing Teller's heart, until Teller finally said "I am."

"Then please," the boy implored, "go get my brother, emjadis. Bring him home, all right? Bring him back to our house."

From behind him, another voice piped up. "And," a small girl begged, "and make our river come back too. Make the fishies come back. And our big tree in the village too."

Sheft bent down and held the boy's cheeks between his hands, his eyes fixed on the child's face. "We want to," Sheft said. "As soon as we can, we will try." He reached out to the little girl, but Abiyat quickly intervened.

"The emjadis will save our land, children, but not right now. Rulve will tell us when."

He gently pushed Sheft and Teller through the crowd and out of the Seani House, leaving by one of the doors that opened onto the east-facing porch. "That must have been difficult for you," the healer said, "but you must not allow a child's plea, no matter how heart-rending, to tempt you to act untimely. Be at ease now, and rest in the wisdom of the Weshnika." It was quite dark, and as they walked through the long rectangles of light cast from the Seani House windows upon the sloping lawn, Abiyat recalled he had promised to check on Hirai's little girls. With enjoinders not to stay long at the hospit, and with orders for Teller to see him in the infirmary before retiring for the night, he rushed back the way they had come.

The pleas of the children still aching in the link between the twins, they walked on until they saw three low, dimly lit windows rise from the slope ahead. The anguish Teller had felt as a child began reaching out of the hospit like a poisonous fog.

BONE-TIRED, TEMA STOOD AT THE OPEN door of the hospit and took in a few breaths of air. They were a welcome relief from the odor of sickness inside, which lingered even under the smell of freshly washed sheets and the scrupulously scrubbed wooden floor. She was alone, for Taisa was spending the night in the nursery to help Se Ukaipa deal with the two extra children recently brought in.

It was too dark to see the great gates down the slope, and only the flickering light of torches in the guard-towers marked where they stood. The stars above shone calmly through the rushing clouds, and the crystalline trill of frogs washed out of the dark meadow all around her, but distant thunder growled in the west. Two seasons would grind past each other this night and brew up a storm.

She went inside to make her rounds and lower the wicks of the oil lanterns. The younger patients were restless, for just about all of them were afraid of thunder. A little girl looked up from her cot, the nearest one to the door and farthest from the hearth. "Will it storm?" Willow asked. "Is it going to be real loud?"

Tema brushed the hair away from the left half of the child's face. The right side of her head was partly bald, and ointment covered the grotesque burns there. "It's just spring coming, sweetie. And I'll be here all night, like always."

"Don't bring the lantern any closer," Willow reminded her.

"I won't."

The child in the bed next to Willow was on all fours, banging his head against the wall, and Tema bent over and gently restrained him. "Listen to the frogs," she said. "Shhh. Hear them singing?" But the boy had been too badly beaten by a morue-crazed uncle to listen for singing.

Beyond him, six-year-old Eshu lay on his pillow, his dark eyes anxious and his face flushed. "When is mama coming?" His throat was so sore he had to whisper. She had told him over and over that his mother was with Rulve, but he never seemed to hear her. Thankfully, he seemed also not to hear the repetitive groans emanating from the farm wife in the bed next to his.

When the emjadis had first been brought into the Seani, Taisa had told everyone in hospit that the twin brothers were sick too. It seemed to help the patients to know they weren't alone in their misery. Some asked what was wrong with the emjadis, and Taisa said they had been wounded by poisoned arrows. Their eyes grew round with sympathy, and Tema wondered anew at the greatness of the human spirit that could, in the face of another's suffering, forget for a moment its own.

She was well aware that children could act with great selfishness and cruelty at times, perhaps mirroring the selfishness and cruelty with which they had been raised, but sickness seemed to soften many a ragged edge.

Except, tonight, her own. Because of the miracle in the Pool of Rulve, four-year-old Narla, the child rescued by Hirai and Ianak, was now safely ensconced in the nursery, and the hospit was the least crowded it had been in months. But those remaining here had been left out. Even with the young men Abiyat had sent to help her, she hadn't been quick enough to get all the children into the Pool, and villagers had brought two others into the Seani hours after the miracle was over. In his zeal to heal the niyalahn-ristas, Rulve had healed many, but had left these patients behind. Innocent victims to begin with, they had been victimized yet again, and—she thought bitterly—by their own Creator.

She went from bed to bed, feeling foreheads and checking bandages. She wiped the face of a farmer, probably not yet twenty-five, who would probably die tonight. In a last-ditch effort to save his life, Abiyat had amputated his leg at the knee, but the creeping suppuration was poisoning his blood. She did her best to calm the thrashings of the ten year-old girl who had been mauled by one of the altern's dogs. The poor lass on the end, at the corner where the new wing turned toward the west, smiled tremulously at her. She was only fifteen, but looked years older. Her blackened eyes were filled with pain from internal injuries Abiyat could do nothing about. "What happened to me," she murmured, "was the will a' Rulve."

Tema wanted to scream at her, "It was the will of a gang of umbraks, not Rulve's," but she had learned not to take away whatever shred of belief that sustained her patients.

Sengor had taught her that. On nights like this one, when she felt particularly angry and overwhelmed, her husband used to brush her hair before bedtime. "Rulve walks with us always," he used to say, "no matter how rocky the path. And we don't always know where that path is going either. Only from the future can we look back and see how the past was heading toward the light." Sengor was not a learned man, but he was a wise one. And he had the gentlest touch.

There was a stir at the far door, and Tema turned to see Sheft standing just inside. He apparently didn't notice her in the shadows down the aisle and addressed the little girl in the cot in front of him.

"Is it all right if we come in?"

"Please do," Willow said politely. She cocked her head for a better look at Teller behind him, and Tema saw how her eyes shone. "You're the emjadis, aren't you? You must be feeling better now."

Tema hurried over and dismissed Sheft's apologies for barging in unannounced. She immediately noticed the strain in Teller's face and the exhaustion in Sheft's, but so great seemed their obvious need, both to give and receive, that she could not deny their request to visit. The four of them—Willow had decided to join the group—moved from cot to cot.

The child Eshu immediately noticed Teller's bandaged hand. He reached up to touch the gap in it carefully with one finger. "This must hurt," he rasped.

The dark emjadi looked at him with a strange expression. It struck her that Eshu was about the same age as Teller had been when he was abducted into Oknu Shuld. Perhaps the emjadi realized for the first time how vulnerable children are. Perhaps he might finally forgive himself for once being just as vulnerable. "Yes, it does," Teller said. "But it's getting better."

Apparently satisfied, Eshu turned his head on the pillow to Sheft. He stared hard at his eyes.

The light emjadi flinched, but allowed the child to study him.

"Can you see out of those?" Eshu croaked.

"I can see fine. Thank you for asking. Do you have a fever?"

The boy swallowed, grimacing at the pain. "I feel hot, and"—he patted his throat—"this hurts."

"I wish I could make it better, Eshu."

A sudden thought jumped into Tema's mind, and she grabbed Sheft's arm. "Perhaps you can. With ice. With niyal'arist ice."

Sheft stiffened. "My ice can't heal. I'm sorry, Tema, but it can't."

"Even if used with compassion?"

"You don't understand. There's—there's more in me than ice."

"You mean roots? Abiyat told me you fear them. But

aren't they part of the blood-seed power? You must at least try." She turned her head toward the boy. "Eshu, the niyalahn-rista is going to touch your forehead. You might feel a little cold."

Looking dismayed, Sheft hesitated, but Tema would not be denied. "You owe them, emjadi," she said. "For the miracle in the Pool of Rulve, you owe them all."

Sheft sat on the edge of the bed and placed his hand on the child's head. The silver eyes softened. After a moment, the other hand went gently over Eshu's throat.

The boy sighed, slumped deeper into his mattress, and stared at nothing. Everything stilled, even the groaning of the farm wife in the next cot. The window was partially open above Eshu's bed, and the frog chorus wafted in from the dark beyond.

"Do you feel any cooler?" Tema whispered to the boy.

Still looking peacefully at nothing, Eshu nodded.

Sheft took a quiet breath and took his hands off the boy. Tema felt the child's forehead, which was still warm, but surely not as warm as before. Excitement fluttered inside her, but she must remain calm and collect further observations. Sheft got to his feet—somewhat stiffly, Tema noticed. He had drawn his cloak closer around him and only a practiced eye would notice he was shivering. Abiyat would not be pleased, for he had told her about the emjadi's reaction after using ice; but every person here showed some symptoms of inflammation and, whether Sheft's ice could relieve them or not, it must be tried. She wouldn't allow anyone to be left out again.

The farm wife was next. When Sheft took his hands away from her forehead, the woman responded with a look of amazed gratitude and said she felt much better, but the shadows under her eyes didn't melt away. Had the poor lady merely responded to a caring touch, or convinced herself that the niyalahn-rista had healed her, or had she in truth been physically relieved? Only time would tell.

The next cot lay in front of the central hearth. Willow turned her back to it and, clutching Tema's tunic, edged past.

Teller noticed. "I don't like that kind of fire either," he said to her.

She looked closely at his cheek. "Is that mark from a burn, emjadi?"

He thought about that, and then finally said, "Kind of."

Tema steered the emjadis to the next bed. "This little girl was attacked by a vicious dog just this afternoon." Her arms bandaged, the child squirmed restlessly on the rumpled sheet. She didn't seem to notice when Sheft sat down beside her and laid his hands on her shoulders. Gradually, however, she quieted down as the light emjadi grew paler, and then she lay still when he at last left her side.

Willow pulled on Sheft's hand. "Me next." She guided him to the next bedside chair, gently pushed him into it, and then climbed onto his lap. "Fix it right here," she said, pointing to the burns on her head.

Sheft glanced up at Tema, his silver eyes filled with a helpless appeal, with a look that seemed to say: *How can I do this and then disappoint them?*

"Do it, emjadi," Tema said.

In a kind of despair, he drew Willow against him, cupped a hand over her burns, and shut his eyes. Deep furrows appeared in his forehead, and Tema could see him tense. After a while, he took a deep breath, opened his eyes, and lifted Willow off his lap. "I really hope it works," he said to the child.

He got to his feet, Tema moved him resolutely along, and Teller followed behind, probably feeling useless. She tried to ignore the pang of guilt at the sight of Sheft's haggard face as he laid his hands on the all the rest of her patients, including the man with the amputated leg. Teller followed closely, his sleeves now rolled up and his cheeks flushed, and she realized the dark emjadi must be feeling all the pain in here just as he did when he was a little boy. Perhaps, she thought, he was part of whatever healing process was going on. Didn't compassion involve taking into oneself the suffering of others?

But then, she suddenly thought, how could anyone who felt such pain manage to survive in Oknu Shuld? Wave after wave of it must have assailed Teller every day he lived there. For the first time she glimpsed niyal'arist power, and awe of it swelled in her throat.

Suddenly the windows flashed into incandescence, and a clap of the dreaded thunder rolled through the building. Eshu bolted upright, big-eyed, in his bed. Willow ran to Teller and hid against his chest while the head-banger stopped rocking and looked around in terror. Sheft gathered him up, and the boy clutched him around the neck. Tema rushed around shutting windows and murmuring reassurances as the rain poured down and thunder cracked and rolled.

The storm finally passed, and she meant to make the emjadis leave, but they stayed to help when Eshu wet his bed, when water began pouring from the roof leak at the joining of the new wing, and when the young farmer took a turn for the worse. Once or twice she noticed Teller glance at the door at the end of the hall and realized he was looking for Taisa to return. But in the rush of things she forgot to tell him her daughter was spending the night in the nursery.

Some time passed before Teller and Sheft finally left. By then the bedsheet had been changed, the floor mopped, and the young man with the amputation had breathed his last. He did so quietly, gazing in wonder at the niyal'arists of Rulve sitting at his side.

CHAPTER 14

A Figure Blocks the Path

Teller followed Sheft out the door, closed it quietly behind him, and stepped onto the wet grass. It must be after midnight, and they were both exhausted. Teller, hot from maintaining the skora barrier, welcomed the cool air on his face. Sheft, on the other hand, was shivering with ice-reaction. They walked through wisps of a ground fog as they made their way up the slope to the Quela.

When they got there, the round table was gone, but a few chairs had been left for them. A gangly young man was using a knife to pry the stump of a burned-down candle from one of the stands. "Don't mind me," he said. "I'm just here to replace the candles." He dropped the stump into a bag slung over his shoulder and grinned at Teller. "You don't remember me, do you?"

Teller searched his memory. "Eiver?"

"The same. I went with Lir to rescue you from the ineerva. Ironic, isn't it?"

"Ironic?"

"Sure was. The missing pages were the ones you yourself copied from the *Tajemjadi*. So this is your brother. Hello, Sheft. I only got a glimpse of you while I was installing the candle in the infirmary, but you sure looked *ba-ad*." He peered into Sheft's face, and then into Teller's. "I really don't see much resemblance, but—yeah, I see it now. It's the hair and eyes that confused me. Twins all right." He beamed at them. "Who'd've thought? This is going to be a different place now that you're back."

Eiver went about his business trimming wicks, all the while talking non-stop. He invited them to a dice game he was arranging for tomorrow night in the barn, told them he suspected Kryshe cheated but didn't know how she did it, and described ways he had devised to add what he called "oomph" to Hirai's latest ale. Teller tried to follow his conversational leaps, but soon got left behind. Sheft stood in dismay, apparently giving up altogether.

"Well, that's done," Eiver said at last. He cast Teller a knowing look. "So, you've met Taisa, have you? She's a sweetheart, but there are, you know, *others* that think the same. Mainly Lir. But no worry, I know a lot of the girls around here and can introduce you. Hands off Kryshe, though—not meant crudely of course, but then again. She likes me, at least most of the time. Anyway, you probably want a hot bath before going to bed. Getting dunked in the Pool of Rulve doesn't really count, there being no soap and all. Just so you know, no one will be using either of the in-hill pools at this hour, and there are plenty of towels and clean clothes in there. Don't forget about the game tomorrow night; but, uh, just keep mum about it. Some people around here have *no* competitive spirit." He went out, banging the door behind him and whistling tunelessly.

They stared after him. "Hot bath?" Sheft asked, clutching his cloak tightly around him. With joints and muscles still sore from the bout with ineerva, and after a day of sitting on a hard chair in a cold hall, and then his prolonged ice expenditure in the hospit, Teller understood how much the idea appealed to his brother. It didn't sound bad to Teller either, whose last real bath had been quite a while ago in Oknu Shuld.

"The pools Eiver mentioned are in the Seani House," he explained, "where everybody goes to take a bath." A memory popped up, and he shared it through the link with Sheft: a gaggle of small children splashing in the warm water, squishing bars of soap out of their fists, and Mena finally hauling them out to be wrapped in the pleasantly scratchy and much-washed towels. "There's a back way in," Teller said as he led Sheft out of the Quela. "That way we won't run into anyone who might still be in the dining room."

"We didn't have baths where I grew up," Sheft remarked as they walked. "We washed in a basin in the kitchen, or in the river." In his turn, he showed Teller his recollection of the first compulsory bath of early spring: goosebumps rising on his arms and legs as he stripped on the stony bank, the shock of the brown, fast-flowing water—"with chunks of ice still bobbing in it."

"Chunks of ice! Our mother made you bathe with chunks of ice?"

Sheft grinned. "It makes a better story that way."

Teller, on the other hand, didn't need to make up horror stories about the baths in Oknu Shuld. He sent images of mold-slick floors, water that smelled like sulfur, and ristas trying to pick fights by pointing out how meagerly other males were endowed.

They took the deserted Red Lantern Way to a path that led to a sunken garden at the back of the Seani House. Built partially into the hillside and enclosed on three sides, the garden was very dark. Someone must have been preparing the flowerbeds earlier in the day because the place smelled like newly turned earth.

"The wall to your right is the back of the pantry," Teller said. "Keppit used to store her desserts along the shelves in there. Eiver once pried out a loose brick from the wall over there, and we'd pull it out to swipe an extra cake or cookie. Keppit thought it was mice."

It had been a magical time when he had been a boy here, when he had known himself only as Teller, Mena's grandson. Taisa had been only a toddler then. Thoughts of who she was now filtered into his mind, thoughts of those brown eyes and of her warm hands rubbing him with oil.

He pushed the thoughts away. Taisa was with Lir. Even if she wasn't, he couldn't burden her with whatever the toltyr would demand. It was he, not she, who had agreed to pay the price of his mission. At the time he had believed it would be paid only once, but now he was beginning to realize it might have to be paid many times.

He pulled open an iron-hasped door, almost invisible in the dark, and they slipped through the opening beyond. There was no one about, and only one light burned. "This is our storage cave," he explained. "It's built into the hillside behind the Seani House. Those blocks of ice were cut from the pond this winter and keep food fresh for months." They passed through the chilly cavern, which smelled of sawdust and root vegetables, and followed the plank wall which partitioned the storage area from the bathing rooms.

They entered a small vestibule, where a lantern hung on a nail in the corner. The room contained three doors, and Teller pointed to the one directly ahead. "That leads into the dining room." No shoes stood outside the other two doors, which meant the baths were empty. He steered Sheft toward the left, where, as he recalled, the pool water was warmer. They pulled off their boots, entered their respective baths, and closed the doors.

The room was just as Teller remembered it. Lanterns lit it almost as bright as day and the rock floor was lined with mats. A natural hot spring took up most of the space. Steam wisped from its surface and fogged the one high window. He took off the homespun clothes he had been given—disturbingly similar to ahn-clothes—placed them in the laundry basket in the corner, and then eased himself into the pool. Finding the underwater ledge that served as a seat, he sank onto it, keeping his bandaged hand out of the water. The warmth lapped against him, and he leaned back, resting his right arm on the edge of the pool, and sighed. Sheft must be luxuriating in this.

One niyal'arist will help the other die.

The memory struck out of nowhere, and he sat bolt upright. Celume's prophecy, uttered earlier that day, twisted a knot in his stomach. But hadn't Nemes explained what she meant? Celume was describing a symbolic truth and not an imminent reality. The Seani had time to discover what Rulve wanted them all to do. And of course one niyal'arist would help the other die. When the weariness of old age no longer held body and spirit together, it was only natural that one twin would be at the other's bedside.

Teller found the soap in its usual stone depression and awkwardly scrubbed his hair and body with his left hand. He rinsed off and dried himself, but even as he put on clean ahn-clothes from a pile of them on a small table and transferred the twisted red and blue cord into his pocket, the sense of foreboding did not leave him. He left the room and waited on the bench outside. Soon

Sheft emerged, his pale hair still damp and wearing clean ahn-clothes as well.

They made their way out of the sunken garden, around an arm of the hillside, and onto the deserted path. All was quiet. The ground-fog had become more opaque, blurring the lanterns into a curve of wispy red spheres that dissolved into the distance. Teller had always thought of the Seani as a safe enclosure, but now he suddenly became aware of the dark primeval forest that surrounded it.

Beside him, Sheft abruptly halted. A tall figure blocked their way. Hooded and silent, it seemed to float in the ground mist.

"Good evening," Sheft said uncertainly.

There was no reply. Teller reached for the skora-sword.

"You would attack your own ancestor, niyal'arist?" The voice was low and that of a woman. She threw back her hood, and her eyes shone out silver as moonlight. They were the eyes that had haunted Teller in the Riftwood.

"Who are you?"

"I am the first of what you are. I am wife to a mage and consort to a king, sister of a star and a star myself. With Rayuel and S'gan, I am the Spera, the hope of the Seani."

Staring at her, Teller touched Sheft's arm. "Her name," he said, "is Marhaut."

Chapter 15

The Mirror Pool

SHEFT WENT DOWN ON ONE KNEE to the woman before them. "You protected Mariat in the Riftwood. You brought her safe to the henge. I can't thank you enough for what you did for us."

Marhaut stood with her long-fingered hands lightly clasped. Her pale face and planed cheekbones gave her an ascetic expression, and her disconcerting, seemingly blind gaze rested above Sheft's head. "It was not only for you, but for many. Rise up, emjadis, and come with me. The Seani is in grave danger."

A strong wind gusted, things turned in the night, and suddenly all three were standing beside the Pool of Compassion. A full moon was reflected in its depths, but no moon was visible in the cloudy sky. Old oaks surrounded them, interspersed with the white buds of star-nuts that peered out of the dark like tiny faces. The statue of the sad mother, made of stone, yet somehow far softer than the stern reality before them, shone faintly against the dark woods. Teller had knelt here only twelve hours before.

The woman's silver eyes turned full upon him. "Do you remember firing your skora into balls of earth, for a use you did not know, or care?"

It seemed years ago, but it had been only months, in Autran's laboratorium. Teller nodded.

"You made abakal, the terrible source from which dark rumors have fled."

Teller recalled obeying Vol Autran's order, but to him abakal meant only muddy balls of earth mixed with dried herbs. It had required a great effort to fire them with skora, to change them into rough, black spheres that glittered in the meager light of the luniku globes.

"Besides morue," the woman continued, "abakal is the greatest weapon the Eyascnu Vora has yet devised. When Vol Shacad attacked the falconforms, he used only three abakal stones of the twelve you made, and they sufficed to send the wind-lords reeling toward extinction."

Yarahe had told him nothing about this attack, even though the young falconform had risked his life to save him, to bring home the man who had played a role in murdering so many of his kind.

"Now the Eyascnu plans to use abakal again. He will come with it against the Seani and utterly destroy it."

The words swooped upon Teller like a bat in the night. "That's not possible! The wards here are strong and will soon become stronger. They surround the entire compound and can withstand any weapon known."

"Not this one." Her long finger pointed at the still surface of the Pool of Compassion. "Look there."

The water hardened, cracked into pieces like a broken mirror, and flew silently into his face. He flinched, then blinked against a sudden light. He was standing with Sheft on the meadow beside the hospit, and a steely sun had just cleared Insheer Cliff. His ears rang, as if he had suddenly gone deaf, and every color was permeated by grey. The dome of the sky, though clear of clouds, was dull and ashy, barely tinged with blue. Faded grasses cast long shadows toward him.

It was, he realized, a vision of tomorrow.

Sounds burst upon him: shouts of frantic people as they ran past him toward the gates, clanging and rumbling from beyond the walls, the crack of a falling tree and the neigh of a horse. Colors surged back as he charged down the slope.

The wooden guard towers that flanked the gates were manned by all the trained soldiery the Seani possessed. Five mottled, forest-green cloaks flapped on the northern tower, one of them belonging to Komond who was clutching the rail with both hands. With him were four other Rift-riders, including Deoner and a woman Teller somehow knew was Kryshe. They held arrows nocked, but weren't aiming them. Neither were Larrin and his five guards in the opposite tower. The enemy must be out of range.

A loud thump from outside the gates was followed by a triumphant cheer. The people around Teller halted and looked up at the sky. A rough black sphere was sailing toward them like a ballooning nightmare. With a scuttering crash, it hit the ward and, for a moment, rendered it visible. It appeared as a great, glittering sheet, half again the height of the walls and rising in front of the guard towers. The ward bent inward at the blow, but smashed the ball into pieces as if it had hit an iron wall. Sparks flew. The ward rebounded with a whoosh and cast the fiery nuggets back onto the enemy. Teller's clothing and hair streamed in and out with the great washes of air and then fell flat.

Screams came from outside the gates, where a few of the lord's soldiers must've been hit by the lethal shards of their own weapon. A cheer came from those around him, but Teller's heart sank. Abakal. First ineerva, and now abakal. Would everything he had made in Oknu Shuld come back to strike at him? But what he had done could not be undone. It was his to atone for and his to deal with now. And he wasn't even certain what abakal could do.

No one seemed to notice him as he raced down the slope, climbed the ladder of the southern guard tower, and ran across the covered platform to the railing. Just beyond bowshot, trees had been hacked down to enlarge the clearing. Umbraks, Sekrew Bloodknots in their muddy red doublets, swarmed among white stumps bleeding with sap.

In the midst of them, a war engine hunkered. The oak arm, taller than a man and thicker than an umbrak's thigh, had already been winched down and the leather sling on the end of it loaded. Farther down the hillside and carrying their round Shields of the Eye, waited the Azanzi Scaths, two hundred of Shacad's most ruthless foot soldiers. Teller had once worn the red cloak hemmed with slate, had once been an officer in that elite group. He recognized Vol Tierce himself, a small figure at this distance, sitting at ease on his horse at the rear with Archon Rigiati at his side.

Teller looked back at the catapult. It was just beyond the reach of Seani arrows, and also protected by a wall of Azanzi shields. Dismay had barely hit him when the subaltern artilleryman barked an order.

A muscular umbrak stepped forward. He grinned and spit at the gates, then struck the lever with a mallet. The metal catch flicked, and the arm sprung up like a scorpion's tail, smashing against the buffer-bag with a loud *whump*. A cloud of dust flew out of the buffer, the engine bucked viciously, and a second ball arced towards the walls. As it did so, the subaltern darted from behind the shield wall to ascertain its course. Teller shot a flare of skora at him, the man's arms flew up as he fell, and the ball whooshed over Teller's head. He grabbed the nearest support just as white heat burst over the gates and the ward once more flashed into visibility.

Shacad's troops roared and the Scaths clashed sword-hilts on shields. Teller held on as the entire tower swayed backward along with the ward, and then rebounded, once more shoveling fiery pieces of abakal back at the enemy. With creaks and groans, the tower settled. A quick glance showed little damage. Its twin across from Teller, however, had not fared as well. One of the roof supports had buckled, and the roof above it sagged. Larrin shouted at Komond across the distance between the towers, but he couldn't be heard above the fray.

Once more the umbraks below were winching the arm down and another artilleryman stood by.

Teller saw that seven of the deadly balls remained on a pile behind the shield wall. One strong flare of skora would ignite them all, would cause an explosion that would wipe out the entire stock of abakal as well as the enemy forces around it—if he could get close enough. He assayed the distance. The enemy archers would make sure he wouldn't even get out the postern.

From behind his protective shields, another red-cloaked artilleryman sneered up at him and thumped his chest in a mock salute. Teller grimly returned it. He had just concluded there was no need for a fatal run toward abakal, because the abakal would come to him.

Teller concentrated on skora, built it up in his spirikai, and fused it into a fiery flare. It took more time than it ever had before. His bout with ineerva, his maimed hand, fever from the hospit visit, whatever—all had taken their toll—and meanwhile the winches were turned and the arm was forced back.

With a *whump* and a cloud of dust, the arm thudded against the buffer and the ball flew toward the gates. Teller took a steadying breath, considered the trajectory, and flared skora just ahead of the missile's path.

Abakal sailed a hand's-breadth above the skora flare and slammed into the ward.

With the sound of a hundred arrows hitting canvas, the ward tore open. It swept the weakened tower so far back that Teller went sprawling. The cracked support beam on the opposite tower collapsed and fell, dragging part of the roof with it in a shower of broken timbers and thatch.

The ward juddered with a peculiar sound, like staccato inbreaths. Its edges quickly re-seamed, and it bounded forward, bending the towers in its wake. Creaking and straining, the northern tower tilted at a dangerous angle. One of the Rift-riders fell and began sliding, kicking frantically to seek purchase. The others clung to the posts and tried to reach him, but he went over the edge. With a loud crack, the tower righted itself.

Hand over hand, Teller hauled himself to his feet and looked across the clearing. The catapult was being reloaded once more.

A DISTANT PART OF SHEFT'S MIND knew he was experiencing a vision, but the sounds and panic were all too real. He looked around for his brother, but screams of terror were coming from the hospit, and he rushed into the building. He dodged aside to avoid the farm wife who was carrying the dog-mauled little girl toward the door.

"Everyone get up to the Quela!" Tema cried. "Farne, get these people out of here! Find the other medicants!"

She pulled blankets off the beds and bundled patients out of their cots. Farne, carrying Willow over his shoulder, headed toward him. Before Sheft could get out of the way, the medicant rushed right through his body, like a gust of red, warm wind. Shocked, Sheft looked down at himself, felt his chest. He was solid, was real.

Willow beat against the medicant's back. "The emjadis!" she sobbed. "Where are the emjadis?"

The bed curtain in front of Sheft clashed open, and a grey-faced boy clung to it, coughing. Sheft reached out for him, but his arms only wisped through the boy's body. Frantic, he lunged for Eshu, who sat whimpering on the next cot. The result was the same. He couldn't pick them up, couldn't help them.

Tema swept up Eshu and ran to the door. "Oh God!" she cried. "Where's Taisa?"

FROM THE NORTHERN TOWER KOMOND SIGNALED to Larrin with a jerk of his thumb toward the ground. "I've got to join the Seah!" Komond shouted. "We've never faced this weapon before, and will need every Se to fight it. Pull back!"

Over his shoulder Larrin ordered his men. "Get down. Get down right now!" The surviving Rift-riders on the other tower had already scrambled down the ladder, but Deoner still remained.

Alone now on the southern tower, Teller clutched the rail as the catapult was winched down on the other side of the wall. He had the range now, but tremors raced through his body, and he didn't know if they came from exhaustion or from the weakened timbers that strained to hold up the tower. The scorpion-tailed beast spit out another ball. Watching its arc, Teller held back the fire. Not yet, not yet ...now!

An arrow thumped into the rail next to his hand just as he loosed skora. He missed.

A tremendous blast shook the tower and knocked Teller off his feet. He held on while the remains of the shredded roof disappeared, planks under him sagged, and the ladder blew off in a whirling cartwheel. Bits of fiery rock rained upon the fleeing guards. Above him, the ward painfully re-seamed, making sounds like a dying man gasping for breath. Teller looked for Deoner on the opposite tower. The floor there had collapsed, and the Rift-rider's still, sprawled body lay on the ground below.

Avia's husband, came the fleeting thought, the young father of twins, but then Teller whirled at the sound of ropes creaking as the catapult arm was pulled back yet again.

A RUSH OF HOT, INCOMING AIR greeted Sheft as he stumbled out of the hospit and up the slope. Fiery black pebbles fell around him and people brushed them frantically off their shoulders as they ran. The pebbles were sucked up and dragged away again by the rebounding ward, but some heavier stones remained and rolled among the grasses. Flames sprang up in their wake.

On the hill above him, all nine Se and their four assistants had gathered on the great lawn. Everyone faced the gates with joined hands, and Sheft could feel them dredging up power, weaving it together, pouring it towards the beleaguered ward. Their faces were fierce with concentration.

A young man rushed up to Hirai. It was her husband Yuin, whom Sheft had met in the dining room last night, and he carried their two-year-old daughters in his arms. These twins were the first niyalahn ever to find safety in the Seani, the first tiny victory in their war against the

Spider-king. Hirai tried to shake her hands free from the group working on the wards, but Yuin shouted at her. "Don't stop helping them! Hirai, don't stop! The girls will be safe in the nursery." He rushed off toward the Seani House. Hirai turned her head to watch them, but Utray, next to her, jerked at her hand, and she returned to her task.

Sheft looked around wildly. There was, he'd been told, another set of twins. With Deoner at the gates and Avia involved here, had anyone taken their babies to safety? Were they even now crying in their domicile? Sheft spied a young lad, brandishing a rake and rushing down the slope toward the gates. "Stop! Help me find Avia's—!" He grabbed at the boy's arm, but his fingers went right through it. The boy ran on, never glancing at him.

Oh God. Oh God Rulve, wasn't there anything he could do?

KNEELING, BREATHING HEAVILY, TELLER HELD ONTO the rail with both hands and watched the 'braks load yet another ball. He should have known how potent abakal would be. He should have dashed out of the postern, tried to get a flare of skora out before arrows felled him. Now it was too late.

With his sweat-soaked shirt clinging to his back, he reached deep into his spirikai for every glowing ember. He breathed in like a bellows to fan them into life, strained to build a flare of skora stronger than the last.

The scorpion tail fully winched down, the order was snapped and the ball loosed. Teller waited for the right instant, aimed just below where the abakal hung for a split-second at the peak of its arc, and flung out all the skora he had. The gout of fire soared like a comet toward the big stone.

It hit dead center.

But even as it did so his heart sank. It wasn't enough. It wasn't strong enough to shatter the ball or even shear a piece off. The projectile slammed into the ward. The explosion blew the ward backward, tearing a long, fiery rent in the air between the hospit and the gates. The ward winked out as skeins of power unraveled. Coming now from the opposite direction, the blast bent Teller's guard tower like a mighty wind bends a tree. He held on as timbers leaned and groaned and snapped. Across from him the northern tower was swept away in a tangle of broken boards, posts, and the remaining thatch from the roof. Inside the Seani, burning shards of abakal hit the ground and scattered, and whatever they touched burst into wind-lengthened flames. His tower shuddered to an upright position, but one corner sagged dangerously while behind him the gathered enemy roared in triumph.

His own rasping breaths blended with the painful *uh-uh-uh* of the ward slowly attempting to knit itself together. It stuttered in and out of sight as the tatters of a hole flapped against the sky. Then it collapsed, and the Seani lay exposed.

Faces rushed through his mind: Taisa's, his grandmother's, Willow's, Druv's. The invaders would slaughter them all.

Again he heard the squealing of the winch, the grunts of the umbraks, the creaking strain of the thick ropes. Somehow he had to fend off another missile, give the Se time to revive the ward. Teller pressed his forehead against the railing and squeezed his eyes shut in a tight and quivering effort to rekindle skora.

A WHISTLING SOUND PULLED SHEFT'S EYES toward the sky. Like an impossible hole in the air, a bristling black ball was becoming larger and larger as it flew toward the hospit. Directly in front of it, at a man's height from the ground, the ball released its full potential. With a deafening, reverberating *PHUNG!* it burst into a blinding white disk rimmed with purple. It streaked past him like flat lightning, cracked the air, shook the ground.

He felt nothing, but the log walls of the hospit flew apart. Beds and people were tossed out like flaming debris. A bundled child, on fire and screaming, rolled down the hillside. Farne and Tema, with the children they carried, were caught by the deadly leading edge. Sheft cried out, rushed to help them, but their burning, bodies passed through his arms.

The air whistled with another in-coming ball and Sheft whirled. Purple flashed—*PHUNG!*—and incandescence took his sight. He tottered away, his arm over his eyes, and when his vision returned, fire was racing up the great lawn. Wailing, the Se ran, but the fiery disk caught them all. Celume and Nemes threw up their hands as they were dragged under. Utray held Hirai in a protective embrace, and the fire swirled them into a horrible dance. Figures writhed like dark shadows in the midst of the flames. The firestorm carried their bodies in a wave of arms and legs and drove them toward the Seani House.

Dazed with horror, Sheft staggered after them, wading unhurt through the burning grass. He glimpsed Druv in front of him, clutching the doorframe, his powerful shoulders straining to hold on, but the conflagration sucked him into the dining hall where tables and chairs ignited with a rumbling *whoom.*

At the door, Sheft stared into an inferno. Flames licked at the walls and rushed up the wooden stairs. A woman, holding two babies in her arms, was trapped at the top. One child was screeching and kicking and a little white sock drifted off his foot. It swirled upward in a rush of hot air. The woman only had time to gasp before the fire engulfed her. It transformed the three of them into a pillar of flames that folded, tottered, and pitched down the burning stairs.

Sheft backed away. He smelled scorched flesh, heard screaming from the floor above, saw the ceiling blacken, like an ink stain spreading. Unable to tear his gaze away from the Seani House, he stumbled backward off the porch and down the slope. The house erupted into yellow and orange flames that swirled into a cloudless blue sky. A figure appeared on the balcony, clambered over the rail, and fell into the fire below. Sickened, Sheft turned away.

Down the hill, the gates burst open. Soldiers poured through and overwhelmed the pathetically small group of Rift-riders, guards, and men with rakes and shovels. They kicked their bodies aside, making way for the umbraks who pushed and heaved at a great wooden engine, its tail raised obscenely.

He had no idea what it was, but soon found out. With a thump-kick and a screaming sizzle, another deadly ball sailed in. It exploded over the Quela with a deafening. *PHU-UN-NG!* The brilliant purple edge sheared the roof off and hit the twelve great trees like an ax. The arched windows blew out in colored fragments, followed by the double doors.

A metal hinge from the door flew by his head and Sheft found himself staring into the hellish interior. Nin, Oko, Dek—all the ancient trees Lir had pointed out to him—were snapping and spitting like mighty torches against the sky. Green wax from the candles, trailing flames, flowed toward Rulve's pool as glowing chunks of the walls slid down. Fire chewed through Welf and Eka, and like weak, blackened logs, they sank down in a fountain of sparks. With an explosive crack, Rulve's green disk split into two jagged halves. The open hands fell apart, and the western wall came down in a fiery cataract.

AS IF HE WERE A HAWK hovering over the Seani, Teller was looking down at a compound that had been completely overwhelmed. Bloodknots and Scaths were swarming like ants through the gates and spreading out, searching for survivors. Vol Tierce sat on his horse near the postern, his throat working as he drank from a flask. At the base of what had been the north tower, a group of 'braks were hacking at the dead bodies with their axes.

The Lord of Oknu Shuld hadn't even bothered to attack the walls. His diabolic weapon enabled him to walk in the front door.

A roil of smoke forced Teller to wheel away, only to veer sharply from the towering pyre of the Quela. Under a hail of embers and sparks, four people were running for refuge toward the Burvena Basin, their robes flapping in the hot breeze. Among them was Taisa. The fire stalked after them, racing up flowering branches and leaping maniacally from tree to tree. A budding, fiery branch raked the top of Taisa's head, and a coil of her long hair ignited. She beat at it as she ran, and the purple ribbon, tied around her delicate brown wrist, flashed in the sun.

He cried out to her, couldn't make her hear him, couldn't reach her.

She and the others jumped into the water of the Burvena Basin and disappeared in its mineral-laden depths. Fire raged around them. Burning tree-trunks and branches fell over the pool, one heavy pillar crashing over another. They formed an impenetrable, red-hot net, trapping those beneath. Pale ovals appeared under the murky water, contorted faces with open mouths, outstretched hands.

Teller rushed toward them, into the flames. "Taisa!" he screamed. "Taisa!"

CHAPTER 16

SUMMONS

EVERYTHING WENT DARK.

A woman's low voice was speaking. "And so it was written, that on a spring morning in Seed, those who dwelt in the valley looked up and saw flames on the hillside. The Sperians in the village cried in secret and the corrupt laughed openly and the Seani burned to the ground. By mid-afternoon only smoke and charred stones marked where once it stood. And even as the ground cooled, the Eyascnu Vora came into his power and there was nothing but death left in Shunder."

Wisps of ground fog curled over the calm surface of the Pool of Compassion.

Teller took a long, tremulous breath, not of acrid smoke and burning flesh, but of damp night air. His hand throbbed fiercely.

Sheft looked at his own shaking hands, and Teller knew he was wondering why they were not smeared with blood and soot. "I couldn't touch them," his brother said. "I couldn't help them."

"In visions of the future and in dreams of the past," the woman said, "we are powerless. Only in the present may we act."

The two silver gazes met, and beside that link, Teller was a bystander. Sheft's eyes held a question liquid with its own feared answer; the woman's reflected the memory of a long-ago sacrifice. "Like balm applied to a wound," she said, "s'rere must go to the source of the hurt."

And where s'rere went, skora must follow. Teller swallowed and his throat felt raw, as if he had been screaming. Every door had slammed shut, leaving open only the darkest. "If we do this," he said to the woman, "if we go willingly to Oknu Shuld, what are the assurances the lord will not destroy the Seani anyway?"

"There are no assurances, emjadi. We are all part of a weaving we cannot yet see. But the vision is clear. If we continue on this present road, there is no doubt where it will take us."

Dread shot through the link like slivers of ice, like sharp darts of fire. There was far more at stake than the Seani's fate. Everything the toltyr stood for—Shunder's freedom, the land's healing, release for the ahn—all of it could be lost if they went to Oknu Shuld. There was nothing to stop the Spider-king from seizing everything they had and emerging with the very powers he had sought for so long.

The woman stood with Marhaut's statue behind her, and even its stone eyes were etched with sadness. "The Seani was once my home. Here I loved my husband and bore my son. I had to leave them, emjadis, in order to save them. I do what I can to protect this place. There were no assurances then, and there are none now. There never can be when people are as free to choose darkness as they are to choose the light." She shifted her gaze from one to the other. "In the vision of tomorrow you accomplished nothing, saved no one. The Lord of Shunder prevailed. In the present, you must keep your word."

An inner cry flashed out of Sheft. It tore through Teller and became his own. *Oh God, Rulve. I agreed to do your will. I want to do it. I will give my life for your good purpose. But to spend everything, and buy back nothing?*

"We are not summoned to relevance," the woman said, "but to do what love demands."

Teller met his brother's eyes. The choice had already been made. They chose to be Rulve's Coin. They chose to trust him to spend them both, however she willed.

"When will they come for us?" Sheft asked.

"They will be waiting outside the back gate one hour before dawn."

In four hours, when the Seani would be steeped in quiet, when Taisa would still be asleep. On the time-candle it was a distance one could measure between thumb and forefinger.

The woman's form hardened, paled, and flowed backward toward the statue. "Y'rulve, emjadis," she said, her voice growing fainter. "Y'rulve."

Now only a white marble figure stood there, shining faintly in the starlight, the blank eyes looking into the distance. Sheft-Teller was alone, yet somehow with each other.

They walked through the thin fog until they were back on the Red Lantern Way, back where they had first encountered Marhaut. All was still. No screams disturbed the quiet night, no flames shot into the sky.

But they had been summoned. First by the voices of children, then by a vision so powerful it stalked by their side as an alternate reality.

Teller remembered that Abiyat was expecting him in the infirmary. They parted ways, Sheft going on toward the Quela. In the Garden of the Sick Teller stood just outside the lighted window. Would Taisa be inside?

What could he say to someone he might never see again? He took a deep breath, and then pushed the door open. His eyes searched the room for her, but found only Abiyat working at the counter.

The healer looked up. "I was just about to walk over to the Quela and get you. Bring the chair to the lantern here and let me look at your hand."

"Sorry I'm so late."

Abiyat unwound the bandage and examined the wound with a clear air of disapproval. "I suppose you did what you thought necessary, Teller, but Rulve doesn't ask for body parts."

No, Teller thought, she asks for the whole thing.

Abiyat sighed. "At least there is no sign of infection. I suppose we have the skora to thank for that." He pressed gently on Teller's hand, where the roots had been.

Pain ran up his arm, but he tried not to flinch. He apparently didn't succeed because Abiyat said, "There's not much to be done about that. It just needs time and some protection. Tonight we will keep the wound open to the air, and it will heal faster. In the morning I will re-bandage it." Shaking his head, he dabbed healoil onto the burn, carefully rubbed a salve into Teller's hand, and then reached for a small bottle filled with a liquid. "Drink half of this just before you lie down and give the other half to Sheft. I want both of you to sleep late, and have arranged that you not be disturbed."

He and his brother must be up well before dawn, but Teller took the potion anyway, intending to pour it out as soon as he left the infirmary. "Thank you, Abiyat," he said, then hesitated. "And," he found himself saying, "extend my thanks to Taisa also."

Abiyat's lip quirked in a crooked smile. "Thank her

yourself, emjadi. No young lady is ever won by reticence, you know."

Evidently, Teller thought, the healer didn't know about Lir. "It's very late," he said, then added, "Isn't it?"

Abiyat waved a hand in the air. "Late, shmate. You young people think nothing of staying up to all hours. Taisa is in the nursery, and I'm sure she wouldn't mind you stopping by to extend your thanks to her. Or," he shrugged, "wait until tomorrow. Meanwhile, not being a young man anymore, I must get myself to bed." Moving toward the door to his room, he wished Teller a good night.

Outside, Teller poured the potion into a bush. There would be no tomorrow.

A sudden desire arose in him, like a shining fish coming up from moonlit waters. No matter what, he had to see Taisa, and he had to see her now. In only hours, he and Sheft would be gone.

Only two days ago, when he had risen half-conscious from the water in the Pool of Rulve, when he had looked in confusion at the people around him and dimly recognized some of them, when the all-encompassing pain was no more, his eyes had been drawn to the beautiful young woman holding his hand. She was keeping him steady in the water then, as she had been keeping him steady through boiling thermals of pain only hours before. Immediately he loved her.

But she belonged to Lir. He saw how Lir's eyes had shone when he looked at Taisa, how he stood protectively over her, how he seemed never far from her.

Lir had ridden through the night and into the dangers of the Bellstone Forest to save both emjadis' lives. Teller, painfully aware of what he had done in Oknu Shuld, would not compete against such a man. He would not interfere in a relationship that looked to be growing, and would not attempt to snatch from Lir such a treasure as Taisa's love.

But she'd done so much for him, and he wanted to give something back. Not, he told himself, to remember him by, not that, but something. He immediately rejected the jade dagger at his waist; it would be an insult to her healer's heart. His fingers touched the red and blue cord in his pocket. It wouldn't be right to offer her a symbol of his despair. And it wouldn't be seemly either; it involved, after all, females other than her. So he had nothing for her, but somehow still continued moving toward where she might be.

The dining room of the Seani House was now dark and quiet, lit only by lanterns on the stairs directly ahead. He went up, hoping that the nursery was still where it used to be, across the hall from the stairway. It was.

The door was ajar, and a dim light shone through. He crossed over to it and quietly pushed the door open. A quick glance told him all six cribs were occupied by sleeping babies and toddlers. No adult was in the room. The door to the Sunrise Balcony, however, was open, and Teller moved to it. Outside, with her back to him, Taisa stood looking out at the night.

Marhaut's vision jumped before his eyes: Taisa trapped in the Burvena Pool, caged in by fiery branches, her face under the water. Would these visions assail him until the day he died?

But, he thought with a great leap of joy, Thank God, she's alive! And Sheft and I are going to do our best to make sure that she, and everyone in the Seani, will stay that way.

She turned. She must have heard him because she turned, and her eyes lit up for him, and he moved quickly toward her with an open heart. But an arm's-length away from her he stopped. He had no business coming here. All he had to give her was a fiercely knotted cord, the tangible remnant of his failure.

"Is it really?" she asked him gently. "Did you really fail them?"

Again he'd been unable to hide his deepest emotions from her. "I didn't save them, Taisa."

"But you tried. And isn't that love?"

"Love isn't futile. It isn't fatal to one and devastating to another."

A sad smile touched her lips. "You spoke the truth, emjadi. Love is Rulve's essence and can be neither of those things."

But wasn't it? Wasn't love fatal to the lover who was called to give up everything and devastating to the beloved who must feel the loss? He stood regarding her, bereft in her presence and aching for her. "I have to give you something, Taisa. I can't—" This time he came down hard and blocked the rest of the thought: *I can't leave you without saying good-bye.*

She couldn't have heard that, but responded to what he had last said. "So give me your hand, Teller."

He knew which one she meant and slowly extended it.

She caught her breath at the sight of his missing finger, yet with great tenderness cradled his hand in both of hers. She held it, looking into his eyes, then gently raised it to her lips and kissed it. "This wounding is love, niyal'arist," she said. "This is what you did in order to take up the toltyr and save Shunder. It was love that helped the little ahn who wore the blue ribbon and love that freed the woman from the red cord. I see these two as my sisters."

In spite of his misgivings, she would accept the knotted cord; in spite of his doubts, she even wanted it. He drew it out of his pocket, crumbled as it was, and laid it into her open palm. For a brief moment the blue and red touched the purple mourning ribbon around Taisa's wrist.

She stared at it, a wondering smile touching her face. "How beautiful, emjadi. The love we share for them connects us." She closed her fist around the cord, and immediately, without thinking, he went to her. They came together, and he squeezed his eyes tight against the top of her head, held her as close as he could against him, while sweet, breathy words in the mind-speech spilled out of both their hearts. He felt them merge, her and him, the desire mounting until it hurt on his part and swirled deeper on her part, and never would he want to let her go.

But then a small pair of arms wrapped themselves around his leg. He looked down to see the child Narla, the one rescued from the village shamana. She must've rolled out of her mat to join them on the balcony. Hugging them both around the knees, she looked up at them with a dreamy smile. "I wov you too," she said.

Reality came rushing back for Teller. Oh God. He must not take Taisa's heart away from Lir when he wouldn't be alive to keep it.

He stepped back from Taisa, who smiled down at the little girl. "What are you doing up so late? It's back to bed for you."

"I'll leave you to it, then," Teller said quietly. He couldn't look at the woman he had just embraced and only managed a rigid nod. "Good night, ladies," he said, and left them.

The hall was almost dark when he walked into the Quela. Only the time-candle and the two tall candles on either side of the Great Disk were lit, and someone had brought in a brazier for warmth. Sheft, with one of the

Seani's brown cloaks over his shoulders, knelt with his back to him in front of the green disk. Teller could feel that his twin was in deep solitude with Rulve, simply being with her, enduring his grief with him, and trying to trust her in what was to come. With a pang, Teller realized his brother was as close to the Creator as he himself once had been and now struggled to be again.

His twin didn't need the extra weight of what his brother was feeling. Teller blocked as much as he could from the link between them just before Sheft turned and saw him.

Sheft got to his feet and looked at him. Then he quickly blocked his end of the link too. Wasn't their connection supposed to divide the anguish, not double it?

"Did Abiyat take care of your hand?"

"He did."

Sheft searched his face. "Was Taisa there?"

"No."

Sheft continued to gaze at him, and Teller was the first to drop his eyes.

"Teller, I have to go alone. This lord seems to want s'rere more than anything else. You need to stay here. You have to use your skora to defend the Seani and—"—he hesitated, but went on—"and protect the woman you love."

But he didn't love her. He shouldn't.

A small table stood nearby, which held washcloths, a basin, a full pitcher of water, and slices of bread and cheese on a dish. Thoughtful Keppit must have provided all that. Teller put Abiyat's empty bottle on the table. "Neither of us can go alone. We are one thing, Sheft."

Sheft turned his head to the side. "Mariat and I were one thing too."

Teller knew Sheft's remark was a memory and not an accusation, but it still hurt. "The lord wants his revenge on me as much as he wants s'rere," he said. "With both of us in Oknu Shuld, he has no reason to use his precious remaining abakal against the Seani."

Sheft said nothing; they both knew there were no assurances. Their mats lay side by side in the dimness of the Marhaut alcove, and they turned into them, facing away from each other.

"If," his brother said, "if something should happen to me, please take care of Mariat in my place."

"I will, Sheft."

His brother wrapped himself in the worn Seani cloak and a blanket, but Teller saw he was still shivering, so he reached over and covered him with his own cloak as well. The skora, alarmed and suspicious, was keeping him warm enough.

The earth floor was hard and the mats lumpy, and Teller almost regretted throwing out the sleep potion. Every time he closed his eyes, he saw the Seani in flames. Their link had slowly opened on both sides, and the two of them tossed and turned to escape their separate yet shared memories of the vision. They eventually managed to push that away, but then the connection between them became charged with scenarios of what awaited them inside Oknu Shuld.

One niyal'arist will help the other die. At first they had assumed this meant one of them would live. But now they realized Celume's words did not say that.

Finally Teller fell asleep. In his dream a young woman ran, her hair streaming, the hem of her robe ablaze. *Taisa! Oh, God, Taisa!* He groaned, turned over, and glimpsed the calm, haloed light of a candle above him. Or was it a small sphere floating?

He stumbled into his brother's dream, where welling brown eyes looked at Sheft-Teller with love. She lay close to him, her arms around him, and then was gone, and he felt her forever loss.

Later, half in a dream, Teller turned to see his brother kneeling once more before the Great Disk, his head bowed almost to the ground.

Chapter 17

Fire Ghosts

Druv had left the Quela hours ago, but still couldn't get to sleep. He lay on his usual side of the wide bed, alone. He could have sprawled out—his wife had been gone for years—but seldom did. Fog pressed against the partially open window next to him, like a forlorn and banished memory. The only sound was the faint ripple of the Westbrook, a sound usually overlaid by the whisper of the wind coming off the Outcrop or by the ancient apple tree scratching at his roof. But tonight the air was still.

A strong smell of smoke trailed through the darkness.

He turned to face his one-room domicile. The fire was banked and nothing smoldered in the hearth. A deep sense of unease crept over him. He made his way to the door, stepped out, and sniffed the air. He smelled nothing but the mist-soaked forest around him.

The fog. It must be keeping the chimney from drawing well. He went back into the house, and the smell of smoke, as if from some half-perceived vision, had faded away. Moving carefully now because of the stiffness that had recently plagued his back, he climbed into bed, drew Leana's cold pillow against him, and put his arm around it. His eyes closed, and slowly the memory of his long-ago wife edged through the open window and sifted into his dream.

IN THE HOSPIT, WILLOW OPENED HER eyes. Something wasn't right. She smelled smoke, more than the usual smell that came from the hearth. The curtain around her bed had been left open, and she could see a few flames licking at the logs in the fireplace. As she watched, the flames turned into a fiery face with smoky hair roiling around it. Its eyes were lit-up slits, and they swiveled to the right and to the left, looking for her. Now they saw her.

Willow gasped and pulled the blanket over her head. She wanted to scream for Tema, but she must not move, must keep perfectly still. Heat was building up under the blanket. Was the fire-face coming? Was it bending over her, breathing on her? The smoky smell got worse and scratched at the back of her throat. Would her blanket suddenly burst into flames? She squeezed her eyes shut. The burn marks on her head crawled.

If the emjadis came again, the fire-face would dart away. It would dash back into the hearth where it belonged, and the smoke would go up the chimney like it was supposed to. She tried to make a picture of the emjadis in the air above her bed that would scare the fire away. She thought of Emjadi Sheft's hair, the color of wheat, and his eyes sort of grey, like the special silver spoon Tema gave them medicine with. She thought of his cool hands and of the gentle way he cupped the side of her head. Hardly anybody ever touched her there; even she didn't like the bumpy feel of her skin on that side. Emjadi Teller had a scar too, a rough one on his cheek. He didn't like fire either, but he wasn't afraid to go past the hearth.

When she was pretty sure she had made a good picture of the emjadis, and that it was hovering over her bed, she opened her eyes. She saw only the close weave of the blanket against her face, and a dim light beyond. Cautiously she peeked out. The fire-face was gone and so was its smoke. She took a deep breath of relief. It had all been real, but the emjadis made it go away.

THE FOG-BLURRED OUTLINES OF PINE TREES surrounded the deserted botanarium. Inside, the only light came from a corner of the room, where the flame of the time-candle stood motionless in its lucent pool of wax. Its steady light illuminated the far sides of the serpent boxes but kept the near sides in shadow. In one box a head lifted and a forked tongue flicked. It detected something. Something that had left its scent, then had withdrawn. Something that still lurked a short distance away. The reptilian coil slowly unwound itself and flowed as far away from it as it could, into the darker side.

IT WAS TIME. THEY WERE COMING, and it was time. Teller sat up, dread heavy in his stomach. The Quela lay in shadows, its alcoves discernable only in side-vision grey. The time-candle stood in its own small circle of light, along with the two other lit candles that flanked Rulve's Disk. The disk itself was a featureless black circle that loomed over the hall.

They drank from the water jug Keppit had left for them, but after the sleepless night, neither could eat the bread or cheese.

Without speaking, they were drawn to the Great Disk, and they knelt before it shoulder to shoulder. The same prophecy flashed through their link: *"You will be wounded; by a child, by your brother, and by the dark."* Different children, different brothers, the same dark.

The flames of the two candles, tied to their wicks, strained upward, and their auras laid golden kisses upon Rulve's hands. As a small boy Teller had once climbed into those hands, and he longed to do it again, to find safety, to hide from what awaited them. A plea for courage twisted out of their link.

He and his brother had taken different paths and chose the turnings, or else did not choose and were driven. Thin spokes of volition and chance, radiating from some solid center, wheeled them to this central place, to kneel before Rulve. Their lives were in his hands.

They rose, put on their cloaks, and left by the Eka-door, the one facing north. A chilly Seed-fog hung in the night and they could hear no one about. They left behind the misty spheres of the Red Lantern Way and followed a trail that led toward the back gate. This took them through a grove of pines, where the sharp smell of resin filtered through the drooping branches, and past the small stone bridge under which Rayuel's Rivulet bubbled and trickled, clearly heard in the fog. A little farther, and the training ground appeared, so filled with fog it looked like a shallow lake. Beyond that emerged the light from a dim lantern hanging beside the back gate. Mist veiled the treetops beyond.

Teller glanced back at the way they had come. Moist air settled on his face as he breathed in the silent peace, the elusive, unmistakable aroma of a spicebush, gone with a second breath. Sheft put out his hand to stop him. A lone guard was passing on his rounds. They waited in the trees until he disappeared in the fog and then approached the side gate.

"We forgot something," Sheft whispered into his ear. "Who will replace the bar?"

"I'll take care of it." They slipped out the gate, closed it quietly behind them, and Teller turned to speak a low command. The bar on the other side settled into place with a soft clunk.

Sheft regarded him with raised eyebrows.

"Something I learned in Oknu Shuld."

They moved forward, into a damp, clinging mist, following a faint down-sloping path as the fog opened before them and closed after them. All was silent.

What if, Teller wondered, last night's vision had only been some strange reaction to ineerva poisoning? What if he and Sheft had only been passing illusions, fears, and nightmares through the link? A warm possibility rose in his heart: that they could turn around and go home, that he could see Taisa in the morning, eat breakfast with their grandmother, go fishing with their new friends; and only his brother would know of their joint delusion.

Sudden figures appeared in the night. Waiting on the path were two Sekrew Bloodknot subalterns armed with swords and four Clawthorn 'braks, their hairy hands resting on ax handles. The Delver, wearing his dead-leaf cloak, stood in their midst. Sheft started at the sight of Vol Kuat's face, as ridged and grainy as the bark of a tree.

The Vol's strange double voice addressed them. "Have you come here of your own free will?"

They had promised to do what love demanded. They were utterly bound as Rulve's Coin. They must enter the only door that now stood open. Both nodded their assent.

"Are you they who claim to be niyalahn-rista?"

Teller felt his brother's heart hammering as hard as his own, but Sheft answered quietly. "We are as Rulve made us."

The subalterns—Teller recognized one he knew only as Eye-patch—stirred uncertainly and glanced at Vol Kuat.

"Bind them," the Vol ordered.

Two 'braks surged forward, pulled off Sheft's cloak, and secured his arms behind him with a chain.

Completely unbidden, skora jumped into Teller's hand, and he found himself brandishing a sizzling, flaming sword.

"What in hell are you doing?" Sheft demanded.

"It—it seems this fire is as protective of you as it is of me."

"You've got to do something about that, or it's going to be a problem."

Which it immediately became. The 'braks behind Sheft grabbed him as a shield and pulled out their axes. The others, weapons in hand, spread out. Teller edged toward the trees, trying to protect his back while whipping the fire-sword from side to side. '

"Stand down," Eye-patch growled at Teller. He pointed his chin at Sheft. "Or he gets an ax in the ribs."

"He won't do it, Teller."

The arc of sharp steel around Teller tightened, but he cut his eyes to the Delver and put on a wolfish grin. "You'd let them spill the blood the lord wants?"

Vol Kuat lifted one hand, and his men halted their advance. He answered Teller, his blank white eyes seeming to reflect a distant fire "Do you choose to fight us?"

Teller hesitated, and then glanced at his brother.

"Is that why we came here?" Sheft asked.

Teller felt his face flame. He had already wavered from the course, already broken his promise to Rulve. With an inward groan, he lowered the sword and wrestled the skora back into his spirikai.

Vol Kuat held out a wood-grained hand, palm up. Teller realized he was brandishing the green dagger. He must have slipped it into his belt before he left the Quela and pulled it out along with skora. It had become part of him: a leaf and a flame in a jade-hilted blade, a nascent toltyr in the only form he had been able to accept. He did not want to give it up.

He looked at Sheft, who only looked back. Teller was suddenly aware of the void where his finger used to be, of the toltyr lying heavily against his chest. Hadn't he cut off the one to take up the other?

He flipped the hilt forward and handed the dagger over.

Braks ripped off Teller's cloak and chained his wrists behind him. They probably reasoned that metal would be harder than rope for skora to burn through. Their deliberate roughness set his hand throbbing.

The guards shoved them forward into the fog, and they followed a trail further down the hillside. It met a narrow track, where a small horse-drawn wagon waited. A pair of 'braks guarded it, their eyes glittering in the light of the two lanterns that hung on either side. The wagon held a low wooden cage, two strides long, barely thigh-high, and barred at the top and sides.

At the sight of it, the skora raged up in fury and again Teller had to hold it back. With umbraks prodding them with ax handles, they were forced to crawl with bound hands into the cage, facing each other. The cage was so low they had to kneel with bowed heads, as if in obeisance to the lord who intended to humiliate them. The rough planks were permeated by the smell of the last occupants, which must have been a crush of terrified pigs.

A 'brak tied the door shut, thrust his grizzled head close to the bars, and bared his teeth in a grin. "A scathi butcher's cage, this is. Headin' for the knives."

With a jerk, the wagon set out down the track. A subaltern walked with an umbrak on either side, a pair of 'braks guarded the back, and two led the horse. Eight armsmen, Teller noted, just for the two of them.

As best he could from his bent over position, Teller looked through the bars for the Delver. He had disappeared, a move characteristic of him. The enigmatic Kuat was often gone from the lord's service for days on end. He was the only Vol without a name, or at least not one he was willing to divulge. The Delver was inhuman, sly, and manipulative; yet for some reason Teller could not fathom, the fact that Vol Kuat had supervised his arrest felt like a betrayal.

Fog droplets settled over his hair and shoulders as the wagon bumped down the narrow track. With every turn of the wheels, he was being taken back to Oknu Shuld. Back to the place from which he had escaped, back to the confining dark, back to the unremitting ahn-pain that must be constantly blocked by a low skora barrier.

Back to the strisnu.

Four steps down, he remembered that; the smell, sharp and coppery; stains on the long wooden table. Oh God, a drain in the floor. Iron rings on the wall. His arms were shackled above his head, a cold point pressed against his back. "That's not my name!" The point popped through the skin, burned and burned on its way down. "That's not my name!"

Sheft's forehead touched his. "I know, Teller. I know."

He was breathing too hard. He was going back there. "No. You don't know."

Wincing, Sheft lowered his head.

There was a grinding ache in his shoulder. But it was Sheft's shoulder, the one that had been hurt in the field-burn accident. The damaged tendons were being strained by the unnatural position of his arms pinned behind his back. The link blurred the difference between them, and he couldn't tell whose grief squeezed his stomach, whose fear rose in his throat.

Chapter 18

Journey

The wagon jolted on. Dampness from floor of the cage seeped into Sheft's pants, and his shirt, wet from the droplet-laden twigs that brushed against the bars, lay over his shoulders like cold hands.

Gradually the light of the oil lanterns dissolved into the grey of a sickly dawn, and umbraks blew out the flames. Teller had described these creatures, and Sheft thought he was prepared, but still an angry knot tightened in his chest at the sight of them. The last thing his wife had seen was their small feral eyes; the last thing she had felt was their bristle-backed hands. Yet it seemed these beasts were part of a land Rulve wanted to save.

The wagon left the hillside track and lurched onto a road. Even as the wheels splashed through puddles of mud, even as last night's rain still lingered in the air as a clammy mist, the ground slowly passing beneath was parched with a deeper thirst. The fog lifted to reveal newly furrowed fields on either side, but the thin soil held little fertility. Without sweet-rue, without its deep roots and green leaves being plowed back into the soil, the land was dying. Farmers trudged to the fields with hoes or bags of seed, but they had no real hope in their eyes.

Sheft couldn't lift his head high enough to see where they were going, but their guards had bestirred themselves so there must be a village ahead. One of the umbraks removed a tambour from its nail, a subaltern called out the charges against them, and the umbrak ended each sentence with a whack on the small drum.

"These claim to be niyalahn-rista," a subaltern sang out. *Whamp.* "Here be rebels against our lord." *Whamp.* "These plotted to steal your morue." *Whamp.* "These claim to be niyalahn-rista." And on and on.

The ache in his shoulder was spreading into the side of his neck, and despite his best efforts to suppress it, Sheft knew the sensation was leaking into the link. He flexed his right hand to convince himself the throbbing there wasn't his. They had to do a better job of blocking these sensations, had to, or they would double whatever torment awaited them in Oknu Shuld.

The first of the houses came into view, and soon villagers began gathering on both sides of the muddy street. The gaped at the cage or yelled insults, while a few made slashing gestures across their throats.

"Hey look! It's niyal'arist pigs!"

"Slice 'em up for bacon; cut'em up for hams!"

Sheft tried not to listen, not to focus on the glee-twisted faces, the jaws slack from the alehouse even at this early hour, the eyes glazed from the addictive morue. When he had agreed to do Rulve's will, he hadn't expected this humiliation, hadn't expected this cage and this crowd. The faces all around him were as full of the same abhorrence and disgust as those at the K'meen Arûk.

"I should have told you," Teller said. "A parade like this is free entertainment. I knew this sort of thing happened, but I never thought about it, never—"

"It's all right. It's not your fault."

"Ghast!" a woman exclaimed, pointing at Sheft. "Ghast, look at his eyes."

"By the twin voras! They're fish eyes."

Sheft quickly looked down, then remembered what Mariat had once told him: *"You don't have to do that anymore, Sheft."* She had given him the courage to look directly into her eyes, to allow her to do the same for him, to let him love her; and now she was gone. That last word sounded like a groan, like the tolling of a bell.

Something flew past his head. A stone. He shrank away, but there was no protection inside the open cage.

Teller couldn't lift his head high enough to see where the stone came from, but as far as the skora was concerned, his brother had been attacked. The fire leaped up. Teller held it in readiness as he scanned the crowd as best he could.

A man to his left was cocking his arm. Teller fired a thin flare of skora that caught him on the wrist. The man dropped the stone and clamped his hand over the burn. "Hey," he shouted angrily. "Hey!"

Another rock flew, but Teller shattered it before it could hit the cage. Some in the crowd liked the display. "Look!" they shouted. "Look! He's using skora!" More people came running and a fourth stone arced. A sudden lurch of the wagon deflected Teller's aim, and the stone hit Sheft on his bound hand. His brother jerked sideways as ice rose on his end of the link, and fire rose higher on Teller's.

Eye-patch reached through the bars and pulled Teller's head back by the hair. "You do that again and I'll cut an eye out. It'll make no difference to the lord as long as I deliver you alive."

Teller shook free and glared at the man. "You try that, subaltern, and your arm's a burned brisket."

The man's mouth twisted into a half-smile. "There's eight of us here, and we'll get you from behind, asshole." He turned away and the wagon rattled on.

A cold breeze sprang up, clearing the sky. Sheft shivered in his damp clothing while Teller, hot with skora, fought to keep it under control. All they had against fear was ice and fire, and neither was doing them much good right now.

Sheft thought of his sheepskin jacket. The last place he'd seen it was on Mariat's pony. Did she have a chance to put it on when night fell? Did it keep her warm until—?

He cut off the thought before it reached his brother. They each had their own torment, and the best they could do for each other was to keep it to themselves.

Some of the crowd had drifted away, but the subaltern's mindless chant drew a few loiterers who attached themselves to the wagon. They marched alongside, shouting the same remarks over and over about butchering the pigs and carving them up. Sheft struggled to block it all out, to picture Rulve's disk, to put his trust into the protective hands. He knew they existed, somewhere far from here.

They were passing a leather shop, and two well-dressed young women emerged, carrying packages. They and their two male companions stopped at the sight of the wagon.

The first lady wrinkled her nose and whisked back her skirt. "Ghast, Preya, look at this!"

With a short laugh, the woman called Preya raised her hand and called to the subalterns. "Stop the wagon for a moment, please."

"Who is this lady?" Sheft asked Teller.

A deep dislike came with the answer. "She's the daughter of Moverik, the altern of Rydle. He dotes on her."

The wagon bumped to a halt. Preya stepped off the walk and bent down to look into the cage. Her skin was flawless, her hair coifed, and her eyebrows plucked into perfect arches that rose above cool grey eyes. Although she was looking at them, she addressed the woman behind her.

"What a shame. These are too good-looking to be ruined in Oknu Shuld. Especially the piss-head. You don't see that color much around here. What's your name, piss-head?"

Sheft stared steadily at the floor of the cage and said nothing. He'd been called that name before.

"Ah, his name escapes him." Her cloak rustled as she straightened.

"Let's try an easier question," her male companion said. "Tell us, O Niyalahn-rista: is the hair on your head the same color as that between your legs?"

Guffaws and snorts of laughter followed this remark.

"I'll wager it is!" Preya's friend cried. "Who'll take me on?"

"Done!" someone in the crowd shouted. "I'll take your bet." Talk of wagers drew other onlookers, who peered into the cage.

Preya tapped a slim finger against her lips as if she were thinking. "But how will we know who wins?"

Her second male companion, a man with long sideburns, suggested that the piss-head should be dragged out of the cage and displayed. Others elaborated. Sheft felt a flush creep up the back of his neck. As if in answer, the skora rose in Teller, and Sheft knew how hard it was for him to quell it.

The first man reached through the bars and plucked at his pants. Sheft could pull away only a few inches, but managed to get a knee into position and shove the hand away. One of the umbrak guards immediately jabbed an ax handle into Sheft's thigh.

"Treat these people with respect, pig," he ordered.

The man who had reached into the cage addressed Eye-patch angrily. "I want this prisoner spread out on the street."

"You'll like it, niyalahn-rista," someone shouted. "You'll like every scathi thing we're gonna do to you."

Hands jiggled the door, pulled at Sheft's chained wrists, pawed at his hair and clothes, but there was no way to get away from them. He fled in his mind to the quiet henge, to find Mariat, to put his arms around her and bury his head in the curve of her neck. But she wasn't there, hadn't been with him for days.

"By the suckin' voras, I said pull him out!"

Inside his heart Sheft remembered: *"You wear my Coin, but will you be my Coin?"* Hadn't he freely consented to be spent according to Rulve's will? And wasn't this journey part of that spending?

Fingers pinched the side of Sheft's neck. "Get a scathi knife," a man shouted, "and cut 'im."

"Hey, sell him to the Scarpi brothers," someone declared. "They'll treat him real friendly." This produced considerable chortling and jabbing through the bars.

"This land is wounded, and I cannot heal it. My children are imprisoned, and I cannot release them. I have no hands but yours, S'eft."

But his hands were chained behind him, and his courage was wavering. Yet the providence of Rulve was relentless, his love unstoppable.

"That's enough!" Eye-patch snapped, pushing the nearest man away from the cage. "These two belong to the lord."

"But surely," Preya said to him in a voice loud enough for everyone to hear, "our sovereign wouldn't object to making a profit from them, would he? They're just a pair of pretenders after all. Nobody really important. So how much, subaltern, for them both? My friends here will find a better use for them than Vol Shacad will." People nearby roared with laughter, and she looked around, her eyes sparkling.

Sheft suddenly realized that, in spite of her manner, Preya desperately needed the crowd's affirmation. And the subaltern was in a bad spot. He had to deal carefully with this favored woman, and drivers in the road behind them were standing up and shouting their displeasure at the delay.

But Preya's attention had been caught by something in a shop across the road. "Oh look at those shoes, Mosca! They'd go perfectly with my gown for tonight." Picking up her skirt, she rushed off, and her party followed her.

Sheft watched her go. Deep inside this Preya was someone Rulve loved. No matter who they were, Rulve cared about them. *"I hear all of them, whether they cry out to me or to the demon in the dark."*

He'd assented to be Rulve's Coin and wore around his neck the sign of his promise; but oh God, he and his brother were just beginning to understand what that promise meant.

The wagon pulled away from the walk and resumed its creaking way through the street. The dead earth, scored by ruts of pain, rolled beneath him. They led directly to a place where there would be nothing but a thin, remote grace.

Chapter 19

Into the Shadow of Insheer Cliff

When Ketiba first encountered the unusually crowded walkways, she was annoyed. She could leave her youngsters with a neighbor only so long, which left her with a limited time to help out at the glassblower's shed. Her friend there had been overwhelmed with orders, and Ketiba had promised to help.

Then, when she heard what the excitement was all about, that the lord had captured yet another pair of rebel twins, she felt angry. She had witnessed this scene before: two brothers chosen at random and dragged away from their farms, their mothers or wives crying and pleading, so that the so-called Lord of Shunder could make an example of them.

As a mother of sons herself, she took care to protect their budding strength and pride in their manhood; she knew how vulnerable such things were. To be caged and displayed in the street would be devastating, almost worse than a sword-thrust. No young man, innocent of any wrongdoing, should have to bear it.

Especially, she thought as the wagon with its guards came into view, these two. She couldn't see the prisoners very well, partly because of the crowd and partly because they were bent over in the small cage, but already they seemed different from the other so-called niyalahn-ristas. Their hands were tied behind them as usual, but with chains, not ropes. And they were enduring their humiliation in silence. They didn't seem simple or insane; didn't shout threats or sob or brag about their non-existent powers. Indeed, one of them looked like he was trying to pray.

Ketiba felt sympathy for the two young men, but when the crowd parted a bit, and she could see them better, her sympathy turned to shock.

They were twins—yet not. They were alike in feature and build, but different in coloring. In a land of single rista births or identical niyalahn twins, they were all three. They were niyal and ahn and rista, an impossibility in Shunder.

Except in one case.

Oh God Rulve, hadn't Hirai hinted they had come? This was barely four days ago, when Ketiba had helped her and Ianak sneak out of the village after curfew.

A chill went through her. These lads were the blessed twins, the niyalahn-ristas called by Rulve to save their land. And this time the Spider-king had truly caught them. She stared at them, and tears gathered.

Before anyone could notice, Ketiba quickly turned away and wiped her eyes on her sleeve. She needed to get hold of herself, but the sight of those two young men had shaken her to the core.

She rushed through deserted alleyways and found herself behind the glassblower's shed. The back wall was made of old planks, upon which had been painted long ago a symbol that was now mostly hidden by tall weeds. The green circle.

She had to get word to her fellow Sperians, to those who risked their lives to paint the green circle as a sign of hope. These included her brewing-sisters, farmers who worked with Se Utray in the struggle to raise crops from a dying land, families who sheltered the medicants, or parents who had had lost, or knew they soon would lose, one of their precious twins to Oknu Shuld. Others turned to secret resistance because they had seen loved ones swallowed by morue, or they themselves fought to escape from its clutches. Some owned small shops and could no longer bear the ever-rising rents and ruinous taxes. The number of Sperians rose after several children died in the music school fire set by umbraks.

Despite their oppression, the Sperians had no real leader, no plan, no weapons, and no fighting expertise. They were part of a cowed and conquered people, crushed under the heel of the rich and powerful and accustomed to bowing under atrocities rather than rebel.

Something lay half-hidden in the weeds beneath the faded green circle: a rusted rake, its handle partly sheared off. Ketiba picked it up and shards of rust clung to her hands. Oh Rulve, it was hopeless. No matter how great their suffering, there was nothing they could do against the might of Oknu Shuld.

Until now.

Now had come the saviors Rulve had promised, the redeemers predicted by the ancient escrimages, the niyalahn-rista twins called forth by the great Bellstone. But they were being taken to Oknu Shuld, to certain torment and a lingering death. Something had to be done, and there was only herself to do it.

Clutching the rake, Ketiba made her way around the shed and entered the glassblower's shop. The owner, a quiet widower, had been one of the first who had secretly painted a green circle. Havek's eyes met hers, moved to the rake, and then back to her.

TELLER'S WORLD SEEMED TO SHRINK DOWN to the chain digging into his damaged hand, to the grating, singsong proclamation of the subaltern trudging beside the wagon. A ragged adolescent, abandoning his task of sweeping the planked sidewalk, pushed his way through the crowd and walked alongside the cage, trailing his broom behind him. He stared at Sheft with an idiot grin, then thrust the broom handle into his ribs.

Sheft flinched and twisted aside, but there was nowhere to go. Realizing this, the boy prepared to jab again, his grin slipping into a far more avid expression. Apparently he'd found someone more helpless than he was and wanted to make the most of it.

Inside Teller, skora jumped up in anger, eager to ignite the broom and the boy attached to it, and it took an effort to keep it under control. Just before the broom handle reached Sheft, Teller managed to pin it down with his boot.

Scowling at him, the boy struggled to pull the handle out of the cage. "Gimme my broom!"

Teller flicked a bit of skora at his fingers and the boy let go. "Ow!" he cried, shaking his hand. "Ow!"

A heavy blow from above cracked onto Teller's left shoulder. An umbrak with a cudgel looked down on him from atop the cage. "You were told to treat the villagers with respect."

The sweep jerked the broom out, spit at Teller, and ducked into the crowd. He left a gob of mucus slipping down Teller's cheek. His shoulder throbbing, the skora raging, Teller wiped his face against one of the wooden bars.

"Did you see that?" someone shouted. "That prisoner attacked an innocent child!"

"I saw him!" a man exclaimed. "It was the dark one." He frowned and thrust his head forward for a better look. "By the suckin' voras! I was at his Acclamation. He was once a scathi *Vol!*" He stepped closer and bent to peer into the cage. "You filthy, ungrateful traitor! Betraying the very lord who raised you up." He pounded on the bars with his fist. "You deserve everything you're going to get, you shit. You hear me? Every scathi thing!"

Angry faces pressed closer. "Mad dogs. They're nothing but mad dogs!"

"Chain that man's neck! Muzzle him!"

From every direction rage clawed at Teller through the bars, and skora leaped to answer. Even Master Keel with his mind-whip, even those who picked fights against skora, even Shacad hadn't exhibited such mindless anger. These people were demented idiots who deserved to be seared and struck down where they stood.

Sheft looked at him, his eyes a bleeding silver. "They feel betrayed. They thought the niyal'arists would come in power to free them, and instead we came in this cage. They hate the cage, Teller.

"All of Shunder is a cage!" he exclaimed. "All of Oknu Shuld!"

The shouts continued, got louder. "How dare they attack us in our own streets!" someone yelled.

"Coward! Killer!"

The cage seemed to constrict even more. The rough-hewn bars pressed against Teller's arms and the back of his neck. Madmen pressed close and spit invectives.

Contorted faces loomed over him. The wagon was rolling through a red tunnel of hate, and skora raged in his spirikai.

'Braks laid about with cudgels to clear a path through the crowd, and Teller was on fire to join them. His hands worked in frustration against the chain around his wrists. He longed to swing a club and feel the satisfying crunch of oak against bone. He longed to smash his fist into every howling face, drive his dagger into fat stomachs, and turn it.

"Stop it!" Sheft cried. "There's as much hate inside this cage as there is outside it." His face was dead white, his breaths coming like unvoiced sobs.

Like a dash of cold water, Teller felt the truth. His fury was the same as theirs, fueled by the same urge to obliterate and destroy. He'd felt it when he lived in the tunnels of Oknu Shuld, felt it with Dahran, with Mochlos, with Shacad. He felt it just as strongly with the ragged sweep.

"He's only a boy, Teller," Sheft said. "A poor half-wit who once was his mother's joy."

He became aware of something lying heavy against his chest, against his twin's chest, the toltyr inside his shirt. His right hand still ached with the cost of accepting it.

The blind rage that choked him dropped away. Now he could see past the frenzied people who thronged around the cage, could see the ordinary villagers in the background who avoided the crowd. A man pushed his way down the boardwalk, frowning at the cage and shaking his head. A woman shouted that madmen should be cared for and not reviled in the street. Several men stood silently at the edge of the crowd, their arms crossed and their eyes smoldering as they glared at the guards. A few people hurried along, seeing nothing but their own misery. One woman at the back of the crowd, holding her cloak tight around her, was crying. Teller twisted his head to watch her turn away and rush into an alley.

He'd cut off the vol-ring, had put the toltyr around his neck, but he hadn't changed. Hate remained a part of him.

He wasn't going to get through this. Rulve had brought him to a trial he had already failed.

THE CROWD BECAME THICKER, SHEFT NOTICED, with people more inclined to focus on their daily affairs. All manner of handbarrows, carts, and wagons jostled down the widening street, and he thought they must be entering the main square. He couldn't raise his head to see, but the way the east-facing shop windows reflected a golden light told him the sun had just cleared Insheer Cliff. Looking sideways, he could pick out the striped purple and grey flags that fluttered over what looked like a military headquarters.

A fenced-off area was coming into view at his left. On the ground lay a gnarled shadow that crawled into sight as they came closer.

His brother stiffened. "It's the Skewrong Grabe, Sheft. The Torture-tree." A flood of images from Teller rushed through the link—a giant dead willow, bloodstained bark, a naked body—but were abruptly cut off when his brother realized what was coming through to his twin.

A clatter next to his head made Sheft jump. An umbrak had detached himself from his duty around the Grabe, approached the cage, and was dragging his ax handle along the bars. He thrust his head closer, his small boar-like eyes glittering with malice, and pointed with his ax at the giant willow. "Lookee there, niyal'arist! Lookee there. See that one nailed to the wood? See how he's squirmin'?"

Sheft followed the ax's trajectory. Shock hit him, then nausea. Swallowing, he turned quickly away. A thin sound, like a breathed-in scream, came from the tree.

"You'll wish you was them up there," the 'brak growled. "Before the day is done, you'll wish you was any one a'them."

Teller's presence, even though numb and wordless on the other side of the link, helped Sheft concentrate on something else, on the slowly moving rows of alehouses and armorsmiths across the road. Yes, being connected in this way doubled the pain, but also could cut it in half, because they were not alone.

They passed the Skewrong Grabe, but its odor trailed after as they drove out of the square. The wagon trundled on, and at last the crowd thinned, then all but disappeared. A few sparrows fluttered in a rain-puddle, only to fly off at their approach. Sheft twisted his head to gaze at the ramshackle huts crammed tightly together on either side of the road, separated by several large houses surrounded by fenced gardens. No one back home in At-Wysher was so poor, no one in Ferce so wealthy.

The wagon sprayed through another puddle. Some of the muddy water splashed on the side of Sheft's pants, but most of it wound up on a barefoot child trudging at the side of the road. He wailed, holding his dripping arms out at his sides, a shivering little figure that no one came to comfort. Thoughts of Willow and Eshu in the hospit flowed through the link, along with a surge of gratitude that the Seani had rescued them from being this child.

The Seani children would be waking up soon, yawning, perhaps going to the door and looking out, and the same sun would shine down on them as on this cage. Their tomorrows would be very different from the ones belonging to the wet little boy in the road.

But if he and Teller could accomplish whatever they had to in Oknu Shuld, could endure whatever awaited them, if they could enable Rulve's providential will to be done, this little boy's world might be changed by tomorrow.

Tomorrow. The word felt strange to Sheft. It was as if such a thing did not exist, as if time were winding down as they plodded closer to the gates of Oknu Shuld. The word slowly moved through the link, ominous and heavy. Tomorrow.

A great house with two towers and surrounded by a dark yew hedge slid by, and then a shack came into view. A grey-haired woman, watching them through slitted eyes, stood in the doorway with her arms folded.

An explanation from Teller came through the link. The woman was the shamana, the so-called healer. Sick people lay in the filthy shack behind her. They were dying. The chain clinked as Teller turned violently away. For thirteen years in Oknu Shuld, Sheft knew, his brother had felt pain like that, the ahn-pain, and in only minutes he would face it again.

Oh Rulve, there was too much agony here. In the people, in the land. How could it be borne? Even the Creator struggled to do that, and needed their niyal'arist hearts to help him.

They were leaving the village. The subaltern fell silent and hung the tambour back on its nail. Oknu Shuld was just ahead. The realization jammed a steel bar of fear down Sheft-Teller's throat.

A sense of unreality filtered over them. The sun, fully risen now, cut every shadow with a hard-edged distinction. Its sharp beams stabbed through the cage. They cast the wooden bars and the profiles of the guards walking alongside into inky silhouettes on a too-bright road. Only the two of them were blurring. Only the two of them were seeping into the darkness under which everything else was veneered.

In the company of a few other wagons carrying helmets and casks and clucking chickens, their own wagon rumbled over a bridge and into the shadow of Insheer Cliff.

Chapter 20

Deoner's Mission

The fog had lifted past the tops of the trees, and Keppit smiled in anticipation of a sunny day. Chilly of course—it was barely the middle of Seed with probably a frost tonight—but still beautiful. She pulled open the door to the Quela and bustled in with her cloth-covered basket. Let the emjadis sleep late, Se Druv had told her, and she had done that; but no one had any business lazing in bed at this hour of the morning.

"Sausages and eggs," she called out, "and some a' that cheese bread you used to like, Teller." Sausage was a rare treat, but it wouldn't hurt to indulge the emjadis a little after all they'd been through.

There was no answer, and she proceeded toward the great disk, looking into all the alcoves. The brazier had gone out, and other than the rumpled blankets and mats, there was no sign of the emjadis. Perhaps they had gone to the Sky Tower to join the Se, who had all eaten already.

Dare she burst in on their work? She sniffed, irritated that Druv would further tax the poor lads with yet another meeting, and on empty stomachs too. The Se loved to talk and talk, usually coming to a conclusion that any sensible person would have reached hours before.

But Teller and Sheft were young men who needed their breakfast, doubly so because they were recovering from such terrible injuries. Head high with indignation, she opened the Eka-door and stepped out.

"Whoops!" She nearly ran into Deoner.

"Are the emjadis inside?" he asked. He looked worried and was carrying two cloaks.

One was Teller's. She had seen him come into the Seani with it and knew their laundress, Susera, had had a terrible time getting it clean. "No," Keppit answered. "I thought they might be over at the Sky Tower. I'm goin' there now. Do you want me to give them their cloaks?" They must have left them in the hospit, for Tema had already told her of their visit there. Such kind-hearted lads, and them so tired after that long Weshnika.

Without another word Deoner whirled and headed for the Sky Tower. Something must be wrong. Keppit wasn't as young as she used to be, but she still got there shortly after he did. She burst through the door just in time to see Deoner toss the cloaks onto the table inside.

The entire Weshnika had crowded into the small tower room. Se and their assistants sat conversing and sipping tea at the table or on the spiral steps, but Keppit couldn't see the emjadis anywhere. Se Druv, as pale as a turnip, sat side by side with Mena closest to the fireplace. He looked like he'd had a bad night.

She herself hadn't slept well either, come to think of it. Kept dreaming something was burning in the kitchen.

WITH LARRIN FOLLOWING TRACKS, AND A villager reporting what she had seen, it took less than two notches for the Se to learn that Sheft and Teller had left the Scani and had been arrested by the Spider-king's men.

"There must be some mistake," Mena protested. "Larrin said the gate was barred from the inside."

Druv looked at her. "A simple task for a powerful Vol."

"What?" And then her expression crumpled as his words struck home. "But why would Teller…? I don't understand!"

Penan chewed his lip and then angrily thumped his fist on the table. "Whatever in God's name possessed them to leave the Seani?"

"The summons, Penan," Celume said. She was gazing at the miniature version of Rulve's disk that hung between the two round windows that opened to the southeast. "Something must have convinced Sheft and Teller that they were summoned. All the doors but one must have closed in the night."

His eyes deeply troubled, Penan held his chin between his thumb and forefinger for a moment and then dropped his hand to his lap. "We were wrong about your vision yesterday. Wrong to make it an easy generalization and not the prediction it was."

Druv pulled at his beard as if he wanted to tear it off. "Yes we were wrong. Now we must inform our allies about what has happened."

"I'll go to the Bellstriker," Deoner said.

THE MORNING'S EVENTS HAD REIGNITED THE fire in Deoner's blood. Born a warrior, he had reluctantly gone the way of peace that the Se had decided upon years ago. Now Sheft and Teller had been taken by the Spider-king, and the Seani had no choice except war. After all these years of restraint, after all their talk of serving the people instead of fighting their oppressor, they were left with no other path.

He itched to get his bow, to ride hard in the company of a determined band, to hurl his strength against the vicious evil of Oknu Shuld. But it would take more than a band, no matter how determined. It would take cool heads as well as hot blood. The Spider-king's army consisted of three divisions, and no one knew how many soldiers served in each, but it was rumored that the Scaths alone numbered at least two hundred men. The Seani Rift-riders and guards, the rakes and hoes of the Sperians, the claws of a few remaining falconforms—the Lord of Oknu Shuld would laugh at these things.

Unless they were joined by the seasoned fighters of Bellstone Forest. Then the lord's laughter might be cut short.

Deoner had just saddled one of the horses lent to Lir by the forest folk and was leading her out of the barn when Larrin stopped him.

The captain of the guards flashed him a warning look. "I know you, Deoner. Your mission is to report to the Bellstriker—and only that. It's not up to you or me to call a muster for war. You know as well as I do that if Sheft and Teller were taken into Oknu Shuld this morning, it's already too late to save them."

Deoner mounted his horse and looked down at Larrin. "It may be too late for them, but not for Shunder. We've wasted years in debate, missed a glut of opportunities to build a fighting force. Now's our chance to unite with the Sperians and the Bellstone warriors and save our land. Now's our chance to build a force that must be reckoned with. My mission is what Druv said it was: tell the Striker exactly what's happened. And that's what I'll do."

He rode out without looking back. What happened to the emjadis was a clear summons to the Seani. Rulve had closed every door but one. There was no time to waste on more deliberations. The Se would see this eventually, but the time to act was now.

Squinting against the morning light, Deoner urged his horse down the hillside. Despite the chill of Seed, the sun felt warm on his face. Acting without explicit orders weighed heavily. But the emjadis had been taken, and nothing weighed more heavily than that.

In spite of his heartbreak for Sheft and Teller, excitement raced through him. He had been born for war, and at last it was imminent. Generations of oppression were coming to an end, and Rulve had called him to be a part of it.

He came down from the hillside and gave the mare her head through the meadow. The Seani possessed less than a dozen fighting men, but they would train others and act as captains. Captain Deoner. The thought sent his pulse racing, but then he felt ashamed. Even if he had no rank at all, he would give his life for freedom. Yes, Avia would rail against war, but her heritage as Se Isavin's daughter would win out in the end. They would be fighting for their children and their land. His wife would come to realize justice must sometimes be purchased at a very high cost.

As he made his way through dried grasses that brushed against his heels, Deoner thought about the niyalahn-ristas' puzzling behavior. Why had they left the Seani? They must have known the deadly danger.

And then it struck him—the only explanation for their action.

The emjadis had realized that handing themselves over to the Lord of Oknu Shuld was the only way to spark all of Shunder into rebellion. It was the only way they could win the freedom Rulve intended. Celume was right: this realization, this summons, had come to them in the night.

A chill ran down his spine. Oh God Rulve, their bravery was incredible. It would be sung about forever. Their sacrifice would be immortalized in all the holy books.

For it would be a real sacrifice, and not just for Teller and Sheft. Ever since the miracle in the Pool of Rulve, the Seani people had become one with the niyalahn-ristas. They all had the same mission, were called to the same terrible sacrifice. Who knew how many of them would survive the bloodshed of war? But the Seani was also the Coin of Rulve, and it too was meant to spend everything it had in order to buy back all that had been taken away.

Anguish for Teller and Sheft vied with his deep respect for them. They must have left the Seani trusting their action would save Shunder, but knowing they themselves could never be saved.

Chapter 21

The Jeweled Spider

As the wagon turned south to skirt the cliff, the horse picked up speed. The wheels jouncing on the stone-paved road caused Teller's hand to throb again. As soon as he became aware of it, he blocked the link.

"Don't do that, Teller," Sheft said quickly. "We should stay connected as long as we can."

"You blocked me first, brother."

They had both blocked the link at some point, but they knew there would come a time when they would have to shut it down completely—a time when neither would want to add what he was experiencing to what his twin was already bearing.

Insheer Cliff towered over them, showing no sign of the stronghold built inside. Here in its massive shadow it was cold, a cold Teller welcomed as skora burned inside him, but a chill that pinched his brother's face.

The road wound between the long curve of the cliff face at Teller's right and the slope on his left that led down to the valley floor. Thorn bushes managed to survive among the debris that littered the hillside: glass from shattered globes, pieces of broken crates and barrels, and the remains of a few wrecked wagons. At the bottom, fetid strands of the Eeron River wound through banks of gravel and weeds. It had been a long time since Sunsink Falls kept the river running clear.

"There's some kind of building ahead," Sheft, who was facing forward, said.

His brother's mouth was dry and his palms wet, Teller knew, just like his own. "It's the entryway to the main gates." Even with his back to it, Teller was familiar enough with the road.

They were approaching the only part of Oknu Shuld that was free of the winter-dried ivy, the western wall of the entrance hall. It was constructed of black granite blocks and jutted only about three wagon-lengths out from the cliff. Deep inside stretched guard stations, the Hall of the Eye, weapon storage vaults, and the endless, interconnecting levels, stairwells, chambers, and passageways of the lord's stronghold.

The wagon was passing the section where two wide stairways ran from opposite sides of the wall to the high, wide porch that fronted the monumental blackwood doors. Vorian guards, wearing purple-plumed helmets and the lord's spider-badge on their purple sashes, stood on the edge of the porch and looked grimly down on them.

As the wagon trundled on, a mosaic bigger than the Quela's jade disk came slowly into view. It took up most of the wall between the two entry stairs. Teller could feel Sheft's skin crawl when his twin saw what the mosaic portrayed: the giant likeness of a morue spider. Squares of polished grey chalcedony formed the lean, predatory body, rubies marked the eyes, and obsidian and deep purple amethysts made up the stripes on its long, pointed legs. In the afternoon sun the jeweled spider would provide a dazzling display, but now, like the hunter it was in reality, the spider lurked in the shade.

It faced downward, its mouth-fangs open, as if it were ready to spring onto the road below. The wagon, like a tiny fly, crawled beneath eight eyes seemingly intent on following its progress.

Aware of the creature's impact on his brother, who was seeing it for the first time, Teller leaned out and touched the side of Sheft's forehead with his own. "Don't look at it," he said. "Look across the valley. From the Seani you can hardly see that thing."

His brother turned his head, and together they beheld a sight very few people in the Seani had ever seen from this side of the Eeron River, their own far hillside bathed in morning light.

His home, and Taisa's. "Your home too, Sheft. But you didn't have time to get to know it."

Actually, neither of them had, and probably never would.

Morning fog was rising from among the hillside trees like plumes of white smoke. It revealed the red-ochre of hard new buds interspersed with a few yellow-misted willow groves. Ancient trees, still bare, stood with upraised branches, as if they were singing a song of praise that no one could hear. In spite of the dying land, they were struggling with heartbreaking persistence to bloom. The distant Seani walls were only a small spot shining in the sun. A sudden memory pierced Teller and then Sheft, of a bright winter day when Se Utray had taken the children sledding on the Great Lawn, their gleeful shouts echoing over the quiet snow. It was a different side of Se Utray, and Teller was glad that his twin had glimpsed it.

They watched the hillside slide past, and Teller, aware of the darkness that awaited them inside the cliff, tried to impress every detail of his homeland into his mind.

But the presence of the hunting spider fingered the back of his neck, and of Sheft's too, and all too soon the road veered to the east, and the Seani passed from their sight.

At the turn, a nauseating smell assailed the cage. The road widened into a clearing in front of the side entrance gates, and across from that lay the garbage heaps of Oknu Shuld. Hill-sized piles of offal cleared from the shit shafts steamed under the sun, along with rotting kitchen scraps and bones. A few round brick chimneys protruding from the heap exuded pale yellow wisps. These were part of the pipe system that vented steam and gasses from the bubbling pools far below the surface.

Near one edge of the massive pile, a swarm of black birds fought with rats over what looked like entrails mingled with torn rags. This was the place where most ahn, once beloved children of villagers and farmers, found their graves.

The wagon turned into the crowded side entrance, creaked past vehicles being loaded and unloaded, and made its way through the heavy gates. It entered the gloom of the military training cavern, where it jerked to a stop.

Teller met his brother's eyes. The metallic taste of fear spurted through the link.

Eye-patch untied the door of the cage and 'braks pulled them out. Both brothers stumbled as their feet hit the ground, and their legs prickled with returning sensation.

A company of Skinners, back in Oknu Shuld from their countryside garrisons for the twice-yearly rotation, stopped their calisthenics and stared. The subaltern in charge turned, his hands on his hips. "What have we here, gentlemen?" he boomed to the crew behind him. "Looks like a couple more niyal'arists for the Vora's dinner." His remark produced a rumble of male laughter that echoed under the cave-like roof.

The subaltern sauntered over, thrust his pockmarked face in front of Teller, and then bared his teeth in recognition. He was "Needles" Noz, one of the ristas who had once tried to kill him. Noz had gone on to receive the subaltern's red cloak on the same day Teller had, except Teller's cloak had been hemmed with slate, marking his rise to the rank of the prestigious Azanzi Scaths, while Noz had been given the cobalt, the more lowly mark of a Skinner. Noz never forgot that.

Now the man's cold eyes raked over Teller's chained hands and mud-spattered clothes. "Well if it isn't Vol Cinc. Dressed like the ahn he loves so much." Triumph glinted in his eyes; the military training cavern was one of three places in Oknu Shuld where all Powers were suppressed, including, Noz was well aware, skora.

Noz was physically the bigger man, and Teller, anticipating what was coming, tensed. He slammed the link down a split-second before Noz's fist plowed into his stomach. Two guards caught him as he reeled backward, gasping.

With a grin, Noz rubbed his knuckles and advanced. "Allow me to welcome you home properly, Teller-of-Lies."

"Get back," Eye-patch snarled, pushing Noz aside. "He belongs to the lord." He dismissed the umbrak guards and motioned to four waiting Skinners. They hustled Teller and Sheft through a doorway, and immediately the ahn-pain hit Teller. It was worse than he remembered. He still tried to keep the link firmly closed, but Sheft must've felt something because he flinched.

The minute they walked through the door, darkness swallowed them. Even for Teller it was a shock. After months under the sky, even the military training chamber, where at least some natural illumination came from the open gates, seemed dim. But here, in these corridors, he felt almost blind. With a firm hold on them, the guards pushed them rapidly through the hall. As his eyes adjusted, the passageway between the weapon-storage rooms emerged into view under the rows of dusty luniku globes that hung from the ceiling.

"Open the link, Teller." There was a tightly controlled note of desperation in his brother's words. "I don't care what gets through."

Teller reopened the connection and immediately took a sharp breath. What his twin was experiencing rushed into his own sensations: the weight of tons of rock inches above his head, repulsion that skittered down his arms at the sight of globe after globe crawling with luniku larvae, and cold terror climbing up the back of his spine.

Teller looked desperately around, trying to find something to describe, to explain, to distract his twin from a panic that threatened to overwhelm him.

Yet he had to prepare his brother for what was coming, for the full shock of Oknu Shuld. He nudged Sheft with his elbow and nodded toward the arches on their left, which gave onto a vast, dark opening. "That's the Hall of the Eye, Sheft. We're on ground level here, but there are five levels above us, so this is called level six." **And the higher the number, the worse it got, until you reached the sub-basement of the shadowy level nine.** "See that red flicker against the pillars over there? It comes from a real fire, the Igneous Eye, the only fire in Oknu Shuld. It burns behind a pane of glass above the lord's throne," **and wherever you turned, no matter how you tried to escape it, you felt that fiery reptilian eye upon you.**

He was back in the past, and memories were swarming in. He tried to suppress them, to turn them off, but only succeeded halfway. "I received the red cloak in this hall; it was crowded and hot and the cloak weighed heavy. Vol Cinc's Acclamation was held here too," when his back felt stiff with barely healed wounds, when his head swam with pain-killing potions. "Here is where I saw for the first time the lord's true face." Red smiling lips, an expanse of skin where there were no eyes, only spirals drawn with charcoal, crazed spirals pulling you in…. He shuddered, and a part of him knew he was talking too much, but he couldn't seem to stop. "His eyes, Sheft, he hides them, hides them under a spider mask. Eight black stones, don't let them look at you! They drill down to the soul; look at the floor," where embroidered morue-spiders crawled in the hem of the lord's robe, in a rock-bound room where a warning chill could erupt in any moment "and that means volghasts, Sheft. They come out of the walls. They reek of mold."

They approached alcoves to their right. Displayed in there were the lord's sculptures. They were stomach turning. "Don't look at anything over there, Sheft. Look straight ahead and not…"

"I won't, Teller. I won't look."

But wasn't his twin forced to look? What one of them saw, smelled, remembered, felt—all of it poured into their link, and the other experienced it too. He had been spilling a noxious stream of his memories into Sheft. "Oh God, Sheft, I'm sorry, I'm sorry. I didn't mean to—"

"It's all right, Teller." Sheft cut in.

But it wasn't.

The guards moved them up a stairway, and they emerged not on the fifth level, but—in the torturous manner of the stronghold where some passages undercut others—on the fourth. They entered the rista student section. The globes were brighter in this part of level four, and the tunnels wider, but a clammy twilight still reigned here, and the ceiling pressed down relentlessly. Blue-robed instructors stared at them from classroom doors, and the rista students inside craned their necks and snickered.

Dead insects and squashed quills crunched underfoot as they were rushed through. A bony ahn, dragging a half-filled waste bag, crawled by as she used a hand-brush to sweep out the dirt caked in the angle between the floor and walls. Horrified compassion washed over Sheft, and then he started as a morue spider darted out of a floor-grate and disappeared into a crevice in the wall. It was a big one, about the size of a skullcap. They turned left and were marched down a now carpeted hallway where various dignitaries kept their apartments and where ahn, their heads lowered, knelt outside closed doors.

One of them tottered out of a side passage, carrying a heavy slop-bucket. Teller recognized Hanat, the matriarch who had helped heal the letters on his back, one of many ahn he had betrayed. She looked at him, then at Sheft, took in their bound hands, and her eyes returned to his in a startled question he couldn't answer. The guards prodded them on.

Briefly interrupted but still desperate, his garbled mind-speech sprung up again. "I'm not sure where they'll take us, Sheft. Maybe directly to the lord. Maybe to his workroom" where he had sickened at the sight of Arachniman, the lord's depiction of a man turning into a spider, its hands now futile claws, with no mouth to scream. "Maybe to his private audience chamber" where the bruised purple and green lights swam in front of his eyes and fear skittered down his neck, where he must kneel to a shadow within a cloud of mist.

His twin kept swallowing, and was shaking. "You showed me a lot of this, Teller. You already showed me."

Teller barely heard. "They might take us somewhere else. Past the luniku chambers," where an ahn, covered with a swarming, buzzing mass, screamed in agony, "or to the strisnu." The memory of his torture came rushing back, as if it were happening right now, Vol Shacad's low, intense voice *"That was the letter T."*

"That's over, Teller! For God's sake, that's all over."

It wasn't. It was just starting. He tried to get hold of himself, took a deep breath, but words kept spilling out. "I don't know what I'm doing here, Sheft. It's not clear to me. You might know what you're supposed to do, but I don't."

Sheft turned his head toward him, and his silver eyes were as desperate as his own must be. "It's what we said, Teller. We said 'yes' to Rulve. We put ourselves on his path. We heard what those little children asked us to do. Marhaut showed us what would happen if we didn't come here. Isn't that what we've been hearing all our lives, Teller? You here, me in Ullar, people crying, the land crying—"

Teller wanted to reach out and shake his brother, but his chained hands couldn't do that. "You're not thinking, Sheft! The first thing the lord will do is seize the s'rere. Don't you know that? And he won't use it to restore the sweet-rue. He doesn't care a turd about that. He'll use s'rere only to cure himself of a disease that's rotting him away, to make himself the strong king that will completely ruin this land. Is that what you want?"

"It's not about what I want or don't want!" His mind-voice was pleading, begging for an understanding Teller didn't have. "I came here to give everything I've got, Teller. To bring everything in me to the source of the hurt. I've got to enter the only door left open; don't you see that? I've got to put my life in Rulve's hands with the only power I have."

A memory came wrenching out of Sheft's mind, of him tucking a piece of paper into Ane's shroud. It was a thank-you to Mariat's mother for loving him when his own mother couldn't. He'd copied Ane's favorite story from the red book of tales, and now words embedded in the very center of it burst into Teller's head: *"You can only save your life if you lose it."*

"I don't understand that, Sheft. I don't want to die here. I have fire and don't want to die in the dark!"

"Maybe that's not it for you. Maybe you're the one who will help the other die."

"I want us both to live!"

"What will happen, will happen, Teller. We chose these toltyrs, we said 'yes,' and everything we are, everything Rulve put in us, everything we chose—all of that has come together now. We're free now, and Rulve will show us what we have to do."

"It's easier for you," **Teller cried.** "You lost Mariat, but I just found Taisa!"

The minute he said the words he wished he hadn't.

Sheft jerked his head up, as if hit. "I didn't lose her, Teller, I killed her! Rulve knew I could never leave her, so he took her. Oh God, I was the reason Mariat had to die."

Sheft must have been hiding that terrible thought ever since he learned his wife was dead. It must have been sawing through him like relentless amputation. Now his own brother had made it real and sent it screaming back at him through the link. What had he done? How could he have added to his brother's already terrible grief? "Sheft, I'm sorry. That's not what I meant at all. I shouldn't—" Appalled, he began to block his end of the link, to sear it shut with skora before he could do even more damage, but his brother cried out before he could do it.

"Don't. Don't lock me out, Teller." **Panic rose from Sheft's end of the link.** "I don't know if I can do this. I don't know if I believe all those things I said. There's no air in here. There's no light, Teller!" His mind-voice was rising, and he looked frantically and yet blindly from side to side.

Oknu Shuld was dividing them, closing in on them, sucking out all hope. It wanted to tear them apart and hurl them dissected into a pit of despair.

Except—

Someone was walking with them, another person in addition to their guards. Sheft and Teller turned their heads and saw no one, but they felt a reassuring presence. It was a gentle woman who wouldn't leave them, a strong youth who would uphold them, and a sage who knew them through and through. "Trust in what I have given you," they said, "and act with an open heart."

Was it as simple as that? To doubt, to despair, but still move forward trusting?

In heart and mind Teller and Sheft leaned into each other. They were linked, embraced, and guided. Everything they needed had been given to them, and now they must freely give it away. Because of who they now were, they would know what to do when the time came, or wouldn't know but would do it anyway.

The terror inside them subsided, the debilitating inner turmoil receded, and it was as if they had awakened from a nightmare and could see again, breathe again.

The passage branched and the guards prodded them to the left and down a wide flight of black marble stairs, scuffed in the center with use. They were on the fifth level, and still the presence followed, unseen but encouraging, familiar and loved.

They approached a portcullis, which the guards winched open, and entered a deserted passageway.

Shockingly different from the relative opulence they had left behind, it was dark, low, and deathly silent. Boots thumped and their chains rattled, but it all sounded muffled. Smells Teller had never noticed in all the years he had lived here—sewer-wisps, mold, and stale, re-breathed air— permeated the passageway.

They stopped at an ordinary-looking wooden door, which opened at the subaltern's coded taps. Inside, four Vorian Guards took charge of them.

Teller knew where the guards were taking them. The skora barrier began to rise and, even though his spirikai churned with fire and his hands were sweating, chills tripped down the length of his arms. The link tensed on both ends.

They entered the most exclusive section of Oknu Shuld. Globes on ebony stands cast silently writhing shadows onto the carpeted floor. The smooth rock walls were covered with tapestries that clung like mildew. Vorian Guards lined the way with unflickering rigidity. They passed through the wrought-iron gate fashioned in the likeness of prickly morue leaves and stopped at the deeply carved blackwood door.

Teller knew that door intimately, and now so did Sheft. Their hearts pounded, a double cadence rolling like a heavy ball back and forth through their link. They could no longer feel the reassuring presence.

The guards opened the door, thrust them into a room rank with a sick, sharp odor, and the door gnashed shut behind them.

Chapter 22

Without Sound or Hope

Three levels down in the isav, Rivere shook the boy lying on the thin mat until his fevered eyes blinked. "For God's sake, Quil," he hissed, "stop moaning!" The thirteen-year-old reached out with a shaking hand, took the wad of cloth Rivere offered him, and stuffed it into his mouth.

There was nothing more that could be done for him, and Quil knew it. The punishment cage had been winched too deeply into the boiling pool, and the lower half of the boy's body had been horribly burned. Rivere sat back on his heels. Should he use the last of his elmwalm to ease the pain of a dying patient, or save it for someone who had a chance to recover?

He seemed to ask himself a question like this every few rotas, but did it really matter? The ahn were brought here to die. They died from burns, beatings, and broken bones; from malnutrition and rat-bites and rape. He had seen delicate tissue torn by perversions of all kinds, heard the rasp of lungs burned by years of working in the sulfurous kitchens, watched flesh being eaten away from morue-spider venom. His years-long apprenticeship with Se Abiyat, as the idealistic healer he once had been, seemed like a distant dream. The isav was reality, and the surest cure here would be a sharp dagger-thrust into the heart.

Liasit's blanket, he noticed, was back in place again. Drab-colored, but the finest in the isav by far, it hung over the other tattered, moth-eaten blankets that curtained off his alcove at the very back of the cavern in which the ahn slept. Liasit and a few others still came to the blanket at night, still smoothed it with reverent hands. Rivere sighed. No use pulling it down. Liasit would only replace it.

It was the blanket Teller had draped over her shoulders before he led her, unmolested, out of his room. That had been maybe a year ago. There was no time here, really, only an endless succession of rotas. Rivere wasn't even sure how old he was now, but the occasional coiled hair he found on his mat was no longer dark brown, but grey. The blanket had once been a symbol of hope for the ahn, a symbol that Rulve had not forgotten them and still cared for them. It was a touchable reality that proved that the niyalahn-rista had appeared among them, that he would free them, break their collars, and lead them home. It had kept Liasit alive after what Vol Autran had done to her.

Now, to most of the ahn, Teller's blanket was only a rag. Vol Cinc had seen to that.

Rivere levered himself to his feet, for he had been on his way to check his store of so-called medicines. Making his way along the rock wall at the back of the isav, he passed through the break in the wooden partition that separated the men's sleeping chamber from the women's. The proctor made sure the partition was kept in good repair at the front, where he placed the younger and still more presentable ahn, but not back here. The subalterns and ristas, when they came down to choose a male or female to degrade in whatever manner they liked, seldom ventured past the first few rows. This suited the proctor perfectly. It meant far less work for him, and he was able to feed the ahn in the back less and stuff himself more.

Rivere moved quietly so as not to disturb the exhausted ahn in the middle of their sleep-shift. Row upon row of them lay on filthy mats, where they found a brief unconsciousness. The few globes allotted to the isav were made of cheap, cloudy glass only partly filled with the thinnest worms, so Rivere had to look closely to find the small opening he had long ago dug out of the wall. It was just large enough to hide his meager stash of herbs smuggled in by the field-ahns, healing molds scraped from nooks and crannies, and the rare bits of non-poisonous residues carefully swept from the laboratorium floor. He used to keep this sad apothecary in his alcove, but moved it when rumors spread that the proctor would be conducting a seldom-held cleanup. Vol Cinc had ordered this, to prevent rats and morue-spiders from endangering the lord's store of slave labor.

Of course Liasit and her ilk saw the order differently. For them, the cleanup, as useless and perfunctory as it had been, was the first step toward their always-postponed salvation.

At a slight sound ahead, Rivere instinctively pressed against the wall. He relaxed when he realized whoever was coming had entered through one of the hidden service passageways. Like the ventilation tunnels, these honeycombed every level of Oknu Shuld, but few of its distinguished residents ever noticed them. Except, perhaps, the mysterious Vol Kuat.

"Rivere," a voice whispered urgently. "Are you there?"

He stepped forward, for it was only Clane, the simple man who worked at the back gates. His eyebrows were raised in a kind of excited delight. "I saw the blessed twins!" he exclaimed. "Down where I was unloading the casks." His eyebrows squeezed together in puzzlement. "But they came in a cage, Rivere, with guards."

"They're fakes, Clane. Madmen. People pretending to be niyalahn-ristas."

"But I saw them! They were tied up, and hurting."

"The guards were bringing in another set of pretenders, another set of rebels. There are no niyalahn-ristas." He sighed. "It's just stories, Clane. You heard what Vol Cinc told us."

Clane wrung his hands and looked appealingly at him. "But Teller saved Liasit. Two times, see?" He pulled a small square of greyish white cloth from his pocket and showed it to Rivere. It had been carefully cut from a young man's tunic and still bore a red-brown stain. "Gorv died for Teller, see?"

"You're getting things mixed up, Clane. Don't you remember what Vol Cinc said? He told us never even to say the word 'niyalahn-rista.'"

"But I saw him! I saw him and his brother." His face crumpled. "Oh Rulve, what should I do?"

He reminded Rivere of a little boy who had once sat on his lap in the Seani, who leaned back against his chest, so close that Rivere could bury his nose in the soft, soot-black hair. Many times he had laid one hand on Teller's forehead and another over his spirikai, for both nodes were wounded with the niyal'arist wound. Teller had twisted around to look up at him, and an eager hope trembled in the dark eyes. *Be my ward-father, Rivere. You could sleep in my cot, and I could sleep on the floor.*

Had he taken the child's hand then? Had he held it warm in his? Years later he sat at Teller's bedside, and the young man had once more extended his hand to him. A hand that trembled under the weight of the vol-ring, trembled with a desperate hope for forgiveness.

But Rivere had turned away, and never clasped it.

Their urgent whispers must have drawn Liasit. "What is wrong, Clane?"

"I saw the blessed twins, the ones sent to save us. I saw the niy—aghl—." He was choking on the name, the name Vol Cinc had forbidden the ahn to say, and his hand clutched his metal collar in an instinctive but futile effort to loosen it.

"Oh, Clane!" Liasit opened her arms, and the man stumbled into them. He wept against her shoulder, in the only way an ahn could: without sound or hope.

Chapter 23

Uprooting

Teller stumbled into a murky chamber blotched with amethyst globe lights. Compound eyes jumped out at them; insect claws reached out of the shadows. His brother gasped.

"It's only the lord's sculptures," Teller said quickly. But these were worse than the ones on level six.

Strong hands, so cold he could feel them even under their moldy leather gauntlets, seized them and jerked them forward. Volghasts. All four had been activated. They were once living Vols, but now their eyes glowed red, and mildew-spotted skin stretched over their skulls. Tight woolen coifs covered their heads and necks, and black cloaks hung over their shoulders like shrouds. Their odor, their very presence, swelled the great *No!* that had been building up in Teller's soul ever since he entered the lord's domain.

A purple-edged mist stirred over the dais in front of them, half-concealing a figure seated on an ebony throne and flowing silently down the three shallow steps. Draperies behind the throne were open, exposing for the first time in Teller's memory the black, undeveloped depths of Oknu Shuld. The carpet that usually lay to the right of the throne had been pulled away to expose a circle of earth in the marble floor. It was the diameter of a tall man, and four iron stakes had been pounded into it.

He felt Sheft's stomach constrict when his brother caught sight of it. The protective fire pushed against Teller's spirikai, but he clamped it down. Only then did it strike him that his power had not been suppressed in this, the lord's private audience chamber. That could mean only one thing. Not even the lord could seize a power that had been barred from this room.

With startling strength, a volghast forced Teller to his knees before the throne. Two others held Sheft while the third cast off his chain and pushed up Sheft's sleeve. A dagger glinted in the purple light, and before Teller could react, the volghast cut his brother's arm. Sheft flinched, and the skora inside Teller strained forward, only to be dragged back once more by an effort of will.

"He does not bleed," a sepulchral voice said.

"Then he is the one." The Lord of Oknu Shuld made a sharp gesture and the volghasts pushed Sheft onto the earthen circle. One of them ripped off his shirt, another secured Sheft's left hand to a stake, the third grasped his right.

"Get your scathi hands off him!" Teller shouted. A wave of rage swept away all reason. It left a wake of sped-up time and he was jumping to his feet and lashing out with skora. The flare hit the volghast kneeling on Sheft's right. The creature turned with a snarl and Teller struck out again as a solid arm knocked him sideways onto the floor. His hands chained behind him, he fell onto his shoulder, but kept firing as volghasts leaped down the steps toward him.

"Teller! Stop!"

He barely heard as he hit another volghast and spun him around. A boot cracked into Teller's ribs. He twisted onto his back and flared at the volghasts above him. They dodged, reeled, quickly recovered. Blinding shafts of skora cut through the dimness as the dark shapes shielded their eyes and dove for him. Teller's flare hit one in the arm, the charred hole trailing smoke, but the creature kept coming,. Scrabbling backwards on the polished floor, kicking at their legs, Teller fired again and again. They were dead already and he couldn't win, but the fire inside him didn't care.

But he did. If they killed him now, his brother would be left completely alone.

At his split-second hesitation, the volghasts grabbed him, jerked him to his feet. One of them hooked its arm against the heartbeat that pounded in his throat, the smell of mold emanating from its sleeve. Teller was breathing hard, but none of the volghasts were breathing at all.

Sheft scrambled to a half-sitting position on the circle of earth, his silver eyes fixed on his twin. Horror at his actions poured through the link.

The Eyascnu Varo stood. "Quite the greeting, Teller-of-Lies."

There was nothing to lose. All was lost already, for both his brother and himself. The lord was halfway down the steps when Teller took a deep breath, slammed down the link, and with all his strength shot a bolt of white-hot flame directly at the Spider-king's chest.

It lit up the room with a crack. Shadows shot to every side. He caught glimpses of the lord's crudely drawn spiral eyes, the glistening red lips, the row of small, pointed teeth. The arm around his throat fell away.

But the darkness he expected never rolled back into the room.

The lord caught the skora flare with one gloved hand. It solidified between them, one end emerging from Teller's spirikai and the other grasped by the lord. Power sparked and jumped along the beam as each tried to force it into the other. The lord took the last step down the dais.

"I want," he said, standing now an arm's-length away from Teller as the beam sizzled between them, "what belongs to me." With both hands he grasped the beam of skora and, no longer pushing, he pulled.

The fire resisted. It clung with burning roots inside Teller's spirikai. Hands chained, bracing himself against the volghasts that restrained him, he held onto his power even as the lord, his leather gloves bulging with effort, pulled relentlessly on it. The air thickened with malice; Teller could hardly breathe.

"Ataya, skora," the lord whispered fiercely. *Come.* "Atay'emi, skora!"

Teller gasped, impaled on a spear of pain, struggling like those on the Skewrong Grabe.

Only inches away, the lord's eyes spun inward like black whirlpools sucking in power. With a grunt of effort, he twisted the beam. The roots of skora tore out like burning hooks. Teller screamed as the Spider-king ripped out his fire, his heartbeat, his strength.

The lord barked a command, and the chains fell from Teller's wrists. The volghasts let go, and Teller pitched forward onto his hands. He choked down nausea, his fingers seeking something to clutch on the marble floor.

A pair of boots stood stolidly above him, then creaked as the Eyascnu bent over. He took a long, quivering breath and released it in a hiss of anger. "Where is my vol-ring?"

"I cut," Teller choked out, "the skewin' thing off!" With his left hand pressed against his spirikai, he raised himself on his right to look up at the lord. "My name was *never* Teller-of-Lies." He felt himself grinning crazily. "Your Vols always got that wrong."

The corner of the red mouth twitched. "I raised you up. I trusted you as I could not trust my own brother. I added you into my hand, into the fist that could grasp all of Shunder, and this is how you have repaid me." His boot came down on Teller's maimed hand and ground it into the floor. Bones cracked.

"Open the link!" Sheft pleaded. "Ice can help you!"

His brother had been trying to reconnect all along, but Teller would not let him feel what was happening. Now, pressing his forehead against the cold floor and careening toward unconsciousness, he still managed to keep his end of the link closed tight.

Icy hands on his neck revived him. "I am not finished, Teller-of-Lies. You will stay with me until I am."

The boot ground down once more. He clamped down on a cry as blood, black in the gloom, pooled out from under it.

Somewhere above him he heard a voice, an echoing voice as if two spoke. "It is time," Vol Kuat said. "The Vora waits."

With a final twist, the boot stepped back. "In a moment."

A volghast grasped Teller's hair and pulled his head up. Something hard, cold, and tight snapped around his throat. An ahn collar.

"Leave him alone!" Sheft cried. "I'm the one who has what you want."

The lord laughed grimly. "As you wish, niyal'arist vora." He gestured to one of the Vols. With a snick of metal, the creature also closed a collar around Sheft's neck.

Teller had told his brother about the collars, and Sheft well understood the meaning of their profound humiliation, yet Teller knew his twin would have borne it alone, and in his place.

Two 'braks, who must have come in with Vol Kuat, dragged Teller to his feet. A third stood in the cavern behind the throne and held a globe-lantern. Teller took a shuddering breath that scraped against his raw spirikai. The ahn-collar was so tight it was hard to swallow.

As smoothly as sheathing a sword, the lord slid the skora blade into invisibility. He took in a deep breath, let it out, and then flexed his shoulders. The charcoaled eyes fell upon the toltyr, which had come out of Teller's shirt. "You chose that over my vol-ring. What a fool. Now you are twice enslaved."

Seeming taller than he had been moments before, the lord ascended the dais steps, not bothering to glance back at Teller as he spoke. "You will have a very long time to regret your choice. Your meeting with the Vora will be quite short in comparison." He reseated himself on his throne and looked down at him. "Afterward, you will become Volghast Cinc. Rotting and obeying, with only enough memories to remind you of life long gone." He glanced at the Volghasts standing stolid and without expression before the steps. "You will never sleep, never die, but the trapped core of yourself will be one, eternal scream." The horrible mouth twisted into a smile. "Like Arachniman, is it not? Before you leave here, however, note how we will deal with your brother."

He waved a hand, and the volghasts swirled over Sheft like carrion birds. They pushed him face down on the circle, tore off his remaining clothes, and shackled his hands and feet to the stakes. Sweeping aside, they left him stretched out on the ground, his naked body, his pale hair, gleaming against the black background.

Sheft raised his head to look up at the lord. "You don't have to do it this way."

"Oh but I do. When I asked, you refused. Now I no longer ask, I take."

Sick anguish curdled inside Teller. He could do nothing to help his twin, only stand here with a ripped open spirikai.

Sheft turned as far as he could to look over his shoulder at him. In response to the plea in his eyes, Teller reluctantly opened the link. It would be for the last time. He tried to block his own pain from entering, but almost immediately knew he failed and had wounded his brother yet again. "Sheft, I'm sorry."

And then a cold slap of dismay struck him: he'd done something much worse. He'd gone far beyond where any apology could ever reach. During the Weshnika, his brother had called upon Teller to help him bleed. He had needed his fire to melt the ice.

Why hadn't he remembered that? Why hadn't they planned for that? The very essence of the Coin of Rulve consisted of one twin's power balancing the other, the two of them together accomplishing the Creator's will. Now all that had been destroyed.

But oh God, oh God Rulve, the Spider-king would never believe how interdependent they were. He would see Sheft's inability to shed his blood as stubborn resistance.

If 'braks didn't have hold of him, Teller would have fallen to his knees. Celume's prophecy battered his heart: one niyal'arist would help the other die. But now that would not happen. Sheft would die without his help, and it would be a terrible death.

All because he couldn't control his fire, couldn't save it for when his brother would desperately need it.

"Teller, don't. You gave everything in you, did everything you had to do. The rest is up to Rulve now. It was always up to her."

Sheft-Teller had believed that every power Rulve had given them—everything they had become, everything they had learned, every "yes" they had wrestled out of themselves—would all spring out in answer to whatever happened here. But what had sprung out of him was a selfish, unforgiveable act.

After all the denials and refusals, after their hard-won final assent, the Coin of Rulve had already fallen to the ground. With his own rage he'd cracked it, and now it lay here in Oknu Shuld, broken and worthless.

From behind his outstretched arm, Sheft's eyes met Teller's. "Even if it's broken, how can something Rulve forged be worthless? Don't we hope, can't we trust and try to believe, that Rulve's power begins where ours ends?"

They had no answer. They had settled into a hidden existence with Rulve, struggled to do the Creator's will, but the presence was no longer with them.

They gazed at each other. Their link swelled with forgiveness on one side and the refusal of it on the other, with wrenching regret and compassion born of love, with the hope for courage, both for oneself and for the other, and finally with the words of parting: "Y'rulve, my brother." Go with God. Gently, feeling for the last time that growing intimacy they could share with no other, Sheft-Teller pulled apart their niyal'arist link.

Somewhere— coming from each other or from the very air; perhaps never really spoken, but only remembered or only hoped for—floated back the whispered thought: *May even this be redeemed.*

Addressing the volghasts, the lord's voice rang out. "Take his blood. All of it."

Sheft's body tensed as the volghasts bent over him; as umbraks pulled Teller into the cavern behind the throne.

Chapter 24

Inside the Vora's Domain

A shudder passed through Sheft, and the short chains attached to his shackles clinked faintly. All his life he had fled the dark circle, but it had kept pace with him, rolling moon-like at his side wherever he walked, waiting in his dreams like a shadow-filled well. It had loomed over him when he stood surrounded by hooded figures during the Rites, and now he lay outstretched on it.

The volghasts set globe-lights around him, one of them directly in front of his eyes. Larvae squirmed within its confines. One crawled up the glass in a blind search for escape, only to drop back into the roiling mass.

A volghast moved to his left and knelt beside him. A knifepoint picked up the cord of his toltyr, and over his body the creature addressed the lord seated on his throne. "Should I remove this?" the dead voice asked.

"Leave him his choice," the Spider-king said. "My collar is a leash far stronger."

"He bears scars," the volghast noted. "The skin will be thicker there."

Sheft turned his head away from the globe as the lord rose and approached him. From his position on the floor, Sheft saw him standing sideways, a black shadow against the bruised light.

"Cut over them," the shadow directed, "an inch at a time, deep enough only to draw blood."

Sheft tensed as a knifepoint circled lightly over his back, as if in a beginning flourish, and then slit into his left shoulder. He took a sharp breath and held it as the point burned down. Without his willing it, his spirikai constricted, and ice rushed out to close the wound.

There was a short silence, broken by the kneeling volghast's hollow voice. "He still refuses to bleed."

"Not a refusal," Sheft rasped. "It's ice. A…a power that won't allow—" A volghast standing on his left kicked him in the side.

"We shall see what won't be allowed," the lord said. "My volghasts are skilled and exceedingly patient. They are dead already, and neither time nor your pain nor any 'ice' you claim to possess has any meaning for them." His sideways silhouette moved closer, grew taller. It raised a languid hand to point at him. "You will now return to me what your forebears stole."

"We didn't steal a thing from you," Sheft said, but his denial made no difference. The volghast engraved a series of cuts onto his upper back, reopening the wounds that his wife had so gently stitched together after the field-burn accident, that the water in the henge had assuaged, that the Pool of Rulve had healed. Still the ice clenched down, and still Sheft could not prevent it.

"He does not obey," the volghast said.

A frozen hand, pressing on the back of his neck, penetrated the pain. Sheft shoved ice into it. but the hand did not jerk away. It remained unfazed, ice touching ice.

The volghast sat back on its heels. "Behead this one," it suggested, "and all will be quickly accomplished."

"S'rere must be alive," the lord clipped. "Red and alive as it soaks into the ground. Ista, volghasti." *Continue.*

A second volghast came to kneel beside Sheft, this one on his right. It cut lines now down his lower back, red lines across his mind as he squeezed his eyes shut. Against every ounce of his will, an icy wave froze the wounds.

The lord's voice, low and dangerously tight, floated from somewhere above him. "I see you do not understand, vora. S'rere is my kingly heritage, given to me to sustain my domain. It once ran through my body. I knew its power. I felt its vitality." The voice slid into a hiss. "Then the niyal'arist voras came against me. They sucked my heritage from me. They corrupted my brother and forced violence upon me. I am rotting away because you seized the very life from my veins."

"We're not them!" Sheft cried. "My brother and I never hurt you, had nothing to do with—" The ahn collar around his throat tightened and choked off his words.

"Do not interrupt me," the lord said. "The wheel has turned, niyal'arist vora. S'rere has come back to me and will no longer be denied. It *cannot* be denied."

The lord was deranged, but he had seen the truth: s'rere must pour out here, no matter how long it took, and by whatever means necessary. Yet Sheft could not bleed. He needed to. It was his only power, the only power he had, and he came to this place to give it away. But oh God, like his brother's skora, so protective and deeply ingrained, ice could no longer be controlled.

The lord folded his arms and gave once more the dreaded order: "Ista, volghasti."

Teller used his good hand alternately to press against his burning spirikai and pull at the scathi ahn collar around his throat. Vol Kuat strode ahead, holding his hand-globe high, while three 'braks, the last one in line holding another light, prodded Teller to follow. They descended a steep stairway that hugged the edge of a black abyss and then traversed a low passage that ended at a barred iron gate. The Delver unlocked it, and the 'braks pushed Teller through. Vol Kuat set the hand-globe on the ground inside and then pulled shut the gate between them with a clang.

After motioning the 'braks away, he withdrew something from his robe and tossed it through the bars at Teller's feet. It was his green dagger.

Teller bent to retrieve the weapon. Why did Kuat return the dagger to him? What use was this against the Vora? He couldn't even hold it in his right hand.

The Delver said nothing, only stared at him with his blank, pupil-less gaze.

Could he be offering him a chance to end things on his own terms? But why? That would risk the Spider-king's rage, for nothing would anger the lord more than an intended "work of art" snatched from his hand.

But what did it matter what the Vol's motives were? As always, he acted inscrutably and manipulated events to suit himself. Teller rubbed his thumb along the edge of the blade. Whatever the Delver intended, the green dagger offered a way out. If things got bad enough, perhaps the only way out.

Small pupils jumped into the Vol's eyes. "Your brother's wife is here," he said, "in the Vora's domain."

"What?" He grasped a bar. "What are you talking about? Mariat is dead!"

"I brought her living into these caverns." The Delver turned and walked away.

"Wait!" he cried.

Without looking back, Vol Kuat disappeared around a bend in the passageway.

THE TWO VOLGHASTS KNEELING ON EITHER side of Sheft now took turns, the first one waiting to see if its cut on Sheft's right arm bled and, when it did not, the other trying on his left. Ice-reaction began to creep over Sheft. What was happening to him now smeared into a past vision, in which he lay spread out upon an anvil, his back on fire from the field-burn injuries. The old man had bent over him. *"Will you trust me, niyal'arist? Will you let me answer your deepest prayer?"* He had cried out "Yes!" because he needed the forge, needed strength pounded into his bones. *"Forge me, Rulve, into your forever coin, to spend how and when you will."* And then as now, pain hammered down.

At last the knives were withdrawn, the volghasts stood and moved away, and the collar was loosened, but it took him a moment to realize this, for pain continued to rush and reverberate throughout his body. Every tremulous breath pulled cuts apart, but the blood within never flowed.

A pair of polished boots appeared in front of Sheft's face. Sounding far off and then startlingly near, the Spider-king spoke, his voice rough with intensity. "We have both possessed s'rere. We have both felt its pull. In a manner of speaking, we are brothers." The gloved hand at his side tightened, releasing a sickening smell. "Are you not called to save the land?" the lord cried. "Every niyal'arist pretender has told me that. But it is only I who can do it."

Clenched and shivering, Sheft groaned inside. The icy power encased him as tightly as revenge and ambition gripped this lord.

"Continue to refuse me," the voice warned, "and you will doom all of Shunder."

"As you said," Sheft gasped, "we are alike. You too are bound."

The lord whirled away with a creak of leather boots. "Ista," he commanded. "Ista, volghasti."

Two other volghasts replaced those who had withdrawn. Their blades incised cuts across Sheft's waist and along the grooves between his ribs. He could not clutch the toltyr for strength, could only clutch the chains, while ice kept its relentless hold on him.

The hem of the lord's robe, crawling with embroidered spiders, brushed over his shackled wrist, and then swirled away, out of his line of sight. "Why do you resist?" His voice was that of a reasonable man, puzzled at being misunderstood. "Among a people divided into ahn and niyal, I embody the ultimate rista. I should be commended, vora. I labor to create a new thing: the nihilarist: the one niyalahn-rista, complete unto itself."

"The niyalahn-ristas," Sheft choked out, "are two. Two sides of Rulve's coin." Pain made it hard to know if he was talking to himself or to the lord or to Rulve. Who wove the pattern, and who were the taut threads being woven?

A bark of derisive laughter. "I am no coin to be spent by another's will. I do the spending."

Chapter 25

Time Sliced into Now

Ice-reaction seeped more deeply into Sheft. He shivered, and it seemed the circle beneath him began to turn, slowly dragging with it the walls, the throne, and the faces of the waiting volghasts.

"In spite of how I was born," the lord's voice continued, "I lean on no one—no god, no Vol, no twin brother. The niyal'arist voras fought to diminish me—two against one they fought me—but I prevailed. Now justice shall finally be done, the justice you denied my brother and me."

"Justice?" Sheft croaked. The man he had for so long believed to be his father treasured that word. In the name of justice the village council had condemned Sheft. But it too was a coin, and its other side...its other side must be mercy.

Suddenly he remembered standing in the Seani, in the crowded dining room, and a little boy was looking up at him. His eyes were moist, round with a plea. *"Please, emjadi,"* he implored, *"get my brother. Bring him home."* Sheft bent down and held the boy's face between his hands. But now it was the boy burning with fever in the hospit, and there was nothing he could do. *"My ice can't heal. I'm sorry, Tema."*

Sheft tried to wipe away the tears in his eyes, but couldn't. He was chained here with volghasts, and they were moving on their knees around him—methodical, careful, their thin blades never going deep enough to kill. They strung him on a taut wire, with beads of agony along its length, and ice rushed to close every wound.

His ice was useless here, useless in the hospit. His blood had produced nothing in the Quela.

In time, it would have. Given time, he would have bled in that holy place. He would have lain in Rulve's house, in the safety of the Creator's hands, and caring people around him would have helped him bleed into the land. One day, they'd told him, s'rere would grow into its full power, and he would be able to give it away.

But the future had been sliced into *now*, into shards of *here*. Here and now his blood must be shed—on this circle, for this lord. This parched and wounded place was the source of all of Shunder's hurt and only his blood could heal it.

The woman kneeling beside him gently opened his clenched hand, and then bent to kiss it. "Don't be afraid, my dear son. The one most bound is the one most free."

It was true. The volghasts had trapped him in a net of agony, and in this place of utter commitment, there was nothing left to decide. He was free now—free to trust Rulve completely. With his arms outstretched, he could cling to nothing but who he was and what he'd been called to do.

But the cuts were coming faster now, across the back of his knees and down his calves, and the ahn-collar choked his screams, and the pain was so great he did not know where he was.

The Delver, Teller knew, never lied. He evaded, he hinted, and he spoke with a double voice; but Vol Kuat never lied. Against all odds, Mariat must be here. "As brother to my betrothed," she once had told him, "you are a brother to me."

Now, somewhere in this darkness, she might be cowering in terror, or enduring the Vora's torment, or lying wounded in some dark crevice. And he had nothing to help her with, except his dagger and one good hand.

Shoving the weapon into his belt, he picked up the hand-globe and held it high, then made his way forward within its dim shell of light. Its meager glow showed the uneven floor of a cavern so large that its ceiling and walls were lost in darkness. Never before had he been so deep inside Oknu Shuld. His spirikai simmered as if it contained live coals, and his right hand burned. Too bad, he thought grimly, none of that cast any light. A glance at the globe told him some of the worms were already dying.

Vivid images of what might be happening to Sheft ground into his stomach. Because of his own stupid zeal, his brother would be enduring an agonizing ordeal. He wouldn't even know his beloved wife had been brought here.

But wasn't it better that way? Wasn't it far better to bear grief already accepted, than be torn apart with anguish for a wife he could not help?

Oh God. Just as he himself, through his own fault, could not help Sheft.

He trudged on, cut away from his twin, collared and without power—a true ahn, a one-sided, worthless coin.

After climbing several wide terrace-like steps, he reached a section where the rocky floor had leveled.

Beyond, a smaller tunnel veered to the left, off the main passage straight ahead. Which way had Mariat gone—if she even had made it this far?

As if in answer, the skora-wound flared with such intensity that he doubled over and sank to his knees. The hand-globe fell and shattered against the rock floor. Frantic, he tried one-handedly to scoop up some of the luniku larvae, but most crawled quickly away, taking their light into crevices and holes. The few he managed to catch were dying. In only minutes, he was left in complete darkness.

CHAINS CLINKED, AND THE PULL ON Sheft's shoulders lessened. It took him several heartbeats to realize they had unfastened his bonds. He got shakily onto his hands and knees, turned his ice-heavy body over, and sat up. The metal collar—or was it the toltyr?—dragged his head down.

Ice-reaction made everything seem foggy and unreal, as if snips were being cut out of time. The floor revolved in dizzy snatches. He looked up, blinking at several pairs of red eyes that seemed to float around him in the purple light.

It couldn't be over, could it?

A gauntleted hand pressed a cup of water to his lips. He took an eager gulp, but the ahn collar suddenly got tighter, and he choked. Someone emitted a hollow laugh, then cold hands shoved him onto his back. His wounds, open yet dry, pressed into the earth. When his fuzzy brain understood what they intended, he resisted with all his remaining strength, but soon his wrists and ankles were restrained again. The volghasts needed a clean slate.

He raised his head to look down at himself. Fear raked through him. His throat, his spirikai, everything between his legs that made him a man, all were now far more exposed in this position.

"Ista, volghasti." The voice echoed through the amethyst dark.

Four wool-encased heads closed over him, the grey skin stretched tightly over the skull. One at a time, one careful inch at a time, blades incised his chest. They held him down when he tried to twist away. He held onto consciousness with both chained hands, and someone was screaming, someone nailed onto the Skewrong Grabe.

A presence was kneeling beside him. Not the woman, but now the young man. How long had he been there? "Have courage, emjadi," he said. "I am here. 'Yes' is only one short word."

"But I have to keep on saying it!" Sheft cried.

PANTING AND CURSING HIMSELF, TELLER WAITED on hands and knees until the worst of the pain in his spirikai had ebbed away, and then climbed to his feet. With the light gone, he couldn't see a thing and had to explore each step forward with his foot. After several moments he realized either his eyes were playing tricks on him or the mouth of the left-hand tunnel gleamed dimly. He veered in that direction, but a faint sound stopped him. It came from the pitch-black tunnel ahead. His eyes darted toward it. He held his breath and listened.

Swish-thump. *Swish*-thump. *Swish*-thump.

Dread skittered like ants down his arms. Something big was humping itself toward him. His eyes swiveled back to the side tunnel, which now glowed with the unmistakable crawling light of a globe.

Was it Mariat? It must be.

He could see nothing in the black tunnel ahead. But the air, until now so dead, stirred with movement. He heard the sound of rasping guttural breaths, and a massive shape began to coalesce.

With his left hand, Teller pulled the dagger from his belt. Globe-light grew brighter in the other passage. He glimpsed an approaching shadow, wavering against the uneven wall.

"Mariat!" he shouted. "Mariat, stay back!"

Echoes jumped out of the dark. *Back—back—back.* They mingled with a woman's startled cry, and then fell into silence.

He cut his eyes back to the black tunnel-mouth. It was filled with a slowly disgorging form. Bulky shoulders emerged. From lower down, bulging white eyes caught a reflection, then disappeared as a creature shuffled forward. It was profoundly hump-backed, carrying the thrusting lump of its head on a level just above Teller's own. Its powerful arms were covered with growths and patches of hair.

Teller edged toward the left. Someone stood just inside the passageway there, a slim figure, wearing a tunic and pants. It was Mariat, clutching a hand-globe, her eyes huge.

"Go back!" he shouted. "Now!" *Now-now-now!*

The great beast swung its head toward her, then back to Teller. A low growl rumbled in its throat.

Chapter 26

Black Tears

Dying of thirst, the soil under Sheft desperately sought sustenance from his dry wounds. It was like the emaciated baby mewlet he had once tried to save, its poor mouth nuzzled against the chest of a six-year-old boy. Deep in his spirikai, the s'rere rose in compassion, but ice blocked it from relieving the terrible need. Clutching the chains, he begged, "Help me, Rulve! Help me do this."

A command rang out, and the volghasts sat back on their heels. Sheft took a quivering breath, and far off, the man on the Skewrong Grabe stopped screaming.

"Inform me," a voice above him asked. "Why did you come here?"

Sheft tried to swallow, tried to moisten his raw throat and speak. The lord must have seen this, for the collar loosened as the polished boots came closer.

"I came to heal," Sheft choked out.

The lord emitted a bitter laugh. "You came here to finish the work of your forebears. You came here to destroy me."

"Not that. To heal."

"Then heal *me*!" The lord tore off one of his gloves and threw it on the floor. It landed beside Sheft's head

219

with a soft plop and exuded the sharp smell of decay. The lord leaned over him.

Sheft focused on the blurry hood. What he saw inside it shocked him. The lips were like a newly cut gash, the skin as finely grained as chalk, but above the lord's nose there was nothing. Where eyes should be, two crude spirals had been painted, as if a child had done it. Oh God, had the lord drawn these eyes himself? Out of his eternal dark? Had he dipped a brush into black ink, and with a trembling hand moved it over the empty skin? Under one of the spirals, a drop of paint had fallen and dried. It gleamed faintly, like a black tear.

At the sight of it, a vision rushed upon Sheft, and as if through a dark mirror, he saw a newborn infant crying. But nowhere on its body could tears ever form. Sickened, its mother turned away, her arms crossed tightly over her breasts. They had expected a miracle, the longed-for, impossible twins, but instead one had been born this screaming eyeless horror. It lay next to its brother in the royal cradle, its tiny hands helplessly flailing. Stiff with disgust, the father left the room. He took with him their other infant, a son whole and loved.

A revelation struck Sheft: from birth this lord was wounded. He was wounded like the land and sought healing from s'rere.

Someone settled down beside Sheft. It was the sage, his eyes filled with compassion so piercingly deep it drilled into Sheft's heart. S'rere must heal, would heal, because it arose from this all-encompassing compassion.

"Yes," the sage said. "I gave my gift to this lord, but he lost it. And now comes one who can restore it to him."

"I need my brother's skora to help me, Rulve, but he was taken away, and only the Spider-king is with me."

The sage smiled sadly. "Just so, my dearest son. Just so."

"Did you speak, vora?" The lord's voice sounded eager, full of anticipation. "Did you say something?"

Had this lord half-heard the mind-speech? But whatever he had heard, Sheft felt the path before him open up. He knew now what he must do. "You have skora now," he croaked to the Spider-king. "Use it to melt this ice."

MARIAT SHOUTED, BUT TELLER BARELY HEARD her. The creature pulled itself toward him on its powerful arms, its backward-facing claws scraping across the rock. Shadows hid its face. The odor of sweat and urine, of blood and decay, prickled in the air.

Like a sudden attack, the skora-wound clawed inside his spirikai, but Teller managed to hold onto the dagger and keep himself upright.

The creature bellowed. Halting words tried to leak into Teller's mind.

Sheft? Was his brother attempting to reach him? He immediately opened the link they had broken, and heard a desperate plea. "Help me."

It wasn't his brother's voice. In a flash Teller was six years old, running out of the postern. He was reaching out to a wounded prisoner, reaching out to Neal, grasping his father's hand.

"Help me."

The same words, the same plea, spoken in the same language of truth.

But it was a lie! Impossible then, impossible now. It was a filthy deception, now as it was then.

The top of the creature's face emerged into the dim light. Tumors swelled over the scaly forehead, and huge white eyes, the pupils dilated under a veined and milky film, focused on him. This thing could only be the Vora.

Teller tightened his hold on the dagger and raised it.

THE LORD STARED DOWN AT SHEFT, his red mouth contorted. "I will not," he grated, "be tricked by a vora again." He leaned over Sheft. "And I *resent*, I deeply *resent*, that you think me such a fool."

"If I'm…the vora you think I am," Sheft gasped, "would I be so…so stupid as to try?"

Waving his arm at the volghasts, the lord whirled away. "Cut him!" he shouted at them. "Across the abdomen. Across the hipbones."

They obeyed, working lower and lower, and Sheft feared where they would go next. Everything there belonged to his wife. *I'm sorry, Mariat! I'm sorry.* But she was gone, and would never touch him there again, never receive anything from him again.

He turned his head toward the dark lord standing over him. "Would you," he choked out, "lose s'rere again? Lose it forever? If you…go on like this, how… how long do you think I'll last?"

"You will live forever! Give in to me, and I will make of your body a simulacrum that will never die."

One of the volghasts spoke. "A skora-blade kills, lord, and he would like nothing better."

"Not a blade," Sheft cried to the Spider-king. "A warm stone. Form it from skora, into your hand. Pass it into my spirikai."

The lord stood motionless.

"Do not trust him," the volghast said.

"You're a king," Sheft groaned, "so act like one. Use the power you've taken."

For a moment the lord did nothing, then motioned to a second volghast who whipped off its moldy cloak and spread it beside Sheft. With a creak of his leather boots, the lord knelt. He extended his gloved hand and stared at it until skora-fire glittered. It appeared in his palm as a spiky burning ball.

"What now?" the lord demanded.

The s'rere inside Sheft scraped painfully against the icy barrier, against all that blocked him from what he was called to be and wanted to give. Already stretched out, already rubbed raw by longing and scraped by grief, his spirikai thinned to the edge of tearing.

Sheft pointed to it with his chin. "There," he gasped. "Lay the skora there."

"I know nothing of gentleness, vora," the lord warned "and I will not let you betray me again."

"Do it however you can!" Sheft cried.

The lord grunted and turned over his hand.

Bristling fire burned into Sheft's spirikai. It skewered into its depths, into everything that was frozen inside him. Ice shattered, and shards fell away. With his scream of agony, s'rere broke through. Blood rushed into every wound, rose to the verge of every cut. It trembled there, about to overflow, awaiting his will.

"It is happening," the Spider-king whispered. "My s'rere is returning to me."

A sudden panic took hold of Sheft. It swelled against the collar at his throat. He was about to lay Rulve's gift at the foot of darkness. He was betraying his deepest call, falling into Wask's every temptation. The lord would make of him some inhuman thing, a slave to evil. His outstretched arms pulled at his chest, and he struggled to breathe. He strained against the chains, against the pounding fear, and the bleeding ceased.

A COLD CHILL RUSHED THROUGH TELLER as two opaque bulging eyes looked down on him. As if in some silent explosion, a series of terrible scenes flashed into his mind.

He saw a man wearing rags, lying restrained on a slab of stone. Suddenly Teller became that man.

Barbed manacles bit into his wrists. The chain around his neck tightened; he gasped for air. "No more potions!" he screamed when his torturer bent over him. "We are brothers!" The man smashed a fist into his mouth; forced bitter everbeast down his throat.

He could not speak, could emit only aching groans and bellows. Thirst racked him. "No water," his tormentor snarled. "Suck from the dead." His brother left him, turning to sneer through the barred window in the door. "This is your realm, vora. The kingdom you deserve."

His brother came again and again and forced potions into him. They poisoned any tendril in him that sought the light. They carved chunks out of his soul, heaped them as lumps upon his body, until there was nothing left but a monster.

A thin chain bound him when he was led above, and he did what the potions commanded him. Limb from limb, he tore prisoners apart, ate their raw flesh and slurped their warm blood. Transformed by everbeast, enraged by fura, his skora heritage turned to ashes in his mouth. He roamed black caverns, his world a reeking pit.

But—still deep inside: the mission. The summons. Still his. Still theirs.

Someone came. The Delver.

"Help me, Kuat!" he begged. "Bring Riahson."

The vision slammed shut.

Teller remembered sleepless nights in Oknu Shuld, when echoing, far-off groans rose from the floor grate in his room. The sounds went on for years. The pain of the skora-wound struck again, as if fiery blocks ground inside him.

The creature shuffled closer, a stained rag wrapped around its mouth. A horny claw reached out, but did not touch him. Deep and hoarse, as from years of disuse, a voice spoke words into his mind. "Do not be afraid. I also am wounded, Riahson."

Riah's son. Staring into the creature's eyes, barely conscious of what he was doing, Teller dropped the dagger.

Chapter 27

A Glancing Shaft of Sun

BLIND PANIC GRIPPED SHEFT, BUT THEN a hand pressed over his pounding heart. It calmed him, and a voice in his head stilled him. The woman knelt beside him and brushed Sheft's hair back from his forehead. "Do not fear, my son. There is nothing here but my grace."

That was so. The warm presence enfolded him. Slowly Sheft eased into trust. His outstretched body lay in twilight, under the quiet, steady seep of grace. He remembered the words engraved into the top of Rulve's green disk, and they glimmered behind his eyes: *My life is in your hands.*

Someone gently kissed him in the hollow at the base of his throat. Mariat, in the henge, after she placed the toltyr over his head. *"Do you think all losses are forever, my darling Sheft?"*

He raised his head but couldn't see her. He could only see the toltyr, dimly, lying across his chest.

Skora burned in his spirikai, waiting for his assent. It was time, and he lay back, lying still under the pain. "Yes, Rulve. Now, my Lord."

He closed his eyes and slowly released the tension in his body. Tenderness spilled into his spirikai, and with a long shiver, his wounds opened. For a moment his hands clenched, anticipating the relentless ice, but it never came. He relaxed. The Spider-king's fire, Teller's fire, was doing what it had been created to do.

Blood began to seep out of every cut. He allowed his strength to drip, and then flow steadily, into the soil beneath him. The long-parched earth drank deeply from him, and the soil crickled as it drank—a comforting, satisfying sound. He leaned into it, deeper and deeper, lying in the hands of the wet, warm dark, fulfilling at last his heart's desire.

He bled for the anguish of lost children, for the grief of a dying land. For the infant born without eyes, for those held in the grip of purple, for every ahn and niyal and rista. He bled for his homeland Shunder and also for distant Ullar, for Tarn who sought justice, for Gwin who loved Mariat, for Parduka who clung to her goddess. Red compassion poured out for everyone hurting, for those who were wounded, and for those who inflicted the wounds. The despair of two lands was washed away by the tide of blood and tears.

He had done it. His blood ran with Rulve's freely into the world. Great waves of joy and gratitude shook him again and again.

He opened his eyes. The amethyst light was fading into grey. The figures around him were dissolving into shadows. He could no longer feel the shackles or the collar around his throat. As with ripples on a serene lake, distant pain was washed away. *Thank you, Rulve.*

His sight trickled away. His hearing, the sensations on his skin, everything flowed into the ground. He let it go.

The pulse in his chest beat slower and slower. *Thank you, my Lord.*

A flicker. *My life.*

A long exhale. *Into your hands.*

Tenderness took him. My dearest son.

His heart stopped in deep quiet, empty of breath.

IN THE HALLS OF OKNU SHULD—DOWN branching passageways and dim stairways, inside the crowded ale-chamber and the sulfurous kitchens—startled ahn looked up from their work. Inside themselves they felt a deep wrench. Their eyes sought those of other ahn and found confirmation: something had happened.

A light had passed out of the world—a bright thing, like a glancing shaft of sun.

IN THE DEPTHS OF THE VORA'S domain, Teller heard his dagger fall. A sudden burst of light blinded him. In pale gold and silver, his brother spun away from him. "Sheft!" he cried, reaching out. "Sheft!"

But he'd gone. Gone without him, without his help. Teller dropped his arm. *Oh, God. Forgive me, Sheft.*

Suddenly, agony erupted in his spirikai, the worst yet. Blackness shut down with a clang, and he pitched forward.

LIGHT WAS SHINING ON HIM, AND light like love was pouring through him. Sheft's spirit stretched up and out, caught briefly on his skin, and broke free. He rose out of the ruined and collared body that had once encased him and looked down at it. It was crushed into the mud, into clinging roots and isolating ice; and all that made the painful difference between him and those he loved had drained away.

The earth in the blood-soaked circle danced with tiny roots. Soon they would produce a wave of newborn leaves, soft to the touch, and the dark circle would become a glowing disk of jade-green, forest-green, every green shining with life.

Great hands cupped him, warm and infinitely tender. They lifted him up, past those who grieved but would be consoled, through rock-levels and root-filled soil, into the sun and air of a fresh new morning.

The hands opened, and he spilled into everything, into the dazzling, shifting pattern of all that was, and it spilled into him. All creation wove through his body: translucent flowers, great rivers of ice, wheels of stars. Every possibility was a promise fulfilled. He looked down as a falcon from on high, laughed as a waterfall that plunged over a cliff, tumbled as a river into the placid sea. He was a tree with uplifted branches, whose roots spread deeply into the earth; he was a great fish that rose for breath and leaped straight into the heart of God.

He was home, where his mother and Ana were waiting to greet him, where Yuin's twin smiled and grasped his hand, where Miramakamen hugged him tightly. People thronged around him, and he ruffled the hair of children long dead and those yet to be born. And in the midst of it all shone a space for his beloved, full of her presence not-yet. Opening and opening, he unfolded into love, into a place of simple love, where everything at last enfolded him.

Rulve pointed to the glittering Sky-path, as excited as a little boy whose blood had once made the sweet-rue grow. "Come see what I made! It's an entire universe, Sheft, and so beautiful."

"Can I wait for Mariat?"

"You don't have to wait, my dearest. It's all now."

He turned, and there she was, radiant and smiling. As if a new sun were bursting upon a new land, he saw that everything that had ever happened, and everything that would ever happen, was an everlasting now. Down there, he wouldn't have understood; down there, she wouldn't have either. But here in the *now*, he took her warm hands. They embraced, and with an effortless tingle, their bodies passed into each other with a closeness he'd never imagined—every part of him in her, and her in him—with pleasure that made him gasp. When they pulled apart, they took Rulve's hands and went with him to explore their true home.

Light erupted in the dim tunnel, so suddenly that Mariat hid her eyes in the crook of her elbow. *What...?* A dear presence brushed against her, held her for an instant, and then the darkness rolled back. Shaken, blinded by the light, Mariat raised her lantern. "Sheft?" Sight gradually returned. She saw his familiar figure standing at the place where the main tunnel joined the one in which she stood. Her heart leaped. He'd found her! Somehow he'd followed her! With a cry of joy she rushed forward, only to see him crumple to the ground before she could reach him.

Chapter 28

Heart-Sight

In Bellstone Forest, across what was left of the Eeron River, Gurvale the Bellstriker took a sharp breath. The heaviness that had been weighing in her heart ever since dawn now swept over her senses. The sun dimmed on this bright and cloudless day, the twittering of birds faded away, and the fresh cold air of Seed flashed into a feeling of deep emptiness. The sensations passed, but the sense of loss remained. Restless, she rose from the log she'd been sitting on and slipped through the trees to the ford.

Long ago the Eeron flowed fast and clear over the shallows here, and tasty sunfish spawned in the gravel. But then the Spider-king had dammed the river to create a reservoir lake, and Sunsink Falls had dried up. Now the filth oozing out of the lord's spider hole fouled the water into a poisonous stew, fit only for breeding mosquitoes. The fisher-folk who had once lived here had melted away, and the only thing to be caught now were the bony, grease-colored eels that fed on whatever could live in the muck.

Across from where she stood hidden in the underbrush, the massive bulk of Insheer Cliff curved to the north, hiding the entrance to Oknu Shuld. Silent and aware, the cliff still brooded in late morning shadow. A passing breeze sent a shiver under Gurvale's deerskin shirt as she watched the enemy band camped at its base.

Clawthorns, they were. The umbrak division of the Skinners, consisting of lithe, lean 'braks experienced in sudden forest raids. Besides their axes, they carried deadly three-pronged slashers at their belts, claw-like weapons that could rake out an eye or ravage a throat. She had seen their ugly work far too many times.

The 'braks had taken care to settle themselves under a few stunted trees out of arrow range, but she could see the glint of side arms as they took their mid-day meat. They knew Rung's archers were watching from the forest all around her, and the archers knew they knew.

Nothing had changed. Both sides waited for night. But something had happened more terrible than night.

Deep inside Insheer Cliff, in his private audience chamber, the Lord of Shunder rose to his feet. The light-haired vora no longer strained against his bonds and lay still. The last red rill glistened as it trickled down his side, and no others followed.

It was done.

The moist soil around the body shivered, urgent with life, and the lord flung off his cloak. "Already the earth dances, my volghasts. Now get this corpse out of the way."

The undead warriors swooped down and unshackled the vora's legs and left arm, but before they could finish, the lord rolled the body aside with his foot. "Hist!" he commanded the earth, *not yet*, and the movement of the soil stopped.

The dead vora was left on its side outside the circle, one wrist still shackled. The ahn collar had somehow fallen off. No matter; he would replace it soon.

The volghasts withdrew into the shadows as the Lord of Shunder retrieved his remaining glove from the floor and put it on. Heedless of his velvet robe, he knelt inside the muddy circle. He scooped the drier earth from the edge into the wet center and scraped every bit of soil from around the four iron stakes to which the chains had been attached. Carefully he mixed it with his hands to form a uniformly moistened mass of rusty black clay. As he worked, droplets of sweat gathered on his forehead.

A TWIG SNAPPED BEHIND GURVALE, AND she turned. None of Rung's men made a sound in the forest unless they chose to. It was young Hewish, back from his stint with Defender Flyn, motioning that she was wanted back at camp.

She followed the boy to Defender Rung's tent, where he and a stalwart with brown curly hair were sitting cross-legged on Rung's thick bearskin rug. They looked up with grave faces as she entered. Glancing at Rung, the Defender of Eerford Glade, one of three glades that comprised Bellstone Forest—and the glade nearest to the Spider-hole—she knew the matter was serious. .

Rung regarded her with his steady blue eyes, his lips a grim line in the midst of his rust-brown beard. "This here is Deoner," he said, "wardson a' Se Utray. He rides the horse Flyn lent to Lir. Se Druv sent him with very bad news. The niyalahn-ristas have been taken by the Spider-king."

The heaviness in Gurvale's heart sank into a lump in her stomach. "I think," she said, "'tis even worse than that."

Deoner turned to her. "What do you mean?"

"T'was a heart-sight I received, only moments ago. I saw a shadow pass over the sun." She bowed her head. "I ken at least one emjadi has already died."

The young man stared motionless at her, as if he were slowly being turned to stone.

"I'm sorry," Gurvale said. "The heart-sight's been with me for as long as I kin remember. But it increased in power three days ago—after I rung the great Bellstone for the first time." Since then she'd been feeling as if she were a fishing-net, a trawling awareness connected by fine, tough threads. And she didn't always like what she caught.

Rung had pressed his clenched fists on his knees in dismay, but now his face hardened and he glowered at Deoner. "So what now?" he growled. "The hopes of our warriors are dashed? Our Bellstone called 'em and yer Seani lost 'em? You let the salvation of Shunder slip through yer fingers?"

"No," Deoner said. His face had gone pale, but now his eyes glinted with fire. "They didn't 'slip through our fingers.' Sheft and Teller left the Seani of their own free will. The niyalahn-ristas deliberately left the safety of the Seani in order to answer Rulve's call. They went to Oknu Shuld freely. And now we know what that cost. They went before us to show us the path, and now one has died." His voice rose. "By God, Rung, we can't let that death be in vain."

Deoner's words rang through the tent, and Gurvale saw how they filled Rung's eyes with hope. "'Tis the spark!" the defender breathed. "The glint of Rulve's sword as she unsheathes it."

"The sacrifice of the niyal'arists is indeed the spark," Deoner said. "It is meant to ignite a rebellion, and for this we must unite and pledge all our strength."

Rung turned to Gurvale. "This must be the meanin' of the Bellstone's word '*One.*' Rulve urges us to stand up and act as one."

Gurvale mistrusted the rising excitement in the tent.

"One in what, Rung? In war'? Killin' will burn Utray's grains and spill Hirai's ales, destroy the medicants and all the Seani stands for." She turned to Deoner. "You think now yer hospit is crowded? Wait 'til the hackin' begins." She waved her hand in a gesture of dismissal. "War has nuthin' to do with what Se Druv's been buildin' the last twelve years. Yer message is no sayin' of his."

"Druv doesn't understand what the niyalahn-ristas have done," Deoner retorted. "The fate of Shunder now rests in the hands of those who do. Of those who will not put aside Rulve's plain call, of those who will never allow the blood of the emjadis to be shed for nothing."

She leaned toward him. "You think the villagers will rise up? That a handful of Sperian rebels will convince a people weak from starvation and achin' for Purple to attack the Spider-king's powerful supporters? This land is riddled with greed and corruption, and you think yer daggers kin cut it out?"

Deoner flushed, but continued to look her right in the eye. "So let the Spider-king prosper? Sit and bemoan your oppression while he grows stronger in his lair?' He glanced at Rung. "Has Rulve put weapons in our hands only to see us toss them away? Tragic as it may be, wrenching as it may be, war is the only coin that can buy back our freedom."

"You forgit yerself, young man," Gurvale said. "I seen years of killin' under the trees, seen our young men spillin' their guts out in the clearin's. I heard the Bellstone speak, for it was me who released its voice, and none of its words was 'war'."

Deoner's eyes flashed. "It mocks Rulve to twiddle our thumbs and call it trust, to turn aside from duty and call it hope. There will be no healing until he who wounds this land is dead."

"You'll kindle carnage in the villages," Gurvale insisted. "Those who profit from the lord, those who grew powerful in his service, they'll murder the resistors as traitors. The Spider-king needna lift a finger."

Rung, who had been stirring restlessly, now spoke. "We canna turn away from what the emjadis stand for. We canna let them die in vain."

Gurvale glanced at him but continued to speak to Deoner. "What happened to learnin',' to workin' together, to changin' hearts and minds? It's the Seani's way, Deoner." But he was too convinced of the path they should go, too young to listen, so she tried once more to reach Rung. "Has war ever built anythin'? Planted anythin'? Has it ever done anythin' but spawn another war?"

Rung stood, apparently having made a decision. "This is an old argument between us, mistress," he said. "But now the emjadis have been taken, at least one is dead, and we must consider these events in council. We will meet with the other Defenders and the elders of the three towns. We leave immediately for a moot at Galensgrave." Calling for one of his men, he ducked out of the tent, followed by Deoner.

Gurvale got to her feet. War would let death loose in Shunder. It would do the same work as the Spider-king, but in the name of Rulve and the niyalahn-ristas. Is this what the Coin of Rulve would purchase?

Heavy with foreboding, she left the tent. If one niyal'arist was already gone, what could the other do all alone? He would die, or face some fate worse, and the two young men would be the first victims of a vicious war that would drag their land into yet more destruction.

CHAPTER 29

HAND AND CLAW

THE MAN MARIAT HAD MISTAKEN FOR Sheft, the man who made her cry out in bitter dismay because he wasn't her beloved, seemed in terrible pain. With some awkward help from the creature's backward-facing claws, she managed to get Teller onto its arms, then edged out of the creature's way as it laboriously carried him past her and into the tunnel from which she had just emerged. Frantic to know what had happened to Sheft, she snatched up the green dagger and followed the monster's misshapen back.

They came to a niche where—hours ago? yesterday?—the Vora had brought her. At least she hoped this creature was the Vora. Perhaps something much worse—the real Vora—might yet appear. But how many monsters could lurk down here? Quite a few, she concluded.

When the thing had first loomed out of the dark and backed her against the cave wall, blind terror almost swept her away. The huge creature, however, merely crouched before her, keeping its face out of her lantern's light. It made mewling sounds in its throat, pitiful sounds full of hurt. It finally dawned on her that that the monster meant her no harm.

With an awkward shuffle, it had led her down a side passage and into a small alcove. It kept its distance as Mariat nervously put the lantern globe onto the floor, and then it reached with a horny claw to touch what seemed like a concave area on the ground beside it. As it did so, ripples spread out, and she realized she was looking at a small reflecting pool. The water was so still and pure, probably having filtered down through layers of rock, that it had been invisible to her. The creature motioned for her to lean over and drink.

She had been horribly thirsty, and found the faint mineral taste was not unpleasant and even seemed to strengthen her. When she looked up, wiping her mouth on her hand, the creature pulled something out of the shadows and nudged it toward her. It looked like a bundle of rags, but the creature demonstrated it was meant to be a pillow. The realization brought a pang of compassion and gratitude. She spread out her green cloak and eventually fell into an exhausted sleep. Teller's cry must have awakened her.

Now the Vora deposited Teller onto her makeshift bed, and Mariat knelt beside him. He seemed barely conscious as she gently shook his shoulders. "Teller, are you all right? Oh God, was Sheft with you?" A medallion had spilled out of his shirt, a toltyr just like Sheft's, and she tucked it back against his chest. It was then she saw an evil-looking metal collar tight around his throat. The collar repelled her, and she tried to remove it, but there was no clasp.

The creature filled a chipped crockery basin with water from the pool and holding it the only way it could, by the wrists, set it carefully beside Teller. Because its head was so bent, she still couldn't see much of its face. It settled itself opposite her and extended its poor claw, making motions that she should take off Teller's toltyr and hand it to him.

"No," she said. If it cost Teller as much to wear it as it had Sheft, she had no business giving it away.

The creature then gestured that she should take off the medallion and drop it into the basin. There could be no harm in washing the blood off, so she did that.

The Vora groaned something at her—an expression of thanks?—and managed to lift Teller's right hand into the basin.

At the sight of it she started. Oh Rulve! Teller's hand was a bloody mess of crushed bones and torn skin. A finger was missing, along with the ring he used to wear. What on earth had happened to him? And where was Sheft?

With great tenderness the creature laved Teller's hand with its claw, all the while making soft sounds in its throat. She watched as the blood from Teller's hand drifted through the water, as it tendriled around the toltyr and the creature's claw.

The hypnotic movement mesmerized her. Everything she had lately endured—the umbrak attack, the anxiety for her beloved husband, her terror at being left alone in a dark cavern, and now Teller's shocking injury—all of it suddenly seemed unreal. She stared at the slow spiral of red and black.

As if in a dream, the colors diffused, blurring the scales on the Vora's horny claw. The water, now pink, appeared to soften the sharp nails and gradually straighten the tight curves of the creature's knuckles and wrist.

Mariat blinked, and with a creaking of bones, the claw began unfurling. This couldn't be happening. Brown-nailed fingers were now scooping water over Teller's hand.

The change crept up the monster's arm. The limb seemed to deflate, and the coarse hair on it thinned. With a long tremor and a sucking, cracking sound, the arm's impossible length retracted into the Vora's shoulder. The creature shuddered violently, knocking over the basin with a clatter.

Before her very eyes, the Vora was changing. With creaks and snaps, the massive form began to shrink. The spine straightened, the neck stretched, and the head lifted. Growths fell from its face and body, plopped into the spilled water, and dissolved with it into the ground.

Mariat realized her mouth was open and closed it. A human figure was now sitting at Teller's side. Bone-thin, it turned its face to the wall.

INSIDE HIS PRIVATE AUDIENCE CHAMBER, THE Lord of Oknu Shuld continued to work with the blood-rich soil in the circle next to his throne. He smoothed a torso, a head, arms and legs. At last the sculpture was complete. It lay inside the circle, its face featureless, its arms at its sides. The lord leaned back to sit on his heels and flex his gloved, tapered fingers. "Soon," he muttered.

He took the thin chain from his belt and carefully passed it under the torso to separate it from the rock. Then he stood and addressed his work of art.

"Surzara," he commanded it. *Arise.*

Chapter 30

A Small Brave Fire

Back in Bellstone Forest, Hewish snapped off a bare low-hanging branch so it would not hit any of the people riding in single file behind him. His companions included the two elders from Eerford Village, the Bellstriker, Defender Rung, and Deoner—all going as fast as their mounts could traverse the winding, boulder-strewn trail to Galensgrave.

Although he had been there before, Hewish had never seen a Bellmoot. The last one had occurred before he was born, after 'braks had burned Sagetown and put a brutal end to the short-lived Niyalahn Rebellion. The elders of Ettebel had called that moot, for they had been the first to smell the smoke from Sagetown and understand what it meant.

He had grown up not far from the holy meeting place, and Pa had taken him twice to visit it. Today would be the first time Hewish would return there since his father was killed a year ago. Pa had died on a sunny day in Seed, much like this one. The obstinate old man knew that 'brak raiding parties were crossing the Eeron, but insisted on taking his hoe and sling bag of 'tater eyes to the sandy clearing some distance from their house. "I'll git the 'taters planted and no pig-man's goin' t'stop me," he'd said. "A fighter's gotta eat sumpin' when he can't take the time t'hunt, don't he? And there's nuthin' like a nice hot 'tater t'fill the belly."

He had found his father's body covered with blood. 'Braks had hacked at him with his own hoe and drove the splintered end into his stomach. At age thirteen, Hewish was now the man of the family.

He'd dug the grave beside those of his two older brothers, near to the honeysuckles behind their house. His ma and little sister cried when he left to join the wood-warriors, but Ma refused to move behind the sharpened log fence the elders had built around Eerford Village. Oh God, the elders should've made her. But she was a stubborn fool, his ma. Just like Pa.

It was almost dusk when they arrived at the clearing that marked the burial place of Galen Greathand, the first Bellstriker. Long ago, in this hidden spot between Eerford and Ettebel, the great leader had called the moot that had, after generations of bickering, united the forest's three glades. Now his bones rested under the circular stone table in the center of the clearing.

None of the others were here yet, and the place lay steeped in quiet. Their whole party knelt for a moment in respect, then everyone turned to their own tasks. Deoner and Rung set up the tents and tie line for the horses, while Gurvale, using a twiggy branch, brushed last year's summer leaves off the stone table. She did the same for the three long benches that formed a triangle around Galen's grave. Carved out of single great tree-trunks, the benches were large enough to seat the entire delegation from each glade.

Hewish was set to building a campfire, which he soon had burning brightly in the dusk. The elders prepared a simple meal for everyone, and the smell of roasting venison floated through the already frosty air.

Earlier that day, when Deoner was meeting with the others inside Rung's tent, Hewish had lingered quietly outside. Gurvale's talk had angered him. The Bellstriker was supposed to fill their hearts with courage and resolve, not with doubt-filled drivel.

Now she must have noticed his stony face, for she came to sit beside him at their supper. "You heard what I said in the tent," Gurvale said.

"I did. But all know what you think. Since you rung the stone, all know how you've changed."

She said nothing for several moments, then touched his boot with the toe of her shoe. He had taken the boots off the 'brak he had clubbed three nights ago. "Killin' that one didna bring your father back. Nor your little sis."

He jerked his foot away and tore a chunk out of his bread. "'Tis one less t'kill another's dad. And I aim t'get at least one more, for her."

"Ah." Gurvale sighed and turned her head away. Almost as if she were talking to herself, she muttered, "There's na end to it, is there?"

The campfire snapped as tiny, sharp flames bit down on the twigs. "There's an end," he said. "When they're all dead, it'll be an end."

Her forearms resting on her knees, Gurvale held a cup of water between her hands and stared into the fire. "And so we keep lookin' for justice and settlin' for revenge."

The sun had already sunk behind the hillside, and twilight was seeping out of the trees, like Rulve's blanket, Pa used to say, coverin' up him and his little sister for the night. The soft settle of evening used to bring peace to his heart, but now it brought only emptiness.

Gurvale levered herself to a standing position and looked down on him. Her eyes were bleak. "I dinna think one emjadi can accomplish what Rulve gave 'em both to do. No single person can bear the justice a' God."

She left him sitting alone. As it so often did when no one was around, his little sister's face formed behind his eyes. If only she was safely dead, lying next to his brothers and Pa. Then he could plant a rose bush over her. He'd looked for one with pink flowers, in sunny places at the edge of the forest, but never found it.

The tents melted into the darkness that gathered under the silent oaks. A cold night crept in, shrinking the size of their camp and encroaching upon their small brave fire.

MARIAT STARED AT WHAT HAD BEEN, only minutes ago, a monster. Now it was a man, or what certainly resembled a man. He sat silent, his head bowed. She caught a glimpse of a brown, age-lined forehead.

Perhaps he could not speak. Mariat rose and moved to his side. He tried to hide his face, but Mariat turned it toward the light and tilted his chin up. He flung up his arm, but allowed it.

For the first time, she saw his mouth. Oh dear Rulve, it had been stitched shut. With his awkward claws, there was nothing he could have done about it. This was cruelty beyond belief.

Gently, she reached out to touch the black threads. "Let me cut these away for you."

The man did not react, so she picked up Teller's dagger, and as carefully as she could, began cutting the stitches away. Because he had shrunk so much, they hung loosely, but still they had to be pulled out. The thread was thick and coarse, and removing it must have hurt him, but the man never flinched.

When she finished, however, the poor man swayed. She dropped the dagger to steady him until she was sure he wouldn't fall over. "All right," she said, "now I'll have to clean off your mouth." She wet a corner of her sleeve in the pool and carefully dabbed at the man's injuries. If only she had healoil or burvena, but her small pack of medicines had been lost. Mariat sat back on her heels and surveyed the man from top to bottom. "I suppose it wasn't important before, sir—you were so bent over and all—but now the matter should be addressed. You have no clothes on."

Slowly, as if his neck were sore, he lowered his head and looked down at himself.

"Here," Mariat said, "use this." She pulled a strip of rag out of the pillow under Teller's head and held it out to him. He didn't seem to know what to do with it, so Mariat wound it around his waist and tied it at the side. "I'm Mariat, Sheft's"—she had to swallow down a sudden lump in her throat—"Sheft's wife. Teller here is my brother-in-law. Who are you, sir?"

He didn't answer, only stared at the toltyr lying among the cracked shards of the basin.

Mariat picked it up, wiped it on her green cloak, and placed it once more over Teller's head. The throat lump swelled again as she remembered doing the same for Sheft, on that beautiful evening when they had been—so impossibly, so wondrously—reunited in the henge.

TELLER OPENED HIS EYES. AFTER SEVERAL breaths he realized that his hand, lying on his chest, no longer throbbed. As far as he could tell in the meager light, the skin was bruised and scraped, but the crushed bones seemed whole again. He could flex his remaining fingers, and the base of the missing one had healed over. What—?

Someone helped him sit up, a weathered rod of a man he had never seen before. Someone else touched his arm. It was Mariat, handing him a cup of water. "I-I thought—" he choked out.

"Drink first, then we can talk."

He started to gulp the water down, but choked against the tight ahn collar.

She touched the metal ring with the tip of a finger. "What is this?"

He pushed her hand away. "A slave collar."

At his tone, Mariat met his eyes. "But you wear the toltyr now," she said.

It was lying outside his ahn-shirt, and even the sight of it, and her kindness, did little to relieve his humiliation. The collar clearly proclaimed what he had always been: the property of the Lord of Oknu Shuld. He felt heat creep up his cheeks. More carefully now, he drained the cup. "I thought you were dead," he croaked. "I thought the 'braks killed you."

"No one hurt me," Mariat said, and as if she had just realized this, a kind of puzzled wonder dawned in her eyes. "I'm—intact." She briefly touched the base of his missing finger. "But you aren't. What happened, Teller?"

He gestured futilely. "The vol-ring. It was the only way I could get rid of it. It's…it's a long story, Mariat. But how did you get here? Did the subaltern—did the 'braks—?"

She told him everything, ending with the strange creature, now a man, who had helped them both. Teller turned to study him. His features seemed familiar: the square face and planed cheekbones, the slightly hooked nose, the lips that would be thin if they hadn't swelled so much.

And then, with a chill of shock, he saw it: This man had eyes. Pale amethyst eyes. That was why he didn't immediately recognize him. "You're his brother," Teller breathed. "You must be the twin brother of the Lord of Oknu Shuld."

Chapter 31

The Simulacrum

THE LORD WATCHED CLOSELY AS THE simulacrum, lying on the now scoured circular depression beside his throne, trembled. The featureless head lifted, the elbows bent. With a faint squelching sound, it sat upright. The lord extended his hand, and as if it were a mirror image, the form did likewise. The Eyascnu pulled his creation to its feet.

They stood close together, facing each other: the Lord of Oknu Shuld and the rusty-black mud-form quivering with repressed roots.

"I would embrace you," the lord murmured. "I would embrace you now." He leaned toward the form, then abruptly stepped back. He must wait; now was not the time.

At his gesture, the volghasts glided to his side. One carried the dead vora's ahn-collar in its leather-encased hand. The lord tenderly placed the collar around the simulacrum's neck. He said a word, and the collar snapped shut.

The lord turned away to address the volghasts. "My Apotheosis will take place at the ninth high-gong tomorrow. Consult with Kuat regarding the arrangements. I want everyone gathered in the Hall of the

Eye: every archon, altern and quad-captain, every rista, resident scholar, and foreign visitor. Command Alterns Moverik and Shulay to summon my loyalists from Rydle and Baenfeld and all the estates between. Make sure they understand that no excuses will be accepted. Now take this form to the hidden room behind my throne in the Hall of the Eye. Guard my living sculpture well until the ceremony."

The volghasts turned the black figure toward the door, and in their midst the simulacrum shuffled out. The lord sank onto his throne. In the dim silence he leaned his head back and spread out his arms, as if to encompass all of Oknu Shuld. Then with a smile he opened them wider, to a now possible far greater realm. He had restored everything that had been stolen from him, and now skora and s'rere were his. He was invincible.

Now he must gather himself for the ceremony next rota. He made his way through the workroom adjoining his private audience chamber and down the secret tunnel that led to a small, unadorned room. There he sat in his cushioned chair and allowed his carefully summoned sight to slip away. There he sat in blackness that passed for dreamless sleep.

Chapter 32

Varo

As Teller gazed into the man's strange eyes, mindwords began flowing into his head.

"My name is Varo," the man said. "My brother and I were born as you were, T'lir: the living toltyr, the s'eft and t'lir of Rulve's Coin."

For Teller, it was as if all the air in the tunnel rushed out. "What!" he exclaimed.

"Our story is told in the Tajemjadi. You copied the words yourself."

Teller remembered the room of the skulls, where Kuat had set him to transcribing ancient pages that alluded to a tragic conflict of the past.

"We were born niyalahn-rista," Varo continued, "born with s'rere and sh'kier, precious abilities to spend on the land, to spend in service to the people. But my brother did not wish to be spent. 'He chose to live for his own will.'"

The last sentence. It was a quote from the *Tajemjadi*. He had carefully inscribed it onto the page, but never allowed it to penetrate his understanding.

Mariat touched his sleeve. "What's going on, Teller? He's not talking, but it looks like you're listening to him."

Teller explained about the mind-speech and what had just been revealed in it, then turned back to Varo. "Can you speak aloud, so she might hear?"

Varo touched his swollen lips with the back of his hand. "I will try." With a finger, he scooped up a bit of the mud formed when the basin had broken and smeared it onto his swollen lips. As it sunk in, the balm seemed to help him pronounce certain words.

"Our names," he continued, "were Eyascamen and V-Varo: 'True-sight' and 'B-beacon.' But my twin spit on his name, for to him it was a cruel jest. He saw compassion as pity, and hated those who gave it. He refused help. Born without eyes, he contrived to see through sorcery."

"What about sh'kier and s'rere?" Teller asked. "What about the powers Rulve gave you?"

Varo stared at the writhing worms in the lantern on the cave floor. "In the violence between us they b-bled away. In our hatred they were destroyed."

"The Lord of Shunder," Teller said to Mariat, "always claimed his brother was corrupted by evil and that he was forced to turn against his own twin. Every rista in Oknu Shuld knew the story. We all had to memorize the lord's autobiography, the *L'garza Wadek*."

Varo passed a long-fingered hand over his eyes. "Rulve created us inter-dependent. To help each other. But my b-brother perceived our twin-ness as weakness. He desired the strength of the whole. He claimed no kingdom could be strong if its powers were divided. To him, I was the favored son, who plotted against him.

As Varo spoke, Teller realized that the Lord of Oknu Shuld, as did every tyrant since the beginning of time, had sought justification for his actions by declaring himself the victim. Celume had been right; the more one studied the events outlined in the *L'garza*, the more distorted they became.

"We fought," Varo went on, "and I lost. We b-both lost. Yet my brother claimed victory. He took the name of Eyascnu, 'no-eyes'. It was defiance, to proclaim that his power was greater than any weakness." Varo's clenched fist pressed against his chest. "I also hated. My twin built upon that. He forced potions down my throat. He changed me. Into the v-vora he was b-becoming. He turned me into the mirror of his soul, and then despised me."

With a start, Teller realized that he had heard Varo's agony. The long years of torture, the groans—he had heard them through the floor vent in his room at night. He'd dreamed—he'd feared—that it was happening to himself, that in the depths of Oknu Shuld he was being made into a monster. And in large part the Spider-king had succeeded, perhaps not as much as he had with Varo, but enough. Shame at what he had done and what he had failed to do swelled against Teller's ahn-collar. He could not condemn the Spider-king without condemning himself.

"Then it b-began," Varo continued. "The slow redemption, set in motion. Vol Kuat heard…my pain. He came to me."

"Out of pity?" Teller looked up in astonishment.

"At my plea. That the evil of Oknu Shuld might be overcome."

"But why?" Teller asked. "Why would Vol Kuat agree to such a thing?" Pain flared in his spirikai, where the fire used to be, and he drew up his knees against it.

"He is Rûk, the king of the Riftwood. He would preserve his realm from any who would destroy it."

"The man who brought me here is king of the Riftwood?" Mariat exclaimed.

"Vol Kuat is no king," Teller protested. "He's the Delver. No one knows his true name. He's the lord's fourth Vol." Yet...yet the lord had always related very oddly to this Kuat. As if he were unknowingly reacting to the power of an equal. The Delver's aloofness, his lengthy disappearances, his strange duality—it all fell into place. Vol Kuat was the shadow-king, delving and devising to protect his realm.

"His consort," Varo continued, "b-beseeched him. Marhaut did not want my twin to destroy the Seani."

"But Varo," Mariat said, "being here for so long, in the dark and alone, how could you know anything about Teller?"

Varo turned his leathery face toward her. "Riah was sent to me," he said. "Rulve sent her." His hands made futile, rolling gestures, as if they could pull out the words. "Riah's sons." He leaned forward to look full face at Teller. "My sons."

Teller sat very still as the cave seemed to tilt and then straighten. His father was Neal. His grandmother had told him that. Ever since he could remember, his father had been Neal, the green-eyed man who loved children.

But a green-eyed man had lured a six-year-old child out of the Seani, had changed into a monstrous wyvern in front of his eyes, had condemned him to thirteen years in the depths of Oknu Shuld.

At his side, Mariat seemed to be struggling. "What are you *saying*?" she breathed.

"I hoped," Varo said in a quavering voice, "that a new Coin would b-be born, to replace the one we lost. New niyal'arists, to do what we should have done."

"You raped her! When Riah was imprisoned in this place. Sheft told me something happened to her here, but…she always said his father was Neal."

Varo stared at her, his eyes shining with tears. "Not rape, Mariat. Never that. To engender. To atone. While I was still human, still a man. To plant in a Se's daughter a seed that could save us all."

Words from the *Tajemjadi* came back to Teller, and he quoted them in a low voice. "*'Evil will fall upon the land. But the people will cry out to Rulve, and she will hear them, and in his mercy she will call forth the niyalahn-ristas always yet again.'*"

What Varo told him answered a painful question that had haunted him for years. On that terrible day, when he was six and ran outside the Seani gates to help the man he believed to be his father, how could the shape-shifting Delver have lied to him in the mind-speech? The fact that he apparently had done so formed the first deep crack in Teller's ability to trust.

But the Delver hadn't lied. He had demanded Teller's help in truth, not only for Varo, Teller's true father, but also for his own Riftwood realm. The Delver had abducted him, stolen his life, stood by to watch his corruption, but never lied to him.

"Varo," Mariat implored, "are you telling me that it was through Rulve's *mercy* that…that my husband, and Teller here, were born? That you are my father-in-law?"

Varo seemed to deflate, and he slumped back against the cave wall. "It was her mercy for Shunder. But for me," he moved his arm to encompass the dim cave in which they sat, "it was his justice."

Teller struggled to encompass Varo's revelations. Varo—the lord's twin brother, the failed niyal'arist, the creature he had heard groaning through the floor vent while he tossed and turned on his bed, the monster who tore prisoners apart and slurped their blood—that one was his father.

The one Rulve had redeemed.

The truth swirled dizzily around him, but another reality was growing in his spirikai. The grinding pain there had intensified, and now it was spreading to his abdomen, streaking down his thighs. It brought the sharp realization that no matter what he felt, it was only a shadow of what his brother was facing when they had parted. He had to go back to him. "Varo," he said. "Take us to where Sheft is."

Mariat turned her head toward him, two grooves digging into her forehead. "What do you mean? Where is he?"

Something heavy filled Teller's throat, and he couldn't answer.

Varo gently touched her hand. "My son is gone," he said.

Mariat looked at him as if through a long tunnel. "Gone?"

Varo nodded.

Teller saw Mariat's eyes change. It was as if she felt what he did: an ominous gap, the numbness between receiving a wound and feeling it.

"Come," Varo said. He reached out to Teller and, with strong hands as dry and creased as old leather, pulled him to his feet. Mariat grabbed her cloak and the lantern, and together they left the alcove.

Following Varo, Teller told his sister-in-law what had happened to him and Sheft since the umbraks had captured her in the Riftwood. He started with his own acceptance of the toltyr and ended with the vision that had propelled the two of them to come willingly to Oknu Shuld. Then he stopped.

Mariat touched his hand. "Please go on, Teller."

He looked away from her anxious face. He couldn't give her any comfort but had to give her what he could. "Guards took to us to the Lord of Oknu Shuld's private audience chamber," he said, still not looking at her. "I lost skora there, Mariat. Then Sheft and I were…we were separated, and," he finished quickly, "I didn't see him after that."

He glanced at Mariat and saw she wasn't satisfied, that questions still filled her eyes. But he couldn't go on, and once more looked stolidly ahead.

Varo led them through the cavern, and although Teller was sure the gate had been locked behind him, it now hung open. From far above came the dim sound of a gong, striking nine times. It had been a high gong for morning, not the deeper gong rung after noon. He could still tell the difference. Oknu Shuld was still with him, still in his blood.

CHAPTER 33

INSIDE

AS THE HIGH GONG STRUCK NINE times, the front gates of Oknu Shuld opened, and the large audience, buzzing with speculations, flooded in. Many had attended numerous Acclamations and Cloaking Ceremonies—events always good for business—but none of them knew what an Apotheosis was, or how it would affect their financial interests.

Some of them had been shivering in the cold for hours as they waited outside gates glittering with frost. When finally admitted, they discovered that, with so many people invited, there was no room for seating. So, to everyone's dismay, they all had to stand.

Huge crimson-veined globes, filled with the brightest luniku larvae, glared down from the high ceiling like bloodshot eyes. They cast red glints off the lord's massive ebony throne, big enough for two men but now empty, ensconced on the wide dais in front. Even more discomfiting than the globes was the artifact built into the wall above the lord's throne. Flames jumped behind the red glass of the Igneous Eye, the only fire in Oknu Shuld. Its hot gaze flickered over the crowd like a probing reptile tongue.

A line of Vorian Guards stood at the edge of the dais, the purple plumes on their helmets stirring as their heads turned to watch the crowd. Three steps below them, level with the marble floor, stood a cadre of military officers. These included the five men entitled to wear the sable cape: three archons who headed the three divisions of the lord's army and two alterns who ruled the towns of Rydle and Baenfeld.

Next came the civilians. First were the foreign guests and scholars residing in the sumptuous apartments on Oknu Shuld's level four, followed by the local wealthy, their eyes constantly scanning to see who had been invited and who had not. Dressed in their finest, they pushed for the front places where they could see and be seen.

This group consisted of town magistrates and aldermen appointed by the Lord of Shunder, landlords who owned most of the houses and shops and set the rents, morue distributors, those who collected license fees from shamans, vintners, and brewers, and tax-collectors whose income included whatever taxes, in addition to those imposed by the lord, that could be squeezed from farmers and small shop owners.

The lord's glover, who controlled leatherworks in both Rydle and Baenfeld, found a place among the most prominent. He stroked his sharp chin as he exchanged pleasantries with Preya. She stood behind her father Moverik, altern of Rydle, who regally nodded at those around him.

Behind these prominent guests, teachers in their blue robes mingled with rista students. Those of lower rank—food distributors, moneylenders, and suppliers of globes, armor, horses, and weapons—were relegated to the back.

Seeking entertainment, soldiers on rotation came and went in the side hall, pushing their way between the arches to see what was going on. Unlucky latecomers, who lived as far away as Baenfeld and had received the summons later than the others, crowded in the vestibule between the guardrooms, blinking as the great doors behind them closed against the morning light. Red-cloaked subaltern guards moved into place at the rear, forming a crimson wall.

The hall was agog with rumors regarding the niyal'arist voras who had yesterday been paraded through the Rydle streets. One of them, someone claimed, was Vol Cinc. Impossible. Many here had witnessed his Acclamation. But where was he? Come to think of it, where were the other Vols? Since nothing was happening yet on the dais, people conversed in low voices, their eyes darting about.

Activity on the dais stopped their whispers. Some in the back rose on tiptoe to see a line of drummers, clad in black and silver, file in and stand against the wall behind the throne. The ceremony was finally about to begin.

THE CLIMB UP THE LONG NARROW steps was arduous at best, but the growing ache in Teller's spirikai forced him to stop all too often. At last they emerged from the cavern behind the lord's private audience chamber.

They stopped behind the lord's throne, which was empty, and under the dim purple light the chamber before them lay in silence. The smell of blood and burned skin scraped across the back of Teller's throat. He reached for his green dagger, but found it must have been lost somewhere in the dark of Varo's prison. No guards were posted, however, and no volghasts lurked along the walls.

"Wait here." Pushing Mariat behind him, he moved toward the circle beside the throne.

All the earth had been scraped out of the rocky depression. Sheft lay on his side at one edge, his back toward them, his tangled hair shining in the light of a nearby globe. Red-brown cuts and streaks of mud covered his body. His right hand was still shackled to the iron stake; his left hand lay open, his fingers slightly curled. The sound of a caught breath behind Teller made him turn. Mariat had followed him. He quickly tried to block her view, but he was too late.

Her hand at her mouth, she stood there, staring. "No," she moaned softly. "Oh no." She pushed past Teller and fell to her knees beside her husband. "Oh God. Oh dear God, what have they done to you?" Mariat reached out to touch him, but stopped with her hands helpless in the air. Anguish twisted her face as her eyes traveled over her beloved's body. "Everywhere they have hurt you! Oh my dearest. Oh Sheft!" She pressed her arms against her stomach, as if it had been cut open, and rocked back and forth.

The sight of his brother's wounds sawed through Teller's stomach. Where Sheft hadn't been cut, where mud and blood hadn't dried, patches of skin gleamed a bluish-white. He knelt beside his brother and gently turned him onto his back. His ahn-collar was gone, to be used on someone else. On top of his other wounds, seared over Sheft's spirikai, lay a raw, red burn.

It could only be from skora. His skora. Wielded by the Spider-king to burn the ice out of Sheft.

Oh God Rulve. He bent and took his brother's shackled hand in both of his. *Oh God, Sheft. I should have been here. I should have been here to help you die. I would have laid the warmth gently on you. I would have helped you bleed, helped you before you endured all this.*

Across from him, Mariat took up Sheft's free hand and, still rocking, pressed it against her cheek. "Oh Sheft," she moaned. "Oh dear heart. You can't stay like this." She pulled off her green cloak and tenderly covered Sheft with it, tucking the edges under his hips and shoulders. With tear-stained cheeks, she looked up at Teller. "My mother gave me this cloak," she said. "Not long before she died. Sheft was there, and it was getting dark, and my father said," her face crumpled, "he said, 'Time you be leaving us, Sheft.'"

Her voice gave out, and shaking with sobs, she stretched over her husband's body and put her arms around him and tears fell into his hair.

Under the heaviness of rock and shadows, Teller's grief carved its painful way through the tightness inside him. Sheft had been the first to take up the toltyr, the first to keep Rulve deep in his heart. *I once had the fire, my brother, but you always had the light.*

After a while, Varo spoke, and Teller raised his head. Sheft's father had placed his hand on Mariat's shoulder and Teller heard the quaver of loss in the old man's voice. "We must go now," Varo said to her. "The power is growing in Teller. My son will not b-be able to wait much longer."

Mariat had pressed her forehead against the base of Sheft's throat and did not look up. "I can't leave him! I won't leave him in this dark place."

"It is not dark where he is."

"We were just married! He was niyalahn-rista. Oh God, his life was wasted."

"Can anything b-be wasted that was poured into Rulve's hands?"

"I accepted his mission. I said put Rulve's will first and then ours. But I didn't know it would be like this!" Another sob choked out of her, and she tightened her arms around Sheft. "I did what Rulve wanted. Now he must do what I want. He must allow me," she broke off, squeezing her eyes shut and her throat working, "to choose the time of my dying." Still on her knees, she straightened her back to look up at the rocky ceiling. "I choose now, Rulve, to follow Sheft."

"You cannot."

She turned as Varo bent over her and looked into her eyes. "Inside," he said quietly. He touched her abdomen. "Sheft-daughter, Mariat-son."

For a long moment she stared up at Varo, unheeded tears coursing down her cheeks.

A memory broke open in Teller. Celume had foreseen this. She saw three Coins: one long broken, one to be spent, and one yet to be born.

"It is a long journey," Varo said, "to the fullness of 'yes.' You helped Sheft endure it. You surrendered to Rulve's will. And now, in different ways, the Creator has granted both of you new life."

Mariat turned back to her husband, her heart in her eyes. She placed her hand gently over his covered groin, then leaned over to kiss him there. "He says you're a father, Sheft. He says we made babies." A tremulous smile played over her lips, but it fell into a contortion of grief. "My dear heart," she whispered. "My beloved heart." She kissed his cheek, his eyelids, and ran her fingers lightly over his mouth. Her face a mask of anguish, she pressed her cheek against his chest and held him.

Varo touched her shoulder. "We must leave, Mariat."

She gave her husband one last squeeze, then knelt up straight and wiped her eyes on the back of her wrists. Tenderly she removed Sheft's bloodstained toltyr and put it around her neck. "Free him," she pleaded, looking up at Varo. "Carry him out of this terrible place."

"He is already free. And long gone from here." Varo stooped beside Sheft and placed his hand on his son's head. "His body is the seed, a healing laid upon Shunder's greatest wound." He turned to Mariat. "Thank you for allowing him to do this."

A pressing imperative rose up in Teller. "I will bury him, Mariat," he rasped. "I promise I will bury him." The words caught in his throat. "And beauty and peace will forever mark his grave." He knelt there bereft, stripped of fire and wearing an ahn-collar; but somehow he would do it.

Mariat looked steadily at him, her eyes swimming in tears, and then climbed to her feet.

But Teller found he could not do likewise. The pain in his spirikai flared up so badly he almost cried out. Deep inside, something was happening to him.

CHAPTER 34

APOTHEOSIS

THE PULSE-POUNDING SOUND OF DRUMS FILLED the Hall of the Eye. From the archway at the right of the dais, guards marched in three prisoners clad in rough grey tunics, their hands tied behind them.

Startled murmurs spread through the crowd. They were Volarachs! Vol Ségun, pale and stick-thin, his fingers bare of any of his famous rings, trembled violently. The feared Vol Tierce stared stonily ahead, a muscle at the side of his mouth occasionally twitching. The third, the one holding himself ramrod straight, why he must be Vol Prome! They had never seen him unhooded, never seen the thick, raised veins and ugly scars that covered his face and bald head.

The drums stopped abruptly. All three Vols were made to kneel on the second step of the dais, facing the empty throne. Behind their backs, whispers rose among the dignitaries. Why had these three powerful underlords fallen from favor? Did this signal a change in the profit web that had benefited them for so long?

The drums rolled again, and four entities seemed to emerge from the tall wall-carvings behind the throne. They stalked forward, like dead warriors recently exhumed, but the eyes that faced the crowd glowed red. Their appearance froze speculation into alarm, and the whisper "volghasts!" swirled around the great hall. The horror that seeped out of them, and the smell, quickly brought silence. It was an uneasy silence, like mist that curled over the deceptively solid surface of a peat bog. Several of the wealthiest spectators moved from one foot to the other, as if they were uncertain of the ground on which they stood.

The tallest volghast stepped forward and raised its gauntleted hand. "Kneel in reverence for the Lord of Shunder." His voice was not loud and held no emotion whatsoever, but it swept like a chill to the very back of the Hall. The audience fell to its knees in one long wave.

With another thunder of drums, a door to the left of the throne burst open. A black mist poured out, covering the dais ankle deep. This had never happened before, and the crowd stirred warily. Vol Kuat emerged and took a place on the far right of the dais.

Next, a reddish-black figure appeared, looking for all the world as if it were made of mud. Entirely featureless and wearing only an ahn-collar, it was escorted by one of the volghasts to the very edge of the round carpet beside the throne. It stood there, unmoving, but every inch of its skin seemed to tremble—or was it a trick of the crawling light? The figure was a disturbing sight, but its ahn-collar reassured the crowd. Whatever it was, the lord controlled it.

The tall volghast flung out an arm. "Behold what remains of the niyal'arist vora. Behold it now in thrall to the lord."

People craned their necks to see. Was this black thing really the niyalahn-rista that killed the lord's brother? Had it been hunted down at last? Was it a vora, disguised as one of those young men who had been dragged through Rydle only yesterday? Glances met among the dignitaries, exchanging disbelief or suspicion or alarm, and quickly leaped away. The creature was what the volghast said it was.

"The lord sculpted this simulacrum with his own hands," the volghast continued. "He formed it into a vessel brimming with s'rere, with the blood that makes the earth dance."

As if with a sudden wind, the mist on the dais swirled, and out of it stepped the Lord of Shunder. He stood facing them from the far side of the carpet. But he was not the same lord they had seen before. His tight-fitting gloves—a fashion affected by many of the dignitaries present and which had enriched the glover—were the same. But instead of a luxurious but relatively plain silk shirt and tapered trousers, he wore a short-sleeved black velvet robe, thickly embroidered with deep-purple morue flowers at the neck, down the front, and around the hem. His usual simple coronet of twisted silver wires had been replaced by a black onyx crown studded with amethysts. His red lips, no longer curved in an affable smile, formed an uncompromising line.

But what caused eyes to widen throughout the hall was the mask. Under the crown, and hiding the entire top half of the lord's face, was a mask covered with short, spiky quills that surrounded eight obsidian stones. How could he see? Yet he strode forward with complete confidence, the round black crystals glittering eerily like spider eyes.

The crowd froze. This ceremony was going beyond a demand for fealty, beyond mutually beneficial business arrangements, and even beyond the search for revenge. This ceremony was frightening them.

"Behold," the volghast intoned, "the Lord of Shunder. With you all to witness, he will now enter into his Apotheosis."

IN THE LORD'S PRIVATE AUDIENCE CHAMBER, one level above and deeper inside the cliff, Teller tried to get up from his knees.

Varo bent over him. "The pain is that of sh'kier, my son. The fire is growing in you."

"It can't be," Teller gasped, pressing both hands over his spirikai. "The lord took everything."

"He took skora. Sh'kier he could not take."

"I don't understand."

"Skora is but the scabbard. That is all my b-brother saw in you, and that was all he took."

Teller tried to remember what Avia had said about sh'kier at the Weshnika. Something about it being the fire, not so much of justice, but of balance, that it came like a lightning bolt to rip through lies and cruelty. The Se used many words to describe it, words that meant nothing compared to what raged inside him.

"I participated in too much evil," Teller choked out, "allowed too much of it to persist around me and never stopped it. If Rulve laid sh'kier inside me, it will be—twisted." The ahn-collar pressed against the swell of emotion in his throat, and he pulled fruitlessly at it.

"Perhaps. Perhaps something of skora will always taint it. But in reality, Rulve's greatest power is her deep love. His providence redeems all things, even what we perceive as intended evil. Did not my b-brother Eyascnu release the sh'kier in you that was destroyed in me? Did he not free your twin from the ice that blocked s'rere?"

For a moment Teller caught the blessed vision: how weakness swirled with grace, failure with salvation. And in very truth, didn't one niyal'arist help the other die?

But then that other part of him, the ingrained darker part that questioned, that needed incontrovertible proof, objected. *If Varo's perceptions were true, what is there to show for it?*

He hurt too much to sort it out. "Sh'kier is too strong for me. I-I can't stand up under it."

"It is your power, niyal'arist, and you must wield it. What do you feel, T'lir?"

His brother's ruined body lay before him, and every wound in it cried out for revenge. Anger flared at the scathi turd-king he had served for thirteen years, at the coward who had murdered an innocent man who desired nothing but to give up everything; anger all the more cutting because there was no skora to carry it, no fire to burn what his rage demanded.

He wanted to cut, burn, kill as Sheft had been cut and burned and killed. Red rage swept over his grief. Teller clenched his fist, as if it held his green dagger, as if the blade were ripping down the Spider-king's chest, to do to him what he had done to Sheft.

"Your anger goes even deeper, my son. To when you were only six years old, when you had just been brought into Oknu Shuld."

Oh God, it went back thirteen years! To the vow made in the rock-bound interrogation room, where he learned to hate. They would all burn. For what they had done, then and now, they would all burn. They had no right, no right to torture and uproot and destroy. No right to seize a six-year-old child and tear out his soul. He'd sear them out of existence for that, burn them alive while they screamed.

Varo touched his arm, and suddenly Teller saw what was happening. Another niyal'arist raged once more, seethed with murder in his veins. The vicious edge of hatred was cutting him away from his promise to Rulvc.

"Go deeper, emjadi. Into the place where 'I" was once "we."

"That place is gone! I was reunited with my brother for less than a week."

"Go to where you used to find Sheft. Go there, niyal'arist."

COMPLETE SILENCE DESCENDED UPON THE HALL of the Eye. The lord stepped around the carpet to face the simulacrum. A languid, ethereal snake of mist curled around and between them. Then a lone drum thudded—*boom-BOOM, boom-BOOM*—like the collective heartbeat of the crowd.

The Eyascnu took a step forward, and so did the black form. Now two drums pounded. *BOOM-boom-boom, BOOM-boom-boom.* With each step, another joined in. As the space between the Lord of Shunder and the simulacrum decreased, all the drums beat louder, faster, sweeping up every heartbeat, until the two figures stood on the center of the carpet, only a hand's-breadth apart.

The mud-form shuddered, its arms hanging at its sides. The lord pulled it close, shoulder to shoulder and knee to knee, and clasped it to his chest. Mud oozed, and with the drums thundering and every pulse racing, the two shapes blurred. The simulacrum wore a crown, the Lord of Oknu Shuld the collar of an ahn. Power trembled over the dais like black sheet lightning, and the two shapes merged.

Abruptly, the drums stopped. No one breathed. An ahn-collar fell onto the carpet. Alone now on the dais, untouched by any trace of mud, the Lord of Shunder turned to face the audience. The blood-red lips beneath the spider-mask stretched into a deadly smile.

"Acclaim your emperor," all the drummers cried. "Acclaim the King of Shunder, the Thakur of the Riftwood and Master of Bellstone Forest!"

The lord flung up his hands. He released his subjects

from their pent-up breath and drove them into a wild and harrowed applause.

LIFE SURGED INTO THE LORD, SWIRLING into his arms, his fingers, his face. It rushed through his veins, pulsing with energy, with the power of the earth. He tore off his gloves, and his sorcerer's vision saw healthy new flesh. Two spots under his mask tingled, in places where eyes soon would appear.

Through the mist, his people gaped up at him. Fear and awe furrowed their faces, but it was only the beginning. They were trembling on the edge of understanding. He was now their king, but would soon be their god.

He swept his arm to the side and the mist around him fled. All must see clearly what was about to occur. He positioned himself directly under the Igneous Eye, removed his crown, and handed it to a waiting volghast.

"Behold the Eyasc-perjabik!" the lord cried, "he of the Piercing Eyes! Behold the Nihilarist, the one, the true, Emjadi of Shunder."

With a sweeping motion, he ripped the mask off.

VARO GRASPED TELLER'S SHOULDER, AND HIS father's compassion shimmered inside Teller. It gently assuaged his complicated emotions. He followed them down, into the deepest place he knew: the spirals of his spirikai.

The end of his link with Sheft remained there, unwinding into the dark. Sheft's memory lingered there, a quiet whisper in the night. *Niyal'arist.*

Just a word, but his only peace. The core of his brother and himself. The word melted anger away and laid bare the essential wound they once had shared.

It throbbed with the pain of a niyal, her most intimate bond forever torn away; with the shame of an ahn, degraded by slavery; with the tragedy of a rista, his power corrupted.

It spilled into the anguish of parents forced to give up their child, of villagers whose honest love for the land had been twisted into compliance with evil. The soil cried out to him. Morue debased him. The abuse of power plowed him into the ground.

This is how Rulve suffered. He ached with the pain of an entire land, with the helplessness of its people. She knew the ahn-collar, tight around her throat. *"I have no hands, T'lir; only a heart."*

But Rulve's desire for healing ran side by side with his own craving for revenge. Oh God, how could he keep the two apart, keep the black current from polluting— once again—the light?

"Remember, my son, what I forgot. You are the servant of sh'kier, not its master."

Teller looked up and searched Varo's lined face. He saw there the bleakness, and yet the hope.

"I understand the challenge, T'lir, even though I did not meet it; for I was t'lir myself."

They were two bearers of Rulve's fire, the father who had fallen and the son now sent to redeem.

Teller fumbled at his neck. He encountered first the metal collar. In Oknu Shuld he had always worn it, in truth if not in fact. It was the part of the toltyr he had most rejected. The part that called for his complete abandonment to a loving will. His fingers then felt the medallion, the flame on one side and the leaf on the other. He grasped it tightly, and all it meant.

There had been enough failure. As he had once done to Rivere, he put out his hand to Varo. This time his true father took it, and helped him climb to his feet.

CHAPTER 35

NIHILARIST

GASPS SHOT THROUGH THE HALL OF the Eye as the crowd stared at the horror that was the lord's face. He had no eyes! Nothing but a smooth elongated forehead above his nose.

By the twin voras, what was this? A few suspected a trick, some malevolent test, and looked toward the doors—solidly guarded. But most people could not pull their terrified, fascinated gazes away from the lord's face. Under the glowering light, a hush descended.

The Eyascnu Varo straightened his onyx crown, held out his arms with a confident smile, and waited. Below his forehead, in the places where eyes should be, two black spirals emerged. They began to circle inward, as if screwing holes into the lord's skin. A red ember appeared in each center, and a hard black sliver grew in its depths. Cries rang out as those closest to the dais saw what was happening.

"Voralmighty!"

"Look there! By Ázu and Rûk, look there!"

The embers smoldered down to pale amethyst irises; the slivers grew into vertical pupils like a snake's. The newly reamed eyes bulged as they filled with liquid. Lids formed, and the eyes blinked. In the perspective of many kneeling before the lord, the two horrible eyes formed the base of a narrow triangle with the great red Eye above. They moved experimentally, looking to the right and left, then out at them all. Intensely focused power burned out from the lord's gaze, and some of his subjects screamed and flung their arms over their faces.

"My friends need not fear me," the lord said. But then his voice changed into a roar. "But my enemies cannot withstand me!"

The soulless eyes turned upon the three kneeling Vols, two of whom shook violently. The lord raised his arm, and again the crowd gasped. He held a sword of fire, a sword with a blade of flame.

Cries of "skora! skora!" fled through the hall.

The lord laughed, stepped forward, and struck. Three heads tumbled to the dais and the bodies toppled after. Blood spattered the lord's polished leather boots and dripped down the steps. "I have no need of such Vols!" he cried. "No need of their plots and betrayals. They served for a time as the fingers of my hand, but now my hand is full of strength!"

A few glances cut to where the mysterious Vol Kuat was standing at the far right of the dais, but he remained impassive, evidently loyal and therefore spared.

The lord raised the sword in one hand and displayed the other with fingers curved like a claw. "The time of laxity is over. No longer shall greedy traitors suck the life from my kingdom! No longer will grasping fingers paw at our rightful taxes and rents!"

He gestured to a volghast, and it stepped forward, unrolled a scroll, and read from it. "The following have robbed the kingdom of its lawful income and are therefore guilty of treason against the King of Shunder." To the accompaniment of gasps and isolated screams from the audience, the creature read out four names. One was the glover's.

Those kneeling around him did their best to sidle away. Preya, however, peeled off her gloves and cast them into the man's shocked face. Several people followed her example, and various gloves flew through the air as the glover and the three others, who included the richest landlords in Rydle and Baenfeld, were dragged forward. Protesting and begging, they were forced to kneel in the puddle of blood from the Vols. With a flash of the skora-sword, they met the same fate.

The audience knelt in stunned silence.

"What you have just witnessed," the king announced, "is justice. No longer shall revenues be shunted away from our coffers. No longer shall rebels terrorize my forests, or pustules of sedition thrive in my villages, or rumors of secret societies disturb the hearts and minds of my subjects. The green circle has never been a religious symbol, but a vile and treasonous one. Every home, shop, or tavern within fifty strides of such a circle shall be reduced to ashes."

Many faces in the crowd paled before his anger, and no one dared raise their eyes.

"My kingdom will triple in size," the king thundered, "and everyone in this Hall will bear both the glory and the burden. Taxes will rise to outfit my army, the Riftwood will be cleared to grow morue for export, and quotas will be set to increase farm production. Breeding will be controlled, not left to mere chance. Chosen parents shall produce high-quality offspring in whom I can trust, for their rista children will be raised in my strongholds and by my surrogates, and all niyalahn will serve the greater good."

He paused, turning his head to scan the crowd, and no one broke the silence. "I make these promises to you," he said, "and as a surety of things to come, I now perform my first official act." The king pointed to a man with broad shoulders standing in the front row, "Archon Rigiati," he ordered, "step forward. I name you Kai Archon, the great archon, and head of all my forces." He raised his arms in triumph. "For in my fist I now hold this land!"

It was obvious what their king expected. All jumped to their feet, and to the pounding of drums, they cheered and shouted as loud as they could. This appointment meant war. Assessing eyes met briefly, then darted away. Many would suffer, the weak and the stupid would be ruined, but the loyal and the cunning would profit. Through all the noise, their king paced across the dais. His red mouth grinned knowingly, his perfect, gloveless hand gripped a sword of fire, and even the boldest flinched from his inhuman gaze.

All acclaimed the Nihilarist, the lord of life and death.

Chapter 36

Orders

Rigiati waited until the applause died down, then moved smartly to stand on the dais only two steps below the king, and gave him a short bow. At last, just after ten high gongs on this fourteenth rota in Seed, justice had truly been done. He turned to face the crowd, which clapped politely, and then glanced down at the headless body of Vol Tierce, his former commander. He allowed himself a secret smile. For years Shacad had accomplished little but pander to his twisted urges and leave all the work to silent, loyal Archon Rigiati. Now the screw had been fully turned. Now he was Kai Rigiati, the most powerful man in the king's army.

He signaled to a group of subalterns to remove the heads and bodies of the traitors, taking the opportunity to glare at the Vorian Guards arrayed on either side of the king. It was high time the skewers did more than preen their purple plumes, but as of now he dared not issue orders to the king's personal guard. Instead he turned his attention to the archons and quad-captains standing stolidly at the base of the dais. In one face he glimpsed hard resentment before it was quickly blanked out. *Too bad, Altern Moverik, but you were never in the race for this position.*

"Kai Rigiati," the king commanded, "form up the officers for my review."

Rigiati snapped out orders. Guards forced the dignitaries back, and the five men who commanded the three divisions of the lord's army and the garrisons in the two villages shouldered forward. Most were careful to show no emotion as one of their own was suddenly set above them.

The Lord of Oknu Shuld, plus much more now, moved to the edge of the dais and surveyed his warrior elite. "The era you have all awaited has arrived. This very rota, at the twelfth deep gong, our army will march out to defend our domain. This very rota we will annihilate our first target. Before darkness falls, the Seani will lie in ashes!" He raised the sword of fire and the commanders roared their approval.

Rigiati, however, stood speechless. This was not what he and the king had planned. The attack was supposed to begin early the next rota, not a mere two gongs from now.

The king smiled at the crowd, his hands uplifted in acknowledgment of their worship, but then transferred his full-bore gaze directly at him.

Rigiati froze. Stiffly, he turned to his underlings. "You heard the king. We move out in two gongs." He nodded at the tough and grizzled Archon Pyk, head of the Skinners. "Order your 'braks to prepare the catapult to use abakal against the Seani. Oil it up and move it out."

"Yessir."

Rigiati looked around for the Skinner subaltern "Needles" Noz and spotted him lounging in the throng near the archways. The conceited, pockmarked ass needed to be taken down a peg. No Skinner would get away with assaulting one of his own men, even if Teller-of-Lies had apparently gone mad. He glanced back at Pyk. "Have Subaltern Noz choose a few men and get up to the Node. Nine balls of abakal are stored there, along with their leather carrying cases. They're heavy. Have the men haul them down, as many as each can carry, to the side gate. The balls may have developed a somewhat harder crust by now, but warn the men to be careful with them." He tossed the gate-key to Pyk, then looked back at Noz. Besides being heavy, balls of abakal were dirty and sharp: they'd surely mess up that fancy shirt of his.

He scanned the crowd to see if they had noticed his irritation with the king, but they seemed oblivious. His eyes sought out the sole remaining Vol. What was his reaction?

But the place where Kuat had been standing was now vacant.

A SLIGHT RUSTLE CAUSED TELLER TO turn; Vol Kuat emerged from the darkness behind the lord's throne. The Delver had a name now, was Rûk the King of the Riftwood; but the Vol's eyes had gone blank and, for the moment, contained no pupils. His face was still as unreadable as a whorl in the bark of an ancient tree. He was still the devisor, still the background shadow who manipulated everything and revealed nothing.

Mariat took one look at him and her face hardened. "Sheft thought I was dead! You arrested him but never told him the truth. You couldn't spare him even that one crumb of comfort."

Rûk raised an eyebrow. "One crumb? It was I who allowed S'eft to travel safely through the Riftwood and into your arms. It was I who took you from the grasp of the umbraks, who spared you from a session with the Eyascnu's mind-probers. The Spider-king would have discovered immediately who you were. Your husband would die as he must, but first would have seen you tortured in front of him and killed. He did not see it, your offspring survived, and that was the 'one crumb' I gave you both."

"Your children had to live, Mariat," Varo murmured.

"These babies are nothing to me yet! If they even exist. My husband was everything." She flung out her arm toward his body and turned her head back to Rûk. "Couldn't you at least have saved him from *that*?"

Rûk regarded her for a moment. "You also could have, as you put it, 'saved' him. You could have insisted he never leave your side, never become who he was. You did not. You loved him more than that. You knew he was called to a destiny beyond you, and you let him go."

Anger drained from her expression, to be replaced by desolation. She searched his face. "Who *are* you, Rûk?"

His gaze grew unfocused, looking at nothing except, perhaps, the past. "You met my servant Wask once," he murmured. "And you fought him. S'eft heard me once, in the Riftwood, when I saved his life. And he saw me once with two others, within the inscrutable aura of God."

For a long while Mariat continued to stare at him, and then sank down on the top step in front of the Spiderking's empty throne and held her head in her hands.

"Everything you did, Rûk," Teller said in a cold voice, "was ultimately for yourself, to keep your kingdom intact. You used us like puppets to accomplish your plans."

Rûk turned his eyes on him. The effect was strange: as if the one he had known as the Delver did not really see him, but saw only everything around him in his preplanned world. It was how manipulation worked.

"You also benefitted, T'lir. Who brought you to the only place where your power could be so fully developed? Who stood in the shadows and protected you from the worst the Vols could do? Who bade you copy the words that snatched your brother and yourself from the ineerva you created? You know nothing about the great design that encompasses even me."

"My brother is dead. I don't need to know anything else."

"Oh but you do. This very rota, the Eyascnu plans to cast abakal against the Seani."

"I've been through all that already," Teller snapped, "courtesy of your consort's vision."

"The events Marhaut showed you in the Pool of Compassion were only that: a vision. What the Eyascnu plans is reality. In the Hall of the Eye, he has just announced it."

Teller's eyes cut to Varo's. "Is this Rûk lying?"

His father—how odd to think of him as that—looked at him with pity. "'This Rûk' kept me alive when my brother would have torn out the last of my soul. Destroying the Seani has long been part of my brother's plans. Now he holds the powers he has always wanted. It would be astonishing if he did not immediately use them."

Marhaut's vision sprung raw in Teller's mind, and then settled like a sickness in his stomach. But what had the vision actually portrayed? The Spider-king's attempt to extricate the niyalahn-ristas, or his triumphant attack after he had already done it?

"You were told," Rûk said, "there are no guarantees."

Yes, they had been told that. So everything he and his brother had endured was for nothing. The hellish abakal still existed, waiting to annihilate the Seani, to engulf Taisa and Mena and little Willow in flames. Sheft had suffered for them, given his life for them, but it made no difference. Abakal would still sear them away.

His abakal. First his ineerva, then his skora, and now his abakal.

Rûk's demeanor sharpened, as if he held a spear aimed directly at him. "The last nine balls are stored in the Node. Two levels above our heads."

Teller's spine turned cold. So this was his mission. This is why he had been spared. He had made abakal; and no forgiveness, no atonement, could eliminate the bitter consequences of that act. He had failed in his niyal'arist mission, but now must at least destroy what he had created.

Igniting nine balls of abakal would obliterate all of Section Thirty-one, and it was clear what would happen to the one who set it off. But he'd come to Oknu Shuld knowing he would never leave it.

Chapter 37

Sh'kier in Deed

There in the lord's private audience chamber, and without warning, Teller's memory of his last moments with Taisa swept over him. Her sweet body in his arms, her hand closing around his blue and red cord. *"How beautiful, emjadi. The love we share for them connects us."* Whatever Rûk intended, destroying abakal would save her, would spare the entire Seani, would right a terrible wrong that he had set in motion.

But it could do more than that.

"I will go to the Node," Teller said, "and destroy the abakal. But you must get these two," he nodded toward Varo and Mariat, "and all the ahn, safely out of Oknu Shuld. All of them. Through your Delver tunnels."

Hard oval pupils jumped into Rûk's eyes. "We do not have time to discuss this."

Teller looked steadily at him. "I think we do, Rûk. I think you will do anything for your kingdom—if I agree to destroy the abakal. It's what you really want, isn't it? Abakal is as much a danger to your Riftwood domain as it is to the Seani."

The Delver's lipless mouth twisted into an ironic half-smile. "The collars you made will not allow the ahn to escape."

Teller had forgotten that. He wanted to forget it, as he wanted to forget many things he had done. Varo leaned toward him and put his hand on his arm. "Sheft took up the collar in love. He died wearing one, so others would not have to. And you also wear the ahn-collar, my son. You both became one with the ahn, with those you came here to save. Rulve will not let that sacrifice be in vain. Niyal'arist power will break the collars."

Looking stretched and dazed, Mariat stared at him. "Sheft is dead," she cried. "One wrist is still chained to the ground!"

"Niyal'arist power will do it," Varo insisted. "It is the way of what must be."

The light in Varo's eyes made Teller's heart sink, and he shook off his father's hand. The years of torture and isolation had finally pushed Varo into madness.

"Is not sowing a seed an act of trust?" Varo asked him. "Is it not full of power?"

"That was my brother's mission, Varo, and he failed."

"And now you have your own mission, T'lir."

"As indeed you do," the King of the Riftwood put in. "You will destroy the abakal because you must, not because of any bargains we can possibly make between us. These ahn are not my responsibility. Apparently you have made them yours."

They stared at each other for a moment. "What you do not seem to understand," Rûk said, "is that I also have failed. All my work, my devisement as you would say, is useless now. You have managed to get your brother killed, and without the two of you my plans are ruined."

Oh God, there were no saviors in Oknu Shuld.-

"You forget," Varo said to Rûk, "that there are two niyal'arists here."

"Your power is long gone, Varo. A generation separates you from T'lir, and now you are only one old man."

"Perhaps. But who knows? That inscrutable God you name so easily? My son wears Rulve's coin, and I will do as his heart desires. *I* will lead the ahn out of Oknu Shuld."

NOZ WAS NOT HAPPY WITH HIS orders. Even on such short notice, he had managed to procure a new shirt for the lord's Apotheosis. It was of fine black linen, with cobalt buttons and trim that exactly matched the Skinner hem on his cloak. Now hauling abakal around would completely ruin it.

He pointed at four of his strongest men. "Didak, Haro, you two there in back, you're all with me." They'd been watching the proceedings from where they had pushed themselves into the archway closest to the dais and now disengaged from the crowd. The last two Skinners were munching on chicken legs.

"Where'd you get those?" Noz barked.

The two looked at each other. Then the one with red hair answered. "Uh, a coupla Sekrews are sellin' them at the side gate."

"Get rid of them. There's a war starting and you're on duty now."

They stuffed the meat in their pockets and wiped their fingers on their pants. Didak, who wore only a jerkin and no shirt—he claimed sleeves chafed his bulging biceps—spit on the tiles when Noz gave his squad their assignment. "Let the 'braks do it," he said. "Skinners is a fightin' force, not a haulin' one." Just in time, he must have realized that they were technically no longer in the Hall of the Eye, where all powers were blocked, because he hastily added, "Sir."

Haro-epet, a wiser man, thumped his chest in salute and kept his mouth shut. He was a northerner, from Opa-Binya, and wore his hair in a long, oiled braid.

"Pyk's orders," Noz said tightly. "Coming straight from our new Azanzi Kai. No surprise there; Scaths have always looked down on us Skinners." He led his squad up the main stairway, quicker than the spiral stair because it bypassed level five.

FOR THE FIRST TIME SINCE TELLER had known him, the Delver seemed taken aback. The hard pupils in his eyes vanished, to be replaced only by the whites. "How? The 'Delver tunnels' T'lir referred to do not exist as he imagines them. There is only a single way to access Oknu Shuld undetected, and for that one must take on the guise of a snake."

"There is another way," Varo said. "Eyascamen found it with his strange sight when we were only boys, getting into everything and exploring our domain." He swallowed. "When we were still brothers."

"Saving ahn was never part of my plan," Rûk stated.

"Now it is, my friend."

Through narrowed eyes, the Delver glanced sideways at Teller, and then back to Varo. "I will go down to the isav with you and this woman. I will order the ahn to follow you, Varo. No matter what you believe, the collars will choke them if they attempt escape, but that is your problem. Then I will leave this place, and if T'lir fails to destroy the abakal, I will prepare my kingdom for the Eyascnu's attack."

Rûk made as if to leave, but something in Teller's heart made him raise a hand to stop him. "There are many who hold apartments across the hallway from the Node—ristas, teachers, foreign visitors. Subalterns man duty stations nearby. I can't allow them to be destroyed by a weapon I never should have created."

Rûk grinned horribly. "Then you must destroy this weapon, must you not?"

"Sh'kier will not destroy the innocent," Teller replied, "nor will I." He knew little about the power growing inside him, but was quickly finding out. Sh'kier belonged to Rulve and was intended to restore the balance evil had upended. It served neither retribution nor revenge, but justice tempered with mercy. He knew this as a certainty.

"So these 'innocents,'" Rûk sneered, "had nothing to do with the evil in this land? These foreigners and teachers were completely free of compliance with it?"

"They didn't know what they were doing."

"The rista who hunted ahn did not know what they were doing? The subalterns who guarded the morue crop suspected nothing of its uses? Scholars who traveled to this place had no idea of what was taught here?"

"If justice means punishment for allowing evil to fester," Varo put in, "then who would ever escape destruction?"

Certainly not me, Teller thought. How could he now claim to protect the innocent, when Keya and Gorv had died because of him, when he had brought children into Oknu Shuld, when the Seani might yet be destroyed by a weapon he so unthinkingly had made?

"These people who so concern you, T'lir," Rûk said, "are all gathered far below us in the Hall of the Eye. Village and military elites are there as well, to witness the Eyascnu's triumph. Many levels protect them from whatever damage may occur in Section 31. They can leave unscathed, whenever they wish, and always could."

Rûk began threading his way past the insect carvings, but stopped at the door. "I will go now with

Varo and Mariat down to the isav. But know this, T'lir: you are not the only one seeking abakal. Only moments ago, the lord decreed that he would lead his troops out of Oknu Shuld at the twelfth deep gong. Already five guards have been ordered to bring the abakal down to the side gate to use against the Seani." He opened the door and glanced back at Teller. "You must get to the Node first."

TRUDGING UP THE MAIN STAIRS, Noz caught Didak's sideways glance. "There's them that says you shoulda been quad-captain by now, sir. Pyk always held you back, kept you an artilleryman."

"Our esteemed archon," Noz grated, "doesn't know how to deal with the greater Powers. He claims Needles contributes to a lack of focus, of courage even. It's nothing but envy."

"Sir, you sure don't lack focus." Didak chuckled. "I seen you narrow your needle-stream so tight it could ream out Pyk's left eye."

"Damn right." His Power made him twitchy and easily bored, and the needles were building up in his gut. He'd stood in that scathi Hall too long, where pent-up Powers grew frustrated. He looked around for an ahn, for soft flesh to hurl his needles against, but there wasn't a single one in sight. "Where's all the scathi ahn?"

"I seen the proctor down in the Hall," the last man in back said, "and the Vols are all gone. So they're probably takin' the opportunity to snore in the isav."

Barely listening, his hands at his sides, Noz rubbed his thumb rapidly over his forefinger in irritation. "Back in our student days I tried to make friends with that arrogant bastard. But Teller-of-Lies stuck up his nose at the rest of us. Sir High-and-Mighty Skora cheated and lied and schemed his way to the position of Vol Cinc while still nothing but a skewin' boy."

"Shacad's pretty boy, most like," someone added.

"It was blatant, blazing favoritism. But the scathi shit finally got what he deserved. We all saw him yesterday, stumbling out of a pig cart in chains. It warmed my stomach, Didak."

Upon reaching level three, they stopped for a moment to catch their breath. Coming down wouldn't be easier, because they'd be carrying heavy weights.

"That beheading business downstairs was a farce," Noz said. "Vol Cinc wasn't kneeling there, and he was the biggest traitor of the bunch."

"They say," Haro-epet put in, "that lord has special thing in mind for him."

The idea pleased Noz, as did the fact he had punched Teller-of-Lies at the side gate. He should have hit him again, harder, while he had the chance.

Cold panic knifed into Teller's stomach. The attack would begin at the twelfth deep gong. That meant noon, and hadn't he just heard the tenth? How could he elude five guards who were probably on their way up right now?

As if in answer, the fire inside Teller asserted itself. No longer just a painful wound or an instinctive defensive reaction like skora had been, it was now a pulsing implacable demand. It arose not only from his response to the wrong that had been done to his homeland, but also from the bitter knowledge that he had been part of that. In this charged darkness, sh'kier flickered like far-off sheet lightning, with thunder yet to come.

Varo moved past him to follow Rûk, but stopped to squeeze Teller's shoulder. "Do not forget, my son: your brother planted the seed, and you must bury it. That is a deed you must accomplish and the promise you made to Mariat."

Out of wild grief he had promised that. It was a promise he made before he learned about the abakal, about the twelfth gong. "Father," he said, "Se Celume told us that 'One niyal'arist will help the other die, and all who bear s'rere must be buried.' But I didn't help Sheft die, and I won't have time now," he made a futile gesture and looked away, "to do anything more."

Varo leaned closer. "You are still Rulve's coin, my son, made to be spent. Trust the Creator. Trust Sheft. Do as sh'kier directs." Varo squeezed Teller's shoulder once more and then followed Rûk, who was waiting for them at the door.

Mariat had risen and was standing beside Sheft. She gazed down at her husband's body, her face almost as white as his. Teller went to turn her gently toward him. "Go with the others. Please hurry, Mariat."

She touched his cheek, and her eyes filled with sadness. "Oh Teller. You are so like him."

He searched her face, the face of one who loved so much. "Good-bye, my sister. Please forgive me." *For abandoning you now. For abandoning your children, Sheft's children, who will one day need a father.*

She pulled away a little, puzzled. "Aren't you coming with us?"

She apparently hadn't heard much of what had gone on. "I want to, Mariat, but I can't." If he could do what he had to, she and the others would escape, would make their way to the Seani—and would see Taisa. His heart swelled. They had embraced less than a day and a half ago, but so much had happened to him it seemed far longer than that. If only he could send Taisa a message, tell her now what he should have told her then: that he would never forget the intimacy they had shared when she was helping him bear the ineerva pain, that he loved her and never wanted to be apart from her. But he had already said good-bye.

Mariat clutched him tightly for a moment, and then followed Varo.

Teller watched the door close behind them. Then, even though the mandate to rush up to the Node prickled inside him, he had to kneel for the last time beside his twin. *I'm sorry, Sheft. I didn't help you when you needed me, and now I won't even be able to bury you. Please forgive me.* The toltyr around his own neck, combined with the collar that marked him a slave, had never felt heavier. Perhaps he had no business wearing the toltyr anymore. Perhaps his father was wrong, and he was no longer part of the Creator's coin.

Sheft had been relieved of all such weight. He had died utterly bound, and now was free. So deeply graced.

Teller's heart wanted to cry out: *I'm trying to follow you, trying to do whatever I can. Please look back and help me.* But Sheft had paid the price and must now be left in peace. He kissed his brother's forehead. *Remember me, Sheft.*

Even as he prayed that, even as grief tore him apart, a thought came upon him like a gentle touch: they were joined by more than memories and always would be. If his twin could speak to him, if he were using their link right now, he would say that s'rere and sh'kier were expressions not only of Rulve's loving will, but also of their own deeply rooted need to express it.

He got to his feet, wiped his eyes on his sleeve, and made his way past the insect sculptures. Even now the glittering compound eyes regarded him, and jointed appendages seemed poised to snatch at him. Outside, the corridor was empty. Sh'kier drove him forward with urgent insistence, down the passageway toward the spiral stairs. They would emerge closer to the Node than the main stairs did.

Chapter 38

The Node

Teller met no one on the spiral stairs and found the passages deserted. The double gates to Section 31 were locked. What were the latest passwords? He leaned against the bars and, in spite of the simmering in his spirikai, tried to concentrate. How long ago had he heard the tenth gong? Could he have missed the eleventh?

His mouth was dry. Sheft would have been just as thirsty and alone, and hurting much more, when he faced his final ordeal. His brother died chained and bleeding, knowing that his twin's skora had made the Spider-king stronger than he had ever been.

Teller ground his forehead against the gate. *Oh, Sheft. My death will be quicker than yours. Rulve, please, grant that it not be for nothing.*

The passwords. He had to focus on getting into the Node. He tried a phrase that could have been replaced weeks ago. "Sek ephra!" To his relief, the gates clicked open, and he pushed past them. They swung shut behind him with a clang, and for an instant he panicked. Were the passwords still the same for exiting?

Scathi fool. There wouldn't be any exiting.

THREE LEVELS DOWN IN THE HALL of the Eye, Rigiati determined to maintain face in front of his archons and quad-captains. The king had arbitrarily changed the time of the Seani attack, but they must from now on stick to their original plans. The most important of them was to make it crystal clear who was still in charge of the Azanzis. "As the king has ordered," he said to his second, "I want my Azanzis ready at the back gate at the twelfth gong. I'm in command of them until I find someone qualified." *Which would be never. Controlling two hundred of the army's best fighters might come in handy one day.*

He noticed that Perius, the most ambitious of his quads, had a smug look on his face, clearly expecting he'd be moved into the Azanzi position. Don't be so sure of yourself, Rigiati silently told him, or you'll wind up digging field latrines.

"The king and I"—he liked that phrase; it implied equality, and he intended to use it more often—"the king and I anticipate that our foray against the Seani will be over by nightfall."

The king scratched a spot on his smooth, chalk-white cheek as he cut his amethyst eyes to Rigiati and then to the rest of his officers. "I want the Se taken alive. I want them turned over to you, Moverik, and I want to see them writhe on the Skewrong Grabe. Impaled or nailed, archon, just make it last."

"That might prove impossible, your majesty," Rigiati said smoothly. *As you should know,* "Abakal is notoriously difficult to control, and its use could engulf the whole Seani compound in flames. Finding anyone alive—"

"You are explaining to me what you cannot do?" the king asked in a silky voice.

Rigiati bowed his head and thumped his chest. "Certainly not, your majesty." From the corner of his eye he caught Moverik's brief smirk, but swallowed his irritation and turned to Archons Burs and Pyk. "The following is our plan for tomorrow's incursion into Bellstone Forest. At six high gongs...." He went on with orders that would result in the forest being swallowed whole, and ending with Pyk doing clean-up. "By 'clean-up' I mean leave no man, woman or child–"

"No." The king turned his head and spoke to Pyk. "Dispatch the crones, the crippled, and males over ten, but I want every woman and child in the forest taken as ahn. I want every Defender and their seconds brought directly to me for punishment. Bellstone has never contributed to my service, and now they will pay their full debt."

With a lift of his chin, Moverik had the audacity to speak. "Since we are attacking the Seani in two gongs, your majesty, shall I send a squad to hold the Rydle Bridge?"

Of course, Rigiati thought in annoyance, this ambitious fool would want to draw attention to himself at this crucial moment. "Hold the bridge against who?" He sneered. "A handful of Sperians? Or don't you have your own town under control?"

The man glowered back at him, his nostrils flaring over his thin mustachios. "Under perfect control, Kai Archon."

Rigiati glanced up at the king for his reaction. Had he even heard Moverik's question? His snake eyes were flicking over the crowd. What were they seeing? Prey? He felt a wild impulse to wave his hand to get the king's attention, but the vision of a serpent striking, burying its fangs into his skin, quickly quelled that action.

He continued addressing his archons. "As to the Azanzi placement—"

Without looking at him, the lord once more interrupted. "I myself will lead the Scaths against the Seani."

What? Rigiati stiffened. This was not what he had just announced, not even remotely part of what they had already planned. Although the lord was a good strategist, he had little experience in the field, and none at all with fighters as good as the Scaths. This, Rigiati thought angrily, is the third time this king has contradicted me—and in front of officers under my command.

Noz AND HIS MEN PASSED THE empty guard station on level three and made a hard right. Half-way down the hall, Noz heard a metallic clang. It came from around the corner. From the gates to Section 31, which were supposed to be locked. He checked his pocket and felt the cool metal of the key Pyk had tossed to him.

He put up his hand for silence, and then he and his men moved quietly forward until they came to the closed gates. Peering through them, Noz saw a man with dark hair striding down the dim passage. Even though he was dressed like an ahn, he wasn't one; they all scuttled around with bowed heads. Noz ducked aside when the man turned his head slightly, but he still caught a glimpse of his face. "By the suckin' voras!" he whispered to Didak. "He's wearing an ahn-collar! But it's Teller-of-Lies, all right. Scathi Teller-of-Lies. Somehow he's escaped and is heading for the Node. And, by Ázu, for the abakal."

He had two choices: report this information back to Pyk or finish what he had started with Teller-of-Lies. He knew which one would give him the greatest satisfaction and make him quad-captain besides. "Let's get this scathi shit!" he hissed to his men. Before entering the Hall of the Eye, their weapons should have been routinely confiscated at the entrances, but he'd bet Haro still had the stiletto hidden in his braid, and Didak had a friend who wouldn't check for the knife in his boot. Whatever, it was five to one. Plus Needles.

Teller thought he heard something and glanced around. It must have been one of Autran's rat spies. They ran free ever since Vol Autran had abandoned working with them and turned to breeding a particularly vicious strain of much bigger rodents. No way did Teller want to encounter any of those.

He made his way through a tunnel quickly becoming thick with bad memories. On his left he passed the laboratorium, where he had so many times assisted Autran. Where he had made ineerva, the very poison that had almost killed him and his brother, where he had made fura that had turned his father into a monster, and where he had made abakal that could burn Taisa alive.

He could smell potions even through the closed door, could still detect the faint hint of smoke that lingered from the fire that had resulted when he fought Autran's last attempt to seize skora.

Mold, encouraged by the steam that rose from the Node's great cauldron when it was in use, slimed the walls and ceiling, growing thicker as he approached his goal. He could see the door, ahead in the dimness. A thin line of light shown beneath it. Sunlight. Autran must have left the shaft, with its great crystal, unshuttered.

Noz concentrated on the figure before him. Teller-of-Lies had halted, making himself a perfect target against the dim glimmer around the door to the Node. The image of rising needle-tips prickled in his veins. He took a deep breath and held it, summoning his strength, focusing his widest beam on the traitor's back. Almost of themselves his hands rose through the bars of the gate, his rigid fingers extended. Already frustrated, already itching inside him, his Power spiked. With a hard grunt, Noz expelled it. A swarm of needles hissed down the passage.

A SUDDEN CHILL BETWEEN HIS SHOULDER blades sent Teller diving to the floor. A metallic swarm whooshed over his head and thudded into the wooden door of the Node. Pointed at both ends, a cluster of five-inch needles trembled there. Eventually they would dissolve and melt away, but right now they were lethal.

Teller glanced over his shoulder. A group of Skinners had rushed through the gate, and now four of them stood behind Noz, who was half-crouching to gather another volley of his Power. Teller jumped to his feet, and remembering at the last minute to shield his eyes from the sudden light to come, burst through the door of the Node.

Sunlight streamed down the shaft as Teller, expecting a second Needles attack, veered to his right just in time. A mass of needles lashed past his neck and, with a deafening clatter, hit the chest-high cauldron across the small room. Teller banged the door shut. The cauldron, half-filled with water, had been pulled aside on its track from under the shaft, so at least the Node was not full of steam. Along the wall, several big rats, half-starved in their cages, squealed in anticipation of being fed and lunged against the slats.

A quick perusal found what he was looking for. In the corner to the right of the door, the lethal pile of rough, slightly crusted spheres, cushioned by wads of hay, stood out black in the bright light. Taking a deep breath, pushing his focus past his pounding heart, he reached inside himself to grasp sh'kier.

The door burst open. Skinners barged in, quickly shielding their eyes. "By the suckin' Voras!" one of them cried.

Teller darted to the wall at his right. He grabbed one of the stout leather bags that hung there, hefted the closest ball of abakal into it, and headed for the door.

The big Skinner, however, had already recovered. Squinting, he rushed toward Teller and swung a fist at him. Blocking it with his forearm, Teller kicked out and hit the big man's knee. With a grunt his assailant went down. Teller quickly placed the bag on the floor as the second and third men leaped forward.

Teller rammed the heel of his palm into the nose of one, then sliced the side of his hand against the other's throat. They both stumbled backward against the wooden rat cage, which cracked open. Rats bigger than cats leaped out. They attacked the first things they saw, which were the two Skinners, one with a bloody nose, who swore and beat at them.

Before Teller could snatch his bag and dash out, another man, a northerner with a braid, reached behind his head and produced a stiletto. Teller fumbled for his dagger, discovered it still wasn't there, and dodged to his left. A rat snapped at the northerner's ankle, and he jumped back. Swarmed by rats, Bloody Nose grabbed at his pocket and wildly threw something that looked like a chicken leg at the pack. Two rats turned aside to fight over it, but the rest clawed at him and the other Skinner for more.

Somewhere in the room, Teller knew, Noz crouched in the shadows, his fingers outspread, waiting for his Power to build up. He'd already fired two salvos in close succession and would need a few heartbeats to fire a third. Intent on Teller, the northerner kicked a rat aside and came at him again. His black eyes glittered, then flicked at something over Teller's shoulder. Teller lunged sideways as needles whizzed past his arm.

The attack narrowly missed the northerner, who jumped aside with an oath. He stumbled over a rat, crashed into a bank of wooden shelves, and his weapon went flying. Glass containers shattered on the stone floor and liquids pooled. "Skew it!" he shouted. Acrid fumes began curling out.

His eyes wild, Bloody Nose stomped at the rodents around him. He squashed the head of one, slipped on it, and grabbed at a wall hanging. The fabric tore away in a cloud of dust and enveloped the top half of his flailing body. On the floor next to him a Skinner kicked at the attacking rodents while trying to wrest something out of his pocket. The northerner staggered toward Teller. At the same time, the big man who had first attacked Teller crawled toward him, his eyes glittering. Teller whirled, spied the bag of abakal through a rising blanket of fumes, and snatched it off the floor. Behind him, coughing and screaming mingled with the squealing of rats as he bolted toward the door. He didn't make it. A hand closed on his ankle and pulled him down.

"I've got 'im!" a voice called out.

Chapter 39

Too Late to Love

Rivere threaded his way through an isav he had never seen so agitated. He had to find Hanat. Rumors claimed that the ahn matriarch had seen guards marching Vol Cinc down the passageway on level four, and then, some time later, the entire ahn community apparently experienced a devastating event.

Now the proctor and his guards had been summoned to a big ceremony above, and the isav chamber was packed with ahn from every sleep session. They had been ordered down from their duties on every level of Oknu Shuld, and even the field workers were present. This had happened before, when the Spider-king had wanted to make sure his emaciated ahn-slaves were hidden from the sensibilities of the clean and well-fed guests attending his various ceremonies. This event, however, seemed very different.

He had just found Hanat in front of the chamber when, without any warning, Volarach Kuat stalked in. With a long gasp, the ahn fell to their knees in a wave spreading away from him. Rivere, sinking down next to Hanat, stared in astonishment at the two strangers who accompanied the Vol: a disheveled young woman and a gaunt, nut-brown man wearing nothing but a rag around his waist.

Vol Kuat mounted the proctor's stand, waited for their full attention, and then spoke in a voice that resonated throughout the isav. "I order you," he said, "to listen to the person who will next address you." The Vol gestured to the gaunt man to step up beside him.

This was extraordinary. Such an event had never happened before.

Stringy hanks of hair hung around the man's face, his mouth was swollen, and a disconcerting light haunted his slightly protruding, amethyst eyes. "We bring a message to you," he said, "from Teller, the niyalahn-rista."

Rivere took a sharp breath. They had not heard the term since Vol Cinc had forbidden its use among the ahn. "But he's dead!" a voice in the rear cried out. "We felt him die."

Vol Cinc was dead? Was that what the ahn had collectively experienced?

"One niyalahn-rista indeed is dead," the stranger said, "and at the hands of the lord. But the other still lives. I and this woman spoke to Teller only a short time ago. He and his brother came here to help you."

Help them? Rivere was no mind-speaker, but even he could feel the confusion that swept through the room.

"They took on the ahn-collars for your sake," the man continued. "Now Teller has begun a dangerous mission to set you free. We do not have much time, so he begs you to listen to me and do what I order."

No one said a word, but now confusion was hardening into suspicion. Who were these people? Vol Cinc wore an ahn-collar? Yet he supposedly wanted to free them? This stranger made no sense, and he could not be trusted.

"And that is not all," the man said. "Teller, the niyalahn-rista, wishes you to follow me." His head turned from side to side as he looked into their eyes. "To follow me and this woman out of Oknu Shuld."

A hiss of disbelief spun through the isav. Out of Oknu Shuld?

Shockingly, without permission, Hanat came to her feet, fear and horror written on her face. She pulled at the metal ring around her throat. "But we cannot leave! Ever!"

"You can, and you will! I know a way out, and we will all go together."

They had lived for this hope, prayed for it every rota, but had never imagined it would happen like this. The blessed twins would come for them out of Rulve's compassion, not send a hated Vol. They would come as liberators, not as ragged strangers. The niyalahn-ristas would lead them out in power, and one would not be dead. And the first sign of the miracle they hoped for would be their ahn-collars falling away.

Those nearest to Rivere turned anxious eyes to him. They were not used to questioning a Vol's orders, especially when a Vol commanded they listen to a stranger. The ahn trusted Rivere to speak for them.

Rivere joined Hanat on his feet and glared at the ragged man. "You say Teller is alive, that you will lead us to freedom, but why should we believe you?"

Then a male voice shouted from the shadows in back. "What is it to you, stranger? You wear no collar. What is it to you if we all die?"

The Vol stirred impatiently, as if he were in a hurry, but the ragged man turned away from Rivere and once more appealed to the ahn. "My name is" —he hesitated a moment— "Beacon, and I ask you: what have you got to lose by doing what this Vol has ordered and what the niyalahn-rista has come to do? Do you love your collars so much you will not dare to cast them off?"

But the ahn weren't satisfied. Rivere could see that by their set faces and the way they shifted on their knees.

Beacon must have seen that too. "It is true. I do not wear a collar. But I suffered a thrall far worse." He stared fixedly at the ahn. His face sharpened with a peculiar intensity, and the entire chamber fell into a sudden listening silence. Rivere could hear nothing, but saw every pair of eyes fasten on the man with rapt attention. Beacon was using the mind-speech.

He never knew what Beacon told them or showed them mind-to-mind. But after that, the ahn looked at him as if he were one of them.

Beacon gestured for Vol Kuat to speak.

"As you will," the Vol said, and turned toward the ahn. "I command you: Obey this Beacon. Do it now. At the twelfth deep gong the Eyascnu will set his war into motion. He will attack the Seani and Bellstone Forest. He will overrun your villages and your fields, and your niyals will be slaughtered. Soldiers quartered here will soon pack the tunnels on their way to the gates, and there will be no escape from this chamber." With that, he swept out of the room, and the ahn clambered to their feet.

"My brothers and sisters," Beacon said, "form now a line at the door. Rivere will help you; listen to him." He turned his head to look at Rivere. "Have them follow me to the first tunnel past the scourery. From there we will exit beneath the level where the soldiers are quartered."

"But sir," someone objected, "that would be level nine, and there *is* no level nine."

He was right. Level nine existed only in legends.

"It is there," Beacon said quietly, "and I will show you. Now, quickly, everyone move out."

Dazed, Rivere looked around. In the blink of an eye, everything had changed. He'd been appointed a leader of the ahn. So be it. They would all follow a half-clothed man down some passage that would lead to a solid dead end. There they'd be trapped and would all die together.

UP IN THE NODE, TELLER HIT the ground, and only a quick twist of his shoulder kept the abakal protected. Under a layer of noxious vapors, he viciously scraped the heel of his boot at the hand that gripped his ankle.

"Scathi shit!" The hand let go.

Teller jumped up and stumbled out the door, keeping the leather bag close to his body and slamming the door behind him. He had to get up to Insheer Cliff. That was his only access to the Node now and his only chance to somehow destroy the abakal.

Breathing deeply to clear his lungs from the fumes, he darted through the passageway to his left. With the heavy bag over his shoulder, he wouldn't make it to the stairs before Noz caught him, but there was an ahn service-tunnel close by.

Behind him, the door to the Node banged open. "Which way?" someone shouted. "I can't see shit!"

"Didak, the gates!" Noz shouted. "Ignore the laboratorium; it's locked. Haro, get to the spiral stairs. I'll go left. Those are the only ways out of this section, and he'll be trapped."

"What about the other men?"

Noz barked out a laugh. "Rat food. I *told* them to get rid of the chicken legs."

The service tunnel, Teller remembered, ran perpendicular to the passage by which he had originally entered. Years ago he'd used it when the Vols had him filling up water barrels. But where was the service-tunnel in this section? They were designed to be discreet, to blend into the natural clefts and angles in the walls. Was that it, in the shadows ahead?

He heard another shout. "Abakal! He's got a ball of abakal!"

"Don't let him bluff you. If it goes, he goes too."

Teller almost passed the opening. He swung into it and immediately cracked his head on the lintel. He'd forgotten that these entrances were so low. The ceiling opened up as he rushed through, trying to make as little noise as possible. If Noz were to follow him in this straight and narrow passageway, his Needles couldn't miss.

Teller ran, hitching the heavy bag of abakal higher onto his left shoulder.

He kept seeing his brother's body as it lay two levels below. *"Is not sowing a seed an act of trust?"* Varo had asked. *"Is it not full of power?"*

But his brother was dead, and the space where he had been ached relentlessly.

He pulled at his ahn collar in frustration, and then, abruptly, stopped running. He couldn't feel the ahn. He couldn't feel their pain; had not felt it, he now realized, for some time.

The emerging sh'kier was blocking their anguish more effectively than the skora barrier ever had. Oh God, were innocent ahn already choking, trapped in a tunnel somewhere? And Mariat, who trusted him, what was happening to her now? Sheft had wanted him to care for her in his place. Now she might dying in the dark, along with Sheft's unborn babies. He had abandoned his brother's entire family into the hands of a madman, one who had convinced him that the ahn-collars would be broken and that he knew a way out of Oknu Shuld. A madman who was his father.

Barbed recriminations twisted inside his spirikai, crowding and tumbling over each other. What if he was too late, as he had been with Taisa? He had left her with three cords, together the ultimate symbol of futility, and walked away from the woman it was now too late to love.

Too late to love? Wouldn't Taisa dispute that? Before they parted she'd held his hand, had kissed the aching spot where his finger had been. "This is love, niyal'arist. This is what you did to take up the toltyr."

As long as life allowed, it was never too late to love.

And far too early to give up. Teller began running again. An inner voice insisted he hadn't failed yet. There must still be a way he could destroy the abakal.

He suddenly became aware that his forearm was stinging. His fingertips came away red. Blood, from a Needle-graze he had barely felt at the time. It trailed down his arm, where the sleeve had been torn. He whirled to look on the ground behind him. A few dark spots disappeared into the dimness. A plain trail for Noz.

While still rushing forward, he tore off the rest of his sleeve and tied it around his arm as a bandage. An old man's voice echoed inside him: *"Will you consent to be spent, and buy back the lost? If you agree, my son, I must take you to a place where there is nothing but my grace."*

Well, this was the place. He fumbled for the toltyr inside his shirt and clutched it in his fist. Trust Rulve. Trust as Sheft had trusted.

The hate he had wrestled down in the pig cart, the anger he thought he had buried at the side of his dead brother, his own self-recriminations—all were still there. But these emotions had changed. Sh'kier had changed them, and now they felt more like burning determination.

He had not helped his brother die, could not fulfill a promise to his widow to bury him, but if he did nothing else, he would get to the top of Insheer Cliff. A ball of abakal—if hurled down the shaft with sufficient force, if it had retained its potency after all this time, if Noz and his men hadn't carted the rest of the abakal away—would cause an explosion that would take his life; but it would also destroy at least part of the mess he had created.

Chapter 40

Vol Zero

Four levels below in the isav, the young woman who had come in with Vol Kuat made her way through the crowd to Rivere. "What can I do to help?" she asked.

Rivere had never seen her before, but a quick glance revealed puffy eyes hinting at a recent crying spell. "Who in blazes are you?" An ahn in some kind of panic was blocking the door, and he had to get over there.

"Me? I'm Mariat. Sheft's wife." She moved her hand to her throat, and an expression of bewilderment passed over her face. "He's—he's dead. Teller will have to bury him."

Teller's name caught his attention. "You know Teller? Where is he now?"

"He's going to destroy abakal, so it can't be used against the Seani. It will be dangerous. Soon he might—might be with Sheft." Tears formed in her eyes. "I'm the one who wants to be with him, but I can't, and Teller's dagger is lost somewhere and," her voice broke as she choked out the rest, "there's nothing left. Oh God, I don't usually lose things."

He had no idea who Sheft was, and Teller as Vol Cinc had abandoned them, so this poor woman must be terribly confused. She was clearly a new arrival here, relying on Beacon to help her, and now was lost. He felt something grip his heart, but pushed it roughly away. They all had lost things.

Hanat tugged at his sleeve. She looked harried. "Rivere, some of the ahn are afraid to leave and they are trying to convince others not to follow Beacon. And the mineworkers don't know what's happening and neither do the ahn on latrine duty. You've got to send someone to get word to them. But hurry! Vol Kuat said to hurry."

"Yes, yes, but I've got to see about that man blocking the door. Send Burken." Rivere pushed his way through a group of crying children and reached the ahn circling the panicked man. His eyes were wild, and he grabbed Rivere's arm. "Our collars are getting tighter!" he exclaimed. "The lord knows what we're trying to do. He knows we're trying to escape!"

DOWN IN THE SERVICE TUNNEL, TELLER hurried past several shallow alcoves that contained buckets, rags, and brooms, as well as items for restocking the laboratorium and the Chamber of Ledgers. From time to time, he shifted the heavy bag of abakal off his shoulder and carried it at his side. The next alcove contained one of the water casks for this section, and thirst forced him to stop. The casks were chest-high, only wide enough to roll through the narrow tunnels. As he reached out to lift the handle on the wooden cover, a sound he'd been both listening for and dreading stopped him: the scrape of running boots. It must be Noz. Just big enough to hold one cask, the alcove offered no place to hide.

He had only one choice. Teller eased the leather bag onto the floor and stepped into the passageway to face his pursuer.

Mariat started when Hanat thrust a woman about Mariat's own age into her arms. "This is Liasit. Please stay with her. She once knew Teller." Grabbing a passing ahn, Hanat rushed off with him, pointing at sleeping mats that had to be moved out of the way.

The two women looked at each other. "I-I wasn't paying much attention when Varo was speaking to us," Liasit said. "So I don't—don't know who you are."

"Nobody seems to. Teller is my brother-in-law."

Liasit only stared at her.

Mariat pulled the toltyr out of her shirt and showed it to the young woman. "This belonged to my husband, Sheft." She was going to add, "He's dead," but couldn't. The reality of that, the lifelong meaning of that, suddenly struck her. She would never sleep next to her dear heart again. Never hold him again, never throw her arms around his strong shoulders again. That one night, those last precious hours they had ridden so close to each other, going home, that was all there was going to be. She actually felt her heart breaking, tearing in two. Oh God, how many more times would that happen?

Blinking away her tears, she looked down at Sheft's toltyr for a moment, kissed it, and returned it into her shirt. "It's the toltyr of Rulve, Liasit. Teller wore one just like it."

Liasit's eyes widened. "Then you knew both emjadis!" She dropped to her knees before her.

"What are you *doing*?" Mariat cried. "Stand up. Just stand up now, miss! I'm nobody special."

She pulled the young woman to her feet, suddenly aware of the people pushing past them. Urgency seemed to fill the chamber like smoke. Most of the ahn were crowding toward the exit, but some were frantically rummaging for blankets or rushing about calling for loved ones. At the far edge of the chamber a woman knelt motionless, her head in her hands, and nearby a grey-headed man cowered on one of the sleeping mats. These were ahn, the people Sheft had come here to save, and she had to help him do that. There was no time for mourning. "Come on, Liasit," she said. "We've got to make sure everyone gets out of here."

TELLER STOOD, HANDS AT HIS SIDES, in the middle of the ahn service tunnel. Startled, Noz halted.

"Turn around, subaltern," Teller said, "and get out of here. Unless you want skora to melt the skin off your bones."

Noz grinned. "Go ahead, Vol Zero." He opened his arms, waiting. "No? The lord owns your skora now, ahn, as he showed us all in the Hall of the Eye. But I have something for *your* skin." With his eyes fastened on Teller's, he eased into a slight crouch and took a deep breath.

Teller lunged to the side, snatched up the handle of the cask-cover, and ducked behind it. The double-pointed needles hit so hard the impact cracked an edge into splinters. Using the needle-studded cover as a shield, he leaped forward. Noz kicked at the cover, his thick boots protecting him against the needles, and the back of the cover jammed against Teller's hand. He almost dropped it as the swipe of a stiletto blade just missed his bandaged arm. Noz must have swept up the northerner's weapon, last seen flying off in the Node. With both hands Teller thrust the cover at Noz, its needle-edge ripping through the man's sleeve, grazing his elbow, and causing his weapon to fall.

"Scathi shit!" the subaltern growled. He ducked around the keg cover and hammered the side of Teller's neck with his fist. Instead of breaking bones, it hit the ahn-collar and jammed it into a nerve. Pain shot down Teller's arm, and his makeshift shield clattered to the floor.

The two of them dived for the stiletto at the same time. The Skinner got there first, and both men rolled on the ground, grappling and pounding each other. Teller wound up under Noz, his left hand straining against the weapon in the other's right, his other arm pinned down. The point hovered inches from his throat. Teller kicked at Noz's legs just as the weapon jerked down and scraped over the ahn-collar, which saved him a second time.

"Skew it!" Noz raised the stiletto again.

Teller jerked his right arm free and smashed his fist against Noz's wrist. Pain exploded in his hand, but the weapon fell. As Noz reached for it, Teller rolled out from under him. Both men jumped to their feet, Noz brandishing the stiletto. They faced each other, panting and moving into position. Noz, Teller knew, was too out of breath to produce Needles, but that would quickly change. The cover lay at Teller's feet. He got the toe of his boot under it and kicked, hoping its edge would slam into the Skinner's ankle. Noz leaped over it easily and turned, but was off balance when Teller rammed his left fist into the man's stomach. Still holding the stiletto, Noz grunted and fell backward.

A look of total surprise bloomed on his face, and then contorted into agony. He had landed on top of a cask cover bristling with needles. The Skinner tried to get up, but sank back with a hiss of pain. A froth of blood bubbled out of his mouth.

Teller reached over to pull him up, but a swipe of the stiletto sent him back.

"Gloat while you can," Noz gurgled. "It won't last long." He fumbled to unbutton his shirt.

"I'm not gloating. Let me get you off that."

"Not," Noz grinned and then gasped, "bloody likely." He tore his shirt open, and cobalt buttons popped off and bounced on the floor. The grin came back, along with a look of triumph. "You'll never kill me, you scathi turd. I'll do it myself." Noz pressed the point of the stiletto against his bare chest, and with both hands drove it in. Breath creaked out of him, his eyes widened, and then they glazed over. A stain spread over his fine shirt, and one hand slipped to his side. Silence sifted over the motionless body.

During Teller's so-called final exam, the ahn Gorv had died like that: by his own hand, in the dimness of a forgotten tunnel, He did it because of who he believed Teller to be. But who Gorv saw and who Noz saw were two entirely different people.

Teller turned, stumbled to the cask, and bent to gulp cool water until he had to stop to breathe. He came up shaking. A man lay dead. It had happened in self-defense, and partly by accident, but still the fact twisted inside his stomach.

He hadn't even thought to use sh'kier against Noz. Unlike skora, it hadn't jumped into his hand; it didn't exist merely for his own personal protection. He was learning, or the power was teaching him, that the nascent fire he was born with had grown into a force that dwelt in him but wasn't his. It was Rulve's power, placed inside him to serve the Creator's good purpose.

What that purpose ultimately was, he didn't know, but the urgency to get on top of the cliff thrummed in his spirikai. He hefted the leather bag over his shoulder, cradled his aching right hand against his chest, and went on.

He remembered the northerner's name: Haro-epet. The Skinner would be waiting for him at the spiral stairs.

Chapter 41

Acorn

From his position on the Eerford Log, one of three long benches that formed a triangle around the stone table that marked Galen's grave, Deoner glared at an acorn that had fallen onto it. The thing should have spent the winter on the ground, putting down roots and showing by now the hint of a sprout. But just like these Bellstone warriors, it was late getting to its goal. Maybe too late. He took a deep breath to dispel his irritation with those sitting on the other two Logs.

The table had been covered with frost when Defender Undering's delegation had arrived for the Bellmoot a little before dawn. Now the frost was gone, the light of a cold day was filtering through the bare trees, and the three Defenders of Bellstone Forest, along with their seconds and two elders from all three glades, were still bickering about a plan.

He glanced at the other observers who sat on two rougher logs behind the others. These included Gurvale the Bellstriker and a group of Sperian rebels from Rydle, headed by a lean man called Havek. A few boys waxing bowstrings or sharpening axes sat cross-legged on the ground near the tethered horses.

It had taken time for the other two glades to deal with their shock at the news about the niyalahn-ristas, and now more time to discuss Havek's report. "Every archon and a stream of red-cloaks have been called into Oknu Shuld," he said. "I'm thinking the Spider-king's planning a big maneuver, and my guess it'll happen today."

Rung frowned. As the Defender of Eerford Glade, the area of Bellstone Forest closest to Oknu Shuld, he was obviously worried. "It'll be within hours then," he said, "while he still has plenty of light."

His neighbor Flyn, the Defender of Ettebel Glade, scratched his black beard. "No gatherin' has been seen among the Clawthorns, and Pyk and Burs are dealin' with tired forces comin' in for rotation. If they was comin' agin' the forest today, we'da seen some sign by now. Mark my words, he's targetin' the Seani. Sorry, Deoner, but that's how it looks."

Rung twisted his lips in thought and nodded. "Mebbe," he said to Deoner, "tis best you leave directly to defend yer home. I know you have a wife and little ones to worry about."

Deoner shook his head. "My family is safer in the Seani than anywhere else. The Se are strengthening the wards, and they can withstand anything the Spider-king can throw at us. I'm not made to hide behind walls, Rung, and I feel we've done that far too long. If this council permits, I would like to be of use here."

Everyone agreed with nods or murmurs, except one of the elders from Bystone, the southernmost section of the forest. "We don't need to be helpin' others," she muttered, "when our own necks are in the noose."

Rung glared at her with his vivid blue eyes. "Didja no hear the Bellstone's word? In this we're One, or we'll be nothin'. I thought we all agreed on that. It's what the emjadis gave themselves up for."

Deoner glanced at Gurvale, the Bellstriker, but he already knew what she thought. Her grim look made it clear that the Bellmoot hadn't changed her opposition to their plans.

Undering, the Defender of Bystone, thoughtfully scratched his clean-shaven cheek. He was the only adult woodsman in the group without a beard, having let it be known that "whiskers did naught but hide a handsome face." He leaned out of his seat and addressed the disgruntled elder. "The Spider-king's interested in more'n the Seani or Rydle. He'll want to control the Gap, ya see, and that means he'll have to deal with all three Bellstone glades. We're all involved, whether we like it or no."

"It's time to sum up," Deoner said firmly. "After much talk"—he did his best not to emphasis that too much—"we've proposed a three-pronged plan. First, when the Spider-king's forces attempt to cross the bridge, Havek's people will block it, at least for a while, by arranging a multi-cart 'accident.' Then, when the lord's men are busy clearing the way, Rung's archers strike from ambush. They pick off as many as they can and melt back into the meadow. Second, when the remaining enemy makes its way through the valley to the Seani, Flyn's men join Rung's to harry the lord the entire distance, striking quickly from cover and then darting away."

"Like mosquitos, eh?" Undering smiled and pointed an approving finger at Deoner.

Glancing around the circle at the others, Deoner nodded and then went on,. "Third, when the lord begins setting up his forces before the Seani, we do like we said. Undering needles his back, and other two defenders his flanks."

"We'll be up agin' the Azanzis, probably," one of the seconds said gloomily.

"So what? They won't be expecting any outside attack, and your men know the ground. Plus the Azanzis are in rotation too, a quarter of them wanting rest and another quarter sent off to take their places."

Havek placed both hands on his knees and looked at the others. "We all knew that winning back our land would take more than one skirmish."

"I ain't so much worried about that big throwin' machine they've got," Undering's second said with a frown. "But I hear now it can hurl them explodin' rocks."

"For god's sake," Deoner said. "There are no such things as rocks that explode. We've got enough to do without fighting rumors."

Rung squinted at the sun, now visible over Insheer Cliff, and then conferred with those sitting at his Log. Because his glade had called the moot, Eerford had the right to end it. The defender stood. "No more talk. What say you about stickin' to our plan, but keepin' some of the lads back to defend the glades, just in case?"

A series of "ayes," a few sober, most eager, came from the three Logs. Only the one elder kept her lips shut tight.

"'Tis done then." Rung cut his eyes to Defender Flyn. "Your Glade is central. Use the woodwinds to start gatherin' our men."

Deoner's heart leaped. The woodwinds, he had learned on the ride from Eerford, were simple flutes that made sounds that only the forest folk could differentiate from bird songs, an ingenious method of relaying messages. Like the great bears of the forest, emerging now from their dens, Shunder was rising up at last.

Everyone stood and headed for the horses, and the last thing Deoner did was to swipe the acorn off the table and onto the ground.

At the end of the service tunnel, Teller cautiously looked out of the shadowed opening and into the circular vestibule. The light from a trio of hanging globes reflected dimly in the highly polished sheen of three blackwood doors that led to three different passageways. About five strides away, the iron staircase spiraled out of the floor of this level and into the ceiling of level two. Striped by shadows under the stairs, the northerner waited, silent and alert. A knife glinted in his hand, probably found in one of the guard stations.

Another assailant. Another roadblock to where he had to go.

Quietly putting the bag down, Teller pushed off from the wall, went back to the last globe light, and removed it from its stand. He needed a diversion to get past the northerner and this was all he could think of. As he carried the globe to the exit, the old aversion came rushing back. The writhing worms inside were separated from his skin by only a thin layer of glass, and the crawling sensation he felt made him almost drop the globe. He jerked his attention away from that, eyed the distance to the stairs, and then lobbed the globe toward their depths.

His aim was way off. The globe didn't crash down the stairs as he had hoped, sending Haro-epet down to investigate the noise, but instead it shattered against a metal rung just above the floor. Teller had made it only half-way across the vestibule when Haro-epet whirled to face him, knife raised.

The Skinner, chewing wyrdroot by the smell of it, regarded him with stony black eyes, his weapon steady in his hand. He was of middle age, tall and lean, his skin weathered, his thick oiled braid disappearing down his back. A necklace strung with claws and bones hung over his jerkin. He ran his eyes over Teller and missed nothing—starting with the bandage around his arm, taking in the ahn-collar, and ending at his missing finger. "Is true," he remarked. "No longer Vol Cinc."

"That's right."

"They say lord took ring back, and finger also." He indicated Teller's hand with his chin. "But wound there not done this rota." The black eyes bored into him. "I think you do it. Before."

Without looking away from him, Teller picked up the bag with his good hand. "I need to get up to the cliff."

The northerner's eyebrows rose. "With abakal?"

"One ball."

The man spit out a stream of black juice.

Raising the bag of abakal slightly, Teller let his eyes travel around the vestibule. "Do you love this place," he asked, "enough to die in it?"

Haro-epet thought about this. "I wish to die under sky, not under ground like mole. You give same answer I think." He leaned against the stairs. "They say you born in Seani. They say you close to heart of Druv."

Close? Se Druv had always been a distant grandfather figure to him. Yet the Se had reached out when Teller lay in agony before the Seani gates, carried him home when he didn't have the strength to walk. Druv saw what he could be and forgave him for what he had been. He'd taken his hand as Rivere could not.

"I think," Teller said, "he knew me better than I knew him." What, he suddenly wondered, would his real grandfather have been like? How did the father of Varo and Eyascamen treat *his* sons? A thought suddenly chilled him. What heritage from his uncle ran in his own veins? What traits hidden in his blood should never be passed down? With one hand Teller rubbed his eyes. He kept forgetting: nothing of his would survive to *be* passed down.

"My father," Haro-epet said, "spoke of one named Druv. He met Se long time back, when Druv coming out of Trey Aughter. Se had young wife with him."

"Se Druv never spoke of his past to me. I was only six years old when I was brought here."

"My father wounded," the northerner went on, "left for dead after Wentuyeh raid. Druv fleeing trouble also, yet stopped at my father's side. Druv must cut off my father's foot, but saved his life. My father never forget. The Opa-Binya never forget." With a swift gesture, he shoved the knife into his boot. "Go to your death in peace. Take morue-weeds with you. Already they are destroying my people."

Teller stared at him, and then began hauling himself up the first few stairs. Part way around the spiral, he looked down on the northerner who stood with folded arms, watching him. "Why did you come to Oknu Shuld?"

The man grinned. "For battles. For weapons of steel."

"Get out of this section, Haro-epet. Take your big friend with you."

"Didak, you mean?"

"Whoever, but get out as fast as you can."

The grin vanished. A turn of the stair took him out of Teller's sight.

INSIDE BELLSTONE FOREST, HEWISH WAS HEADING toward his mare when Defender Rung grabbed his shoulder. "Where you think yer goin', lad?"

"With you, to Rydle Bridge."

"No." Rung walked around him to his own mount. "It's no job for a hot-headed striplin'."

Hewish pointed to his new 'brak boots. "No hot-head striplin' coulda' got these. I'm goin'."

"No. Think of your mother. Yer all she's got left, lad."

"If my brothers were alive, my ma would push 'em forward. She'd be proud to have all her sons fightin' to save our forest."

"Yer stayin' here with the lads Flyn left to defend the Glade, and that's the end of it." He vaulted onto his horse and spoke over his shoulder to his second, who was already astride. "There's not much cover under the Rydle Bridge, an' we'll do what we can. But when the enemy breaks through, I'm thinkin' …"

The group rode off, and Hewish glowered after them, kicking at the ground. He had lost two brothers and a sister to the Spider-king's forces and had every right to seek revenge.

But then an idea sprang into his mind, and he looked around for a couple of his friends. Also left behind, they also looked peeved, and Hewish motioned them over. "I think I know a way," he said, "that we can make ourselves useful."

Chapter 42

Eyasc-Perjabik

Meanwhile in the Hall of the Eye, Rigiati was becoming aware that, while he had been dealing with the king's sudden change of plans, the audience had been growing restive. It consisted mostly of soft civilians, who had been standing for some time and now were aching to sit down. Many probably needed to relieve themselves, but the high-nosed ladies in particular wouldn't want to use the troughs set up in back, overseen as they were by smirking guards. No refreshments were in evidence either, even though it was approaching midday. These arrangements, Rigiati was beginning to suspect, were deliberate.

The lord turned back to the crowd, and silence descended. He smiled at them, their gracious sovereign once more, the ruler they knew. "Many of you may be wondering," he said, "what happened to Vol Cinc."

As far as Rigiati could see, most weren't wondering that at all. A few people glanced anxiously at the guarded doors and others arched their sore backs. Many stopped listening as the lord launched into his autobiography, the *L'garza Wadek,* and how it described the time "when scathi voras crept into my very house." At one point the king thrust his face forward for emphasis. "They changed my own brother into a monster." He paused for effect. "And then they came for me."

He waited for the crowd's horrified reaction, which was duly produced.

"Vol Cinc stole my fire," he went on, "but I snatched it back. He defiled my vol-ring, but I crushed his hand. He plotted to destroy our future, but I saved it! I used my power to wrench history around like a recalcitrant horse, to twist it with my own hands toward the path of justice." He stopped, and those under his eye straightened up. "The evil vora was brought before me. He was forced to see what I was forced to see, to endure what I was forced to endure," he chopped the air with the edge of his hand and emphasized each word, "his brother's slow destruction!"

The lord continued his oration with increasing passion, clenching his fists in front of his chest, throwing a gesture to the Igneous Eye, captivating, appalling, and inspiring the crowd until many became visibly moved. The king was making his grief their grief, his victory their victory.

Rigiati smiled to himself. His suspicions had been correct, and he admired the king's technique. He was playing with the crowd, eliciting their emotions and, at the same time, demonstrating his power over them, warning any who would dissent that his strength extended beyond s'rere and skora. The audience was swept along.

"During all my suffering," the king said, "it was art that inspired me. You have seen my sculptures, in the passageway outside this room, in the Statuary Hall next door. Out of mundane metal, I created life-like forms. Out of wood and clay, I created works that inspire pity, that inspire awe, that enable the viewer to see the essence beneath the veneer."

He took them in with his gaze. "And so shall it be with the remaining niyal'arist pretender. The wheel of justice will now turn back upon the one who tried to destroy it." Clasping his beautiful hands together as if in anguished thought, he paced the dais; then stopped and spoke in a voice hoarsened by passion. "But at last a savior rules in Oknu Shuld. I spared the Cinc's life."

Not a sound broke the silence; no gaze wandered to the side.

"Through my art, right here on this dais, I will transform his evil. I will create a living sculpture that will stand throughout history as a sign of redemption. And you, my subjects, will be the first to witness, with your own eyes, the powerful rite of the Cinc's salvation."

Now the lord held the crowd in his hands. Now every gaze was glued to his face. Something bad was going to happen to Vol Cinc, and they were eager to see the show.

Hewish took his two friends aside. All three had been left behind when the Bellstone Defenders rode off. "Last fall," he said, "I found somethin'." He'd been looking for a rose bush with pink flowers, to plant in memory of his little sister, but he didn't tell them that. "I found an openin', hidden behind a thicket, along what musta once been the bank of the river. I passed there before, but this time I spotted a bat headin' in there."

"A bat?" Stemmer asked, running a hand through his red-brown hair. "They hang around the Knobbles mostly."

"I *know*. That's why I followed it." Raising his eyebrows, he glanced from one to the other. "And that's when I found the tunnel."

"Tunnel!" The other boy, named Lim, snorted. "There ain't no tunnels in all of Bellstone Forest. We'd 'a found 'em long ago."

"Well, mebbe not exactly a tunnel," Hewish said, "but more like an openin'. And like I said, there was this big thicket in front of it."

"So what?" Lim said. "You found some muskrat's den."

"Don't be stupid. I got down on all fours to peer through the bushes, and what I could see way back in there looked man-made, like a big pipe mebbe. And damp air was comin' out."

Now the other boys raised their eyebrows.

"Any tracks?" Stemmer asked.

"No. The thing is, that tunnel looked like 'twas headin' under the river, right toward the spider-hole."

"Why didn't you report it?" Lim asked.

Hewish looked down at his feet. "I forgot—what with findin' my pa and all." And not finding his little sis.

"Yeah," Stemmer said, "and with yer brothers gone too. Bad time for you, Hew."

No one said anything for a moment. Then Lim suggested, "Was it a chimbley of some kind?"

"They're on *top* of things," Stemmer said. "Not goin' under no river."

"We gotta take shovels and axes out there and find out," Hewish said. "We cut down the thicket and clear out the openin'. If I'm right, and the tunnel's headin' toward Oknu Shuld, then we start a big fire just outside. We keep it goin', which makes anythin' lurkin' in there mighty uncomfortable. The smell of smoke could filter up and worry some people inside. Mebbe," he shrugged casually, as if didn't care, "even serve as a diversion from what our warriors will be doin' outside."

His friends seemed impressed, and with hands in pockets as if they didn't care either, they talked about it for a while until Stemmer said, "I'm in, Hew. At least it's doin' somethin'."

Lim said he was in too, but was worried about following orders.

"Just go over and tell the man in charge," Hewish suggested. "Tell'im we're off volunteerin' to patrol along the river."

In a few minutes the three of them, with axes and shovels, quietly rode off.

WITH THE STRAP OF THE HEAVY leather bag digging into his shoulder, Teller climbed the spiral stairs, the air becoming colder as he reached the topmost level of Oknu Shuld. A wide passage on his right led to morue packing. On his left, the thick, metal wall-door had been left partially retracted into its slot. A spider dangled in the opening; grease, dirt, and dry leaves crusted the track on the floor. Around the corner stretched the silent corridor which housed his first room in this vacant, poorly lit area of Section Nineteen.

The past clung to him like cobwebs. He'd been the six-year-old who had pounded on the other side of that sliding door, a door always kept locked. They had left him walled up in an area few people knew even existed. He'd awakened not knowing where he was, aching from the mind-probe, from terror, from homesickness. He remembered another room, where the walls swam in and out of focus, where Vol Nosce had twisted his memories of home into nightmares.

Ahead, a ramp and then a ladder went up to the surface. He pulled himself up the ladder, the rails greasy from many hands. Squinting against the dazzling light and struck by the cold air of Seed, he emerged into the guard shack. It was nothing more than a small roofed shelter open halfway up the walls. Except for a guard's cracked mug left on one of the narrow shelves, the shack was empty.

Teller stepped into the high sun and hard-packed earth atop this section of Insheer Cliff. He took a deep breath of fresh air, trying to rid his vision of the dim passageways beneath his feet. They seemed more real, somehow, than the bright, flat world of sun and sky and distant mountains that shone with such dream-like clarity. He swiveled his head to the west, to the distant place on the hillside across the valley where the Seani lay hidden among the trees. Taisa's face sprung before his eyes, so vivid he took a sharp breath.

But his urgent mission clawed inside him, and so he wrenched his gaze away and turned to the east. After crunching past ventilation pipes and half-way between the guard shack and the morue fields ahead, he came to a thigh-high iron railing. About two arms'-lengths across, it encircled the top of the deep shaft that ended at the Node. Easing the bag onto the ground and squinting against reflected sunlight, Teller looked down. His chest tightened.

The crystal lens was still there. Dusted with earth and a few small stones, its cracked surface lay about six feet deep, resting atop a rock rim. He thought it had been removed, awaiting a replacement on its way from Trey Aughter, but apparently the new lens hadn't arrived yet. If he threw the abakal down there now, it would explode against the lens before it could ever get deep enough to reach level three.

Scathi shit, he cursed to himself. Damn scathi shit.

RIGIATI GLANCED AT HIS ARCHONS, AND they too seemed to be drawn in by the king's clever promise of a show. The king gestured with the back of his hand over the four volghasts standing behind him. "Volghast Cinc shall not be as these others, without mind or memory.

He shall know himself, will understand what he has become. He will pant for death, feel the pain, bear the wrenching hopelessness of his unbearable condition. Is this not justice?" The last question he shouted, but for the next he came to the edge of the dais and in a low voice asked, "Is it not mercy?"

It was so quiet in the hall Rigiati could hear the sticky rustle of the masses of larva that writhed in the globes above his head.

The lord turned and pointed dramatically at the volghasts. "Go," he ordered in a loud voice. "Go to the Vora's lair and bring me Teller-of-Lies. He has been a guest there for some time, so you may need a pallet." The volghasts whisked away as, far off, the high gong rang eleven times.

The lord faced his audience once more. "Shortly the traitor will be brought here before you. As my loyal subjects"—he extended his arms to them—"as, yes, co-creators of the most glorious kingdom the world has ever seen, you shall all"—he swept his arms up—"see and then celebrate the transformation of Volghast Cinc!"

The audience erupted into tremendous applause. A celebration would mean a banquet, so they cheered, whooped, and stamped their feet. The Vorian Guard began the chant, and those in front joined in. "E-yasc-per-*jabik*!" they cried, and it spread throughout the hall. "E-yasc-per-*jabik*." Lord with the Piercing Eyes.

Rigiati scanned the crowd. He met the figure of the foreign necromancer Methe Sinese. The man was standing by the second arch, his folded arms hidden in flowing sleeves and only his sharp chin visible beneath the shadow of his hood. Sinese moved forward slightly, and their gazes connected.

As Teller looked down at the crystal that blocked the shaft, a bulky shadow appeared beside his own. He spun around. Didak loomed right behind him, cocking a meaty fist. Oh God. He was caught between him and a low rusty railing, the only thing, should the already cracked crystal break, that prevented a fall down three levels.

He opened both hands, palms out, and looked Didak in the eye. "Listen. I'm not your enemy. Just let—"

"Skew you," Didak said, and swung. Teller blocked the blow, but with the wrong arm, and the whomp against the bandage made him gasp with pain. Even then, he saw this man didn't fear the abakal; Didak was certain Teller would never destroy himself by using it. And in a way, he was right. The weapon was for something more important than either of their lives, and Teller had to keep it from going off prematurely.

He backed away from the ball as if he were thinking of running off, but instead edged around the shaft and away from the leather sack. Didak followed and took a swing at him, but Teller ducked under it. Didak whirled, the big man's punch brought him down, and Teller's cheek hit gritty soil.

Showing no ill effects from the blow Teller had given to his knee in the Node, Didak aimed a kick at him, but Teller twisted aside, rolled to his feet, and the two closed in. They exchanged blows, and in spite of Teller's best efforts, crashed into a section of railing. It sagged inward, but at least they were opposite the leather bag. As they both went down, the big Skinner beneath, Teller landed a punch that made the man grunt.

Didak shoved Teller aside and both climbed upright. The Skinner pulled out a knife, his eyes blazing. "Your ass is mine," he rasped through bleeding lips. "I'll have your cock for a trophy."

Teller instinctively reached for the dagger that again wasn't there, and then Didak was on him, followed by a blur of dodging and grappling and bursts of light. At one point the blade glittered in front of Teller's eyes, but he chopped at the man's wrist, and the knife flew out of the big Skinner's hand. Didak lunged for it, but Teller grabbed his arm, wrenched him around, and landed another clear punch on the man's mouth. With a yell, Didak retaliated with fierce one-two jabs to the chest. Teller staggered back, then lunged at Didak's knees. They both fell and rolled in a flurry of blows until Teller threw the Skinner off him and the two, breathing hard, stood facing each other. Didak's burning eyes were focused on Teller's face as the Skinner wiped his mouth on the back of his arm.

"Didak," Teller gasped. "Get off this cliff. I don't want—"

The rest was lost as Didak rammed into him. The two traded blows until Didak's fist smashed into Teller's shoulder and knocked him face up onto the ground. Didak dived on top of him, and their thrashing bodies hit the damaged section of the railing, which now bent almost horizontally over the shaft.

Teller tried to pull himself out from under Didak, half-rolling, pushing at him, dragging the Skinner along and getting him down as far as Teller's knees, but now Didak's calves were jutting over the edge of the shaft. "Watch it!" Teller cried.

Didak whipped a look over his shoulder and tried to climb over Teller's body, but Teller managed to raise his knees and push. Didak grabbed at a part of the railing, missed, and momentum sent his legs over the edge. The Skinner frantically scraped his boots for purchase against the inside of the shaft, and while still reaching for the rail with one hand, grabbed Teller's ankle with the other. His weight began dragging Teller toward the shaft. Teller managed to hook an arm around the bent rail as he slid toward the hole. It felt as if his leg was being torn off as Didak slipped further down. Teller turned his head toward the man's sweaty face and extended his free hand. "I'm not your enemy, Didak!"

His big body dangling, holding onto Teller's ankle with one hand, Didak tried to swing his other hand over to him. Teller strained out as far as he could to reach it, but off-balance, Didak fell. His bellow echoed up from the shaft.

Teller scrambled away from the edge and staggered to the intact section of the railing. Didak's body sprawled over the crystal, his neck at an impossible angle, his blood spattered over the thick glass. The impact had lengthened the crack. As Teller stared, it spider-webbed further and, one by one, pieces of the crystal began to drop away.

IN THE HALL OF THE EYE, a wind whistled in the floor vents, slammed a door along the side passageway, and then settled into silence. It was as if a great window in Oknu Shuld had suddenly opened, but there were no windows in Oknu Shuld. A strong gust from the southeast, Rigiati surmised, must have come through the side gates. With a gesture, he ordered them closed.

With his toothed smile, the lord spread out his arms and, looking from side to side, addressed the crowd. "Did you hear, my people? Oknu Shuld stirs out of its long sleep. It takes its first breath of the power to come, of vengeance against those who would destroy us."

The wind died away and the audience responded to their king's gracious, upwelling gestures with renewed cheers. In the midst of his triumph, the king stepped back and beckoned for Rigiati to approach him. The red smile disappeared, and the gaze of an intent reptile stared out of the chalky face. Rigiati bowed to cover his repulsion. "Yes, my king?"

The king spoke in a low voice. "Make sure the subalterns in back allow no one to leave this hall. My people must...."

Rigiati blinked. The king went on, but Rigiati didn't hear him. A row of what looked like tiny pointed blisters had sprung up on the back of the king's left hand. In this bilious light, they looked green. They reminded him—he frowned at the unpleasant thought—of grain-tips emerging from the skin.

One of his quad-captains pulled at his sleeve, and Rigiati took the step down to join him. "The Scaths are ready, Archon," the man said.

"What about the abakal?"

"No sign of it, sir."

No sign? It should have been down by now. "Send some of our men to get those Skinners *moving*."

Hoping the king hadn't heard about this setback, Rigiati looked up at him. He couldn't see any marks on his perfect, upraised hand. It must have been that scathi light from the Igneous Eye.

Chapter 43

Down the Drain

One level down, but deeper inside the cliff, Mariat helped Liasit steer hesitant, dazed, or terrified ahn toward the isav doors. Rivere had soothed the panicked man by pointing out that no other ahn was choking, and that it was fear that made him feel as if his collar was tightening. Liasit, however, had whispered to Mariat that almost every ahn was terrified the lord would discover what they were about to do, and that the poor man's imagined choking could become a terrible reality.

The gong had rung eleven times already, and Hanat stood at the door, waving everyone toward the spiral stairs. "This way now. Follow Beacon. Please hurry."

"Someone's coming!" a woman in the passage screamed. "The proctor's returning."

"The Azanzis! It's the Azanzi Scaths!"

"No!" Hanat shouted. "It's ahn coming down from the mine. Just follow Beacon. He's wearing Liasit's blanket."

Two or three ahn in front of Mariat stumbled in their haste, and one man fell. The woman behind him helped him up. Ahn seemed to be encouraging each other in that mind-speech of theirs, while smaller children trustingly held an adult's hand, and other ahn,

Liasit said, were praying to Rulve. Finally it seemed everyone had filed out. Mariat and Liasit rushed down the rows of abandoned mats to make sure no one had been left behind.

Someone had been. In the shadows of a back corner, Mariat spied a little girl, thumb in mouth, sitting on a mat and rocking back and forth under a blanket. The child paid no attention to them as they approached. "This is Wosie," Liasit explained. "She's not an ahn."

Mariat had already seen she didn't wear a collar. "Why is she here?"

"'Braks brought her in from a raid on Bellstone Forest. There was some kind of clash at the side gate, and she slipped away from them. Hanat found her hiding in the statuary hall. For months we've been able to conceal her from the proctor, but—we're afraid that can't last." Liasit caressed the child's cheek. "Poor Wosie. You can't hear the mind-speech, can you? You have no idea what's happening."

Mariat gently turned back the corner of the little girl's blanket. "Come with us now, sweetie," she said to her, "and you'll be all right. Bring your blanket."

Hurrying along hand in hand, they were the last to leave. As they turned into the passage, a panicked little boy ran directly into Liasit. She caught his arms. "What's wrong, Aron?"

"Where's Wosie?" Aron cried. "She's not anywhere and—" He caught sight of the child. "Where *were* you? I looked *everywhere*!"

Not answering, but giving him a beaming smile, Wosie draped her blanket around her neck and took Aron's left hand at the same time Liasit took his right.

"This is the little boy Teller saved," Liasit explained to Mariat. "Later I'll tell you about it."

The four of them half ran to catch up with the others. As they rushed down the spiral stairs, Mariat noticed that the strange odor of this place had gotten stronger. "What's that smell?" she asked Liasit.

"What smell?"

"Like spoiled eggs. And it's getting warmer down here too. You'd think it would be the opposite."

"I don't smell anything. Maybe because I'm used to it. Further down are the steam pipes, though. They heat up water for cooking and for the baths. The pipes go off to a big chamber where mud bubbles up." She frowned. "It's dangerous there."

Grinning, Aron tugged at Mariat's hand. "It's where Oknu Shuld farts. Sometimes it lets out a real big one. And then we *all* smell it."

TOWARD THE FRONT OF THE LINE, Rivere stood on tiptoe to peer behind him. Beacon had ordered every tenth person to grab a hand globe, and the ragged line of ahn glowed in the passage with spots of wavering light. They had passed tunnels that led in different directions to the scourery and the baths, but this darker passage ended just beyond the dungeons and the strisnu. Did this Beacon know they were heading toward a dead end? The sulfuric pools and hissing steams that lay at the noxious base of Oknu Shuld roiled in a chamber only a few walls away. As a healer, he knew no one should inhale much of that.

From further ahead, Beacon stopped and turned. "I need four strong men," he called out. "The rest of you hug the walls so they can get through." The request was passed down, and soon a few big ahn, looking wary, made their way forward with Rivere.

Leaving the others behind, the six of them rounded a bend where the passage ended in a storeroom stacked with old crates full of debris. Rivere glimpsed broken globes, a moldy boot, and a chair leg, all probably forgotten in their journey to the garbage heaps. Behind the crates loomed a rough rock wall that marked, Rivere surmised, the southern extent of the entire fortress. Fumes had collected in this backwater and were rankling against the back of his throat.

"The air here is poison!" he cried to Beacon. "Are you trying to kill us?"

The man ignored him and gestured to the four ahn. "Move these aside," he ordered, pointing to a pile of crates in the corner. "Quickly, please." They needed no urging and soon exposed a metal circle on the floor about two strides across. Beacon directed them to grab the handles on either side of the cover and, with metal scraping against the rock floor, they dragged it off. Cold, dank air wafted out.

Rivere looked down in horror. This was an access-hole to the drainage system of Oknu Shuld. "We can't take them down there! The drain may be water-logged, or full of rats, or even blocked."

"It was none of those things," Beacon said, "when last I was down there."

"But, but," Rivere spluttered, "that was years ago!"

"It's the only way," Beacon said. "Trust Rulve." He turned to the ahn behind him. "Send word down the line: we are about to enter a tunnel."

Murmurs passed through the crowd as Beacon descended a short ladder into the hole. "It's dry," he called up, his voice echoing, "and the air is better. That means this drain is open, Rivere, just as I remember it. There is not much room, but it is enough. Start sending everyone down."

Only one person at a time could climb down. Rivere tried to hide his misgivings as he handed ahn after ahn down the ladder. Most exclaimed at the tight fit, but at least the sulfur fumes in the chamber seemed to have alleviated a bit, as if some air current had drawn them out when the drain cover had been removed. As more ahn went down after Beacon, Rivere could hear their anxious, high-pitched voices. He wanted someone with common sense stationed in the middle of the line, so he passed word to let Hanat through from the back.

When no one was left above—Mariat ran back a way to make sure—he ushered her, Liasit, and the two children down the hole. Wosie, her eyes big, wrapped her arms around Mariat's neck as the young woman climbed down.

RIGIATI EXPECTED TROUBLE WHEN A SINGLE volghast swept onto the dais and bowed before the king. Like all four of the creatures, this one not only stank like the corpse it was, but also brought with it an aura of hollow gloom.

"Teller-of-Lies is not to be found in the Vora's domain," the thing said. "Nor is the Vora itself. We found nothing but the traitor's green dagger." He laid it at the king's feet.

The king stood very still, and a chill ran up Rigiati's back. If the king's proposed "work of art" had somehow escaped, if Cinc had somehow dispatched the Vora, then his majesty was about to be hugely humiliated in front of his people. Mistakes had been made, and Rigiati would be the first in line when the Eyascnu's reptilian eyes sought someone to blame.

THE PASSAGEWAY WAS ACTUALLY A LARGE pipe, so they had to walk single file on its up-curved floor. Carrying Wosie, and having to bend her head at times, Mariat followed the white-clothed figures ahead of her. Aron and a few of the other ahn children seemed to think this journey was a great adventure, and they had started some kind of chase game in which they squeezed their way past legs or hid to the side and jumped out at each other.

Along the way Liasit told her that Teller had saved Aron's life, but then he had seemed to abandon the ahn and became Vol Cinc.

"He's not Vol Cinc anymore," Mariat said. "I know that, Liasit. He cut off his finger to be rid of the vol-ring. I doubt he ever really *was* a Vol, deep in his heart. And like Beacon told you, Teller is right now up on the cliff, risking his life to try and save all the ahn."

No one nearby in the line said anything until a man muttered, "Well, he hasn't done it yet, has he?"

The line moved slightly downhill and straight ahead, sometimes passing under other openings in the ceiling. Puddles collected here, and everyone had to step gingerly through them. That meant the line slowed or halted altogether and then went ahead so rapidly they had to rush to keep up.

The line halted under one such opening, and Mariat looked up. "Er," she said to Liasit, who was directly behind her, "is something more—solid—likely to plop down on our heads?"

"Something solid? Oh, I understand. No, I don't think you have to worry. We have separate shit shafts leading to ground, and these get shoveled out before much of the, the *juice* I guess you'd say, can leak down here.

The line started up again, and thankfully Wosie had no objections when Mariat put her down and took her hand. "You were getting a little heavy there, sweetie," she said.

The child took her thumb out of her mouth. "No 'weetie," she said. "Wosie."

"All right, Wosie."

"No! *Wosie.*"

Before they could get any further with this conversation, Mariat quickly had to pick the child up again. They'd come to a puddle that smelled like rancid soap mixed with urine, which Liasit said must have come down from the baths. She tiptoed through, wrinkling her nose. After that, the ceiling lowered even more. Occasional cries echoed back to them, perhaps from someone stumbling or striking his head, or maybe from a child caught in the chase game; but most of the time all Mariat could detect in the confined space was the shuffling of worn sandals and the smell of frightened people. The line ahead was dotted by hand-globes, but they didn't seem to illuminate very much. Even with Liasit's globe right behind her, she could only see the nearest faces.

They shuffled along, and in spite of the long line of ahn, Mariat felt alone. Would this drain be like the rest of her life, a long confined darkness without Sheft? She heard Liasit ask Rivere, who was behind her at the end of the line, "Where are we? Shouldn't we be going uphill by now?"

As if in answer, word came down from the front: "Beacon says not to be afraid. The drain goes under the Eeron River and ends in a catch basin on the other side. Then we'll be free."

The idea of going under a river alarmed Mariat, but she concentrated on keeping up. Liasit's hand-globe was barely glowing, the luniku dying, and Mariat dreaded the time when the lights ahead would go out altogether.

Up on Insheer Cliff, Teller watched the crystal cave in, its sharp edges screeching against the shaft and taking Didak's body with it. The Node's hot air rushed up against Teller's face, along with a caustic whiff of the potions that had been spilled during his fight with the Skinners.

Another man had died because he couldn't save him, only hours after Sheft had given his life to save them all.

The shaft was clear. And if his conscience was not, he would pay for that life with his own. He took a deep breath, reached down to the leather bag, and pulled out the ball of abakal. He raised the ball high, and then with a quick prayer—*In your justice, Rulve; in your mercy!*—hurled it down. Gripping the rail, he closed his eyes and waited for nine balls of abakal to explode beneath his feet and drop the ground from under him.

After two breaths, nothing happened. He opened his eyes, waited for one long tense moment, and then leaned over the railing. All was silent down in the dark, yawning hole.

Didak's big body must have cushioned the ball just enough to prevent it from exploding. Or the abakal had become too encrusted with time to be so easily set off. Or more likely, the whole idea had been impossible from the start.

CHAPTER 44

THE GHOSTS OF OKNU SHULD

TWELVE HIGH GONGS RANG THROUGH THE Hall of the Eye. The arrival of the Azanzis at the side gate, Rigiati knew, would distract the crowd from the escape, even if temporary, of the king's "work of art." But nothing would distract the king if abakal did not appear. Rigiati, his stomach fluttering, scanned the archway for his messenger to inform him the abakal had arrived, but didn't see him,

The king turned his ghastly smile upon the audience. "Ah," he said. "It is time. My warriors await me." In an aside, he spoke to the volghast in a low voice: "I want Teller-of-Lies apprehended immediately. Join the others and search for him. As soon as the traitor is found, bring him to my workroom. Keep him alive, bound to the table, to await my leisure." He returned to the crowd and extended his hands. "Our grand moment is at hand!" he cried. "With the Azanzi Scaths at my back, with my loyal subjects cheering us on, we will take our first step toward a glorious future. Subalterns will escort you out of the hall to line up along the road, so you may stand in an orderly manner and cheer our march to the Seani. After our victory, Vol Cinc's transformation will be part of a celebration none will forget."

Rigiati flinched. What if the abakal had not been brought down yet? He turned to the king with an excuse on his lips.

But the words he was about to say stuck in his throat. A shadow had appeared over the lower half of the lord's face. Even as he watched, it spread up to his cheeks.

"What are you gaping at?" the king asked sharply.

"Your—your beard, my king." But the color was wrong. Horribly, unmistakably, wrong.

"I have no beard, you fool!"

Bile rose in Rigiati's throat. This time the shadow was no trick of the light. It was growing with incredible speed into a patch of what looked like—by the twin voras!—tiny blades of grass.

The king rubbed his chin. His fingers came away stained with green. Frowning, he wiped them on the front of his robe and then stared at the back of his hand. Like a horrible rash, tiny spikes burst through the skin, spread rapidly over the royal fingers, and then up his wrists. "Hist, s'rere!" the king commanded. "Hist!" *Stop.*

Green tips popped up on his forearms.

Rigiati leaned closer. "By Ázu, majesty, do something!" The green beard was half an inch long now and creeping over the smooth, white cheeks.

The Eyascnu seemed not to hear him, but a dagger of skora leaped into his hand. The king swept the fire-blade over his arm, shearing the green poking through his skin. An outgrowth of tiny dicots rapidly followed the blade. He caused skora to vanish and used both hands to scratch fiercely at his cheeks and neck. Though torn, his beard continued to grow. Faint red streaks rushed across his forehead. He scratched at them and produced rows of emerging seed heads.

"S'rere hist!" he cried. "Hi—" The command ended in a mumble as moss crawled over the lord's lips.

THE CHILDREN'S GAME HAD ENDED, AND with no distractions, worries crawled out of the dark and into Mariat's head. We're the ghosts of Oknu Shuld, she thought, shuffling through this drain, and no one knows we're down here. What if Varo climbed up some other access hole and abandoned us? What if he was really a madman who thought he was a savior? The air down here was supposed to prove that the drain was still open at the other end, but what if not? What if it branched into other pipes only a rat could get through?

With Wosie clutching her skirt, Mariat bumped into the ahn in front of her. The line had come to a halt. Ahead she could make out only the nearest white-clad shapes. Behind her, past Liasit and Rivere, stretched only the empty, pitch-black drain.

A sound froze her heart. A gurgling hiss was making its way back from the front of the line.

Liasit's hand, ice-cold, found hers. The sound came closer, resolved into a wave of gasps, and it wasn't water flooding in, which she at first had feared, but something worse: wheezing sobs and horrible gurgles. With a strangled cry, Liasit let go of Mariat's hand and clutched her ahn-collar.

She was choking. All the ahn were choking. They'd gone too far, and their collars would let them go no farther.

Guttural rasps filled the darkness. Clutching at their collars, ahn writhed frantically in the close confines of the drain. Hand-globes smashed to the floor, and all down the line lights winked out. Wosie threw her blanket over her head and crouched against the wall. A little boy—oh God, it was Aron—crawled past her and grabbed Liasit's ankles. "Heghlp me!" he cried. But she couldn't.

Rivere snatched up the boy and shouted at those ahead. "Everyone come back! Turn around and come back!" He turned and ran with the boy, as if he could find some invisible line where the collars would let the ahn breathe. Mariat pulled Wosie and Liasit after him as the ahn dropped her globe-light and clawed with both hands at her collar.

Horrified, Mariat held the meager light high with one hand and tried with the other to keep Liasit on her feet. Wosie clung tightly to her leg as panicked, suffocating ahn squirmed past them to follow Rivere. They crawled over those who had fallen, only to fall themselves. Oh God, those further behind would never make it. The dying were blocking the drain against those who fought to live.

Help us, Rulve! Don't abandon us here in the dark.

NINE LEVELS ABOVE HER, UP ON Insheer Cliff, Teller stared into the still-breathing depths of the Node shaft. Nothing arose from it except the whisper of yet another failure. Which was followed by the distant sound he had been dreading: twelve high gongs.

An ache squeezed his throat. He was too late. The abakal would be gone; the Scaths would be setting out for the Seani. Suddenly the ache became a noose around his neck. The ahn collar tightened. Teller grabbed at it, but there was no room for his fingers to get a hold. He was strangling. The ahn must be strangling. Little Aron and Hanat, garroted and betrayed, their hope stifled.

Yet even as black spots danced in front of his eyes, sh'kier burned and pressed in his spirikai. The abakal was still there, and Rulve's fire knew it.

The fight in the Node must have broken up the Skinner patrol. Didak was dead, Haro-epet gone, and the two others might not have made it against rats and fumes. Only now would the archon be missing his weapon.

Trying to reach the bag at his feet, trying to suck air past what felt like a stone stuck in his windpipe, he fell to his knees. Only his heart, before all went black, was able to cry out to Rulve.

RIVERE STOOD HELPLESS AS THE AHN around him gagged and twisted and wheezed in an eye-bulging struggle to breathe. Aron flopped like a dead weight in his arms.

Down the narrow drain breaths rattled. They could no longer cry out. Countless times he had told the badly wounded to be quiet, to stop moaning, had given them rags to stuff in their mouths while he tried to save them, tried to keep the proctor from slitting their throats.

A scream of protest rose inside him.

RIGIATI BACKED AWAY AS THE VORIAN Guards rushed in to form a protective circle around their king. They shielded him from view as he tore grass out of his cheeks.

"Majesty," the Vorian captain cried. "What should we do?"

"By the twin voras," another exclaimed, "what is happening to him?"

The guards reached out anxiously as the king clawed at leaves unfolding from his ears and knuckled a white flower out of his nose; moved along with him as he lurched toward his throne. Abruptly their sovereign halted and looked down, one foot poised. His boot creaked, swelled. Leaves tumbled over the top, then a mass of ivy burst through the leather.

Skora flared as a sword in the king's hand, and he hacked at his boot as if trying to cut it off. Even though the smell of his burning flesh made Rigiati recoil, the king seemed too frantic to notice and still tried to burn himself clean. Skora jabbed through the air, and the Vorians on the dais dodged and jumped out of its way.

No one noticed the ahn-collar lying on the carpet. It was the collar that the simulacrum and the king had, for a moment, shared. It was the collar many lived and died with, borne also by two young men in solidarity with the ahn they had come to save. No one saw it until a wild sweep of the king's skora—a power that had been shared for a moment with Teller and that had released a power in Sheft—cut the metal circle in half. The two pieces flared, melted, and burned into ash.

Chapter 45

Exaltation

Liasit sucked in a deep breath. She pulled at her collar and the thing came off in her hand. Puzzled and blinking, she could only stare at it in disbelief. What in Rulve's name—?

She suddenly realized that the ahn in front of her were gulping down air, that the drain was filled with gasps and the hiss of in-breaths. Everyone was pulling off their collars. Metal clattered onto the stone floor. A young man threw his collar to the ground and stomped on it as if it were a snake. Another screamed out years of pent-up hatred and tried to tear the metal apart with his bare hands.

All down the drain, dim light still trailed in worm clumps on the floor.

She turned to look behind her. Mariat had thrust her globe-light into Rivere's hands and grabbed Aron away from him. She pulled off the collar from around his neck, put her mouth over his, and blew short puffs into his mouth. After a moment he sucked in a gasp, opened his eyes, and started breathing on his own.

Rivere looked blankly from him to Mariat. "The—the collars," he stammered. "How—?" A wild-eyed ahn grabbed Liasit by the shoulders and shook her. "We are free," he shouted into her face. "The niyalahn-rista freed us! Listen! I can say it. I can say the forbidden name. The *niyalahn-rista* set us free!"

All down the line people were shouting the beloved, the saving, the wondrous name; thanking Rulve, thanking Teller. Full of emotion, Liasit burst into tears.

Aron pulled away from Mariat, looked around, and spotted Wosie peeking out from under her blanket. She was still pale and frightened, but being without a collar, unhurt. Aron squirmed out of Mariat's arms and onto his feet. Grabbing Wosie's hand, he slipped through the crowded tunnel with her, pointing out all the pretty lights crawling on the floor.

Someone up the line was trying to be heard above the noise, and Liasit wiped her eyes. A message was coming down, and she repeated it through her hoarse throat to the two people behind her. "Beacon says everyone's safe; that it was a miracle. He says hold onto each other now, move forward, and pray."

"That last part," Mariat replied in a shaking voice, "is good advice in any situation."

She helped Liasit extricate those ahn who had fallen into a tangle of arms and legs, and who were now somewhat hysterically laughing about it, and soon the line began inching forward. Soon another message came down. It sounded urgent, but almost everyone's throat was still scratchy, so what Liasit heard didn't make a lot of sense. Rushing to keep up with the line, she tossed back the message as best as she could make it out. "Beacon says to hurry." That part was clear. "Then he said something about 'a living seed' and 'T'lir has to bury him.' And that they can't wait much longer."

"What?" Rivere shouted from the rear. "A living what?"

Mariat grabbed Liasit's arm. "Oh," she cried, "it's about Sheft!"

With a whirl of her hair, Liasit answered over her shoulder. "It's about Teller," she exclaimed, "and he's still alive!"

TELLER'S EYES SPRUNG OPEN. IN RAPID succession he realized he was breathing, that his throat was sore, and that the tight metal around his neck had loosened. He pulled at the ahn collar and, to his astonishment, it came off.

He held the circle in his hand and knew that the same thing had happened to every ahn in Oknu Shuld. He took a deep breath of the cold Seed air, and gratitude spilled over him, shot through with an impossible joy. The ahn were free.

His father said they would be. But how had that happened?

Sh'kier pounded inside him, and suddenly his question didn't matter. The ahn-collars had been broken, and his father could lead to safety those who had been forced to wear them. Now, no matter what he himself had to do, the ahn would not be hurt. *Oh God Rulve, thank you.*

Relieved of that tremendous burden, he climbed to his feet and turned to stand over the shaft. Focused now on the one thing necessary, he concentrated on the fire that surged up in his spirikai. It filled him with energy and light. It was Rulve's gift—the wrenching, extravagant necessity of love.

For the first time, he willed to release it. Sh'kier streamed out of his spirikai and leaped before him as a single rod of light. It blazed with wild exaltation. Awe struck him with such force that he almost sank down in worship before it. But that would be wrong, for sh'kier was not Rulve, but only belonged to him. It was lent out of her compassion and righteousness, a power Teller must both use and be used by.

Take my hands, Rulve.

Teller grasped the rod of white fire, and even though he could see through it, even though he could feel the terrible thrumming of its energy in his grasp, it felt only as warm as a stone in the sun. It poured its relentless strength into his chest and arms and shoulders, full of Rulve's passion to sweep up the sin of the world and bring justice down like rain.

On the floor of the Hall, several altercations had erupted. Powerful supporters of the king, accustomed to obedience and respect, resisted the arrogant red-cloaked ruffians who were insisting on herding them like cattle into lines. Angry, indignant, and hungry, they assumed the action up front came from the king demonstrating skora to the guards gathered around him.

Surrounded by the helpless Vorian Guards and shielded from view by almost everyone in the Hall, the king whirled in front of his throne, waving skora wildly in hands mittened by gloves of grass.

"Scathi gods!" one of the Vorians cried as the king's magnificent robe bulged and ripped open with greenery. Others tried to pull handfuls of grass poking out of the lord's fine shirt, but mindless streaks of skora pushed them back.

A quad-captain, the last man to join the Azanzi force at the side gates, glanced back. He took one look at the chaos on the dais and leaped to the wrong conclusion. "Treason!" he cried. "By Ázu, the king is being attacked!" A few of his men heard this and rushed back to help. Shouting, they and their captain climbed onto the dais. Already on edge, the Vorians turned with a bellow to defend themselves.

"No!" Rigiati shouted, "Stand down! No one's attacking..." Being pushed and shoved in the melee, he saw the king open his mouth. Like some obscene tongue, the tip of a vine poked from between his mossy lips. The scuffling soldiers on the dais stopped in their tracks as the King of Shunder, the Thakur of the Riftwood, and the Master of Bellstone Forest threw back his green-leafed head and, with the vine in his mouth whipping horribly back and forth, emitted a screeching animal ululation.

AS IF HE WERE A NARROW cleft through which a mountain river flumed, revenge churning into mercy, doubt swirling into certainty, and failures cresting into gain all swept through Teller's body and became one with sh'kier.

For Taisa, for Sheft, and for Mariat, for Rivere and the Vols and the ahn, for his grandmother and his father and for all of Rulve's people, he raised the rod and drove it down the shaft.

Even as sh'kier blazed down, blind instinct made Teller turn and run. He pelted toward stable ground where no tunnels honeycombed the cliff, and the nearest place was the rocky bed of the former Sunsink Falls.

He heard his own gasping breaths, his thumping boots; then purple light flashed behind him. Immediately followed a muffled series of *phung! phung! phung! phung! phung!* and then a long, ragged mutter. He snatched a look over his shoulder. The surface behind him heaved like an emerging hilltop. Earth, stones, and morue sprouts rolled off it, and then with a boom, it burst open. He put his head down and kept running. A rain of gravel spattered over his shoulders and pieces of the rusty railing whirled out in front of him. Earth crumbled beneath his heels as the ground behind him collapsed.

A SERIES OF BOOMS RUMBLED THROUGH the Hall of the Eye, followed by a hot wind that whirled down the side hall. A much greater wind than before, it billowed cloaks and sent grit whirling into people's eyes and hair. It swept in the smell of soil and the sound of a rumbling hiss as from a distant sandslide. The crowd scattered out from the lines they were being herded into.

"Earthquake!" some shouted. "A whirlwind!" Others, frozen with fear and staring in horror at the swinging globes above their heads, were jostled by people pushing their way toward the great locked doors.

SEVERAL QUICK, DULL THUDS THUMPED FROM above, and Mariat cringed as a cold drop of water fell into her hair. Screams jumped through the semi-dark, and the line of ahn came to a halt. A puff of damp air suddenly touched the back of her neck, then was gone.

"Something cracked!" a male voice down the line cried. "Something gave way above our heads."

"Oh, God," a nearby ahn whispered, "the drain is going to cave in!"

Mariat reached to clutch the sleeves of Sheft's sheepskin jacket. She'd been wearing it under her cloak ever since she and her beloved had been separated by the umbrak attack in the Riftwood. But it wasn't there.

She had lost it. In all the terror and heartbreak, she had left it behind somewhere. Wearing it had given her courage for what must have been days. Other than the cold toltyr, it was all she had left of his warmth and his love. She turned, bumped into Rivere, and cried out, "I have to go back!"

But go back where? Once out of the drain, she'd never be able to trace her way back through the confusing network of passages and levels. What if she were caught? What would happen to Sheft's babies?

It was too late, and there was no going back.

ACROSS THE VALLEY TO THE WEST, two abutting timbers squealed on Rydle Bridge. Standing on the village side, the rebel leader Havek turned his head. An earthshake? He looked up at Insheer Cliff, but the view from here was too foreshortened to see the surface. A cloud of dust rose, but small whirlwinds were common up there. There was no time to puzzle over it, however, He and several other Bellstone warriors went back to loading the wagon that would block the bridge. At any moment the Azanzis would round the curve of the cliff, and their whole plan depended on them being stopped, at least momentarily, right here.

FARTHER WEST, INSIDE THE WALLED SEANI compound, the surface of the Pool of Compassion trembled briefly, even though there was no wind. Taisa smiled a little when she saw that. She sat on the stone bench beside the pool, her hood up against the cold, and the trembling brought to mind her first minor earthshake. She'd been about three, and some of the children in the nursery had made a fuss. But she and Teller had laughed with delight as her red ball, all by itself, rolled across the floor.

Taisa turned on the stone bench to face Marhaut's statue, then lowered her head and clenched her hands on her lap. Teller had been gone not even two days, but she could actually feel the wound in her heart.

TELLER SLID INTO THE FORMER WATERCOURSE ahead of him, then turned, panting, and propped himself up with hands on his knees. About a stone's throw behind him, earth thick with morue roots tumbled over the edge of a giant sinkhole. Above it a cloud carried dirt, bits of paper, sparkles of glass, and what looked like the legs and tail of a charred rat. Because most of the force of the explosion had occurred three levels down into rock, the cloud, dropping dust, dissipated in a few minutes. When it all settled, Teller brushed himself off and stumbled past a vent pipe that smoked like a chimney. Keeping well back from the edge, he looked into the crater.

Dirt still hissed down in many places while sunlight revealed glimpses of truncated corridors and the ragged edges of floors. Cut off walls mingled with tumbled heaps of rock and worktables and stair treads, all sparkling with globe-glass. For the first time since it had been tunneled out of the rock, a giant hole gaped through a section of the top three levels of Oknu Shuld.

"THE QUAKE IS OVER," RIVERE SHOUTED up to everyone from behind Mariat. "Don't panic. We're safe down here."

Safe? Mariat thought. She didn't feel safe. Whatever happened far above was bound to affect them all in this narrow, ancient drain. Aron and Wosie had returned to her side, and she held their hands tightly until a murmur came up from the front: "Beacon says to move forward! Move, move, move!"

The line forged ahead. Liasit's hand-globe had somehow survived, and Rivere held it up, but the blackness outside its dimming circle dogged their steps like a stalking presence

People ahead of her pressed to the side, allowing someone to edge past. It was Varo.

"What happened?" Mariat ask him. "What was that noise?"

"Whatever it was, we are intact. I came down the line to make sure no one needed help." He looked aside and then back to his daughter-in-law. "It was as I said, Mariat. The niyalahn-ristas have freed the ahn."

She didn't know if she had ever doubted him. Still did not know what really had happened.

Wosie tugged on Varo's hand. "How," she piped up, "can you see in the dark?"

He bent to look gravely down at her. "Practice, little girl. I have had plenty of practice."

Now Aron had a question. "How come the luniku didn't crawl away? Usually they do that when a globe breaks. But now they're kind of like, lighting our way."

"I don't wike them," Wosie stated firmly.

"They are innocent creatures," Varo told her. "Baby moths you could say. They were created to become the glowing moon-moths that grace the night. But my bro— the king changed them into something bad. Now my sons are redeeming them. Everything is being redeemed."

He moved on to speak to Rivere.

"What's 'wedeemed'?" Wosie asked Aron.

"I don't know. Maybe it means bringing things back to what they're supposed to be. All I know is that Teller saved me when I was in the torture chamber. Maybe now he's saving the luniku too. Maybe they will go back to being good moths again. Now that they're free instead of stuck inside here."

It all sounded so fantastic, Mariat thought, but Sheft could certainly have had something to do with that. He liked bugs.

After Varo passed her, returning to the front, she heard him repeating the same words as he moved farther and farther away. "Have courage. You are free. Trust Rulve."

She didn't understand; found it hard to trust; but hope, maybe, she could manage.

IN THE HALL OF THE EYE, the alarming disturbances went on for several heartbeats, and then gradually subsided. A faint whiff of smoke, however, trailed through the hall. The red-cloaks in back formed ranks against the crowd, assured everyone to remain calm, and ordered them to return to their places in line. Eyes still wide with trepidation, the king's supporters hesitated but began to comply.

But that was forgotten when, shockingly, everything changed. Someone near the dais shrieked.

All over the hall heads turned toward the front. People craned their necks and cried out, "What's going on?"

"Oh my god!" a shop-owner shouted. "Look! Look at the dais!"

"I can't see!"

Those closer to the dais gaped at the place where only moments before guards had been encircling their newly acclaimed king. Now they seemed to be...dancing around him. At first many couldn't comprehend what they were seeing, but then more screams peppered the hall as others pushed forward and got a better look.

The king was staggering under the weight of some kind of clinging, living suit of, not armor, but greenery. His torso was rapidly disappearing under a man-shaped mound of it. Skora-flares burst from within as the mound fell and writhed on the ground. The Vorians darted in to reach it, but were driven back by random streaks of fire.

Screams and questions ran like a tide through the hall. The drummers fled from the dais and pushed their way through the crowd, their instruments banging against their chests.

Archon Burs reached up and grabbed Rigiati's arm. "Stop this!" he ordered. "You must—!" A Vorian fell between them, a skora burn across his face.

Their purple cloaks billowing, the rest of the king's guards jumped off the dais. People who had fought to move forward now fled back, and a wealthy landowner in front, after taking one look at the king, vomited.

TELLER STARED INTO THE HOLE BENEATH his feet. The rolling gate from level one, twisted from the explosion and hanging over the abyss, broke loose and fell. It crashed into rubble at the bottom of the hole. Smoke billowed out from a corridor on level three, where abakal must have started a fire. Gone were the laboratorium and the Node, and Section 31 had been severely damaged.

He stood there as dust settled into silence, repeating over and over, *Thank you, Rulve. Thank you I could do this.*

After a moment he moved away and looked toward the Seani, that small place across the valley that was his home and Taisa's. No one there could know what he had done, but Taisa and everyone else were safe now. The great walls stood solid, the Pool of Rulve glittered untouched, the great jade hands still offered comfort. All of it stood in witness that, at last, the terrible weapon he had made was redeemed. Close to tears, he sank to the ground. What he should never have made in the first place, sh'kier had finally destroyed. Abakal was gone.

He stayed for a moment with that relief and joy. But then he remembered. The Seani was Lir's home as well as Taisa's, and the man who had risked his life for him had the first claim upon her heart.

Chapter 46

Twice Given and Yet Again

Taisa had come to Marhaut's statue to be alone, but someone was crunching over last fall's leaves, and she turned her head. It was Lir.

"A bit of a tremble we had there," he remarked.

"A bit."

He took a breath, then asked, polite as always, "May I sit with you for a moment?"

Lir had been there for both her ward-mother and herself when their beloved husband and father had been brutally killed by 'braks. She turned on the bench to face him, pulled her cloak closer, and nodded.

He sat next to her. Neither spoke, and then Lir leaned over to look into her face. "Taisa, are you all right? You were a pain-bearer for Teller, and it must be hard for you now."

She slipped her hand into the pocket of her cloak, where she grasped the red and blue cord Teller had given her late that night in the nursery. She had held his wounded hand, had kissed it, and all too briefly they had clung tightly to each other. Now she must constantly swallow her worry for him and push away the feeling of dread that he would never return, that his short visit had served only to say good-bye. She averted her head, waited until the swelling left her throat, and then managed to say, "I'm all right."

"As well as any of us are, I think. With both emjadis gone." He hesitated a moment, then said, "I stopped by the infirmary this morning, but you weren't there."

"I was helping Ukaipa in the nursery. She's getting better, but that cold sapped her energy." She smoothed out a wrinkle on her cloak. "I'm sure you were tired too." He'd ridden through an entire night in a race against time and had endangered his life to save Teller's. Then he had to take part in the exhausting discussions during that long meeting at the Weshnik'Aseah.

"I'm fine. Abiyat didn't mind, so I caught a nap in the infirmary while—" He broke off and looked away.

While waiting for her, she guessed. She glanced up at his profile, that of an intense young man who never said much. Yet he was probably destined one day to take Se Druv's place as head of the Se. According to her ward-mother, he lived a hard and even dangerous life, often setting out alone on mysterious missions for Druv. It was said that, while only a boy during the Seani's darkest time after Teller had been abducted, Lir had quietly saved the eldest Se from a debilitating despair.

But, she decided, admiration and compassion weren't what Lir needed from her, weren't what he deserved. "I have to get back to the hospit," she said gently.

"I understand." A muscle worked in his jaw, and then he glanced over at her. "I've found that being with you is important to me, Taisa. I think it gives both of us strength."

Again there was a silence between them. Then Lir

cleared his throat. "Deoner believes Sheft and Teller deliberately left us. That they turned themselves over to the Spider-king so we and the forest warriors and the village rebels would join forces against him."

Yes, she'd already heard that. If it were true, their departure must be what Rulve wanted, and it was right and heroic and noble of Teller to leave her. But it meant her love for Teller had been greater than his love for her.

Lir took her hand. "I think about you, Taisa. More every day."

As gently as she could, she pulled her hand away. "I'm sorry, Lir. It's not like that between us."

"But it could be."

"You need—you *deserve*—more than what I feel for you." He certainly didn't deserve a detestable, jealous woman who couldn't seem to help begrudging the decision her beloved had made.

"Give me time. And just a little hope."

Taisa bit her lip. "Please don't do this. I don't want to hurt you."

For a moment he said nothing, but then a strain entered his voice. "I see. It's Teller, isn't it. He shows up, and suddenly there's nothing for me."

Incredulity flooded her. "How can you say that? He was hurting, and it was my duty to help. You of all people should understand."

He looked her in the eye. "I can't compete with a niyal'arist, Taisa. No man can."

With a pang of sorrow—whether for Lir or for Teller or for herself, she couldn't explain— she turned her head away.

He thumped his fist on his knee. "I'm a fool," he murmured. "He's only been gone a short time, and here I come pressing my suit. I'm sorry, Taisa. I just wanted to say—just wanted you to know—that I care for you. I'll wait, no matter how long it takes. And if he never… well, I'll be here. If you can only give me your second best, Taisa, I'll take it."

There was nothing she could say. She didn't deserve either Teller or Lir, but oh Rulve, now both had touched her heart.

Quietly Lir stood up and left her.

THE SOUND OF BOOTS CLANGING ON the metal ladder woke Teller up. His dream of Taisa's light-filled brown eyes fled, and he fastened his gaze on the still untouched guardhouse.

One by one, four volghasts were emerging into the cold sun atop Insheer Cliff. Like ghastly marionettes, they all together turned their cowled heads toward him.

He stood and backed away as the volghasts skirted the sinkhole and spread out to surround him. The four undead stopped only feet away, and the tallest one spoke. "The king has plans for you. You will come with us, Volghast Cinc."

The words felt like acid thrown against his heart. "No," Teller grated. "I'm not one of you. I'll never be one of you."

"It is the king's command."

"Too bad."

They grabbed hold of him. He struggled, twisted, and kicked, a part of him knowing how useless it was, but the rest of him not caring. There'd be no more dark passageways leading into namelessness, no more windowless rooms, no more of his life scraped away by tightly gloved hands. He would not go back.

They dragged him, fighting all the way, around the smoking sinkhole and toward the guardhouse. They had cut the life out of his brother, inch by inch, and that searing knowledge kept on fueling his rage. Again and again Teller tried to break free, until, tightening their grip, they halted.

"That is enough," the tall volghast said. Expressionless, it stood in front of him while two of the creatures pulled Teller's arms out and the third gripped him by an elbow around his neck. "As forever the least of us, you will learn now to obey us."

The creature hit Teller in the face, its red eyes impassive, then methodically proceeded to strike him, first with its gauntleted right fist and then its left. It stopped when Teller's knees gave out, and he hung half-choked among the three who held him.

They hauled him toward the guardhouse, their moldy boots crushing the morue sprouts; and their smell of the grave, mingled with that of morue, turned his stomach. The guardhouse loomed closer, opening to dim tunnels that led to a desiccated, dusty eternity beneath the ground, to an iron subjugation forever imposed upon his will.

So where are you now, Rulve? Where are the fire and the power when I need it? I can't feel your presence, and it's as if you never existed, and God damn *you, Rulve, if you abandon me now!*

And then, incredibly, out of his depths a laugh bubbled up. Not a solitary bark of bitter despair, but one that realized the utter absurdity of what he had just said to his Creator. He laughed, and the two of them laughed, one at his own brash foolishness and the other with utter delight in the honesty that had provoked it. They chuckled in pure chagrin, with a human-divine emphasis on the grin.

Rulve knew him down to the core, and that intimacy would sustain him forever, no matter what they did to him. He existed with his Lord in a fundamental connection that ultimately made all things well.

Atayami, skora! the king shouted. *Power of fire, come to me!* But the ivy collar around his neck choked back his order, and the fire did not come. Grass sprouted out of his ears and the corners of his eyes; he gasped for air through the leaves flapping in his mouth. He was blind and deaf, an itching, erupting mass.

Stems entangled his feet, and he fought to kick free. A woody knob twisted out from between his legs. With thick hands he groped for the traitor's green dagger to plunge into his heart. The volghast had dropped it at his feet, but now he could not find it. He pounded his head viciously against the marble tiles, attempting to splatter his brains out, but oh god Ázu, he was too encrusted. He tried to order: *Kai Archon, cut off my head! I command you!* but only a long, throaty screech came out.

A voice broke through his agony. Even in his panic he could hear it: someone speaking directly into his mind. It was the voice of a young man. "You are feeling s'rere, the power you have so long sought. It is yours at last, running through your body. Now you truly know its power."

He was losing his reason. It wasn't enough that thready roots wormed into his veins; that his skin crawled like a nest of ants. *Oh God kill me! Take my life.*

"Give it to him, Uncle," the young man pleaded. "You are brimming with life, now give it to Rulve, and she will save your people."

The words in his head were madness, proved he was going insane. He had no brother. He was no one's uncle. There was no Rulve.

"I too was once afraid of s'rere," the voice said. "Afraid of roots, of the power Rulve gave me, of what my heart wanted to do."

Somehow, in his mind, he could see who spoke to him. It was the light-haired vora, the twin brother he had killed, kneeling beside him. He had left the twin's body a bloody mess, but now it was strong and shining.

Now he himself was sprawled on the earthen circle beside his throne. But hadn't he used up the soil inside it? With his own hands hadn't he formed the simulacrum? But where was it?

"It's inside you, king. It's doing what you created it to do."

His skin split open down his back and he crawled forward to escape the pain. *No! I never created it to do this to me.*

"You thought you could control it. But the only way to do that is to let it go. Of your own free will. You must release s'rere into the soil beneath you, and just let it go."

Never! By the Lord Ázu, there is nothing *I must do.*

"You're wrong, Uncle. Skora and s'rere have to be given away. You can't hold onto either one. Only when you release them will you be free."

No. He'd given too much already. Oh God he was born without eyes! He grew up amidst pity and disgust. Wasn't that enough?

"Self-pity has no place here. Are you the king or not?"

He was. He was the king.

"Then do what you were born to do. It's not too late."

It was far too late. Moaning, he rolled his grassy forehead over the ground, and the moan rose to a squeal as his fingers stretched into long fleshy roots.

"Niyalahn-rista." Whispered right in his ear, the word was both an affirmation and a plea. It was like the breeze that came from between earth and sky, a breeze that rippled tree leaves like a wave, rustled like a creek through the grasses.

"Yes, Uncle. Hold on to that image."

But how did he know what such things sounded like? He never remembered hearing them. He had chosen an underground fortress, safely swathed, protected by the dark.

The kneeling young man bent over him, and there was something inside him, inside the one who spoke directly into his mind. It was compassion.

No! In utter rejection of anyone's pity, his whole body flailed in protest.

A hand touched him. On the shoulder. A hand reached through the festering mass and touched him.

Nephew.

The young man had come back for him. The king saw the light in his silver eyes, saw the breeze ruffle his pale hair.

What would such a breeze feel like?

"It feels wonderful, niyalahn-rista."

He remembered that word. Roots were filling his skull, probing into his brain, but he remembered that word.

"You released the ahn, niyal'arist. You broke their collars."

I did not! I created their collars.

"Your skora destroyed the simulacrum's collar. My collar. And therefore those of all the ahn."

He groaned. *I don't remember that. I-I tried, oh God, I tried to burn myself clean, to scrape off these growths, but...*

"Destroying the collars was a good thing. It arose from the goodness Rulve placed deep in your heart. Whether most of you intended it or not, you did the will of God."

There is no goodness in my heart. There is no goodness anywhere!

Now the hand moved to his arm and gently squeezed it. Somehow his nephew could break through the vines and grass and weeds and touch him. Somehow....

"You helped me when I needed it, Eyascamen."

Oh God, that name! His true name. He'd forgotten it.

"You were the one niyal'arist who helped the other die. May I now do the same for you?"

I didn't help you! I burned you, out of impatience and greed.

"And also—admit it—with a small bit of compassion."

I don't need your help! I'm going to die anyway, eaten alive.

"But how you die makes all the difference. To you and to Shunder. Just say the word. Say 'yes' to Rulve and she will do the rest."

The place beneath his ribs swelled painfully, insistently, and his lungs burned. He could not say the word, could not even nod his giant, infested head.

"I said it, and you can too. 'Yes' is only one short word."

Something inside him struggled to assent, but the word was taking too long to say. His finger-roots burrowed desperately into the soil under him.

His nephew's hand moved to the center of his back and pressed down. The king felt earth, cool against his abdomen. The hand pressed gently against his resistance, strong with a power king to king. "Say the word, Eyascamen. Say it, niyalahn-rista, and make the earth dance."

From deep inside him something broke. It surged and rose, but he could not say it. The pent-up word stuck in his throat. But now two hands moved through the thicket that encased him and cupped his head, and in one long exhale, his mind released the word: *Yes.*

The last vestige of skora spurted out of his hand. S'rere spilled out of him and into the ground. He let them go. They were powers bestowed and lost and stolen, gifts twice given and now again, a long, sweet emptying into the dark.

The pain was gone. His entire body suckled the earth. *Let it be, this rest.*

And it was. For how long he did not know. Then the voice spoke once more to him. "Come now with me, niyal'arist, and we will go up."

Chapter 47

The Rolling Crown

The stony ground suddenly sprang closer, and it took Teller a moment to realize he had fallen onto his hands. Then a second realization penetrated his pain-filled brain: the volghasts had let go of him. He looked up at them. They stood rigid around him, staring vacantly at nothing, their red eyes dimming, the cold, cliff-top breeze tugging at their mold-spotted cloaks.

The tall one blinked, and for an instant something human looked out, startled, as might a long-time prisoner suddenly released. It looked down at the soil, as if seeing it for the first time, then up at the sun-washed winter sky. "It is so bright," he said in a puzzled voice. The eyes went dead, the skin withered against the skull, and the volghast collapsed like a boneless rag. The other three disintegrated likewise, their clothes fluttering to the ground, their leather gauntlets lying palms up, like empty hands.

Teller pushed himself into a sitting position. Battered and exhausted, he could only stare blankly as a breeze rippled their cloaks from underneath. After a while, he looked up. Across the valley, a few cloud shadows flowed up the Seani hillside and across the darker green of the pine grove. As a boy, he always liked the sound of the wind shushing through those branches. Now the topmost spires would be thick with tightly closed cones, but in another month or two, after the sun had been shining warm for several days, the cones would open with tiny cracks and pops and spill their spores into the quiet air.

He liked that sound too. And the piney smell.

Something trickled down his cheek and he wiped it absently on his sleeve. It left a red stain. Sore all over, he drew up his knees and rested his forehead on them. Every emotion had drifted far away. Even the deep-down laughter was barely a memory, something felt by someone else. Down in the valley, a lone spring bird warbled.

After a moment he lifted his head. Rulve had saved his life, but now—*God help me*—sh'kier was rising inside him once more.

DOWN IN THE HALL OF THE Eye, the heap of greenery on the dais ceased its thrashing. The king's crown rolled out, as if a convulsing foot had kicked it free. It clattered down the steps and stopped at Rigiati's feet. He looked down at the sparkling amethysts and saw his face reflected in the curve of black onyx.

Two other reflected faces appeared alongside his. They belonged to his rivals: Moverik, the altern of Rydle, and quad-captain Perius. Both had stepped up behind him, but Rigiati acted first. He snatched up the crown and, holding it high, turned to the dazed and frightened faces of the crowd. "The King of Shunder is dead," he cried. "Long live his successor!" He jammed the crown onto his head. "The lord's last act was to pass his crown to me, his Kai Archon. Every man and woman in this hall is witness that I alone now rule."

There was dead silence as the captain of the Vorian Guard cautiously moved up the steps and approached the mound of greenery in front of the throne. It rustled slightly, still growing; but the vaguely human form beneath lay still when the man prodded it with his booted foot. The captain turned to Rigiati, and the two of them faced each other on the dais.

"Serve me," Rigiati said in a low voice, "and prove yourself the patriot that stopped a civil war. Acknowledge me as king, and you will become the second most powerful man in Shunder."

The captain hesitated, and then went down on one knee. "My lord and king," he cried in a loud voice. He turned to glare at his men, and they too knelt.

Rigiati turned toward Moverik and Perius, their eyes burning, their stances defiant. The Vorian captain and his men rose and faced them. Slowly, their expressions rigid, Moverik and Perius knelt as the others did.

Rigiati turned to address the audience that now belonged to him. Some terrified and others wary, no one spoke. The eyes of his subjects jumped from him to the mound of greenery on the dais and back to him.

He held his arms out and wiggled his fingers. "Don't tell me you are afraid. Afraid of mere plants? Of leaves and stems? A flare of a torch will burn them away. You all know that. The shrewder among you also know that a new era has come to Oknu Shuld. The more intelligent among you know that a new king has arisen, one stronger, more powerful, than the old." He jerked his thumb toward the green mass. "See what s'rere has accomplished? See what skora has failed to do? The old powers have passed away, and today is *my* Apotheosis!"

Guarded faces looked up at him. Although all of them believed themselves to be shrewd and intelligent, they weren't certain about a new regime. But they soon would be.

"Behold a king with human sight," Rigiati thundered, widening his eyes at them. "With eyes that look far ahead and see nothing but glory for this land. Behold a king that will lead with fire! Yes, ladies and gentlemen, real fire; and not some magician's trick." Without turning, he flung his hand up at the Igneous Eye behind him. "That will become the true symbol of our reign. It will burn away the past and lead us into the future. Our destiny has not changed a whit, my people, nor have our plans. We still have weapons and the best fighting force ever to arise in Shunder. We still have this fortress, rock solid, from which our soldiers will soon march forth. Within three days, every rebel in our land will be crushed. Tomorrow we will obliterate the Seani; the day after we will cleanse Bellstone Forest; and on the third day we will hunt down the village rats that nibble at our greatness. You will show us who they are and where they hide, and they will run squealing out of the flames, and our troops will hack them to bits. Then shall every rebel leader keep long company on the Skewrong Grabe!"

He could see people in the audience adjusting to the new situation, weighing its merits, thinking how it would work to their advantage. Many drew closer to the steps from which they had backed away only moments ago, and interest kindled in their eyes.

"We still have the business connections between us," he went on, looking at the most influential one by one in the eye, "the long-standing arrangements with landlords and tax-collectors and morue distributors. In this too, nothing has changed. Except one thing."

He waited in the expectant silence of their rapt attention. "I will open the old king's hoard, and its riches will flow in a torrent to my loyal supporters right here in this Hall."

That did it. Everyone in the Hall immediately became a loyal supporter, and they all cheered wildly. Whether the old king had a hoard or not, these people believed that he did. Rigiati basked in the adulation of his subjects, basked in the dizzying knowledge that a man who had once been called Shacad's lickspittle had emerged as King of Shunder. They didn't know it yet, but His Majesty King Rigiati would extend—and deepen—his power far more than the old king could ever have imagined.

His mind turned to the missing Vol Cinc. The volghasts would find him soon, if they had not already. Rigiati looked around to find Methe Sinese. Somewhat startled, he saw the shrouded figure only an arm's length away. Good. The man knew the spells that produced the living dead, and with careful handling, he would prove very useful. Under King Rigiati's control, Sinese would see to it that Teller-of-Lies fulfilled the destiny the old king had planned for him: a compliant tool when needed and a living sculpture when not.

And he had a better plan than the Skewrong Grabe for the defeated Seani leaders. At the hands of Sinese, all nine of them would be formed into volghasts of his own, a secret loyal militia that would roam the countryside to do his will.

All that was visible under the necromancer's hood was an inscrutable thinning of his red lips. With a slight nod, Rigiati acknowledged the unspoken agreement between them.

Chapter 48

Falls

Sh'kier's urgency pulled Teller to his feet. Not far away lay the earth and boulder mound of the West Dam. It choked off what had once been Sunsink Falls, the crystal torrent that had graced the entire Eeron Valley. It had turned a sparkling river, a source of beauty and inspiration, into sludge. It obliterated the land's entire fishing industry and caused many to starve. It created shallows where mosquitos swarmed, bred, and spread disease. The only purpose of this dam was to provide Oknu Shuld with a private lake to stock fish and to irrigate the lucrative morue crop.

He thought he'd come to the end of his strength, but now sh'kier needed—*he* needed—to restore the river Rulve had created and the Spider-king had desecrated.

Keeping the giant sinkhole to his right and pressing his intact sleeve from time to time against the seeping cut on his cheek, Teller made his way up the dry watercourse, skirting weed-filled potholes along the way. At a spot about twelve strides from the base of the West Dam, he climbed out of the watercourse and turned to look at the dam at an angle. Here at the shallow end of the lake, the dam rose in a mound a little taller than he was. Grass grew between its boulders; and the lake, filled with spring run-off from the highlands beyond, had risen almost to the top of the barrier.

Sh'kier burned in his spirikai, waiting for his will. "Yes," he whispered. "Let's do this."

Like a released arrow, the fire raced up his arms. No shining rod appeared, but instinctively he raised his power-heavy hands and extended them toward the dam. With a hiss, lightning shot out of them, followed almost instantly by a bang of thunder right over his head. He stumbled backward as the blast punched a hole at the base of the mound. A stream of lake water squirted through the breech. More of the mound crumbled on either side until the entire center caved in. A lumpy, brown wave, thick with a slurry of muddy pebbles and smelling of ozone and algae, rushed into the watercourse. Rocks rolled in the torrent, smashing into each other and getting stuck in potholes until knocked free.

"WHAT WAS THAT?" ONE OF FLYN's men asked, peering at the sky through the bridge slats above their heads.

"Lightnin' hit something," another said. "I just saw lightnin' up there on Insheer Cliff."

"But there ain't hardly a cloud in the sky."

Ineed there wasn't, the rebel leader Havek noticed. Along with Defender Flyn and ten of his men, he stood calf-deep in the murky water under Rydle Bridge. They were well hidden, he hoped, in the shadows of its stout timber posts. The broken-down wagon was in place, blocking the village end of the bridge, and they were all watching the road that curved around the base of Oknu Shuld. Everything so far was going according to their plan, but the Azanzi force had not yet appeared, and the men were on edge.

"What in Rulve's name...?" Flyn breathed. Now he too was looking up at the cliff.

Havek craned his neck in time to see the top of Insheer Cliff blur slightly, as if it shivered. With a low rumble, a few rocks cascaded down the dry wash, and one rolled almost to the river's edge. This was the second time in less than an hour that something odd had occurred on the cliff, and he didn't like it. "Something's going on up there, Flyn. Get the men out of this river right now!"

TELLER STUMBLED ALONGSIDE THE FLOOD IN time to see the earthy debris reach the edge of the cliff and tumble over. The sound of rocks grating over stones mingled with the slurp of mud, all of which gradually changed into a wild chattering as the water that gushed out of the lake ran clearer and clearer. With deep satisfaction, he watched the freed river scour soil out of crevices, uproot weeds, and gradually wash the dull rock into shimmering ochre, slate, and red. For the first time in three generations, water poured over the cliff, and the newborn falls tossed into the sky a living plume of mist.

Teller stood beside the rushing stream while droplets wafted against his face, and a water-fresh breeze riffled through his hair.

"Thank you, Rulve," he breathed. "Again I thank you for what sh'kier has done."

How Taisa's eyes would shine at the sight of this waterfall. Later, the sunset would turn it into a golden veil, and surely everyone who lived in the Eeron Valley—in villages, on farms, in Bellstone Forest, in the Seani—all of them would rejoice. Would Taisa know he had done it, that sh'kier had done it? Even now currents must be prodding the dying river into life: pulling islands of weeds apart, whirling mats of algae out of sloughs, and restoring the water to its ancestral banks.

First abakal and now the Eeron River, and both had been redeemed.

AFTER LIR LEFT HER, TAISA WALKED over to the hospit to collect a posset Tema had prepared for one of the children. Taisa had almost reached the Seani House when a far-off crack broke the silence. Such sounds were common at this time of year, when a sudden thaw could snap a tree branch. She climbed the steps to the Seani House porch and pulled open the door to the dining room just in time to see Ukaipa appear at the top of the stairs. She was holding one of the children, and her face was beaming. "Everyone!" she called down to the others in the room. "Come up and see this. You won't believe it!"

The four people who had just finished a very late lunch looked up. At the young woman's urging, Taisa's friends Hirai and Ianak joined Se Druv and Se Penan as they hurried up the stairs. Taisa was the last to follow and turn into the nursery. Ukaipa stood at the other end, at the door to the Sunrise Balcony, and gestured madly for them to come through. Taisa put the posset on a shelf and quickly stepped onto the balcony. Se Mena and her students from the schoolroom next door were already there. Two of the little ones were taking their naps in the nursery, but some of Mena's younger students ran along the balcony, which extended the entire length of the second floor, eagerly pointing and finding better views.

Ukaipa was so excited she was almost gabbling. "I was playing on the floor with the children and we all heard this big popping noise; and I thought it was ice thawing or a tree falling and so I went out and saw *that*!"

Taisa followed her pointing finger. She stared, blinked, and then a lump formed in her throat. Across the valley, a long, shimmering ribbon could be seen cascading over Insheer Cliff.

"It's Sunsink Falls!" Penan exclaimed, his eyes fixed on the sight. Without turning he spoke to Mena's older students who had gathered around him. "Boys and girls, after all these years, it's Sunsink Falls."

"Oh my God," Se Mena breathed. "Oh dear God, how beautiful!"

They stared silently for a moment until Ianak, clutching the handrail with his prominently knuckled fingers, spoke up. "The dam up there must have burst." He turned to appeal to Se Penan. "Right?"

"Evidently," Penan said, his brow furrowed as he gazed ahead.

"It's sh'kier!" Hirai whispered into Taisa's ear. "It can't be a coincidence. The emjadis went there, and it must be sh'kier."

Taisa's heart leaped, and she pushed next to Se Druv at the railing. She reached out to grasp his arm, to squeeze it with a wild hope, but something in his face stopped her.

Druv had gazed at Insheer Cliff hundreds of times, but had never marked what he saw now. At first, overcome with disbelief and then awe, he couldn't take his eyes from the falls. But then he noticed that the water was plunging over a section of cliff slightly higher than the section immediately to the south of it. That meant that Insheer Cliff did not, as he had always thought, run in an unbroken block from its edge to where the land formed a plateau to the east and gradually descended into distant Trey Aughter.

He pointed this out to Penan, who squinted at the looming bastion across the valley. "Look there," the scholar said after a moment. "That lower section seems to be made of a different kind of rock, lighter against that darker granite on the north side. We must get Utray up here, but it looks to me as if Oknu Shuld was built into a different, slightly lower, rock formation than the rest of the cliff."

Neither said anything for a moment, until Druv spoke to Penan in a low voice. "Earlier Celume mentioned that the Pool of Rulve had trembled slightly, and then I myself thought I'd glimpsed a cloud of dust up on the cliff."

"And now," Penan said thoughtfully, "the cliff has released an ancient waterfall."

Taisa, standing next to Druv, spoke up. "What does that mean for Tel—the emjadis?"

Druv looked into her worried eyes. "I don't know," he said slowly. Troubled, he put his arm around her shoulders and turned his head back toward Oknu Shuld. Across the valley, the jeweled spider that marked the entrance to the Spider-king's stronghold glinted sharply in the sun.

As sh'kier fell back into his spirikai, Teller took several deep breaths and staggered to the edge of the falls. He plunged both arms in past the elbows, then his head. After shaking water out of his hair, he scrubbed his neck where the ahn-collar had been. Scrapes and cuts he didn't know were there stung when the water touched them, but he felt better when most of the blood and grit were washed away. At last he drank his fill. Although the water still tasted faintly of mud, it was sweet.

Bone-tired, he sank cross-legged onto the ground. The length of his shadow told him it was probably early afternoon. He'd done everything Rulve wanted, he was still alive, and now he could go home.

In a moment perhaps. After he rested. In spite of the cold air, the sun up here on the cliff felt warm on his head and shoulders. The water beside him burbled along, and he closed his eyes. He had missed so many sensations while growing up in an underground stronghold: the hiss of rain, the earthy smell it released from the ground, the sight of a curved green leaf cupping a crystal raindrop.

Taisa was running through the rain to him, laughing, and he caught her in his arms and wiped away the drops from her cheeks as tenderly as if they were tears.

His head nodded, and that sudden movement woke him up.

He didn't know how long he'd been sleeping—from the position of the sun, perhaps half a notch on the time-candle—but he sensed that something was happening down in the Hall of the Eye. Fully alert, he got to his feet. So far, the six layers of rock that separated the clifftop from the Hall of the Eye must have deadened the relatively surface effects of abakal and the opening of the West Dam. Now, however, something had changed.

Even as one malevolence inside the cliff had passed away, another was taking hold. A toxic root still remained deep inside Oknu Shuld, and it was growing.

Sh'kier rose inside him, making the toltyr feel hot against his chest. The pendant hung like a heavy, ripening seed under his torn shirt.

What is it, Rulve? What more must I do?

His eyes were drawn to the monstrous bulk of the East Dam ahead.

CHAPTER 49

GOING HOME

LIM LOWERED HIS AX AND CAST Hewish a sour look. "Seems this thicket is worse of a tangle than you let on."

"Quit grumblin'. We're almost through."

In Bellstone Forest, where a curve of the massive cliff hid both the front and side gates of Oknu Shuld, the three boys had been working for at least an hour. A stone's throw away from the river, they were axing a path through a thicket to the tunnel that was their goal. The depression in which they worked caught all the sun, but at the same time blocked even a breath of mid-Seed's chilly breeze that could cool them off. Equally as bad, the thicket seemed to consist mostly of thorn bushes. All three boys were sweaty, scratched, and itchy.

Stemmer stood up, wiped his forehead, and waved away a cloud of tiny, annoying midges. "It's too early for these things," he complained.

Still hacking away, Hewish said, "Sun musta brought 'em out."

"Who cares what brought 'em out," Lim stated. "They're here now, ain't they?"

Hewish dropped his ax and glared at the other two. "All right, all *right*. We've almost reached the mouth of the tunnel, but mebbe it's time for a rest." He walked over to his water flask and took a swig from it.

After the others did the same, Lim announced he'd be right back and headed for the river. "Eeron's so scraggly," he said over his shoulder, "a tad a' pee might help."

It was an old joke, and neither boy bothered to respond. In a few minutes, however, Lim called back to them. "Hey! You gotta see this!"

The river wasn't quite so scraggly anymore. They hadn't heard its gradual rise, but now an actual slow-moving current was nudging a mat of sludge downstream.

"It's crept up from when we first got here," Stemmer observed. "Mebbe that was what disturbed the midges."

Lim frowned at the river. "I don't like the look of this."

"Just some runoff from the snowfields," Stemmer said, glancing at Hewish. "It's nigh on spring, you know."

"Look," Hewish said. "If you don't want to be here, Lim, ride on back. Me and Stemmer are finishin' up here." He turned and tramped back to the thicket, Stemmer right behind him.

Reluctantly, Lim followed.

MUCH OF THE WORM-LIGHT IN THE tunnel had finally winked out, leaving everyone practically blind. Her neck and back aching from stooping over, Mariat found herself searching for any spark of light still carried by a surviving larva. She spied a small cluster of them and focused on it as she shuffled past. Suddenly she realized that the floor of the drain had stopped heading downward. It had leveled out.

Oh Rulve, were they walking under the Eeron River now? She tightened her hold on Wosie's hand and tried not to visualize the ceiling above their heads cracking open; tried not to think of water, cold and unseen, rushing upon them, filling her nose and mouth and— No, she cried to herself, stop that! You'll frighten the babies.

She blinked. She hadn't thought about them much since Varo told her they existed. Maybe they didn't. She didn't feel any little ones in there, didn't feel particularly motherly. A wave of yearning passed through her. *Oh, Sheft. Oh my dearest heart. I'm not ready for this! Why did you have to leave me?* She dashed the tears away, then shed more when she realized how stupidly self-centered her thoughts had been.

With one fear pushed down, another darted out. Under the shuffling of many feet, had she actually been hearing something over her head? A steady, barely discernable gurgling? She reached up to touch the ceiling. Oh God, it was damp! But not wet, not dripping. Maybe it had always been damp, and she just hadn't noticed. From somewhere ahead a child wailed. "I want to go home!"

"We are, sweetheart," a strained voice answered. "We're all going home now."

Were they really? Mariat wondered. Maybe that child had a home, but without Sheft, she and the babies had none.

She moved along, putting one foot ahead of the other, and then began trudging up a slight slope. An excited commotion burst out ahead. The line stopped and bunched up. Mariat raised her head and sniffed, caught the smell of mud and worms, and—oh Rulve could it be?—the tang of cold, fresh air.

The ahn around her must be mind-speaking, for they glanced at one another with a light in their eyes. The line, however, did not move. She heard low cries ahead, followed by raised voices, groans, and terse orders.

Behind her, Rivere swore and began squeezing himself forward. Something must be wrong. They waited, pressing together until there was barely enough room to breathe, and still no word came down.

Then came a whiff of—of smoke. And then the screams began.

HEWISH STOOD UP FROM WHERE THEY'D been piling brush outside the mouth of the drain and took a deep breath. "We cut enough of this kindlin'," he said. "Stemmer, light it up." If anyone could get a quick blaze going, it was him.

Stemmer thrust a wad of dry grass under the edge of the pile and struck his flint. He babied the flame until the grass caught. The twigs around it began to crackle, followed by the thicker stems. Soon they had a bonfire, and the tunnel, as they all had hoped, was drawing like a granny sucking on a pipe.

Hewish let out a yell of triumph. His plan might actually work! They might actually distract some of the soldiers in Oknu Shuld long enough to save the lives of even a few Bellstone warriors.

A long wavering wail emerged from the black mouth of the tunnel, then died away.

"What was that?" Stemmer asked, his eyes wide.

"A haunt!" Lim cried, backing away. "That tunnel's full a' haunts!"

"There ain't no such thing," Hewish said. He sounded brave enough, but it still took him a moment before he bent over and shouted into the opening. "Who's there? Who's lurkin' in there?"

"I want to go home!" a young voice cried.

Other panicked voices followed this demand, broken by Hewish's yell. "No foolin' about! We're twenty men here, with axes."

Voices babbled, terrified and pleading, until one male voice rose above the rest. "Most of us are ahn. We have no weapons. Who are you?"

"We're Eerford men, under Defender Rung. This is a foul 'brak tunnel, and we're smokin' it out."

"No! There are women and children here. We are trying to escape from Oknu Shuld! Please, water is coming in from somewhere, and we can't get past these bars. Break up your fire!"

"I want to go *home*!" the young voice insisted.

"Don't sound like 'braks to me," Stemmer muttered.

"Me neither." They nodded in agreement, so he and Hewish kicked aside the flaming brush while Lim ran to the river to fill his boots. After a few trips the fire was doused and the branches pushed aside. Aware that he made an excellent target against the light, Hewish cautiously approached the tunnel exit.

"Thank you!" the male voice cried. "Now help us get this gate open. It's warded shut, but only on this side."

Hewish crouched in a little closer and saw the square-barred gate. Beyond it he made out several worried, dirty faces. He turned his head to Stemmer. "You stand by the side here with yer ax. Lop off any 'brak head that pokes out."

He looked down at his own ax and figured its butt end might not fare too badly against the rusted iron bars. "Step back," he ordered and hefted the ax. As he did so, a thin stream of water, which had not been there seconds ago, snaked out of the center of the drain.

FOR YEARS TELLER HAD BURNED WITH skora and thought he knew what fire was. But sh'kier was to skora as a white-hot forge to a cottage hearth. Pure incandescence, it radiated inside his spirikai with a grim imperative. He stood on the partially ruined roof of Oknu Shuld, the newly released waterfall spilling off the cliff behind him, and gripped the toltyr with an inward groan. His work on Insheer Cliff had just begun.

Beneath his feet, tunnels ran through the rock like mold through a cheese, and sprouting morue still contaminated the clifftop. Section 42, where ahn were forced to hide as rista hunted them for sport, still existed. The strisnu, with its shackles hanging from the walls and its drain in the floor, still stood untouched. The smoldering Igneous Eye, the isav, the pitiful chests full of confiscated children's toys, the punishment cages hovering over the scalding hot springs, the grotesque sculptures in the lord's private audience chamber—all these and a hundred other obscenities cried out to be destroyed.

But it was his brother's unburied body that pulled at his heart.

Mariat had shrouded her husband in her green cloak, but the soil, the very earth that had for all of Sheft's life called out to him for salvation, now must cover him. *All who bear s'rere must be buried.* He had promised Mariat that he would do it. And there was only one way he could.

He clamped his hand over the eager fire in his spirikai and turned his steps toward the East Dam. From time to time the wind whistled over the sinkhole behind him. It passed right through Teller's thin shirt, but no matter how cold it was, it wouldn't be winter forever.

Teller reached the edge of the dry ravine that ran out from the dam and perpendicular to the cliff edge some distance away. Irrigation furrows had been dug out of the ravine and through the rows of morue, which were barely poking their obscene heads out of last fall's mulch. When one of the irrigation gates was opened, or if there was a hard rain, this ravine was responsible for the weeping walls that leaked at the back of almost every level in Oknu Shuld.

He raised his eyes to the head of the ravine, massively blocked by the East Dam. One of his first orders after he'd been named Vol Cinc had been to repair the dam after a minor earthshake. Now, yet again, he had to undo something he never should have done to begin with.

Far bigger than the mound sh'kier had just opened, this dam kept the deepest part of the lake from sweeping into the wash by means of cribs and buttresses. The cribs—constructed of thick, hand-hewn timbers and packed with boulders, stones, and debris of all kinds—were shored up by stout oak braces twelve feet high.

A few weeds had already sprouted in the sunny southwest corner where the right hand buttress met the ravine. Lake water inevitably seeped there, and even now two wasps toiled in the resulting patch of stony mud.

Sh'kier raged at the sight of the dam. It didn't belong here. It served only to enable a corrupt stronghold to thrive. For years Shunder had suffered and prayed, and now Rulve's relentless love demanded that their prayer be answered.

Answered through him.

Teller took a breath and grasped the toltyr. The power inside him strained for release, and the Creator of the world waited upon his will. An emerging pattern was grinding its way toward a new configuration, and the last coin must be handed over. He let the toltyr fall onto his shirt and opened his hands at his side. *Yes, Rulve.*

Sh'kier surged out of his spirikai. Twisting and crackling, it leaped into a dazzling spear of fire before him. Its might was too much for him, its intensity too great. He took a step back. But then a sudden awareness engulfed him, of deep resolve and mercy, of father and uncle, brother and son, all in some fantastic union, all with him and in him, who would take hold of the fire and help him bear it.

He stepped forward and planted his boots on the ground. With determination and a fierce joy, he hefted the spear and aimed at the top of central buttress. But the spear dragged itself down and to the right, pointing directly at the southwest corner. Yes! The weakest spot. With all his power and his hearts' desire, with a cry that reflected a combined strength not entirely his own, he hurled the spear into the abomination that was choking the Land of Shunder.

Sh'kier rammed into the crevice with blazing white power. A thunderclap threw him down, but he rolled to his feet as the base of the far right buttress erupted into giant splinters. Its timbers squealing, the crib behind it bulged as it fought the force of the lake behind it and failed. Rocks crashed into the ravine, rolling on pebbles that had been packed around them. A gush of water shot out, undermining the cribs above it. One by one they caved in, and the right side of the dam collapsed. A wave as tall as a barn burst through. Tumbling jagged timbers and bone-crushing boulders, the giant flume blasted into the ravine.

A CLAP OF THUNDER CAUSED HEWISH to look up at the cliff. He couldn't see the top of it, but a feeling of urgency did a somersault inside his stomach. He and his friends had been helping people out of the drain for some time, but it was a slow process. Children emerged blinking at the light and several people insisted on hugging Hewish and the other boys after they climbed out. Some knelt to pray, sobbing. Others hung about, calling for loved ones and getting in the way. They were all exhausted, shivering in the cold air, and streaked with mud.

To his horror, Hewish saw that the water in the drain was now inches deep. It was rising, and there were still people inside, screaming and pushing to get out. "Lim!" he cried. "Ride back to camp for help. Hurry!"

Lim leaped onto his pony and rushed off. Hewish and Stemmer stepped up the pace, hauling people out of the drain as fast as they could. Those who had already gotten out helped others who were panting and stumbling, and they urged everyone to climb up to the higher ground.

"How many more?" Hewish gasped, but people either didn't hear or shook their heads.

An old man in rags stood across from Hewish and kept calling into the tunnel. "Do not panic. We are all going to make it. Do not block the exit after you get out."

A little boy tugged frantically at Hewish's arm. "Did you see Wosie?" he cried. "Where is Wosie?"

"I don't know." His arms were sore, and Hewish was having a hard time pulling up a man who had fallen. "Maybe she's out already."

The boy ran off toward the crowd of escapees just as a man with greying curly hair emerged from the drain. "There's only a few behind me," he panted. "I'm a healer and will do what I can." He staggered after the others.

Next came a pretty lady, the bottom of her ahn-pants wet to the knees. She stopped just outside the drain and turned with her hand outstretched to someone inside. "Take my hand, Mariat!" she cried. She pulled out another lady who was carrying a little girl.

"I'm the last one," the lady called Mariat said. She turned to Hewish. "The water's rising. You and your friend get to higher ground."

The ragged old man climbed out of the depression with the two ladies. Hewish grasped Stemmer's arm and followed them.

Ahead of him, the little girl being carried by Mariat lifted her head from the lady's shoulder. Her eyes began to dance as she looked at him, and then she gave him a wide smile. "Hoowish!" she cried. "Hoowish!"

"Rosie?" He stopped, then rushed up to her. *"Rosie!"*

His little sister squirmed to get down, and Mariat set her on her feet. Rosie ran to him, hugged him at the knees, and Hewish lifted her up high. "My little Rosie! I thought you were—Oh, Rosie, are you all right?"

"Now I am."

With a sob, he lowered her to his chest, and squeezed the small body tight. She was safe, back with his family. Come spring, he'd find that pink rosebush and plant it at home for her delight. He didn't care who saw the tears running down his cheeks.

Chapter 50

Log Jam

A rumble reverberated through the Hall of the Eye. A few people in the audience glanced uneasily at the ceiling, but most heads had turned toward the pile of greenery on the dais to Rigiati's right. Something was happening around the king's dead body. Hairline cracks were shooting out from it. Even as Rigiati watched, stunned, roots snaked along the cracks, sending the marble tiles askew. The roots swelled, and like impossibly quick moles, delved deeper and pushed further. Behind them green sprouts jumped up.

The audience he had just calmed down now flared up again. Groups shoved past each other to see what was going on, but then surged back as the cracks widened. The sprouts burst into mosses, quackgrass, and weeds. Rigiati yelled to regain the attention of the crowd, tried to settle them down, but he couldn't be heard above the spreading alarm. The web of greenery was quickly covering the dais, and his sudden fear of it forced him to jump off.

Officers surrounded him, clearly shaken and shouting questions. "We're going to stop this," Rigiati cried, and pointed to a quad-captain. "Get a squad to start a fire outside and bring in torches. Burn anything green."

Vines were now darting down the steps, and the group of officers quickly moved away, struggling to regroup against the churning of the crowd. Shulay, the altern of Baenfeld, jumped in front of him. "It's the traitor!" he screamed above the noise. "The volghasts died before they could stop him."

"What?"

"Vol Cinc is doing this," Shulay exclaimed. "He's a powerful Vol and wants revenge!"

"There's something going on atop the cliff," one of the quads shouted. "And Teller-of-Lies was last seen heading up there."

"Pyk!" Rigiati cried. "Moverik! Get some men and follow me!"

The archon and five Scaths appeared at Rigiati's elbow, and they all headed toward the stairs. Rigiati glanced over his shoulder to see scattered groups pushing their way toward the doors.

TELLER STOOD ON THE WESTERN BANK of the wash and stared at the wreckage scraping and groaning past him. The force of it jittered the ground beneath his feet.

With only one buttress down, water was rushing into the irrigation ditches, which would soon overflow and flood this side of the bank. A quick look over his shoulder showed that the sinkhole was some distance away, but directly behind him. His gaze flicked back to the dam. The two remaining supports were shaking. When they gave way, which looked to be in only seconds, he would be swept into the very hole he had created.

He would not die in Oknu Shuld. He would not.

Before any more cribs were torn free, he had to cross over this rampage and onto the higher bank on the other side. Running abreast of the surge, he reached a section where the first of the timbers had piled up in a heaving logjam. It was half propped up—for now—by upended supports.

With water frothing around them, the huge timbers were shifting in the current. Among them they could crush an ox. But the situation would only grow worse. He measured the distance to the nearest relatively flat timber. Better to be mangled under the sky than be swallowed whole by Oknu Shuld.

His leap got him onto the timber, but it dipped dangerously, and water splashed his ankles. He grabbed an upended log for support. Its splintered edge cut across his palm, but he managed to hold on, then take a long step onto the next bobbing log. Water rushed under the rocking pile as he picked his way over the wood, half crouching, testing each piece before he put his weight on it, then catching himself. His foot slipped on an algae-covered log, got caught between it and its grinding neighbor, but he jerked it free before it could be crushed. His sudden movement made the log dip, but, waving his arms, he recovered his balance.

The sound of the river beneath him suddenly changed timbre. He glanced up as a gust of wind hit him. The gust accompanied the watery fist that punched through the central buttress.

With a roar, the second wave, a brown monster with splintered timbers in its teeth, bore down on Teller. He leaped off the debris and onto the other side as the log pile behind him smashed apart.

WATER FROM INSHEER LAKE SHEETED OVER the morue fields and cascaded into the huge sunlit hole that had not been there barely an hour ago. Unimpeded, it channeled morue sprouts, mulch, and soil down to level three. There the undamaged rocky floor forced the raging water to surge down dusty halls.

With no outlet, the deluge shoved air ahead of it. The combined force plunged down to level four where it wrenched doors and gates off their hinges; tumbled globes, chairs, and chests in its wake. It devastated empty classrooms and foreign student apartments, swept away the treasure piled in the storage room, sent shelves of tankards in the ale room crashing down.

Down in the Hall of the Eye, everything happened at once. A strong downdraft blasted through the arches. Smelling of fetid water, it tore a tapestry off the wall and sent someone's cape swirling through the air like a clawing ghost. Grates jumped on the floor-vents, puffs of grime rising from them, and the great front doors rattled and boomed.

The globes overhead swung wildly. Several crashed into each other; broken glass and larvae spilled onto the floor. The unlucky people beneath screamed and tried to scramble away, slipping on worms and crying out as they fell.

Defying Rigiati's order, Moverik, the altern of Rydle Village, grabbed his daughter Preya by the hand and pulled her through the panicked dignitaries. They joined a mass of shrieking people who were fleeing toward the doors. The guards saw them coming and rushed out, leaving only one of the doors unlocked. The mob jammed the single exit.

With the floor cracking open behind them, people pushed their way over shards of glass as slippery as ice. A corpulent landlord fell and was trampled; injured people bled and stumbled on.

IN MINUTES THE AVALANCHE OF ROILING water reached level five. It plowed into the lord's private audience chamber, mauled his sculptures, obliterated his throne, and ripped away the stake to which the wrist of a young man was chained.

The wind abated as the flood, finding no outlets to the cliff face, swirled back on itself. It ran down hallways and tunnels toward the back walls of Oknu Shuld. Rock ceilings groaned as the increasing weight forced rivulets, and then streams, to flow down the weeping walls. Several began to crumble.

RIGIATI HAD JUST GOTTEN TO THE main stairway when Archon Burs, out of breath and red with exertion, grabbed hold of his arm. The wind had died down, but the panic had not. Now the entire level was quivering.

"I have my hands full at the back gates," Burs said. "Bloodknots deserting. Scaths ready to bolt. Angry civilians demanding answers. I need more—"

"You need to take care of it yourself." Rigiati pushed the man's hand off him and dashed up the stairs. A quick turn gave him a view of the passage behind him.

A group of long-time residents, more familiar than the others with how the fortress was laid out, clogged the hallway leading to the side gates. Just after Archon Burs fought his way through, someone shrieked as a life-sized statue of King Jebeth the Seeker was knocked to the floor. It blocked the hallway, and several ristas tried to push it aside even as others squeezed past the person caught under it.

Rigiati continued his rush up the stairs.

Chapter 51

Unfettered

A QUICK GLANCE SHOWED TELLER THAT water churning out of the broken West Dam was chewing away at the base of the third and last bastion. The whole thing would go in a heartbeat, and he had to get out of its way. He whirled, grabbed a clump of dockweed above his head and began to pull himself up the slope.

He was too late.

To his left, with enough force to shake the entire clifftop, the last buttress gave way, and the now completely unfettered lake thundered into the wash. The sounds of roaring water and of logs screeching against each other rammed into his ears; dust and mist swirled into his eyes. Half-blind, with the vicious timbers gnashing behind him, he felt the dockweed pull out by the roots. He slipped down, cold water slapped at the back of his leg, and something hard hit his head.

As the torrent from Insheer Lake ground through the crevice, water and mud began to ooze through a corner of the back wall of what was left of level one. A trickle was the only warning, and then the wall exploded in a gush. The ceiling collapsed onto the floor, which in turn broke through the ceiling below. Walls buckled, and each chamber with its added weight crashed into the level beneath.

On the ground floor, the flame of the Igneous Eye winked out, and the red glass blew off the wall. The ceiling ripped open. An inundation—of water and mud; of cracked tiles and broken chairs; of smashed globes, casks, and statuary—burst into the Hall of the Eye. It propelled Rigiati and his men off the main stairs, and tore the spider-crown off the Kai Archon's head. It caught up those few still inside the hall and, bearing their flailing bodies, thrust them through the great gates. From some distance down the road, Moverik's daughter screamed and reached for her father's hand as, with the sound of a dozen thunderstorms, their whole world fell.

Inside the hall, under the meager shelter of a broken wall, one bright body had tumbled down from level five and come to rest. Wrapped in a green cloak, it lay next to the mass of plants still growing out of what had once been the Lord of Shunder. A backwash gently shrouded them in sand and buried them side by side.

HIS EYES GLUED TO THE CLIFFTOP, Druv stood beside Utray on the crowded Sunrise Balcony of the second floor of the Seani House. As word spread that something big was happening atop Insheer Cliff, people filled the balcony and gathered on the entry porch below it. Others were rushing to join the guards and Rift-riders on the two lookout towers on either side of the front gates.

A burst of blinding light had flared over the top of the cliff, followed by a clap of thunder. The ivy that covered Oknu Shuld shivered in a green wave. But this was no storm coming down from the cloudless sky. Instead of diminishing, what had at first sounded like thunder continued as a long juddering boom. The central section of the cliff face trembled, and what looked to Druv like pebbles, but which must have been enormous boulders, fell and bounced and rolled amidst tails of dust.

Then the adjoining section of the cliff, south of Sunsink Falls, began to sag like a decomposing body. The movement caused the bottom of the cliff to bulge outward. Reflected sunlight from the jeweled spider mosaic set into the cliff, that ugly symbol that marked the Spider-king's lair, was suddenly snuffed out.

Penan, almost out of breath, pushed his way to him. "Druv!" he cried. "The falconform Yarahe just reported. The West Dam is collapsing. He says there's a giant hole up there and the lake is pouring into it. "

Utray grasped Druv by the shoulder, and they looked into each other's eyes. "My god," Utray breathed. "If that is so, we haven't seen anything yet."

Suddenly, even half-dazed as he was, Druv understood. Sweat broke out beneath his armpits. Within minutes the cold water of Insheer Lake was going to hit the hot fissures in the deepest level of Oknu Shuld.

Chapter 52

Elementals

Teller opened his eyes. How long had he been out? His head hurt, but worse was the dizzy feeling that the ground beneath him was slipping sideways. Deafening sounds pounded in his ears, of rocks screeching against each other, of a constant threatening rumble. A violent shaking brought him to his knees and he looked around. Disorientation made his head spin.

The land to his left no longer resembled the clifftop he remembered. The flat surface, the vast expanse of widening cracks, soil, and boulders, all seemed to be slipping imperceptibly downhill. The irrigation channels and the dangerous wash he had managed to cross only a short time ago had become a shallow lake that was pouring into the sinkhole he had created. Ahead and to his right, impossible cliff faces had risen like ancient giants out of the ground.

What was happening? He couldn't hear himself think against the noise, couldn't make sense of what his eyes saw.

And then, suddenly, everything came into focus. The cliff faces weren't rising; it was this section of the cliff that was sinking. The weight of the water inside Oknu Shuld was dragging it down. Level by level, the dark fortress that had held so much evil was collapsing, peeling away from Insheer Cliff, and listing with massive inevitability toward the valley.

And taking him with it.

His heart racing, he climbed to his feet and almost fell as the ground under his feet crumbled and sagged. He stumbled toward the face of the newly emerging cliff. It was raw and rugged and now almost thirty feet high. Sheets of dirt fell like waterfalls from the top of it, cracks opened at its base, but he had to get to the stable plateau far above his head. He staggered along its face, looking for a way clear of falling soil. The relentless movement under his feet threatened to pull him away from a cliff that seemed to grow higher even as he watched.

He spotted a small projection and jumped over a crack to grab it. Hanging there, he found a foothold, then groped above his head for something more to grab onto.

He did this over and over, searching with his hands and scrabbling with his feet. His missing finger made an awkward grip; falling gravel hit him in the face. At one point he found a narrow ledge. Taking several deep breaths and gripping tightly to his perch, he glanced down over his shoulder. Fear, cold and sick, flooded into his stomach. He was clinging to what was now a dizzying drop of fifty feet and growing.

He turned back to face the cliff. Time and again he dug the toes of his boots into tiny holes in the rock, forced his fingers around sharp projections. Sun beat against the back of his neck while rock dust swirled into his eyes. At times that queasy sensation seized him, as if the cliff were rising under him, growing ever higher as he struggled upward. And all the while disintegration juddered and groaned behind him.

He found another perilous hold and had to rest. Thirsty, his arms and legs trembling with effort, he leaned against the rock face. How much farther to the top? He dared not lean back to look up and, given his previous experience, didn't want to look down. But he couldn't help a brief glance. What he saw was like a punch in the stomach.

Oh God Rulve. The steam vents.

The last of the water from Insheer Lake was whirlpooling down the sinkhole. Very soon, if it hadn't already, it would make its way into levels beneath the Hall of the Eye, beneath the isav and strisnu, and into the very basement of the stronghold. Where hot mud-pots gargled, where bubbling pools kept kitchen pots boiling, where steaming cracks produced sulfurous fumes.

When icy snow-fed lake water gushed into the fiery cauldron at the base of Oknu Shuld, he didn't want to be clinging to this cliff. He must make it onto the safety of the plateau above and had only minutes to do it.

Teller climbed. The raw edges of the new Insheer Cliff scraped away the bandage over his arm and reopened the cut on his palm. The blood made his grasp slippery, and he had to keep hanging on with one hand while wiping the other on his pants. As fast as he dared, he inched up further, always a little further, sweat stinging in his eyes. Black tatters passed over his vision, and he suddenly sensed he was falling backward. He shoved his forehead against the serrated rock and clung to it, desperate for solidity in this rumbling, shaking world. A thin breeze wafted over the back of his neck, and the illusion of falling passed.

He scrambled onto another foothold and then felt a crevice into which he could jam his hand. Oh God, how much further? He glanced up. Gnarled and black, a nightmarish wyvern claw hung over him. His heart tripped; he lost his grip and slipped down, the toes of his boots grating against the cliff face, his fingers clawing.

His right hand encountered a rocky knob, and he grabbed onto it. His left boot dug into the scree, and he clung, gasping, to the rock face once more.

Blinking sweat out of his eyes, Teller risked snatching another look above his head. The claw was only a bleak, windswept tree. A wave of relief almost made him black out, but now he knew he was not far from the top. Trying to increase his pace, he grabbed onto the half-buried roots and clumps of weeds that began to appear, until at last—one final low ridge. He heaved himself over it and collapsed face down.

He felt it coming, felt it in the trembling in his hands, the grating of the soil against his cheek. In a place far below, all the great elementals were coming together into one massive force.

Water and fire flashed into steam and, with a deafening roar, blasted a mountain of rock into the sky. The plateau heaved. Tossed like a child, he hit the ground tumbling and rolling. Above him, a pale half-moon careened wildly, surrounded by pain-stars. The sky shut down and turned from blue to roiling brown to black. The ground dragged under him like a grating waterfall.

Terrified of being swept over the cliff, he fought against the torrent. The toltyr dug into his chest. Taisa's face flashed before him, then spun away into a jumping, sliding, thundering world.

Sh'kier left him, vanished into a bright haze in front of his eyes. From the back of his head a blackness rushed in.

Rulve! Into your hands!

In sudden silence he watched himself fall, his body getting smaller and smaller as it plunged toward the dark.

Into your hands, he thought; and midnight dropped over him like a blanket.

Chapter 53

Far-off Graves

A DUSKY CUMULUS ROILED UP FROM the top of Insheer Cliff, inflating and expanding in uncanny silence. Aghast, Druv turned to those around him. "Hold on!" he cried.

Barely had he warned them when the sound of the explosion rolled out across the Eeron Valley. The grinding rumble bored into Druv's head, going on and on while the balcony shook and people screamed.

He clutched Utray's shoulder, unable to tear his gaze away from the spectacle in front of his eyes. Spewing brown fountains, cut through with gouts of earth and steam, the cloud billowed into the blue sky, up and up like a dragon unfurling lethal wings. At the base of the cloud, geysers erupted—blinding gold, white, peach, flaring up in glory, collapsing into steaming rivers, only to flare again.

With ponderous majesty, a vast deposit of limestone slid out of the massive arms of the granite plateau. Tearing away sheets of trailing ivy, it crumbled into an avalanche of earth, rock, and gravel that plowed down to the Eeron Valley. Druv caught a glimpse of the new granite face of Insheer Cliff, of a dozen gleaming rivulets rushing down onto what was now a hillside heaped at its foot, until a churning cloud of dust obscured everything.

He stood dumbfounded, his mind unable to take in what his eyes had just seen.

The long reverberation finally rumbled away. The cloud, its top pure white, continued to tower into the sky while the bottom, like a dark reflection in sepia and ochre, shed soil and dust in ragged shreds.

Inside the nursery behind him, a child was crying. Ukaipa ran off to him. With a quick glance around the balcony Druv saw no one had been hurt. Mena, however, stared starkly at the wreckage, her throat muscles working. "My grandsons," she whispered. "Oh God. My grandsons."

TAISA DID NOT SEE HOW HER beloved died. She stayed with the terrified people in hospit while the cliff rumbled and the ground shook. Only later, when the earthshaking had ceased and everyone had calmed down, was she able to go to the door. Her eyes traveled over the devastation that surely had taken Teller's life, and then she lifted her gaze to the sunset-tinged cloud spreading over the new face of Insheer Cliff.

When ineerva had been tearing Teller apart, when she first placed her hands on him to help him bear it, he had cried out in the mind-speech: "I don't want to hurt you! Oh God, don't let me hurt you!"

And he did not. Somehow he had controlled the skora that raged inside him and allowed her to enter his suffering. In that intimate connection, with her one hand over his throat and the other over his spirikai, they were more open to each other than most married couples ever could be. She stayed with him when ineerva convulsed him, when pain nailed them together. She beheld the wounded greatness of his heart, and lost her own heart in the process.

She pulled the blue and red knotted cord out of her pocket. They had never said good-bye, not really, but he had left her this. It was a symbol of those he had tried to save: a little girl and a helpless ahn.

She laboriously picked out the knots, smoothed the ribbon and cord, and braided them together with her purple mourning ribbon, the one she wore after the death of her ward-father. Tears flowed down her cheeks as she wound the braid around her wrist and tied it there.

The door banged open, and she quickly wiped her eyes on her sleeve as a distracted Abiyat rushed in. "Push the cots together," he ordered, "and make more room. I'm afraid we are going to be very busy very soon."

ABIYAT WAS RIGHT. AS DUSK GATHERED, bringing in a cold night of Seed, lines of torches marked where men from Bellstone Forest, led by Havek, were carrying in the injured. The Eeron River had flooded the town, but a band of the forest warriors, who had been secretly preparing an ambush at Rydle Bridge, had suddenly found another mission. They'd rushed out of hiding to save many lives.

As the next hours passed, Taisa was astonished that more individuals than she would have thought possible managed to survive the fall of Oknu Shuld. These even included people who had been attending a ceremony of some kind inside the stronghold: wealthy villagers, foreign dignitaries, rista students, and teachers. Most were too dazed to know what had happened and why they still lived. All these, including some of the Spider-king's soldiers who had cast away their weapons, filled the hospit, the infirmary, and even quarantine. The Rift-riders, along with Larrin and his guards, had to set up bonfires and tents on the Great Lawn to accommodate everyone.

But none of the innocent ahn, it seemed, had escaped. How, Taisa raged, could the merciful Rulve have allowed that? Yet he had, just as the Creator had allowed the gruesome death of her own ward-father at the hands of the 'braks.

Abiyat put her and Farne in charge of the tents rapidly filling with injured survivors, so she was kept too busy to think, yet she found herself glancing up as each new group arrived. None of them had heard anything about Teller, and some didn't even recognize the name. Still, she scanned every face, hoping against despair to see his soot-colored hair and the dark flash of his eyes, all the while fearing that she never would.

Disjointed tales abounded about what had happened, but none of them eased her heart. Yet it leaped when deep in the night she heard a glad shout. It was Larrin, rushing up the hillside with a torch. "I can't believe it!" he cried. "Ahn are coming. Scores of them, from Oknu Shuld!" He grabbed one of Taisa's helpers. "Get Abiyat. His old friend Rivere is leading them!"

The bedraggled group was just arriving—exhausted and muddy, yet alight with the thrill of freedom—when both Abiyat and Yuin rushed in. The healer, in a show of emotion Taisa had never before seen, fell upon a haggard-looking man with curly grey hair and wept. This must be Rivere. He had been Abiyat's apprentice thirteen years ago, when he had been kidnapped along with Teller into Oknu Shuld.

Yuin was soon surrounded by ahn who told him how his brother Gorv had taken his own life to save Teller's, how a lowly ahn had therefore been a major part of the Creator's plan to free them all.

So, Taisa thought, they believed the Creator cared about the ahn and saved them, but Teller was gone.

Wearing a ragged blanket, a strange old man, leathery and gaunt, was the last of those who came in with the ahn. He sat on the ground just outside the largest tent, apart from the others.

"Are you hurt?" Taisa asked him, although he didn't seem to be, and a medicant inside the tent was urgently calling for her assistance.

The man turned bruised-looking eyes up to her. "I am Varo," he said, "and I have everything I need. Everything but my sons."

She patted his bony knee, briefly regretting she did not have time, nor the inner strength, to ask about his sons right this moment, and rushed off. Soon after, she noticed Druv and Lir speaking earnestly with the old man in a quiet corner. She felt distantly glad they were offering him comfort.

Taisa worked through the night, setting bones, cleaning wounds, making sure each tent was visited regularly by one of her helpers. Sooner than she could imagine, word had gotten out to the villages that the ahn had escaped, and farmers and townsfolk streamed in to look for their sons and daughters. Taisa passed many who had found them, who hugged them in the tents with tears of joy, but others sat grief-stricken on the grass, weeping for children who had died long ago or only yesterday. Taisa witnessed many happy reunions that night, but her own heart lay within her like a stone.

At one point, Abiyat hurried in with two women who had come in with the ahn group, one near Taisa's age and the other much older. They had apparently been to the baths already, for they wore clean shirts and pants from the laundry, and their hair was still damp.

"I introduce Mariat and Hanat," Abiyat said in his formal way. "Both have some experience in caring for the sick and have offered their assistance. I'm sure you can use Mariat here, but Hanat I must whisk off to help in the infirmary."

Mariat followed her instructions, said very little, and worked tirelessly. Blank with exhaustion, Taisa noticed nothing remarkable about her until Mariat bent over a wounded man and a medallion she wore under her shirt fell briefly into view. It looked exactly like Teller's toltyr.

Taisa drew Mariat aside and learned the toltyr had belonged to Teller's twin brother Sheft. "This pendant meant so much to him," Mariat said. "But he is—he is dead, Taisa. I can't even bury him. We were married"—her voice quavered and she looked away—"for only a day."

Sudden resentment surged up in Taisa. "At least he *was* your husband," she blurted out.

Mariat looked at her through her tears, then searched Taisa's face for several heartbeats. Expecting an angry retort, Taisa felt herself shrink inside. Instead, Mariat reached out to touch her arm. "Oh," she said, "you loved him! You loved Teller."

Gratitude at her kindness flooded over Taisa and she could hardly speak. "Thank you for noticing," she choked out.

"I'm so sorry, Taisa."

"No one else knows how I feel about him. I'm not even sure if he loved me back."

Mariat seemed to understand—and forgive—the complicated emotions that wracked her. She took Taisa's hand in both of hers, then told her how Teller had witnessed their marriage, saw into the Vora's heart, and stood tall under grief and a growing fire.

"Teller convinced Vol Kuat to lead us all to safety," Mariat said, "and then he had to leave us." She touched her abdomen in an odd, gentle way. "All of us. He had to do something hard, Taisa. I think that's why he couldn't tell you he loved you. The two of them gave themselves up to save this land, and I think both of them knew they would never come back."

Taisa bit her lip against tears.

Squeezing her eyes shut, Mariat looked away. "My husband bled to death only a few levels above where I was being held. And I never felt it." She put a tight fist against her mouth, and then moved it down to her throat. "Oh Taisa, I was so close! But I couldn't help him, couldn't be with him," Her voice broke. "Couldn't take away any of his pain."

Taisa stepped closer to Mariat and put her arms around her. Not trusting her voice, she could only whisper into her ear. "You weren't given that great gift. But I was…for Teller." She pulled back, and even though the memory served only to sharpen her anguish, told Mariat what she had been able to do for her beloved only days ago.

They were called back to their separate patients, yet united in grief. It was as if, walking in a long and empty hall, they had somehow found each other. But as the night wore on, both Taisa and Mariat found themselves glancing over the heads of their patients. They gazed toward the west, into the night that held the far-off graves of the young men they loved.

Chapter 54

At Enlen's Roots

In the grey before dawn, Taisa gave up trying to sleep and made her way to the Seani House. A part of her was drawn to the cozy still-lit lanterns of the dining room, and another part sought only to be alone, but her practical self knew she would be useless to her patients if she didn't have breakfast. The place was crowded and she ate most of her bowl of oatmeal standing up.

Se Druv was standing on the porch when she left. They watched a lone falconform sailing above the devastated area across the valley, sweeping back and forth in a fruitless search for anyone still alive. The part of the cliff that had held the great fortress of Oknu Shuld was now only a sprawling hillside.

Se Utray and Ianak came up. They must have just gotten back from Rydle and were full of news. Normally Taisa was interested in news, but now she had to concentrate on what they said. The restored river had carved a new course around the hillside, destroying not only the bridge, but also the entire half of the village west of the main square. People living there were having to stay in tents on higher ground or with sympathetic folks who gave them shelter. The Seani would have a lot of work to do helping the villagers rebuild their town. The silver lining of this cloud, Ianak remarked, was that the new river would likely bring back Heeringone Marsh, a beautiful fenland that had dried up when the dams were built. Maybe, Ianak hoped, the stately blue stilt-birds would return.

They talked about how bands of 'braks had been seen returning to their homeland of Trey Aughter, that the garrison in Rydle was gone, and that there was no news about Archon Moverik, or indeed of any the archons. Druv told the others what Taisa already knew, that a few wounded soldiers had found their way to the Seani.

"Larrin checked them for weapons," he said. "None were armed, and none were of a mind to cause trouble. One of them even asked to join our guards."

They stood quietly for a moment as a nearby robin, probably just waking up, tentatively sang a few notes. Taisa was about to leave the group—most of what they were saying couldn't seem to hold her attention—when Ianak spoke up.

"There's something else, though," he said, looking down at his boots. "The Sperians know that a heavy evil has passed away and are eager to plan for the future." He sighed and looked up. "But some of the wealthy are as mad as hornets. They made a living from Oknu Shuld, and now it's gone."

"The village will survive with fewer morue distributors and tax-collectors," Druv said. "Let these people turn to farming and feed Shunder's hungry children."

"More easily said than done," Ianak muttered. He rubbed his long, beaky nose. "At least the morue fields are gone."

"Indeed," Utray said, "but we saw an undamaged alehouse on higher ground, and it was packed all night with people guzzling down the last of the spirits. We also heard that fights broke out over the purple leaf stored in the distribution warehouse."

Ianak snorted. "Would you believe people were already talking about digging up that big spider mosaic? Some think it had been encrusted with jewels. I'm sure a few of them will be rushing out there with shovels."

With a slight groan, Utray eased himself down onto the top step of the porch. "I wonder," he said, "if most of the population hereabouts even realize what the niyalahn-ristas have done for them."

"Then it will be part of our job to inform them," Druv stated firmly. "The Sperians know, and so do the Bellstone people. We all understand that Teller and Sheft did not lose their lives, but spent them."

Taisa tried to swallow the lump in her throat that kept her from saying anything, but it did not seem to go down.

"We heard all sorts of rumors," Ianak said. "Before the cliff collapsed, the Spider-king supposedly lopped the heads off all the Vols and then embraced some kind of black sorcerer, or the sorcerer embraced him. The story is that something happened to the king's eyes, and he became more powerful than ever." He hesitated, frowning. "They say he wielded skora."

Teller's skora, Taisa thought with a pang. Pulled out of him with what suffering she could not imagine. A sense of despair joined the grief in her heart, forcing her at last to speak. "You make it sound as if the emjadis died for nothing!" she burst out. "As if nothing has really changed."

Druv looked up at her, his eyes hollowed with sad wisdom, and maybe a glimmer of hope. "The niyalahn-ristas have done what they were born to do. They have done the will of God. The ahn are free, and the morue fields are gone. Our land is reborn. We will never forget. When it comes time for each of us to use what gifts we possess in the struggle against evil, Teller and Sheft will be our inspiration. But what happens next is up to us. Living in freedom is a never-ending struggle."

Perhaps it was. But so was this constant aching in her heart, this numbness, this vague wondering if she would ever love again.

Making some excuse, she left them and went alone to the Quela. Behind her the sun was rising over the new Insheer Cliff. Every bird in the forest seemed to have awakened, and they were filling the air with songs, tweets, and chirps.

Inside, the tall candles were burning low, and only a few other people sat apart in the shadows, quietly praying in Rulve's presence. Taisa sat with her back against the great tree Enlen. At its ancient roots Teller had buried the remains of the vol-ring, a thing he hated, but other than the cord she had braided, it was all she had left of her beloved. She put her hand over the spot. No matter what memorial stone they later set up for him, she would always come here to grieve.

CHAPTER 55

THE THIRD DAY

As Taisa was leaving the Quela, she caught sight of Mariat and the old man who had come in with the ahn. They were sitting on mats under the grey and pale blue window of the Chrysalis Alcove, the one on the south side closest to the doors. Mariat motioned her over and patted an empty spot beside her on the mat.

"I can't stay long," Taisa said as she sat. "I've got to get back to the infirmary." She noticed that the old man, now that she had a good look at him in morning light, didn't seem so decrepit.

"We'll only keep you a minute," Mariat said. Still looking at Taisa, she put a hand on the old man's shoulder. "Taisa, this gentleman here is Varo, my father-in-law."

It was as if a grey veil in front of her was swept aside, and Taisa saw in Varo's strange amethyst eyes yet another person's grief. Now it struck her what this man had meant by "my sons." He was Teller's father, the sorrowing father of both emjadis.

Speaking in a low voice, Varo explained many things to her, particularly that Sheft and Teller were not the only niyalahn-ristas of her time. "My brother Eyascamen and I were also niyal'arist. We failed utterly.

We fought each other and lost our gifts. Yet, my dear, I believe we were part of a beautiful design. We were all woven into an iterating spiral of events, in which a pattern is unfolded, built upon, and expanded. This happens in a myriad different ways, and it creates yet another, even more intricate, design. Eventually and unknowingly—perhaps at times even unwillingly—we, too, were part of Rulve's gracious providence. We helped the new niyal'arists succeed in our place." He leaned forward and touched her hand. "I offer you these words in the hope it will comfort you."

Varo turned his head to look at the nearest great candle, as if the quiet flame were a source of peace. "All who bear s'rere must be buried," he murmured. "And this is what my son Teller has done. For my brother and for his."

Mariat reached out to take Taisa's and Varo's hands. The wife and the father were united in sorrow, and Taisa's own heart ached, but it was hard to join hands with them in their mourning. She had known the adult Teller only a few days, but she loved him far longer than that, since she was a little girl. If their desolation was greater than hers, she did not know how they bore it.

WHEN TAISA RETURNED TO THE INFIRMARY, she was dismayed that their obnoxious patient was still there.

The foreign woman had suffered nothing worse than a badly sprained ankle, but had complained so loudly about sleeping in a tent that a patient in the infirmary offered to give up his bed and take a mat on the floor. The woman glared at Taisa and pointed to Se Abiyat. "I demand to be treated by *heem*," she insisted, "not some underling. I am Dowanjura, of thee House of Pil."

As if we've haven't heard that a dozen times, Taisa thought.

Dowanjura was one of a small number of foreign dignitaries who had escaped the destruction, and at first Taisa felt sorry for her. The woman was all alone in a strange land and had no idea how she was to return home. Her servants had not survived; or as Abiyat opined, had seized the opportunity to run off. But Taisa's sympathy evaporated when she learned why the woman had been in the Spider-king's stronghold to begin with: to learn the black arts.

"Your leg will be treated by my valued assistant," Abiyat said to her, "or not at all. Taisa, please proceed."

Dowanjura moved her shoulders like a ruffled hen and addressed the ceiling. "Have they notheeng here but asseestants and underlings?"

Ignoring her, Taisa unwrapped the bandage and applied burvena to the ankle. The bruises, she had to admit, probably did look alarming to this pampered woman, but they would soon heal.

Abiyat, meanwhile, had returned to his conversation with Taisa's ward-mother Tema. Most of it, however, was drowned out by Dowanjura's loud description of her restless night and the paucity of her breakfast.

"…that working with the sick tends to alleviate the grieving process," Abiyat was continuing. "But Mariat has time yet to decide where she wants to help."

Of course Mariat needed time, Taisa thought. The light in her life had just been extinguished forever.

Taisa wiped her hands on a cloth and re-bandaged the ankle. "Come now, Madam. Let me help you into the garden."

Naturally, the woman had objections, until finally Tema persuaded her to be wrapped in a blanket, helped out the door, and settled into a chair. Abiyat gave a deep sigh of relief.

Taisa glanced at the vacant bed, and a dart of pain suddenly struck her. This was the very bed in which Teller had been placed when he first came home to the Seani. It was where she had been with him in his suffering, where later she had kneaded the tension from his body. Now she would never be able to touch him again.

It had only been three days since Oknu Shuld had finally taken him. How could she live the rest of her life if everything she saw reminded her of him?

She looked up as two village volunteers carried yet another patient through the hallway door. It was a grey-haired man who looked as if he had been pulled from a shallow grave. If he had just been dug out of the debris, after three days, it would be a miracle if they could do much for him.

Abiyat moved quickly to the bed vacated by Dowanjura. "Here," he ordered and then turned to get a basin of hot water.

The two gently deposited the old man on the bed and stood back. Was he even alive? Dirt and a fine, grey dust completely covered the man's face, hair, and torn clothes. It dulled the bloodstains on his shirt and pants and caked the pendant he wore on an ash-colored cord around his neck.

A pendant. A chill passed through her, then a strange darkness that turned into light. Suddenly short of breath, Taisa moved to the side of the bed and looked closely at the new patient's face.

He wasn't an old man at all. Under all the ash and grime, he was her beloved Teller.

HE DIDN'T KNOW WHERE HE WAS, only that Taisa was with him. He saw her and loved her but couldn't touch her. She was hugging him and sobbing, and he tried to reach up and put his arms around her, but didn't have the strength. He tried to hold on to the sight of her beautiful face, but it swam and in out of fog.

He dreamed he was desperately clutching the base of a tree trunk, that dirt rained onto on the back of his neck, that gravel poured over him and weighed him down. He thought he was dead, that they had buried him. For a long time his grave was quiet, except for the scree of a falconform high above. The gravel rattled when sharp claws pulled him out of it.

FIRM BUT GENTLE HANDS PRESSED AND prodded him, a voice gave orders. He was dimly aware of a steam-filled room. "This might hurt, Teller," someone said. "But it will only be water cleaning out these cuts and scrapes. Abiyat can't fix what he can't see, right?"

They eased him into the warm bathing pool, and he took a sharp breath at the pain. Gradually it subsided. They washed him, his face and hair, for which he was deeply grateful. Hadn't he and his brother been in these pools not long ago? But not now. Sheft was dead.

They took him back to his bed. His body was so drained it seemed to filter down into mattress as he lay there. Time passed. More probing. A tight bandage around his chest. Warm soup on a spoon. Taisa smiling, stroking his face, her eyes shining and teardrops sparkling on her long lashes. Her warm hand in his.

Oh God Rulve, he was home.

Chapter 56

A Strange Liturgy

Under Abiyat's watchful care, Teller began to regain his strength. He learned that he owed yet another debt to the falconform Yarahe, whose sharp eyes had spotted him amidst the piles of debris. He learned that every ahn had been freed and that Mariat, Rivere, and Varo had escaped, thanks to a Bellstone lad named Hewish.

Taisa stayed with him as much as she could. From his bed he watched her as she moved around the infirmary. One day she noticed and sat beside him.

"Your heart is in your eyes," she said.

He knew it was. He could feel it there.

He wanted desperately to ask her to be his wife, but understood he must not. He took her hand between both of his. "Taisa," he said, "I thought of you all the time when I was in Oknu Shuld. If you would have me, I want to spend the rest of my life with you. But..." and the words he must say came hard, "but my brother handed the care of his wife to me. Mariat is bearing Sheft's child—children, Varo says. I have to help her and the little ones as much as I can. There is no end to the debt I owe them. In my whole life, I could not pay it back. But my heart, Taisa..." In his weakness he could not finish. He clung for a moment to her hand and then let it go.

Her throat quivered, and tears rose up in the well of her eyes. Their gaze connected them for one long moment, then it, too, broke away. "I understand, Teller," she said, "I understand."

"Well, I don't," someone behind him said briskly.

Teller twisted his head around to see Mariat standing just outside the open half-door. How long had she had been there, and how much she had heard?

Mariat pushed the door open and came to sit across from him on the other bed. She looked each of them in the eye. "To answer the questions both of you are too polite to ask: Yes, I have very good hearing, and yes, I heard every word. You two are being very noble. Thank you, but Rulve has given you your own lives to live."

It was as if she threw him a bright rope of hope, and Teller longed to reach out and grab it. But he could not. "You don't understand, Mariat. Sh'kier is gone. And my twin is dead. I'm not me anymore." He turned his eyes to Taisa. "It's not fair to offer you only half a man. All I have left is my duty to Sheft."

The woman he loved more than anything in the world said nothing, but tears leaked out of her lowered eyes and her lips quivered. He squeezed his eyes shut at the way he had to hurt her.

"Teller, my dear brother-in-law," Mariat said, "can't you see we're all half-people here? Me without a husband. Taisa wearing the mourning ribbon for her ward-father. Mena missing a grandson. Varo missing a son. Then there's Tema and Se Penan and many, many more in this devastated land. All of us are wearing a mourning ribbon, if only around our hearts. But that connects us, doesn't it? If we allow it, I think we "halves" can find a kind of wholeness together. There's healing when one raw and wounded edge touches another."

Teller opened his eyes, but he couldn't face either of the women beside him.

"Look around you, Teller," Mariat went on. "I don't need you in the way you think I do. There are plenty of people here to help me and care for the children. So many, in fact, the twins would be in danger of getting spoiled."

"Mariat, I promised Sheft that—"

"I know, Teller. Rulve brought me and Sheft together when we thought all had been lost. And against all odds, Rulve has brought the two of you together as well. Don't throw that miracle away. What would your brother say if he knew you used his words to make both of you miserable? He didn't grow up here, Teller, and probably didn't realize what an extended family the Seani is."

"That's true, Mariat, but he—"

"Surely an Uncle Teller and an Aunt Taisa would help the three of us settle down here more than two unhappy people ever could? Mena has asked me to live in her domicile with her, and won't a Grandma Mena help too?" She smiled at both of them. "And probably a Grandpa Varo as well. Not to mention all the Se uncles and aunts."

Teller looked up at his beloved. "You gave so much to me, Taisa, when I was lying on this very bed. How can I give you only half of me back?"

Taisa wiped her tears. "I'll supply the other half, my dearest. Then we can be one."

"I know what you two are doing," Mariat stated. "Talking in that mind-speech. Good. So now listen to me, Teller. I'm your sister-in-law. You witnessed our marriage and made Sheft and me very happy. It is my duty to make sure the same happens to you." She stood up, folded her arms, and looked sternly down at him. "Now go ahead, Teller. Ask Taisa to do what your heart really wants."

Teller stared at her. There was no doubt in his mind that, if need be, she would stand there for days. Her look was so officious and stubborn and motherly that it began to tickle inside him. It emerged as a half-suppressed chuckle and then burst into a long, hearty laugh—something he thought he'd never do again. Managing finally to restrain himself, he glanced at Taisa, and her eyes were dancing.

"All right, milady," Teller said to Mariat. "But grant us a little privacy, if you don't mind. In other words: Mariat, will you please get out?"

With a regal tilt of her head, she answered, "I'd be happy to," and swept out the door.

THE LITURGY, HELD THREE DAYS LATER in the Quela, was strange. Rulve's house was full of Seani people, Sperians, Bellstone visitors, a few soldiers even, and as many villagers as could fit in. They all sat on the floor or perched on the great tree roots, crowded in the alcoves, or stood at the back and outside the open doors. Celume and Yuin conducted a ceremony that began with a funeral for Sheft and all those lost, then continued with thanksgiving for all those found, and ended with songs of gratitude for what the emjadis had done for Shunder. After a brief intermission to allow emotions to settle, Druv announced a wedding that promised a new beginning for a sore but healing land.

Mariat cried along with everyone else when Teller and Taisa chose each other in marriage, but her tears were bittersweet. Nevertheless, she joined in the cheers when Druv confirmed their vows.

Keppit and her helpers served a simple meal afterward in the Seani House. The line to greet Teller and Taisa was interspersed with people who expressed deep sorrow for the couple's loss and those with hearty congratulations for their gain of each other, or a fervent combination of both. "Praise be to our Creator," one man said, "who wipes tears from our eyes and puts joy in our hearts."

Families reunited with their ahn lined up to thank Teller or kiss his hands. Ahn after ahn tried to kneel before Teller and Taisa, but the bride and the groom didn't allow that. Little Aron was there, along with his smile-wreathed parents, who had come to take him home to Baenfeld. Liasit squeezed Teller tight in a hug, and then left with her niyal sister. Hanat stood on tiptoe to kiss both of Teller's cheeks. She would be staying at the Seani to help Tema in the hospit.

Mariat found herself exchanging glances with Mena, Penan, and others whose genuine smiles for the newlyweds mingled with a touch of grief in their eyes. This included a dark-haired young man by the name of Lir, who, she had learned, was in love with Taisa, making him, at least temporarily, yet another "half."

She left the celebration early, desperately lonely for Sheft. This feeling came especially at night in Mena's domicile, where Mariat slept in the little alcove that had once been Teller's when he was a child. If only she hadn't lost Sheft's jacket in Oknu Shuld, for she longed to slip into it when she felt so alone.

She tried not to dwell on her loss, but like a torch dropped into a deep, dry well, her husband's light had disappeared.

CHAPTER 57

GREENMIST

As TIME WENT ON, MARIAT was kept busy with Ukaipa in the nursery and with Mena in the schoolroom. Teller spent time with Lir, Havek, and many others down in Rydle helping build temporary housing for the flood victims. At night he bent over the big table in the common room with the village planning committee, drawing up a design for a new town center west of the old town. Mariat often sat with them, doing mending and occasionally offering suggestions.

On a warm spring morning late in the month of Greenmist, Utray and Ianak, grinning with some secret excitement, insisted that Mena, Varo, Taisa, and Mariat come with them to Insheer Hill. Along the way, they persuaded Teller to leave his workmen at the new hospit site and join them. They crossed the river on a foot bridge, still smelling of new-sawn wood, that had replaced the much wider bridge that had been destroyed when Oknu Shuld fell. There would be no more trade in that direction now, and the village was concentrating on business with Baenfeld. Everyone stopped to admire the big hillside meadow that now ended at the bottom of Insheer Cliff.

Under the bright sun, the entire area was covered with grasses and spring flowers. Airy, pink-veined harbingers were nodding in clouds, along with windbells, yellow crocus, and clumps of lavender love knots.

"See those little areas of lacy blue-green leaves?" Utray exclaimed, sweeping his hand toward the south. "That is rue! No flowers yet, but sweet-rue is sprouting again! Small patches of it so far, but growing amazingly fast!" He was more excited than Taisa had ever seen him. "In a week or so we are going back with some of the farmers. We will collect seedlings and plant them wherever we can."

"Insheer Hill will one day be an extraordinarily beautiful place," Ianak told them. "You can't see them from here, but two little springs are bubbling around the curve over there. Tree saplings are already popping up. It's amazing! Impossible!"

"It is s'rere," Varo said. In spite of the warm sun, he sat in his hooded brown cloak, gazing at the meadow. "It is Sheft's gift. It marks the place where two niyal'arists sowed their blood, and helped each other die."

One, they all knew, was Varo's brother and the other was Teller's. The group watched in silence, Mariat wiping her eyes, then followed Utray to see the springs. Teller, however, still getting tired more quickly than he wanted to, found a bit of shade. It was under a small sapling that grew in a place already covered by meadow grass.

He lay face up in the grass and listened to the wind whispering around him and bringing the fresh smell of the waterfall a little to the north. A movement caught the corner of his eye, and he turned his head. Something fluttered from the ground not far off. He sat up and went over to it. A frayed piece of cloth lay half buried under another tiny sapling. Carefully steadying the little tree, he pulled the cloth out of the soft ground around it, then smoothed it out on his knee. About the size of a handkerchief but thicker, it looked to be torn from a forest-green cloak.

The same color as the cloak Mariat had tucked around Sheft's body.

His heart jumped, then steadied. The cloth could have belonged to anyone. More such things would surely be found as the ground settled.

He returned to his resting place and lay back. Barely an arm's-length above him, newly unfolded leaves, translucent green under the sun, moved gently in the breeze. A feeling of peace settled upon him. He rolled onto his side and placed his hand on the warm and fertile ground. A grove would soon appear here. It would always mark his brother's grave. Whether the cloth had come from Mariat's cloak or not, Sheft's body had surely found a resting place somewhere on this hill.

Chapter 58

Flowers in Footprints

"I feel so big and clumsy," Mariat confided to Taisa. It was a blustery evening in late Hawk and they were among the last having dinner in the Seani House dining room.

"Well," Taisa said, "there *are* two of them in there. Are they squirming around?"

"They sure are." Mariat put Taisa's hand over her abdomen, and the two women smiled in a kind of conspiratorial wonder.

Abiyat thought the babies would come soon, certainly before the night of the Spera Setting in Candle. That was when the three great stars of hope were precisely framed in the windows of the Quela's green disk. People from all over Shunder would crowd into the hall, for it was a time to celebrate with prayer and song Rulve's great blessing upon Shunder. Mariat, however, hoped the babies would come right now.

A week later she got her wish. Mariat went to bed on a bitter cold night. She hadn't been feeling well for a while but didn't mention that to Abiyat, who tended to be something of a fussbudget. She'd never been pregnant before, after all, and assumed feeling exhausted and sometimes a bit feverish was normal.

Now she was shivering and having contractions, and desired with all her heart that Sheft could be with her. *I know you'd have wanted to see your babies, dearest, wanted to hold them close. I think they're coming. I hope you'll be able to see them from where you are with Rulve.*

In the middle of the night, a delicious warmth spread over her, and she snuggled into the extra blanket Mena must have tucked over her. Sometime later, a big contraction woke her, and she called out for Mena, who felt Mariat's abdomen, threw on a cloak, and rushed out the door. It was then that Mariat found it was no blanket that had covered her in the night, but a jacket. A sheepskin jacket.

She pressed it against her nose and inhaled deeply. It was Sheft's; it smelled like him, undefinably but unmistakably. Somehow he had been here, was here now, would always be with her. She buried her head in the sheepskin and cried.

Thank you, my dearest heart. I don't know how you did it, Sheft, and I don't care. But thank you, thank you, thank you. She stuffed her arms in the warm sleeves, but soon was feeling very hot and had to take it off. Next thing she knew Teller and Rivere were carrying her to the infirmary, and stars shone huge above them all the way.

IT WAS A LONG, LONG NIGHT. Abiyat felt her forehead and ordered everyone out of the room except Rivere and Tema. Tema held her hand when the contractions became harder, when Mariat's chills rose into a fever which then fell again into chills. She got sick and had to use the basin, and then felt she was burning up. They tried to get her to swallow something, but the very smell made her sick again. All throughout, the pain kept coming, grinding relentlessly inside her. Abiyat examined her from time to time and then said something in a low voice to Rivere.

"Are the babies all right?" Mariat gasped.

"They're doing fine, Mariat," Tema whispered to her. "Don't worry about them, my dear."

But Mariat knew something was wrong. She held tightly onto Sheft's toltyr, which she always wore around her neck. At one point she noticed three quiet figures standing in a dark corner. She couldn't make them out very well, but two were male and the other one was her mother. Abiyat must have let them in.

But Ane was dead, wasn't she?

It seemed like hours and the pain kept getting worse, and then someone was moaning and screaming until, thank God, it was over, and the noise turned into the piteously sweet wailing of two little babies. Suddenly Taisa was there, weeping and laughing, and Teller looked like he was trying to swallow a lump in his throat as he gazed at Sheft's children, all wrinkled and bloody and beautiful beyond belief. Taisa helped Abiyat wash and swaddle the babies and then put them into Mariat's arms.

The fever turned blinding, and she could barely see them. One, the tiny son, already had a shock of black hair; and the other, a daughter, only a fuzz of gold. Mariat nuzzled their little cheeks, and their skin felt so very soft. The infant boy, with his father's silver eyes, seemed fascinated by the play of light and dark on the ceiling; but the girl's eyes, a deep blue that Abiyat said would turn brown like her mother's, were held by the bedside lantern. All the while the three figures in the corner came closer, smiling. One held back a little, but the others drew him along. She could see them better now: Sheft, Ane, and Varo's twin brother.

"Come here beside me," Mariat said to Sheft, but Teller and Taisa thought she meant them. Mariat held the babies close and kissed the tops of their little heads. Gazing with a smile into their eyes, she murmured, "Mama and daddy love you so very much." But now they were getting heavy. "Hold her, Teller," Mariat said, offering him the baby girl.

Carefully he received the tiny body. "Look how she fits in my hands," he marveled, looking tenderly down at the child.

"Taisa," Mariat said, her voice now sounding far away. "Hold this one please." She could barely lift the infant, but Taisa took him into her arms and cuddled him.

Mariat closed her eyes, her strength burning away, but opened them when Sheft came to kneel beside her. He took both of her hands and leaned over to kiss her forehead. "Oh, sweetheart," he said. "They're so beautiful! Thank you, my dearest wife, for making them with me."

She grinned at him and weakly squeezed his fingers. "It was a pleasure," she whispered. She turned her head toward the window—it was full of the grey sky of morning—then back to the dear man beside her. "Will our babies be all right?"

Abiyat must have thought she was talking to him. "Yes," he said. "We can already see that Teller and Taisa will treat your babies as their own."

"Oh," Mariat murmured. "I almost forgot." She kissed Sheft's toltyr and then, with Abiyat's help, pulled it from around her neck. "Keep this in Rulve's house," she said to him. *So everyone would remember,* she wanted to add, but could not.

Sheft smoothed her hair and caressed her cheek. "Come with me now, sweetheart."

Mariat sat up, leaving her body behind. "Oh, gladly, dear heart. Gladly!" He took her hand, and her spirit rushed with his into the embrace of dawn.

TWO AND HALF YEARS LATER, IN late spring, Taisa brought the twins to where Varo and Mena sat on a blanket at the edge of the Great Lawn. "Would you watch the children?" she asked. "Only for a little while? The delegation to Baenfeld just got back and, uh—" She hesitated, her cheeks turning pink.

"—and you're eager to see Teller," Mena finished blandly, noting that certain light shining in her daughter-in-law's eyes. "Go on."

With a big smile and a thank-you, Taisa rushed off toward the domicile she shared with her husband.

"This 'while'," Varo remarked to Mena, "may not be so little."

"They're young, Varo, and have been apart three whole days. You've got to understand these things." She raised her eyebrows at him, and he shrugged, and Mena reflected, not for the first time, that Varo had turned into quite a good-looking man. Patting the blanket, she turned and smiled at the children. "Come and sit here with Grandma and Grandpa."

"First we *wun*," the little girl said, and proceeded to run around the blanket.

"We *birds*," her brother informed them, flapping his arms and following his sister.

Mena and Varo watched them for a while. Then Varo remarked, "The villages have finally managed to put together their first Council of Shunder."

Mena picked a nearby clover and put it to her nose. "That's good," she said.

"They wanted Teller to be their king."

"It was bound to happen, I suppose."

"He told them no more kings. That it was time for people to rule themselves."

"Of course he did."

They sat back in contentment to watch the children play. Barefoot, shouting to one another, the twins tumbled and rolled on the grass. Silver-eyed brother and golden-haired sister squealed and laughed as they ran through the meadow, and the sweet scent of flowers rose up from their footprints.

The End

Questions for Discussion

1. Now that the *Coin of Rulve* series has ended, which volume did you like best? Why?

2. In *Leaf and Flame,* several characters are not who at first they seemed to be. Vol Kuat, the Spider-king, and the Vora monster are revealed in their true identities. What did you think about this? How have Sheft and Teller themselves changed since the beginning of the series?

3. Two major characters die in *Leaf and Flame*. Share with your group your reaction to that.

4. In the *Cosmos: Possible Worlds* TV series, Astrophysicist Neil deGrasse Tyson states, "Even from the tombs of lost hopes, dreams can rise." How would these words pertain to events in *Leaf and Flame?* How are they true in your own life experience?

5. In the *Coin* series, the twin protagonists endure many hardships. In *Blood Seed*, Sheft is expelled from his village. In *Dark Twin*, Teller loses his identity. In *Time Candle*, the brothers suffer from a deadly poison. In *Leaf and Flame*, the Spider-king gets what he wants. In the series, how do such dark events ultimately align with Rulve's redemptive design?

6. "In reality," the character Varo says to Teller, "Rulve's greatest power is her deep love. His providence redeems all things, even what we perceive as intended evil." Some people might

disagree. They might say God's greatest power is connected to justice—punishing evildoers and rewarding good deeds. What do you think? Have you seen in your own life how a person can find grace in spite of weakness or deliverance after failure?

7. After Teller accepts the toltyr, the brothers see each other with different eyes. "Teller saw in Sheft a finely wrought nobility of soul, and Sheft saw in him an unrelenting perseverance, and…now the link between them flowed with the deep humility necessary for interdependent strength." What does humility have to do with interdependent strength?

8. What do you see as an underlying spiritual theme or idea that runs through this book? How does (or does not) the Creator Rulve correspond with your idea of God?

9. Take a look at the three quotes at the beginning of the book, right after the map. Which one resonates most deeply with the *Coin* series? Which one most appeals to you personally? Why?

Thank you for spending time in the Coin of Rulve world. If you enjoyed the series, please let your online friends know that and consider posting an honest review for any of my books on Amazon and/or Goodreads. Whether in person or online, word-of-mouth referrals are an author's best friend and much appreciated!

I invite you to sign up for my private email list for giveaways, sneak peeks, and notices about my books. I won't spam you or share your address with anyone, and you can unsubscribe at any time.
http://eepurl.com/bGCRQf

About the Author

Veronica "Vernie" Dale, a former librarian, writes genre-bridging fiction that includes dark fantasy, romance, psychological intrigue, and the spiritual journey. She is the author of a short story anthology and four novels, and is working on her sixth book. Her work has received commendations from Writer's Digest, Reader's Favorite Book Review, Midwest Book Review, and Writers of the Future. Vernie holds two master's degrees and has twenty-six years of experience in social justice pastoral ministry. She is an established author with Detroit Working Writers, is a member of Phi Beta Kappa, and an Ethical Author with the Alliance of Independent Authors. "I love dark chocolate," she says, "and am a fan of what you might call the Holmes-Data-Spock archetype."

See more about Dale and her books at www.veronicadale.com

About the Coin of Rulve Series

COIN OF RULVE CONSISTS OF FOUR novels that comprise one story arc. It is about twin brothers Sheft and Teller, born in a small resistance community called the Seani. They are the promised redeemers, called to save their homeland from the reign of terror imposed by a brutal lord. In order to protect them from the despot who hunts them, the brothers are not told who they are and grow up in separate lands. Surrounded by cruelty and suspicion, Sheft and Teller each feel a call they cannot understand and struggle to believe in their own power for good. They desperately need the help of the Seani, as well as the strength of two extraordinary women, to undergo the trial of the heart to which the Creator Rulve has called them.

A tale of terror and tender love, told against the plots of the powerful and the providence of the Creator, *Coin* describes the spiritual quest as a dark journey toward the light.

What readers are saying:
"A new approach to this genre."…"The story keeps getting better and better."…"a page-turner"…"wonderfully sympathetic characters and gifted prose"…"Wowza!"

The Must-Read Novel That Launches the Series
Blood Seed
Coin of Rulve Book One

Growing up as a despised foreigner in the backward village of At-Wysher, eighteen-year-old Sheft hides a dark secret. He is being stalked by Wask, a deadly entity that haunts the nearby Riftwood. He keeps himself apart; yet beyond what he had ever dared to dream, he and Mariat fall in love. Sheft can't bring himself to tell her the truth about his deepest fear, nor can he share with her the devastating realization of who he is discovering himself to be. But when he must take part in a secret annual rite designed to protect the village from Wask, he confronts the true magnitude of the evil arrayed against him. It threatens to strip away his life, but will first break his heart.

What readers are saying:
"*intense, powerful, and compelling*"…"*an impeccable read with a troubled hero and highly imagined mysterious entities that are sure to engage readers on many levels. Highly recommended.*"…"*To readers who enjoy dark fantasy settings, but who still prize romantic fiction above all else: you won't be disappointed!*"

POWER, INTRIGUE AND HEARTBREAK IN THE DEPTHS OF AN UNDERGROUND WORLD
DARK TWIN
COIN OF RULVE BOOK TWO

BORN IN A LAND DEVASTATED BY a reign of terror, Teller is snatched as an innocent boy into the brutal lord's subterranean stronghold. Mind-probes twist his memories of home, and he grows up as an eighteen-year-old dark rebel. He simmers with hatred for the extended family he believes abandoned him and the lord's four Vols whose mission is to corrupt him.

But when he discovers within himself the legendary power of fire, the beautiful slave Liasit demands he decide who he truly is. But of the three names among which Teller must choose, one will break his heart, another will break his will, and the third will condemn what is left of his soul.

What readers are saying:
"Firmly rooted in the fantasy genre yet laced with intrigue, political purpose, and moral and ethical issues."..."Pacing, action, tension, conflict: it's all here."..."I don't often read fantasy, but I'd read this entire series straight through."..."I can't wait to read the next books!"...written by "a master of description who keeps all five senses a-tingle."

When Saviors Need Saving, It's a Race Against Time
Time Candle
Coin of Rulve Book Three

When twin brothers Sheft and Teller finally meet in the deadly Riftwood, Teller must decide if he will obey orders to bring his brother into the Spider-king's underground stronghold or lead Sheft back to his home in the Seani. His decision results in disaster.

What follows is a tale of risk, heartbreak, and courage, plus an urgent search for the antidote for a mysterious poison that has left the twins with only thirteen hours to live.

Mariat, meanwhile, strives to outwit the fierce boarmen who have captured her and then must face the most wrenching decision of her life.

What readers are saying:
"Lovely and dark, yet full of tension."…*"Oh boy! What a cliffhanger!"*…*"Timeless and spiritual."*…*"I felt the hope and urgency on every page."*

ALSO BY VERONICA DALE
NIGHT CRUISER:
SHORT STORIES ABOUT CREEPY, AMUSING OR SPIRITUAL ENCOUNTERS WITH THE SHADOW

WHETHER IT'S A WHISPERED INVITATION FROM the basement, a lost but dangerous wizard, or a spirit that has haunted a family for generations, ten different people must deal with the dark side. These insightful, award-winning tales flip from fantasy to faith, and from horror to humor to hope. We all have a shadow, a part of ourselves we'd rather not see, but only by dealing with it can we find the inner light.

What readers are saying:
"If you're intrigued by clever writing, crave fascinating stories that pack a lot in a short space, and appreciate an author who never lets religion get in the way of her highly spiritual and deeply psychological message, take a wild ride on the Night Cruiser."…"The stories are fun, spooky, and strange."

Made in the USA
Columbia, SC
21 November 2022